From the author of
CRIMSON FIRE, NIGHT BIRDS' REIGN and CRY OF SORROW

BOOK FOUR OF THE DREAMER'S CYCLE

HOLLY TAYLOR

Medallion Press, Inc.
Printed in the USA

DEDICATION

To Michelle Velona, who fights her battle with courage, dignity and grace. Thank you for teaching me how to be a friend.

Published 2009 by Medallion Press, Inc.

The MEDALLION PRESS LOGO
is a registered trademark of Medallion Press, Inc.

Cover Illustration by Arturo Delgado
Interior map by James Tampa

Typeset in Adobe Garamond Pro
Printed in the United States of America

ISBN#978-193383657-7

10 9 8 7 6 5 4 3 2 1
First Edition

If I break faith with you,
May the skies fall upon me,
May the seas drown me,
May the earth rise and swallow me.

A Kymric proverb

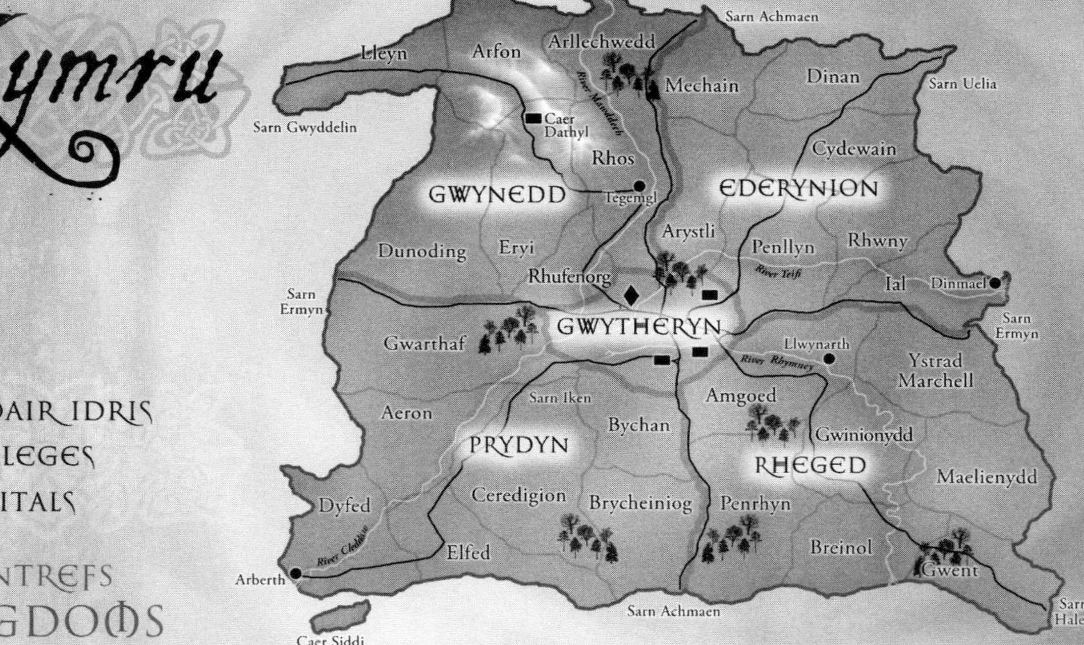
Kymru
CADAIR IDRIS
COLLEGES
CAPITALS
CANTREFS
KINGDOMS
Sarn Achmaen
Lleyn
Arfon
Arllechwedd
Mechain
Dinan
Sarn Uelia
Sarn Gwyddelin
Caer Dathyl
River Mawddech
Rhos
Cydewain
GWYNEDD
Tegemgl
EDERYNION
Arystli
Dunoding
Eryi
Penllyn
Rhwny
Rhufenorg
River Teifi
Ial
Dinmael
Sarn Ermyn
GWYTHERYN
Sarn Ermyn
Gwarthaf
Llwynarth
River Rhymney
Ystrad Marchell
Sarn Iken
Amgoed
Aeron
Bychan
PRYDYN
Gwinionydd
RHEGED
Maelienydd
Dyfed
Ceredigion
Brycheiniog
Penrhyn
River Cleddau
Elfed
Breinol
Gwent
Arberth
Sarn Achmaen
Sarn Halen
Caer Siddi

LIST OF CHARACTERS

IN KYMRU

Y Dawnus (the Gifted)

The Dreamers

Gwydion ap Awst var Celemon: Dreamer of Kymru
Dinaswyn ur Morvryn var Gwenllian: former Dreamer, Gwydion's aunt, Myrrdin's sister
Cariadas ur Gwydion var Isalyn: Gwydion's daughter and heir

The Dewin

Myrrdin ap Morvryn var Gwenllian: Gwydion's uncle, Dinaswyn's brother, former Ardewin and Arthur's guardian
Rhiannon ur Hefeydd var Indeg: former heir to the Ardewin, mother of Gwen
Elstar ur Anieron var Ethyllt: Ardewin, daughter of Anieron, wife to Elidyr
Llywelyn ap Elidyr var Elstar: Elstar's oldest son and heir
Morwen: a former teacher at Y Ty Dewin, a prisoner in Afalon
Trephin: an accomplished doctor, a prisoner in Afalon
Morgan ap Tud: a prisoner in Afalon

The Druids

Cathbad ap Goreu var Efa: Archdruid, Myrrdin's cousin
Aergol ap Custennin var Dinaswyn: Cathbad's heir, Dinaswyn's son
Sinend ur Aergol var Eurgain: Aergol's daughter and heir
Menw ap Aergol var Ceindrech: Aergol's son
Ceindrech ur Elwystl: teacher of astronomy, mother of Menw
Aldwr ap Tegid: teacher of mathematics
Madryn ur Dyrys: teacher of religion
Yrth ap Cyndyn: teacher of the almanac
Hywel: assistant teacher of the almanac

The Bards

Elidyr ap Dudod var Llawen: Master Bard, husband to Elstar
Dudod ap Cyvarnion var Hunydd: Elidyr's father, Rhiannon's uncle
Cynfar ap Elidyr var Elstar: Elidyr's youngest son and heir
Elivri: an accomplished harpist, a prisoner in Afalon
Maredudd: an old friend of Dudod's, a prisoner in Afalon

In Gwytheryn

Havgan: the Warleader, Bana of Coriania, conqueror of Kymru, the Golden Man
Sigerric of Apuldre: Over-General of Kymru
Aelfwyn: Princess of Corania, Havgan's wife
Sledda of Cantware: Arch-wyrce-jaga of Kymru
Eadwig of Pinenden: Arch-byshop of Kymru
Arianrod ur Brychan var Arianllyn: cousin to Gwydion and Rhiannon, Havgan's mistress
Arthur ap Uthyr var Ygraine: High King of Kymru, Penerydd of Gwytheryn
Gwenhwyfar ur Rhoram var Rhiannon: Rhoram's daughter by Rhiannon
Torgar: an old sailer in Havgan's army
Hild: a wyrce-jaga, formerly stationed in Maen, Prydyn
Edwald: a guard at Caer Siddi
Sigald: commander of the guards on Afalon
Rhufon ap Casnar: Steward of Cadair Idris
Tybion ap Rhufon: Rhufon's son
Lucan ap Tybion: Rhufon's grandson

In Gwynedd

Madoc ap Rhodri var Rathtyen: traitorous King of Gwynedd, Lord of Rhos
Tangwen ur Madoc var Bri: Madoc's daughter
Catha of Pecsaetan: Coranian General of Gwynedd
Arday ur Medyr: mistress of King Madoc and General Catha
Ecgfrith of Deorby: Byshop of Gwynedd

Ygraine ur Custennin var Elwen: King Uthyr's widow
Morrigan ur Uthyr var Ygraine: true Queen of Gwynedd (House of PenHebog), Lady of Rhos, leader of the Cerddorian
Cai ap Cynyr: Morrigan's captain
Bedwyr ap Bedrawd: Cai's nephew and lieutenant
Susanna ur Erim: Morrigan's bard, mother of Gwyhar
Gwyhar: bard, son of Susanna and Griffi
Neuad ur Hetwin: Morrigan's Dewin
Duach ap Seithfed: a Cerddorian, Uthyr's former doorkeeper, Lord of Dunoding
Greid ap Gorwys: Master Smith of Gwynedd
Dywel ap Gwyn: Gwarda of Ardudwy, brother to Bledri of Rheged, a Cerddorian
Isgowen ur Banon: Lady of Arfon, leader of the Cerddorian in Coed Arllech
Menwaed ap Medyr: traitorous Lord of Arllechwedd, brother of Arday
Gildasa ur Caw: Lady of Llyn, Tangen's aunt, a Cerddorian
Cian ap Iaen: Lord of Eyri, brother of Griffi, a Cerddorian
Cynwas Cwryfager: Gwarda of Aberffraw, a Cerddorian
Teregund ap Moren: Gwarda of Arllech Uchaf, a Cerddorian

In Prydyn

Erfin ap Nudd: traitorous King of Prydyn, Efa's brother
Penda of Lindisfarne: Coranian General of Prydyn
Eamer of Geddingas: Master wyrce-jaga of Prydyn
Whitred of Sceaping: Byshop of Prydyn
Ellywen ur Saidi: Erfin's Druid
Rhoram ap Rhydderch var Eurneid: true King of Prydyn (House of PenBlaid), Lord of Dyfed, leader of the Cerddorian
Geriant ap Rhoram var Christina: Rhoram's son and heir by his first wife
Efa ur Nudd: Rhoram's second wife, sister to King Erfin
Achren ur Canhustyr: Rhoram's captain
Aidan ap Camber: Achren's lieutenant
Cian ap Menw: Rhoram's bard, a prisoner in Afalon

Cadell ap Brathach: Rhoram's Dewin
Dafydd Penfro: Rhoram's counselor
Lluched ur Brathach: Gwarda of Creuddyn, sister to Cadell, a Cerddorian
Siwan ur Trephin: Master Smith of Prydyn
Rhodri ap Erddufyl: former King of Gwynedd, Rhoram's uncle, father of Madoc and
Ellirri
Marared ur Canhustyr: Lady of Brycheiniog, sister of Achren, co-leader of the Cerddorian
in Coed Gwyn
Dadweir Heavy-Hand: Lord of Bychan, father of Sabrina of Rheged, co-leader of the
Cerddorian in Coed Gwyn

In Rheged

Morcant Whledig: traitorous King of Rheged
Enid ur Urien var Ellirri: Owein's sister, Queen of Rheged
Baldred of Tarbin: Coranian General of Rheged
Saebald of Laewes: Master wyrce-jaga of Rheged
Oswy of Gwyrin: Byshop of Rheged
Bledri ap Gwyn: Morcant's Dewin
Owein ap Urien var Ellirri: true King of Rheged (House of Pen-March), Lord of Amgoed,
leader of the Cerddorian
Sanon ur Rhoram var Christina: Owein's wife, Rhoram's daughter by his first wife
Rhiwallon ap Urien var Ellirri: Owein's younger brother
Trystan ap Naf: Owein's captain
Teleri ur Brysethach: Trystan's lieutenant
Sabrina ur Dadweir: Owein's Druid
Esyllt ur Maelwys: Owein's bard, March's wife
Gwarae Golden-Hair: Gwarda of Ystlwyf, a Cerddorian
Isgowen Whledig: Owein's steward, sister to Morcant Wheldig
March Y Meirchion: Esyllt's husband
Hetwin Silver-Brow: Lord of Gwinionydd, a Cerddorian

Cynedyr the Wild: Hetwin's son, a Cerddorian
Menestyr ap naw: a cloth merchant, a secret Cerddorian
Llyenog ap Glwys: Master Smith of Rheged
Tyrnon Twrf Liant: Lord of Gwent, co-leader of the Cerddorian in Coed Sarrug
Atlantas ur Naf: Lady of Maelienydd, co-leader of the Cerddorian in Coed Sarrug
Feina ur Clustfeind: Gwarda of Llannerch, a Cerddorian
Annyaws ur Menw: Gwarda of Iscoed, Cian's sister, a Cerddorian
Brys ap Brysethach: Gwarda of Mabudryd, Teleri's brother, a Cerddorian
Rhun Rhywdd: Lord of Gwarthaf, a Cerddorian

In Ederynion

Elen ur Olwen var Kilwch: captive Queen of Ederynion (House of PenAlarch), Lady of Ial
Talorcan of Bernice: Coranian General of Ederynion
Guthlac of Cyil: Master wyrce-jaga of Ederynion
Cuthwine of Cyncacestir: Byshop of Ederynion
Iago ap Cof: Elen's Druid
Regan ur Corfil: Elen's Dewin
Lludd ap Olwen var Kilwch: Elen's brother, leader of the Cerddorian
Angharad ur Ednyved: Lludd's captain
Emrys ap Naw: Angharad's lieutenant
Talhearn ap Coleas: Ludd's bard
Llwyd Cilcoed: Dewin, Queen Olwen's former lover, brother to Alun Cilcoed
Alun Cilcoed: former Lord of Arystli, a Cerddorian, brother of Llwyd
Naf: a Cerddorian in Lludd's teulu
Efrei ap Gwifan: Master Smith of Ederynion
Eiodar ur Ednyved: Gwarda of Iscoed, sister of Angharad, a Cerddorian
Llawra ur Erim: Gwarda of Cynnlaith, sister of Susanna of Gwynedd, a Cerddorian

Drwys Iron-Fist: Lord of Dinan, leader of the Cerddorian in Penbeullt
Sima ur Naw: Gwarda of Is Feychan, sister of Emrys, a Cerddorian
Cilyddas ur Cors: Lady of Rhwny, a Cerddorian
Meilwen ur Neb: Lady of Cydewain, a Cerddorian

Historical Figures

Bran ap Iweridd var Fabel: Fifth Dreamer, Guardian of the Spear, one of the Great Ones of Lleu Silver-Hand
Mannawyddan ap Iweridd var Fabel: Fifth Ardewin, Guardian of the Stone, one of the Great Ones of Lleu Silver-Hand
Taliesin: Fifth Master Bard, Guardian of the Sword, one of the Great Ones of Lleu Silver-Hand
Arywen ur Cadwy var Isabyr: Fifth Archdruid, Guardian of the Cauldron, one of the Great Ones of Lleu Silver-Hand
Bloudewedd ur Sawyl var Eurolwyn: wife of Lleu Lawrient, lover to Gowrys of Penllyn, imprisoned in Drwys Idris by Bran the Dreamer
Lleu Lawrient (Silver Hand): last High King of Kymru, murdered by Bloudewedd and her lover

The Shining Ones

Aertan: goddess of fate, The Weaver, wife of Annwyn
Agrona: goddess of war, twin to Camulos, Y Rhyfelwr—the warrior twin
Annwyn: god of death, Lord of Chaos and the Otherworld, husband of Aertan
Camulos: god of war, twin to Agrona, Y Rhyfelwr—the warrior twin
Cerridwen: Protectress of Kymru, Mistress of the Wild Hunt, Queen of the Wood, wife of Cerrunnos
Cerrunnos: Protector of Kymru, Master of the Wild Hunt, Lord of the Animals, husband of Cerridwen
Grannos the Header: god of healing, Star of the North
Gwrach Y Rhibyn: The Washer at the Ford, incarnation of Agrona, a harbinger of war

Mabon: King of the Sun, Lord of Fire, god of the Dreamers, husband of Nantsovelta
Modron: mother godess, the Great Mother, goddess of the Druids, wife of Taran
Nantsovelta: Queen of the Moon, Lady of the Waters, goddess of the Dewin, wife of Mabon
Sirona of the Stars: goddess of stars, wife to Grannos
Taran: father god, King of the Winds, god of the Bards, husband of Modron
Dormath: the hound the guards the door to Gwlad yr Haf

IN CORANIA

Aesc: brother to Emperor Athelred, Warleader in Havgan's absence
Peada: Eorl of Lindisfarne, Penda's father
Readwyth: Penda's son
Athelred: Emperor of Corania
Athelflaed: Empress of Corania
Aesthryth: sister of Aesc and Athelbald, the former Queen of the Franks

Part 1

A Song of Freedom

The sun rises when the morning comes,
The mist rises from the meadow,
The dew rises from the clover,
But, oh, when will my heart arise?

From Bran's Poems of Sorrow
Circa 275

Prologue

Neuadd Gorsedd & Cadair Idris
Gwytheryn, Kymru
Helygen Mis, 500

Llundydd, Lleihau Wythnos—night

Sledda of Cantware, Arch-wyrce-jaga of Kymru, sat back in the Master Bard's chair with a satisfied smile on his cruel, pale face. His silken black robe lay loosely against his bony flesh as he perched there like a night crow come to pick over the remains of the dead.

His remaining eye glittered as he surveyed the Great Hall at Neuadd Gorsedd, the place that once was the college of the Bards. On the whitewashed stone wall above the Master Bard's sapphire-studded chair hung the wyrce-jaga's banner of black and gold. The velvety sable background shimmered in the torchlight as the tree stitched in golden thread glimmered in the flickering flames. Long gone was the Bard's banner of white and blue; tearing the banner down had been one of the first things Sledda had done when he had been given this place for his own.

Black-robed wyrce-jaga filled the tables set for the evening meal. Once, blue-robed bards had sat at those tables—but no more. Bards had not lived in Neuadd Gorsedd since the Coranians had come to Kymru. The Coranians had easily conquered those witches, driving them out of their colleges to hide in the mountains and forests of defeated Kymru. Soon, very soon, Havgan the Warleader would crush them all, and Kymru would truly belong to the sons of Lytir, the One God.

Sitting in the ornately carved wooden chair that had once

belonged to Anieron Master Bard filled Sledda with an even greater satisfaction—a far more personal one. For Sledda had been the one to kill the Master Bard in the dark dungeon of Eiodel those many months ago. It was Sledda who had had the honor of plunging his knife into the Master Bard's heart, killing both the old man and the song he had been singing, a song heard within the mind of every man, woman and child in Kymru—Coranian and Kymri alike.

Yet, though it had brought him satisfaction, killing the Master Bard had not even come close to the payment Sledda craved for the eye lost a few years ago to Ardeyrdd, the High Eagle of Kymru. The eagle had snatched away Sledda's eye with its cruel claws, and that was something that the witches of Kymru must still pay for. He would never, never rest until the last one of them lay dead at his feet. And only then would he feel that something like true payment had been made.

And payment would be made.

True, Cadair Idris, the mountain hall of the High Kings of Kymru, was once again occupied. This was a problem, but not an insurmountable one. Arthur ap Uthyr might sit on the throne in that mountain and claim to be High King, but it did not matter. For Kymru still belonged to the Coranians, belonged to Havgan, not to Arthur.

And what could one man and a handful of witches do against the might of the Coranian Empire? Resistance was, and had always been, futile. But the people of Kymru would recognize that the fight was over when the last of the witches, those that were called Y Dawnus, the Gifted, were dead. Dewin, Bards, and even Druids, the ostensible allies of the Coranians, would fall. And one day soon the Dreamer himself would die.

And on that day Sledda would take the witch Rhiannon ur Hefeydd and do to her all the things he had dreamed of for so many years. She would not survive such treatment long, but it would be long enough.

Her humiliation, her pain, her terror would consume him with pleasure and then, after a time, he would kill her. But that last gift from him would be long in coming. He had many, many things he must do to her first. Thoughts of her, bound and writhing beneath him consumed his mind. Thoughts of lashing her sweet, tender flesh until she begged and screamed for mercy set his body on fire. Thoughts of forcing her to pleasure him over and over again made him sweat and shake with longing.

He would have her. And he would allow no one—not even Havgan—to stand in his way.

He drank deeply from the crystal goblet of bardic blue that rested on the table in front of him. The fine wine of Prydyn trick-led down his throat, easing, for the moment, the fire within him.

They would cleanse this land of the taint of the witches. They would do it yet, and crush the Kymri beneath their heels once and for all. The Cerddorian, those ragtag bands of warriors that hid in the mountains and forests, would cease their futile resistance and surrender wholly to Havgan's hands. Soon, the Dreamer him-self would be captured, and brought to Havgan. Soon, Rhiannon would be his. Soon—

Shall there not be a song of freedom?

He started, almost dropping his wine cup. Where had that thought come from? Of course, he had been thinking of the day he killed Anieron, and that phrase was from the song the old man had been singing. But it had not felt like a thought, had not felt even like a memory. For it had come to him as though sung by hundreds of men and women. And that was not possible.

The other wyrce-jaga, their attention caught by his sudden movement, paused in their meal to stare at him. Coolly he stared back, his thin face impassive. For he would not let them guess that something had gone wrong.

And nothing was wrong. Nothing. Surely what had gone through his mind was only a memory of that cursed song. It could not have been—

Silence will be your portion.
And you will taste death
Far from your native home.

The voices in his head were louder as the song rang through his mind. He did drop the cup this time and it fell to the stone floor and shattered. Blue shards of glass glimmered up at him, glittering slyly.

""Master,""one of the wyrce-jaga said hesitantly, rising from his seat. "Are you well?"

"I—I am well. Nothing is wrong. Nothing," he hissed between clenched teeth. "Nothing."

And then the song came and took him again, crashing through his mind again, almost making him cry out.

Shall there not be a song of freedom
Before the dawn of the fair day?

Sledda gasped, his hands clutching his head in agony.

"Master!" the wyrce-jaga cried. "What is it? What is wrong?" The other wyrce-jaga in the hall jumped to their feet, looking around wildly for the source of Sledda's distress.

"Can you hear nothing?" Sledda managed to choke out. "Can't you hear the song?"

"There is no song, Master," the wyrce-jaga said, in a voice meant to be soothing. "There is no one here but us. No one singing."

But there was. There was. The song in his head increased in volume. He thought that his head would split open with the force of it.

And I am manacled
In the earthen house,
An iron chain
Over my two legs;
Yet of magic and bravery,
And the Kymri,
I, Anieron, will sing.

Anieron's song rushed through his head. Splitting, whirling, and crashing into him with such violence and pain that he could not bear it. He lurched to his feet, shaking off restraining hands.

"Anieron!" Sledda screamed. "You cannot do this! You are dead!"

But the song continued, slicing into him from all directions at once.

Shall there not be a song of freedom

Before the dawn of the fair day?
Shall this not be the fair day
Of freedom?

"No!" Sledda howled, clutching his head. "No!" He ran from the hall, not knowing where he was going, only running to get away, get away, get away from this torment. He blundered down the length of the hall, through the doors and into the main hallway as the song rang in his head.

And I am manacled
In the earthen house,
An iron chain
Over my two legs;
Yet of magic and bravery,
And the Kymri
I, Anieron, will sing.

Not even knowing where he was going, he raced up the stairs, panting and moaning, the song of the dead man ringing in his ears, driving him up and up and up in a doomed attempt to outrun this torture.

Shall there not be a song of freedom
Before the dawn of the fair day?
Shall this not be the fair day
Of freedom?

He raced up the three flights of stairs to the watchtower at the very top of Neuadd Gorsedd and flung himself into the narrow tower room. His one eye desperately scanned the northwest horizon where Cadair Idris lay. He knew, even in his pain and madness, where the song emanated from. He knew.

You of Corania
After your joyful cry,
Silence will be your portion.
And you will taste death
Far from your native home.

"Arthur!" he screamed up into the night sky. "I know it is you! Arthur ap Uthyr, release me! Release me, witch!"

But there was no release. The faint glow of the far-off mountain of Cadair Idris shimmered on the darkened plain and he screamed again.

"Stop!" he cried. "Stop! I will do anything you want! Just make it stop!"

But the song continued.

Shall there not be a song of freedom
Before the dawn of the fair day?
Shall this not be the fair day
Of freedom?

"Stop," he sobbed again, his body straining towards distant Cadair Idris. "I beg you. Stop. I'm sorry. Sorry I killed the Master Bard. Please make it stop."

Shall there not be a song of freedom
Before the dawn of the fair day?
Shall this not be the fair day
Of freedom?

"Arthur!" he called out in anguish, reaching out over the low walls of the open tower to the distant glow on the horizon, his body arching toward Cadair Idris. "Mercy!"

It was then the stones on which he leaned gave a sudden, sickening lurch and he felt his body pitching forward out into the night sky.

"Arthur!" he wailed as he fell from the tower.

The song stopped.

And the last thing Sledda heard before his body hit the ground far below and shattered, was a single voice.

It is finished.

ARTHUR AP UTHYR released the Bards from his mind, one by one. As he let them go, he murmured words of thanks to each and every one of them. For he knew them all now. He knew the Bards of Gwynedd, from the mountains of Eyri to the plains of Llyn. He knew the Bards of Ederynion, from the depths of Coed Ddu to the sandy beaches of Cydewain. He knew the Bards of Rheged, from the deep forest of Coed Coch to the plains of Ystrad Marchell. He knew the Bards of Prydyn, from the cliffs of Arberth to the hills of Haford Bryn. They were his people now, the Bards of Kymru, and they would come to his call.

The last ones he released from his mind-hold were the ones physically here with him in Cadair Idris—Elidyr Master Bard, his son and heir, Cynfar, and Elidyr's father, Dudod.

At last, Arthur opened his eyes. He rose from the golden, eagle-shaped throne. Brenin Llys, the hall of the High Kings, gleamed with a pure, golden light. The clear water in the fountain in the center of the chamber sang softly against the glowing stones that held it. The Four Treasures—the Stone, the Sword, the Cauldron, and the Spear—stood next to the fountain, glimmering steadily with an inner light.

Gwydion and Rhiannon stood at the foot of the stairs leading up to the throne and waited for him to speak.

"We have done it," he said.

"Anieron is avenged," Rhiannon agreed.

"Yes. It is finished," Arthur replied.

"No," Gwydion said quietly. "It has just begun."

Chapter One

Cadair Idris & Eiodel
Gwytheryn, Kymru
Helygen Mis, 500

Meirgdydd, Lleihau Wythnos—night

Arthur ap Uthyr, High King of Kymru, Penerydd of Gwytheryn, stood quietly in the center of the Taran's chamber on the eighth level of Cadair Idris. He craned his neck to gaze up through the clear roof at the stars wheeling overhead. His eyes focused on the constellation of Eos, the nightingale. For the nightingale was the symbol for the Bards, and his revenge for the death of Anieron Master Bard, just two days ago, was still fresh in his mind.

The wyrce-jaga, Sledda, was dead at last, and Arthur had been the instrument of that death. Through him the power of all the Bards of Kymru had been focused and brought to bear on the man who killed Anieron. They had sung the Master Bard's death song to his murderer, and justice had been served.

It was this, after all, this for which a High King was born. To bring justice, using the ability to focus the power of the Y Dawnus into a weapon to be used against the enemy. And this was a power he had come to accept. This was the reason for which he had been born.

He had once thought that he would do anything—anything at all—to turn away from this destiny. He had once twisted and raged against the turning of the Wheel. But he would run no more. Because Kymru needed him, and that reason alone was, at last, enough.

With a steely hiss, he drew his sword, Caladfwlch, from the

jeweled scabbard at his side. With both hands on the eagle-shaped hilt he rested the point of the huge sword on the stone floor. The eagle's bloodstone eyes glittered in the starry light and its onyx studded wings shimmered coldly.

It was time now. Time for the next step in this deadly end game. Although he knew what the result of this night's work would be, he was, nonetheless, compelled to try to turn the Warlord from the path Havgan had chosen. Something, he didn't really know what, demanded it.

Still staring up at the stars, he calmly reached out and gathered to him the very essences of those that waited in the throne room, seven stories below him.

He took the Bards to him first—Elidyr Master Bard and Dudod, Elidyr's father, as well as Cynfar, Elidyr's son and heir. Sapphire blue shimmered before his eyes as he drew in their power, and he felt Taran's Wind rush cleanly and sharply through his soul.

Then he reached for the Dewin—Rhiannon, Elstar the Ardewin, and Elstar's son and heir, Llywelyn. They glowed softly like pearls, as Nantsovelta's Water flowed through him, cool and clear.

He gathered the Druids—Gwenhwyfar's raw, untrained talent, Sinend, heir to the Archdruid's heir, and Sabrina of Rheged. He felt the roots of the fruitful earth claim him, twining through his body, lacing him in the emerald green glow of Modron the Mother.

Last, he gathered the Dreamers—Gwydion, whom he had once hated, Dinaswyn, the former Dreamer, and Cariadas, Gwydion's daughter and heir. The heat of Mabon's Fire burst deep within him, bathing him in an opal-like shimmer as the flames burst through him.

And then he was ready.

Wind-Ride, he called, to the Dewin in his mind. And then he was there, in Havgan's fortress. In Eiodel.

Havgan sat in the Great Hall at Eiodel, his brooding black fortress just a league away from Cadair Idris—just a league away from the mountain that now glowed in the night, its golden light proclaiming that a High King had once again returned to its halls.

Havgan knew that light well. Every night in the past three months, he had gone out to the battlements and stared at that mountain that continued to defy him. He would focus his hate-filled amber eyes on the glowing doors that had refused to open to him for so very long, the same doors that had opened for Arthur ap Uthyr just three months ago.

Later, after the meal was over, he would again go to the heights of Eiodel and take in the sight of that glowing mountain. And his hatred for the Kymri would burn even brighter.

His warriors feasted and drank noisily, filling the hall with their coarse jests and loud boasts. The fire in the pit in the middle of the hall cackled and danced. The dark walls were stark, relieved only by the torches set in their brackets and by a few banners whose rich jewels glittered darkly. The banner of the Warleader of Corania, a golden boar on a field of blood red, shimmered in the light of the fire. The boar's ruby eyes seemed to gleam maliciously in the uncertain light of the smoky hall.

He took a deep drink from the golden goblet in his hands. He had, of late, begun to drink heavily. Because things were slipping away from him, and he knew it.

His victory over the Kymri two and a half years ago was turning sour. The Dreamer, his false blood brother, had snatched the Treasures Havgan had sought. The mountain had not opened for him, in spite of all his efforts. He had captured hundreds of Dewin and Bards and imprisoned them on the island of Afalon, but the victory was hollow, for the leaders had escaped. He had captured one of the Kymri's testing tools, that strange device which demonstrated who of the Kymri were Y Dawnus, the witches of this land—yet the device had not identified a witch in many months.

And Sledda, Havgan's wyrce-jaga, had been killed just a few days ago. Sledda had thrown himself off the highest tower at Neuadd Gorsedd, seeking to escape something. Exactly what, he did not know. But that it was something sent by the witches, he had no doubt. That the witches had been led by Arthur ap Uthyr, the self-styled High King, he also knew.

For Arianrod, Havgan's Kymric mistress, had explained to

him the purpose of a High King in this land. And what a High King could do with the power of the Y Dawnus in his mind.

And worst of all, the thing hardest to bear, Gwydion ap Awst was still alive and free. And that angered most of all. For Gwydion's death was Havgan's dearest wish.

But the game was not over yet. One day, one day soon, he would have Gwydion's life in his hands. And it would take Gwydion so very, very long to die.

A soft, light touch on his arm roused him from his reverie. "You are pensive, my Lord," his mistress said.

He turned to her as she sat by his side. Her honey-blond hair cascaded down her shoulders, held back from her face by a band of topaz. Her amber eyes were soft and beautiful and her sultry mouth invited his kiss. Her gently rounded belly strained slightly against her shift of tawny silk. The child would be born near Calan Llachar, she had told him, one of the eight festivals of the Kymri, the time when they honored Cerridwen and Cerrunnos, the Protectors of Kymru. It would be a boy, she had said. For she was a Dewin and had a way of knowing these things.

His mistress was a Kymric witch. One of the Y Dawnus, one of those that he had come to Kymru to kill. And he loved her as he had never loved a woman before, as he had never loved anyone on this earth before. She was what he had been looking for all his life. She was the other part of him, just as the wyrd-galdra cards had foretold back in Corania. Just as Holda, the Goddess of the Waters, had said. No matter what she was, no matter what happened, no matter who stood in his way, he would never give her up. Never, witch or no.

He took her hand and kissed her palm and he felt her shiver with passion. He smiled at her, but did not answer.

His eyes cut to his wife, sitting on his other side. Aelfwyn had said no word to him this entire evening, a fact for which he was grateful. Exchanges with Aelfwyn wearied him. But it was through her, the daughter of the Emperor of Corania, that he had gained the power to subdue Kymru. He could, and did, ignore her and occasionally taunt her, but he could not send her back to

Corania—not if he wished to keep the warriors of the Empire at his side. And so she stayed, though he did not fully understand why. That she had come to plot against him was obvious. But just exactly what her game was, was not. She intended to bring him down, he knew. But how was not clear. Perhaps she did not know herself, and stayed in Kymru knowing an opportunity would, sooner or later, present itself.

Since she had come to Kymru, some months ago, she had not even attempted to interfere with his plans. She stayed in Eiodel, riding out to Cadair Idris occasionally to gaze at the mountain. Sometimes she visited Neuadd Gorsedd, where the wyrce-jaga were lodged, and more often she went to Y Ty Dewin, where the preosts of Lytir had made their headquarters. Occasionally she would visit Caer Duir and talk with Cathbad and Aergol. She had briefly visited his generals in the four kingdoms, but not one of them had anything suspicious to report. She wrote no letters to Corania. He saw her only at the evening meal. She did not demand his company. She did not demand that he send Arianrod away. In fact, she did nothing. And it was that which made him most wary.

She sat now quietly, her green eyes cold in her flawless face. She wore a silken shift of white beneath a kirtle of the same color. Diamonds sparkled in her light blond hair. Steorra Heofen, they called her, Star of Heaven, and he had always agreed that was so. For she was as beautiful, as cold, as distant as the brightest star in the sky.

Sigerric sat on Aelfwyn's right. Havgan and his Over-general rarely spoke of anything but the business of Kymru these days. Once, Sigerric had been his dearest friend. Through all of Havgan's years of struggle to obtain the warleadership, Sigerric had been there, supporting him, helping him, loving him. But since they had come to Kymru all that had changed. For Sigerric had no stomach for the killing of witches. And, too, Sigerric knew Havgan. Knew him very well, and approved of nothing Havgan had done in the past few years.

Once, Sigerric would have tried to turn Havgan from his

course. Once, he would have urged Havgan to give up and go home. But Sigerric did not even try to do that anymore. His brown eyes had long ago lost their sparkle and luster. Even the hunger with which he always gazed at Aelfwyn seemed to be merely a ghost of the love Sigerric was once capable of.

Havgan lifted his goblet of gold and rubies, and raised it again to his lips to drink. These dark thoughts were no matter. For he would defeat the Kymri, one way or another. And his son would rule this land after him.

And it was then, just as he began to drink, that Arthur came.

ARTHUR'S IMAGE MATERIALIZED within the hall and the sight of him caused the warriors there to cry out. The men scrambled for their weapons and some leapt toward Arthur. But at Havgan's stern gesture they halted their advance, their spears at the ready as they formed a half circle behind Arthur.

Arthur stood before the high table. His sword was pointed at the stone floor of the hall, and he rested his hands on the hilt. The golden eagle's head flickered in the uncertain light of the fire. He wore a tunic and trousers of black, and around his neck was the High King's torque—an opal, a sapphire, a pearl, and an emerald, clustered around a figure eight studded with shadowy onyx.

Havgan was dressed in gold and rubies and, unlike the people around him, he did not leap to his feet at Arthur's appearance. Instead, he sat in his high-backed chair, his strong hand gripping his goblet so tightly that the gold began to bend slightly beneath the pressure. He stared at Arthur with his amber hawk's gaze, but did not speak.

For a moment, just for a moment, Arthur felt something familiar about the Warleader of Corania. And for a moment, just for a moment, a similar, bewildered recognition flashed in Havgan's eyes. And then the moment passed.

The others at the table were on their feet. Arianrod rose, gripping the edges of the table to steady herself. Her sensual mouth was widened in surprise and fear showed in her amber eyes as Arthur gravely returned her terrified gaze.

Sigerric had risen slowly at the sight of Arthur. He had drawn no weapon, unlike the other warriors. He merely stood, staring from Arthur to Havgan, then back again. His brown eyes glittered feverishly and the grooves at the sides of his mouth deepened.

Princess Aelfwyn had leapt to her feet, and her hands were clasped in front of her mouth to hold back the scream that hovered there. It was the first real emotion—besides hate—Havgan had ever seen from her.

Arthur waited, standing inviolate before Havgan, until the people in the hall quieted. Havgan slowly rose to his feet and faced Arthur. The flickering light of the torches played over the Warleader's golden tunic, his honey-blond hair, his amber eyes.

Arthur drew the power of the Bards to him, and Wind-Spoke. "Havgan, son of Hengist," he intoned solemnly, "I am Arthur ap Uthyr var Ygraine, High King of Kymru, Penerydd of Gwytheryn, heir of Idris, heir of Macsen, heir of Lleu Silver-Hand. I call on you to leave this land."

"Your land is mine, Arthur ap Uthyr var Ygraine, heir of nothing," Havgan replied harshly. "And always will be."

"It has never been yours," Arthur said, shaking his head. And he called to him the power of the Druids and the hall shook, spilling flagons of wine from the tables. The fire in the pit leapt up behind him and the flames licked hungrily at the ceiling. The torches flared. The boar banner shivered as a cold wind rippled through the hall.

Havgan's warriors cried out in fear as the hall shook and wavered. But Havgan did not move. And he did not take his eyes from Arthur.

"Even your hall will do my bidding, because it rests on the earth of Kymru," Arthur continued, as he allowed the hall to stop shaking and the fire to die down. Havgan's banner gave one last shiver, then subsided. "Even Eiodel belongs to me."

"Come and take it, then," Havgan challenged. "Come and take it from me."

"All in good time, Havgan," Arthur replied. "For I have already taken your Master-wyrce-jaga, and will take you when I am ready. Sledda died by the power of the Bards of Kymru, in revenge for Anieron's death. See, now, how it was. Watch the Time-Walk, and see his last moments."

And with that, Arthur called the Dreamers to him. With the powers of the Walkers-Between-the-Worlds, the events leading up to Sledda's death were superimposed on the now-roaring flames of the fire. Havgan's warriors cried out as the flames grew and images formed in the dancing light: images of Sledda clutching his head, running to the uppermost tower of Neuadd Gorsedd, and falling to his death. Then the fire sank down again.

"This is how it was with him," Arthur said quietly. "We sang the song of Anieron to him, and he died trying to escape from us. But death was the only escape for him. I offer you a better choice."

"For Havgan there is no choice," Sigerric said quietly, his eyes sad. "Did you not know that?"

Arthur turned to the general. "Every man has a choice."

"And he made his, long ago," Sigerric answered. "He will not turn back."

"Nonetheless, I offer him a chance."

"He has had many chances," Sigerric said sadly. "And refused them all."

"Havgan," Arianrod said urgently to her lover, "listen to Arthur. Take whatever choice he offers you. Please! Listen to the High King."

"I am the High King of Kymru!" Havgan shouted, grabbing Arianrod's arms and yanking her to him. "I rule here!" he screamed inches away from her face. "I do!"

Arianrod, the tears streaming down her face, wrenched away from him, and placed her hand on her gently swollen belly. "Havgan," she whispered. "Please. I could not bear it if you died. I could not."

"See the faith your mistress has in you, my husband," Aelfwyn said coldly. "But then, she is a Kymric witch, is she not? And knows, like no other here, what the Kymri can do to you."

"You will close your mouth, Aelfwyn," Havgan said in a voice more terrible because it was suddenly quiet. "If you do not, I will close it for you. Permanently."

Aelfwyn did not reply, but the contempt with which she looked at her husband spoke volumes.

"You say this land belongs to you, but your Y Dawnus belong to me," Havgan said as he turned again to Arthur. "Those Dewin and Bards taken when we raided the caves of Allt Llwyd live in misery and terror under my guards at Afalon. They wear the collars, the enaid-dals; they suffer terribly and they die. Have you forgotten them?"

"I have not forgotten them," Arthur said quietly. "Yet, still, they do not belong to you. They are mine, and I will take them back when I am ready."

"Brave words," Havgan sneered. "But still they are captive."

"A choice I offer you, Havgan, son of Hengist. Do you wish to hear it?"

"It will not matter," Sigerric said dully. "He will not listen."

"Yet offer it I will, nonetheless. Leave Kymru. Be on your way to the coast tomorrow morning. Call your warriors out of our land. Leave this island. And you will live."

"I will not leave," Havgan said between clenched teeth.

"If you will not leave, then you must stay and fight me. And if you do, you will die."

"So be it, then," Havgan said. "But I do not think it is I who will die."

"You are wrong," Arthur replied as he allowed himself to fade away from the hall at Eiodel. "You are wrong, Warleader. Again."

His spirit back in the highest chamber of Cadair Idris, Arthur released the Druids, the Dewin, and the Dreamers from the grip of his mind. But he retained the Bards, and with them flung his message to the dispossessed rulers of Kymru. He Mind-Spoke to King Rhoram in Prydyn and Prince Lludd in Ederynion, to Queen Morrigan in Gwynedd and King Owein in Rheged.

I charge you to send your warriors to watch the coasts. You will see to it that not one Coranian ship leaves this island. Havgan will send for no reinforcements. Burn every Coranian ship in our harbors.

Ensure they build no others. No word leaves Kymru. The final battle is near.

Gwydion stood wearily in the Dreamer's Alcove in the High King's hall. Soft light from some unknown source glowed, playing across the glittering walls of gold. The High King's golden throne, shaped like an eagle with wings for armrests, shimmered in the golden light. A fountain played in the middle of the hall, bubbling and laughing as the light gleamed on the clear water.

Next to him, his daughter, Cariadas, took a deep breath and wiped a faint sheen of sweat from her brow. Her red-gold hair cascaded down her back in its usual tangles. Next to Cariadas sat Dinaswyn, Gwydion's aunt. As always her face was cool and composed, and her frosty hair was pulled back from her thin face with a band of black silk. But Dinaswyn's cool, gray eyes were weary from the efforts they had made for Arthur just a few moments ago.

In the Druid's Alcove Gwenhwyfar sat down abruptly on the floor. Her golden hair was drenched with sweat and her hands shook. Sinend, heir to the Archdruid's heir, leaned forward from where she sat on a bench and gently laid her hand on Gwenhwyfar's shoulder. Gwen turned slightly and smiled wearily up at Sinend. Sinend's pale face was composed but her gray eyes, so like her grandmother Dinaswyn's, were shadowed and sunken in her pale face. Sabrina, King Owein's Druid, shook her black hair back and her green eyes were dull with fatigue. Yet she smiled at Sinend and Gwen and nodded, to indicate that they had done well.

In the Bard's Alcove, Elidyr Master Bard, his father, Dudod, and his son, Cynfar opened their eyes, at last released from Arthur's grip. Cynfar sank to the floor while Elidyr gripped his son's shoulders to steady him. Dudod's fading brown hair seemed to have become a little grayer but his penetrating green eyes were clear. Dudod grinned at Gwydion and gave him a jaunty wave to indicate that Arthur's messages had been delivered.

Gwydion looked over to the Dewin's Alcove. Elstar Ardewin had sunk down on a bench, her legs unable to hold her after the effort she had made. Her son, Llywelyn, after a glance across the hall to Cariadas to ensure himself that she was well, stood unsteadily by his mother, mopping his forehead with his sleeve.

At last he allowed his gaze to rest on Rhiannon as she stood next to Elstar. Rhiannon's dark hair was held back from her face with a band of pearls. She wore a kirtle of black over a white shift. Her Dewin's torque of pearl glowed around her slender neck. Her green eyes met Gwydion's gray ones, and she smiled wearily. Her hands shook slightly as she absently fingered the folds of her dress.

More than almost anything in the world Gwydion wanted to go to her. He longed to give her his arm to lean on as she recovered from the drain on her strength. He longed to touch her beautiful face and tell her the truth—that he loved her. But he could not. He no longer really thought he could, in spite of how much he wished to.

And so it was her Uncle Dudod that went to her and gave her his arm to lean on. And Gwydion turned away, because he knew he should have been the one to do that.

Rhiannon smiled at Dudod then went to the Druid's Alcove to kneel by Gwen as she sat wearily on the floor. Gwen allowed her mother to help her up, and even smiled her thanks.

For a moment Gwydion wished that Myrrdin were here. Myrddin, with his wise heart and piercing eyes would have made Gwydion do what he had so longed to do. But Myrrdin, along with Rhodri, the former King of Gwynedd, was in Rhiannon's old cave in Coed Aderyn. It was their task to guide those Arthur called here through the maze of caves they had discovered that led straight to Coed Llachar, the forest next to Cadair Idris, and from there to an underground entrance that took them within the mountain itself.

The doors to the hall opened soundlessly and Arthur stood there. The weariness and trembling that the Druids, Dewin, Dreamers, and Bards experienced was not at all evident in the High King's face, or his stride. Indeed, Arthur walked across the hall to his throne with a spring in his step, as though energized, not wearied, by tonight's work. As he walked by the alcoves he stopped for a moment, thanking the men and women whose gifts had made possible what had been done that evening.

He lingered for a moment next to Gwen and his hand almost touched her golden hair, but he moved on before he had done so. He smiled at Rhiannon and kissed her palm. He gave Dudod a hearty slap on the back, then moved to the Dreamer's Alcove. Cariadas rose to her feet and smiled at the High King.

"It was good, wasn't it?" she grinned. "The Time-Walk."

"It was very good," Arthur grinned back. He turned to Gwydion. "Havgan did not heed me."

"You didn't think he would," Gwydion pointed out. "And neither did I."

"There is," Arthur went on, after hesitating for a moment, "something about him. Something familiar."

Gwydion's silvery-gray eyes sharpened. "Ah, you felt it too?"

"Yes. Something. But I don't know what. Not really."

"Nor do I. I never have."

"Perhaps we will before this is done."

"Perhaps."

Arthur turned then mounted the eight jewel-studded steps that led to the throne—topaz for Cerrunnos, Master of the Hunt, and amethyst for Cerridwen, Queen of the Wood, the Protectors of Kymru; blood-red ruby for Camulos and Agrona, the Warrior Twins; emerald for Modron the Mother and pearl for Nantsovelta of the Waters; opal for Mabon of the Sun and sapphire for Taran, King of the Winds; and lastly onyx for Annwyn, Lord of Chaos.

"You have all done well, my friends," Arthur began, as he seated himself on the golden throne. But he stopped as the doors to the hall opened once again.

"High King of Kymru," a familiar voice said, "I bring guests to your hall."

Arthur stood, trying to make out who had come, unannounced, into Cadair Idris.

Gwydion, recognizing Myrrdin's voice, gestured for Arthur to stay where he was, and hurriedly made his way to stand before the doors. For Myrrdin was accompanied by six figures dressed in robes of brown, their hoods pulled low over their faces. Rhodri followed behind them, his hand hovering over his sword, his blue eyes watchful.

"Myrrdin," Gwydion began, "who have you—"

But Myrrdin, his gray robe gleaming in the golden light, held up his hand for silence. His wise, dark eyes were calm and he was smiling slightly.

"High King of Kymru," Myrrdin continued, "I bring you allies. I bring you friends."

Within the Druid's Alcove, Sinend stirred and tentatively took a few steps forward, her gray eyes wide as she took in the featureless visitors who wore the robes of Druids.

"Friends, Myrrdin?" Gwydion asked, gesturing to the six figures that stood quite still in the golden doorway. "Druids? And you led them here? Are you mad?"

"Certainly not," Myrrdin said crisply. "Arthur, I beg to present to you—"

But Myrrdin did not finish the sentence. For Sinend flew from the alcove, skimming across the golden floor and flinging herself into the arms of one of the figures.

"Menw!" she cried, as she embraced a thin, slight figure. "Brother!"

The boy's hood fell away from his face as he grinned and held his sister tightly. "Sinend," he cried as he stroked her reddish-brown hair. There were tears in his dark eyes, but he smiled as he held her.

"Why are you here?" Sinend asked as she put her brother from her, holding his hands in her own and looking searchingly into his young face. "How did you ever get away from Da?"

"He didn't," one of the still figures said, pulling his hood back from his face.

"Da!" Sinend gasped, as she realized that Aergol, the Archdruid's heir, one of the foremost traitors to Kymru, was here in the hall.

The others poured out of their alcoves, standing before the steps leading up to the throne, forming a human shield in front of Arthur. Elidyr Master Bard and Elstar Ardewin; their sons, Llywelyn and Cynfar; the Dreamers, Dinaswyn and Cariadas;

Dudod and Sabrina, with Gwen in the forefront, they stood fiercely, ready to do battle for their king.

But Rhiannon did not join them. Instead, she came to stand beside Gwydion as he stared at Myrrdin and Aergol.

"How could you do this, Myrrdin?" Gwydion asked, his voice harsh. "How could you bring the Archdruid's traitorous heir before the High King?"

"Because this is where he wished to be taken," Myrrdin said simply.

"You compelled Myrrdin to do this thing?" Gwydion snapped to Aergol. "You forced him to bring you here?"

"I did not force him," Aergol said, as he stood unmoving by Myrrdin's side. "I asked him."

"Myrrdin, have you lost your wits?" Gwydion began, but he was cut off as Arthur's voice rang through the hall.

"Aergol ap Custennin var Dinaswyn," Arthur said solemnly, "you have come to see the High King and I am here. What is your business with me?"

Aergol bowed to Arthur, then gestured to his companions. "I bring with me some of the most powerful Druids in the land, our most honored teachers at Caer Duir. Ceindrech, our teacher of astronomy," he gestured, and one of the Druids pushed back her hood. Her brown hair spilled down her back, and her dark eyes were proud. "Aldwr, our teacher of mathematics," Aergol went on, as another Druid pushed back his hood. The man's hair was gray, and his green eyes were keen in a sharp face. "Madryn, our teacher of religion," Aergol said, as another Druid pushed back her hood. Her hair was blond with streaks of gray at the temples, and her brown eyes were sharp. "And Yrth, our teacher of the almanac," he said, as the last Druid pulled back his hood. Yrth's gray eyes were calm and patient in a weather-beaten face. "And, of course, my son, Menw ap Aergol var Cendrech," he finished, gesturing at the boy. The six Druids bowed, then fixed Arthur with their eyes.

"These Druids, High King, have come to offer you their services," Aergol went on. "They are yours to do with as you will."

For a moment, no one spoke. Gwydion moved forward to

stand directly in front of Aergol. "You must be very sure that Arthur will win, Aergol," he said, his voice full of contempt, "for you to decide to throw in your lot with us."

Aergol, his dark eyes never leaving Arthur's face, smiled bitterly, "On the contrary, Dreamer, I believe that Arthur will lose. He cannot win with the might of the entire Coranian Empire ranged against him."

"Then why have you come? For you must know that the might of six Druids will not be enough to kill Arthur. He will take the power you hurl against him and destroy you all."

"We have not come to kill the High King," Menw said, his young voice shocked. "We are Kymri!"

"A fine time to remember that!" Gwydion shot back.

Arthur did not speak, but merely held up his hand, and those in the hall again fell silent. "Tell me," Arthur said quietly to Aergol.

Aergol took a deep breath. "High King, we can no longer go on as traitors to Kymru, or as traitors to Modron the Mother, our goddess. She cries out against us, and haunts us in our dreams for what we have done. And so we come to you."

"Why now?" Rhiannon asked, her green eyes narrowed in suspicion.

"The Archdruid has done terrible things to Kymru. And we have helped him do that. But what he proposes now is too much for us to stand by and watch."

"And what does Cathbad propose to do now?" Gwydion asked, his voice terrible. "What could be worse than what he has already done? What could be worse than to work with the enemy, to hunt your fellow countrymen, to revile and reject Modron, to give the secret of the enaid-dals to the Coranians? What could be worse than that?"

"He plans to use the tarw-casglaid, the bull-gathering, to proclaim Havgan true High King."

Sinend gasped and her face turned white. "No! He would not risk the Mother's anger so!"

"He will," Aergol said softly. "He will do anything. He proposes a mock ceremony, a sham, where he will pretend to dream that it is Havgan whom the gods have chosen to rule our land. He plans to mock the Mother. It is too much. So we have come to you, Arthur ap Uthyr, the true High King of Kymru."

"My son," Dinaswyn said, as she glided across the golden floor to stand before Aergol. "You have all mocked the Mother, since the Coranians came, and you began to teach the religion of Lytir, the Coranian god. It is too late, I think, for her forgiveness."

"It is too late, Mam, for her to forgive me. But it is not too late for the others. What we have done will be on my head. And I alone will pay for that. The Mother will accept my life as the sacrifice, and my daughter, Sinend, will be the Archdruid of Kymru. She is blameless of what we have done, and Modron will forgive the Druids, when I am dead."

"Da," Sinend whispered as she let go of her brother's hands and came to stand before her father. "Da, you will give your life? You will kill yourself?"

"That is for the High King to do. In the name of justice, Arthur ap Uthyr, I call for the death of one of the traitors to Kymru. Draw your sword, High King, and kill me for what I have done. And may the Mother accept my sacrifice and cleanse the Druids of their darkness and shame."

Arthur rose from his throne, Caladfwlch in the scabbard by his side. As the people before the throne parted to let him through, he drew the sword with a hiss of metal. The eagle's eyes on the hilt gleamed as Arthur came to stand before Aergol.

"Take my life, High King," Aergol said, his head held high, his dark eyes gleaming. "Send me to the Mother for her to punish. The rest are innocent, for they followed me. And I followed Cathbad, for he had taught me that he was right to join with the enemy. I believed it was right for the Druids to be the only power of the gods in the land of Kymru, just as we had been in Lyonesse. I believed the Mother would reward us if we made it so. But I was wrong."

Arthur held Caladfwlch steady in his hand. But he did not move to strike.

"Behold," Aergol called, his voice suddenly huge in the still hall, "behold my daughter, Sinend ur Aergol var Eurgain! For she is the true Archdruid of Kymru. And those Druids who long to be free again will answer to her as their true leader, after I am dead."

"No," Arthur said calmly.

Aergol, his eyes wide with shock, gasped, "No? I tell you, Sinend is blameless! She has never had a part in—"

"I know it," Arthur said, cutting Aergol off. "And Cathbad is not the true Archdruid of Kymru, and has not been since he first betrayed the Mother. Hear me, Aergol. You may not step back from your responsibilities now. For neither is Sinend the true Archdruid of Kymru. You are."

"I cannot be," Aergol gasped. "It is too late for me. The Mother—"

"Will take you in her own time," Arthur interrupted briskly. "Until then I have need of you. You will lead your Druids to take back this land. And rest assured, Aergol ap Custennin var Dinaswyn, we will see to it that Cathbad dies for his mockery of the tarw-casglaid and the Mother. I will not kill you. You will live until the Mother calls you home."

"I tell you, she has called me. I will go to her, and offer myself up to spare the others. She has called me."

"Then she will have to wait," Arthur said crisply. "You have offered yourself to my service, and I call on you now to keep that promise."

"High King, I—"

"There are Smiths of Kymru who suffer on the island of Caer Siddi. And they have need of you and yours, Aergol ap Custennin."

"You will trust me?" Aergol said his eyes wide and incredulous.

"I will, Archdruid. I will. For now."

Chapter Two

Kymru
Helygen Mis, 500

Haford Bryn, Kingdom of Prydyn

King Rhoram shivered briefly atop the icy hill amd drew back his bow. His arrow flew through the chilly air, speeding over the snow-covered ground, and came to rest in the exact center of the knothole in the trunk of the distant, gnarled oak tree.

"Ha!" he crowed to the captain of his war band. "And you said I was too old."

"You are," Achren said coolly, and then she let her arrow fly. It sped through the wan afternoon sunlight and, with a loud crack, split Rhoram's arrow in two.

But Rhoram, undismayed, pulled his last arrow from the quiver on his back. "My dearest Achren," he said as he fit the arrow to the bow, "would you care to make a wager?"

Achren grinned, her dark eyes challenging. "And what might you have to give me that I could not take for myself, King of Prydyn?"

Rhoram grinned back. "Me," he replied, as in one swift movement he drew his bow and let the arrow go. And, of course, just as he had planned it, the arrow embedded itself within her arrow.

For a moment Achren was silent, and Rhoram had enough time to wonder just how badly he miscalculated.

"Fool," she said lightly, as she swung her quiver to her shoulder. "The King of Prydyn does not offer himself to women. Women offer themselves to the King of Prydyn."

"But if I waited for you to offer yourself, I'd die of old age," he said with a smile. But he meant it.

"So you would, my King."

"Achren—"

"Choose your words carefully, Rhoram ap Rhydderch," she said, fingering the dagger that hung on the belt at her slim waist.

"Achren," he said, "you are the only woman I know who would threaten a man who declares undying devotion to you."

"Don't be a fool, Rhoram. I know a passing fancy when I see one. One day you will thank me for paying no attention to you." She turned away and he reached out and caught her arm. But he let her go almost immediately, as he felt her tense.

"Without a doubt, Achren ur Canhustyr, you are the most exasperating woman I have ever met. You think a stone is where my heart should be. And you are wrong."

"I am not wrong," she said, her dark eyes flashing.

"You are," he replied, his voice steady and quiet, the truth of his heart in his blue eyes.

For a long time she was silent, gazing up at him, taking his measure. At last she said, "When once again you reign in Arberth over all of Prydyn, when once again fortune favors you so that you may have the choosing of any woman of Kymru, offer again, if you still wish it."

"And then?" he asked, his blue eyes alight.

"And then," she replied crisply, "we shall see." She turned away, wrapping her fur cloak closer to her. Her dark hair, braided closely to her skull as always, shone briefly beneath the pale sun.

"You can be sure I will ask again," he muttered to himself as she left him there. How long had it been, now, since he knew he loved Achren? Not long. Only in the past few months had he come to understand that. Yet it seemed to him now that he had loved her, without knowing it, for many years. That had always been his problem—that he did not know his own heart. But he was older now, perhaps a little wiser, and he knew that he loved the captain of his war band. And that he always would.

Perhaps the worst part of knowing that he loved Achren was the fact that she would never believe it. And who would? After all, for so many years now his heart had remained untouched, inviolate, since he had made that terrible mistake and let Rhiannon go, only to find that the woman he had left her for was not worth a moment's thought. Since that time he had never again given his heart. He had dallied with women to their mutual enjoyment, and then gently let them go. He had not thought he would ever love again. But he did.

Rhoram sighed. Well, she couldn't hold out against him forever. Or could she? He had never known a woman as stubborn as Achren, and that was saying something.

"Da!"

He turned from his blank contemplation of the distant oak tree and waved to his son as Geriant came running up to him through the snow. The sunlight caught in Geriant's golden hair and his blue eyes were shining as he halted in front of his father.

"Da, there has been a message from the High King."

"Ah. And what, besides burning Havgan's ships, does he wish from us now?"

"He says we are to meet him on the south shore of Camain in three and a half weeks."

"Who is to meet him?"

"You, Achren, and twenty warriors."

"And what is it he would have us do?"

"He would not say. He would only say to be on time."

"Then be there we will. Are you ready, then, to do the High King's bidding?"

Rhoram had expected Geriant's eager assent, but the enthusiasm on his son's face faded and his expression became still. "Geriant?" Rhoram asked in concern. "What's the matter?"

"Da, I—I had the Bard ask the High King when Enid will be rescued."

"Ah," Rhoram said gently. "And what did he say?"

"He said that her freedom was in the hands of her brother."

"Hm," Rhoram said in a neutral tone. He hardly knew what to say. A year ago Geriant had been hand-fast to Enid, Princess of Rheged, and they would have been married by now, if Enid had not had other plans. For that poor, foolish girl had left her brother Owein's camp in the dead of the night and journeyed to Llwynarth, there to beg Bledri the Dewin to give up his traitorous ways. Enid had actually loved Bledri, and been convinced that he had loved her. But Bledri had given her over to King Morcant, the pretender to the throne of Rheged. And Morcant had married Enid, giving himself a better claim to his throne, and brutalizing Enid in the process, if the stories were true. And Rhoram had no reason to disbelieve them. Morcant had always been a pig.

And here, almost a year later, poor Geriant still loved Enid, and thought of nothing but rescuing her, killing Morcant, and making Enid his wife.

"He said that the release of Queen Enid would be the task of her brother," Geriant went on. "And her rescue would be soon and I told him I wanted to be a part of that. And he said I must speak to Owein."

"Of course."

"And he said that he didn't need me to go with you. He said that, if Owein agrees, and if you agree, I could join Owein in Coed Coch and help them to get her back."

"Geriant," Rhoram began gently. But he barely knew how to go on.

"No, Da," Geriant said firmly. "You don't have to tell me what I already know. When we get Enid back, she will not be the same girl she was before she left. But it doesn't matter. I love her. And I always will. I know she doesn't love me. But I want to take her away from Morcant for her sake. Not for mine. And then I will return here. Alone."

Yes, Geriant was like his mother, Christina of Ederynion. Direct, forthright, knowing what was in their heart, knowing the truth from the beginning.

"We must speak to Owein, then, and get his permission for you to join them. For you have mine."

"Thank you, Da," Geriant said with a grin. "I did that already."

Rhoram raised his brows. "You were so sure then that I would allow you to go?"

Geriant smiled. "I was so sure."

"You know me too well. And what did Owein say?"

"He said it would be at Bedwen Mis. And to come to Coed Coch at any time in the next month. And that my sister would be glad to see me."

"I'm sure she would," Rhoram said, smiling. How relieved and grateful he had been when Sanon came to him at Cadair Idris as he and the other rulers prepared to return to their camps, after witnessing Arthur pass the Tynged Mawr and become High King. Sanon had said that she would not be returning to Haford Bryn with Rhoram, but going to Coed Coch, with Owein. And the joy on her fresh face had been just as much as the joy in Rhoram's heart, that his daughter had found love and peace at last.

"Then you must not go with us," Rhoram said firmly, "but rather go to Coed Coch and help Owein to bring his sister out of her prison. Not forgetting the truth of what you have said. She will be changed."

"That does not matter. Because I have not. And never will."

Coed Coch, Kingdom of Rheged

Owein waited for Esyllt to break contact with the Bard at Haford Bryn. When she had done so, she looked up at him with her deep blue eyes.

"He is coming?" Owein asked.

"He is," Esyllt replied, absently stirring the slumbering campfire in front of Owein's tent.

"I must tell Sanon," Owein said and turned to go.

"Owein, I beg a favor of you," Esyllt said quietly.

Owein turned back to her. Snow lightly dusted the thick branches of the trees overhead, but very little sifted onto the forest floor. The trees of Coed Coch were too thick for that. But the ground was cold and wet and the dead leaves were soggy beneath his feet.

Owein wore brown leather tunic and trousers, lined with wool and, even walking just a few feet, seemed to instinctively blend in with the trunks of the dark trees. The lines of heartache and pain that had once been carved into the stone-like countenance of his young face were smoothed away, though his blue eyes held a sadness still, the remembrance of his mother and father and brother. That sadness would always be there, but now there was joy, too, since Sanon of Prydyn had come with him to Coed Coch to share his exile and his heart.

"A boon, Esyllt?" he prompted. "And what do you wish?" He stopped himself from asking what she could possibly want now, for Esyllt wanted many things, most of which he had no power to give her. But it was in her nature to demand, as beautiful women sometimes will. And he was used to it. For he understood, as many did not, that Esyllt ur Maelwys, wife to March y Meirchion and lover to Trystan ap Naf, Owein's captain, was merely afraid, and it was her nature to seek out any who would promise, or seem to promise, to care for her.

"Trystan is in Ystrad Marchell, leading the Cerddorian in burning Havgan's ships, as the High King has ordered."

"Yes," Owein agreed, knowing full well where this was leading.

"I beg you to order him back to Coed Coch."

"I need him where he is, Esyllt. You know that."

"Owein—"

"No." He was silent as Esyllt slowly turned away. "Esyllt," he said softly as she turned from him. "Your husband, he is almost well."

"Yes," Esyllt said dully, not bothering to turn around. "He is almost well."

"Go to him, then. For he loves you."

"As Trystan does not."

"That I cannot say."

"Cannot or will not?"

"Cannot," Owein said firmly. As she slowly walked away, he couldn't help but notice that Esyllt had not asked if she could go to Ystrad Marchell to be with Trystan. Esyllt had never been brave. But she was his Bard, and had been his father's Bard. And he was sorry that he could not help her.

He walked away from the clearing with its ring of tents, so well made that they were warm and snug, even at this time of year. He needed to tell Sanon the news. He smiled to himself, because he would have gone to find Sanon now, in any case, news or no news. For she was his heart's delight, the only delight he had ever really known, and he always longed to be with her, though that never prevented him from doing his duty, for that was not his way.

He knew where she would be. She would be with Teleri, his lieutenant, practicing her work with sword and dagger. Sanon was already an accomplished bow-woman, but she had, as she explained to Owein, never given her attention to the art of swordplay. Before the enemy came, her time had usually been given to the making of tapestries, to weaving, to embroidery, because that was what she liked. She could have trained for combat, had she wished, but she had never wished it. And after the enemy came, she had done nothing, she told Owein, for the last two years. She had been consumed with sorrow for the death of her intended, Owein's elder brother, Elphin. She had taken no interest in life, had, she said, wandered the caves of Ogaf Greu like a pale ghost.

But now, she had gone on to explain to him that first night together, her dark eyes honest and truthful, her golden hair spilling over his bare chest, she wished to learn to fight. Because she was Queen of Rheged now and she wanted to fight with him, shoulder to shoulder, to drive the enemy away from their land.

And he had said, bitterly, that Morcant was the King of Rheged, and that his sister, Enid, was the queen. And Sanon had sat up so quickly she had startled him, and glared down at him as he lay within the blankets, and her dark eyes had flashed.

"You are King. And I am your queen. And, soon, Morcant will be dead by your hand and your sister will be returned to you."

And he had not argued with her, but had pulled her down on top of him, and kissed her anger and his bitterness away.

"Like this, my Queen," he heard Teleri say. And he heard the whoosh of a knife blade flung through the cold air, and the solid thunk as it embedded itself in the trunk of a tree. He crept up to the clearing where his wife and his lieutenant stood.

Sanon wore brown riding leathers and a wide, red belt around her slender waist. Her calf-length brown boots clung to her shapely legs. She shook back her golden hair from her face, narrowed her dark eyes, and threw her dagger in an underhanded cast. The blade whipped through the clearing, burying itself in the tree trunk.

"Good," Teleri said as she walked over to the tree and pulled both daggers out of the wood. "That's what you want to do to get them in the belly. Now, the overhand throw is good for getting them in the back." Teleri's petite form was always at odds with the relish in her voice when she spoke of the best ways to kill. Her gray-green eyes were alight as she began to instruct Sanon on how best to throw the knife to kill as efficiently as possible. Sanon's dark eyes were grave as she listened.

"And then we can move on to slitting the throat. Remember, always do that from behind them. If you are in front, you will take a blood bath, and that can be tiresome."

"And messy," Owein added, as he slipped into the clearing.

Sanon's dark eyes held laughter as she turned to him. "Watch," she told Owein. And she cocked back her arm and cast the dagger across the clearing. With a solid smack it embedded itself in a trunk.

"A good cast, *cariad*," Owein said as he kissed her. "We will make a warrior of you yet, won't we, Teleri?"

"The Queen does well," Teleri agreed.

"*Cariad*, I have news for you," Owein went on. "Your brother is coming."

"Geriant? Here? To Coed Coch?"

"Indeed. He has asked for, and I have given him, permission to aid in Enid's rescue."

"Oh, Owein," Sanon said slowly. "Do you think he truly understands?"

"From what he said through the Bards, I believe he does. He does not expect Enid's gratitude or, indeed, anything from her at all. But he wishes to help, and the High King and your father have given permission. As have I."

"Well," said Sanon doubtfully, "it might do him good. And then again, it might not. He may say the right words, and even believe them, but his heart will be forever set on Enid. It is his way. When will we leave?"

"Leave?" Owein asked blankly. "For where?"

"To rescue Enid, of course."

"We?" Owein asked quickly, startled. "You are not coming."

"I am," Sanon said firmly.

"You are not—"

Sanon laid the palm of her hand lightly over Owein's mouth.

Owein sighed and gently removed her hand, kissing her palm. So this had been the point of all this knife throwing. "I see. So, Queen of Rheged, will you always tell me what to do?"

"Only when you need telling, *cariad*," Sanon said with a smile.

"Which I hope is not too often," Teleri said with a wicked grin and a dig to Owein's ribs. "You must have at least learned a little about what to do by now."

"Oh," Sanon replied with a wicked grin of her own, "as to that, he needs no telling."

And then Owein did something he had not done in many, many years. He blushed.

Coed Ddu, Kingdom of Ederynion

LLUDD AP OLWEN var Kilwch, Prince of Ederynion, clenched his jaw and stood, unmoving, in the center of the clearing. With all his will, he concentrated on not letting his rage pass his lips, not letting his boiling anger out into the wan morning light.

But enraged he was, and everyone knew it. They waited for him to speak, and, as they waited, they were silent and still.

Angharad, his captain, her green eyes blazing with her own anger, her glowing red hair muted by the dense trees which kept out the sunlight from fully penetrating the forest, waited for Lludd to speak. Alun Cilcoed, Lord of Arystli, was scowling, his dark eyes thunderous. Talhearn, Lludd's Bard, waited quietly, his blue eyes wise and sharp in his lined face. Emrys, Lludd's lieutenant, stood stiffly, holding the bloody dagger in his hand, his eyes angry, filmed with unshed tears.

Lludd stared down at the corpse at his feet. Naf, one of the best of his men, had died in surprise. His eyes, still open and staring, were lightly dusted now with snow. Naf, whom Lludd had known ever since he was a boy, had taught Lludd the rudiments of knife fighting. Never again for this turn of the Wheel would Naf wield a blade with joy in his eyes. For his soul had gone on to the Summer Land, to await rebirth.

Lludd did not, could not, move as he looked down at the murdered body of his friend. Just a few moments ago Lludd had been on the edge of waking from a dream of Queen Morrigan of Gwynedd, the High King's sister. He had seen her for the first time in the caves where the leaders of Kymru had gathered those few months ago, to view the Treasures, to meet Arthur, to follow him to Cadair Idris and watch as he tested his soul.

Since that first moment that he had seen her, he had few moments when he was not thinking of her. Her long, rich auburn hair, her dark, shining eyes, her beautiful smile which so easily turned to a grin, her easy competence with knife and bow, these things had reached out to him, captured him, and he was not sorry to be bound.

Someday, he had thought ever since then, someday, when the enemy was gone, when his sister wore the torque of Ederynion in freedom, when his work here was done, he would go to Morrigan, whether she willed it or no. And he would lay his heart at her feet. And perhaps, just perhaps, she would accept it.

But that sweet dream, the dream that sustained him as he fought and schemed and led his warriors, and despaired of ever freeing his sister, that sweet dream had been broken this morning. By this.

"So, Llwyd Cilcoed is gone," Lludd said at last.

Angharad nodded. "Sometime in the night. When we found Naf, he had already gone stone cold. Been dead at least six, maybe seven hours."

"And my brother has had that much time to run," Alun Cilcoed said, his dark eyes glittering. "My prince, I beg you, let me go after him. I will find him. And this time, I will kill him."

"No," Lludd said quietly.

"Prince," Alun pleaded, "I must. How else can I live with this shame? My brother deserves death, and I must be the one to give it to him."

"Perhaps you will, Alun," Lludd said, still looking down at Naf's corpse. "My heart says that you will have your chance."

"Then—" Alun began eagerly.

"No. You may not go after him."

"Why?" Angharad flared. "I will go with him. Between the two of us Llwyd Cilcoed is a dead man."

Lludd looked up then, his swift gaze crackling in the air like summer lightening. Angharad, who feared nothing, fell silent.

"I will waste no warriors on Llwyd Cilcoed. We have a mission to complete. Perhaps some of you have forgotten." No one answered him. He had not thought that they would. "Havgan's ships are burning up and down the coast of Ederynion. And the job is not yet done. This task is more important than Llwyd Cilcoed's worthless hide."

Lludd did not want to say what he said. He would have given almost anything for the chance to run Llwyd Cilcoed to earth and gut him. The others thought, perhaps, that his hatred for Llwyd was a pale thing. But it was not. For he hated his mother's former lover with all his heart. He hated Llwyd Cilcoed for his desertion of Queen Olwen when the enemy came. He hated Llwyd Cilcoed for the hold the man had once had on her. He hated Llwyd Cilcoed, not for the slights he had given Lludd, but for the slights he had given Elen, Lludd's sister. Had Llwyd Cilcoed thought that no one had noticed the way he used to look at Elen? Had the man truly thought no one could see the lust in his eyes as he looked at the daughter of his lover? True, Olwen herself had never seen it. But Lludd had. And Elen had. They had known his thoughts and his thoughts had been vile.

Since Llwyd Cilcoed had come here, thrown himself on Lludd's mercy, and pleaded to be protected by him, almost a year ago, he had served diligently. For Llwyd Cilcoed was Dewin, and for that Lludd had spared the man's life, knowing that the man could be of real use. But Lludd had not trusted him, not for a moment. He had set a guard on Llwyd Cilcoed, a warrior who shadowed him, watched him, saw to it that, in raids on the enemy, Llwyd Cilcoed did what he was told.

And last night, Llwyd Cilcoed had killed his guard and slipped away.

It was then that Lludd began to think. "Why?" he asked Talhearn.

The old Bard's blue eyes sharpened. Trust Talhearn to truly understand the question. "Indeed. Why now? Who has he been Wind-Riding with?"

Angharad shook her head. "We can't know the answer to that. None of us here has that talent."

"Perhaps he hadn't contacted anyone yet," Lludd said softly. "Perhaps he had to go in order to get close enough to the one he wanted to see."

Talhearn nodded. "He could contact another Dewin up to thirty leagues away. No more."

"Eiodel is further than that," Lludd said quietly.

"So it is," Talhearn agreed.

"Talhearn, contact the Master Bard. Tell him to tell the Ardewin what Llwyd Cilcoed has done. Let them seek him out. He cannot hide from the Dewin."

"He can," Talhearn corrected. "But not for long."

"And when you are done with that, contact the High King. Tell Arthur what has happened here. And tell him that we will be leaving Coed Ddu somewhat sooner than we thought. We must leave before Llwyd Cilcoed betrays our location. Our hiding places in Ial are almost ready, and we can make do. That Dewin never knew anything about that."

"It shall be done, my prince," Talhearn said, bowing his head.

"And tell him one more thing."

"Yes?"

"Tell him my sister has been prisoner long enough. Tell him that I will not obey one more order from him until she is freed."

"Lludd, I cannot—" Talhearn began. But before he could finish, the old man sank to his knees, his eyes wide with surprise.

Lludd leapt across the clearing and took Talhearn's arm. Heart attack, he thought incoherently. He's dying.

"The High King," Talhearn gasped. "He speaks to us."

"By the gods," Angharad murmured. "All the way from Cadair Idris?"

"He is High King," Alun murmered, his eyes alight.

"What does he say to us, Talhearn?" Lludd demanded.

"He says you are to do your duty to him, whether he rescues your sister or no."

Lludd's brown eyes blazed with rage for a moment, and then he bowed his head. "It shall be as the High King wills."

"But Arthur says that he will not make you wait much longer. In a few days he will send us someone who can help us. Elen will be free by Bedwen Mis. Even if he has to come himself to free her."

"The High King is generous," Lludd said, his voice breaking slightly. "Even after my harsh words. Give him my thanks."

"It is done," Talhearn said. The Bard relaxed, leaning against Lludd.

"You are hurt," Lludd said, his anger kindling again.

"I am not," Talhearn said with a smile. "I am only tired. I tell you, boyo, I have never felt such power. Never doubt it, Kymru will soon be free."

Cemais, Kingdom of Gwynedd

Queen Morrigan quickly made her way up the gently swelling hills of south Cemais. A stiff wind nipped at her, bringing the blood to her cheeks, whipping back her auburn hair to fan out into the winter afternoon.

Snow dusted the rolling hills, glittering like diamonds beneath the coldly shining sun. Less than a league away, to the east, was the camp her Cerddorian had made when they had arrived here from Mynydd Tawel. But though she knew it was there she saw no sign of the camp, so well was it tucked away in the folds of the land, artfully concealed beneath the tall, thick brush. She wished her brother was here, so she could show him how well they had done.

Morrigan sighed. She had barely begun to know Arthur before he had irrevocably changed. He had been taken by Gwydion to be raised in secret when she was only two years old, too young to remember him. The first time she had seen him to remember was the day he and the Dreamer, with Rhiannon and Gwenhwyfar, had come to Mynydd Tawel.

Her throat tightened, for thinking of Arthur reminded her of her father. He had been dead now these past two years, killed in battle with the Coranians. And still she missed him so. She dismissed her tears and swallowed. She was the Queen now, and tears were not for her.

Then she smiled. For she knew what was for her—Lludd, Prince of Ederynion. She wanted him and she would have him. She did not think he would have an objection for she had seen the light in his eyes, even if he had barely spoken to her at Cadair Idris. She knew it and she was forthright enough to admit it.

And why not? She was no Cai, longing for someone but too frightened of loss to speak. She had seen how he looked at Susanna. Susanna's son, Gwyhar, did his best to urge the captain, but Cai was stubborn. Strange how a man could be so brave in battle, but such a coward in matters of the heart.

And in matters of the heart, even a man as wise as Myrrdin could be a fool. For Morrigan had seen the light in her Dewin's eyes at Cadair Idris. She had known that Neuad was in love with the man who had once been Ardewin of Kymru. And she knew what Myrrdin thought. For Myrrdin was old enough to be her father and Neuad was young and beautiful, and any man could be hers for the taking. But Neuad did not want any man. She wanted Myrrdin. And Morrigan knew her well enough to know that Myrrdin was as good as caught. No matter what the old man thought.

In matters of the heart, Cai's nephew, Bedwyr, was not much better. She knew why Bedwyr brooded so much, and over whom he brooded. For Tangwen, daughter of Madoc the Usurper was in a truly unenviable position indeed. Her shame at her father's deeds led her to spy for Morrigan and her Cerddorian. Yet she loved her father, even as she betrayed him.

A change in the sound of the wind alerted her and she turned. The sun lit Susanna's red-gold hair to a fiery sheen as the Bard traversed the last few feet and came to sit on a snow-dusted rock at Morrigan's feet.

"My Queen," Susanna said, inclining her head.

"If you wish to be formal, it's best to do that with my mother," Morrigan said with a grin.

"Less formal now, don't you think?"

"She is, isn't she?" Morrigan agreed. "Because?"

"She has seen her son again. Her hope returns. Her sacrifice from years ago now has a purpose."

"Will I ever, ever, be as clear sighted as you?"

Susanna laughed. "My Queen, it is not necessary that you be wise about others' hearts. Only that you listen to those that are."

"Then I will always listen to you."

"And Lludd, too, I think. For he is no fool."

Morrigan blushed, but smiled. "He is going to be mine."

"So he is," Susanna agreed.

"Why did you follow me here?"

"I Wind-Spoke to your brother."

"He is well?" Morrigan asked eagerly. "He has a new task for us?"

"He is well," Susanna said gravely. "And he has no new task. I told him that Havgan's ships were being burnt along the coast as he ordered. And that we would be moving to Coed Dulas in a month's time, as agreed."

"The better to be close to Tegeingl. So we can take it back," Morrigan said fiercely. "We are ready. And I am more than ready to topple false Madoc from his bony backside and back into the muck where he belongs." Susanna did not answer for a moment and Morrigan's heart beat fast. "No, oh, no. He didn't!"

"Didn't what?"

"Forbid me to fight. He didn't. I'm old enough."

"Almost sixteen," Susanna gravely agreed.

"I know what I'm doing. I know how to fight. And I know

how to lead a battle. I will not stay behind!"

"No, you will not. He said nothing of that."

"Susanna! How dare you frighten me!"

"He did give me a message for you."

"He did? What did he say?"

"That he loves you."

Morrigan bowed her head so Susanna would not see her tears. But Susanna knew.

"Yes," the Bard said gently. "He loves you very much."

"And that was all of the message?" Morrigan asked harshly. For her voice would shake if she did not.

"All that you need to know."

"He knows about the spy in Tegeingl, then. The one you know about but have told no one. Until you told him."

"He is the High King," Susanna said simply.

"And I am your queen. Why, why won't you tell me who it is? You won't even tell the Master Bard."

"Anieron knew. He bade me to tell no one but the High King, should he return to us. And hold that secret safe until it is time."

"It is as dangerous as that?"

"It is as dangerous as that."

"Well then," Morrigan said firmly, but brightly, for there was no malice in her, "we must see to it that the time is soon. For I will take back what is mine before the spring is out."

"So you will, my Queen. So you will."

Eiodel, Gwytheryn

HAVGAN SAT STRAIGHT and unyielding in his golden chair in the Great Hall. He was dressed in gold and rubies and a circlet of gold held his honey-blond hair back from his grim face. His amber eyes glistened while Gram, the Bana's sword, lay unsheathed across his knees. The bright blade etched with three boars' heads glittered, as did the blood-red ruby on the black iron pommel.

His mistress stood to the left of the golden chair. Arianrod wore a kirtle of amber, which lay gently over her swollen belly. Topaz glittered at her ears and slender throat. Her honey-blond hair was held back from her face with a band of amber stones.

Aelfwyn sat on a chair to his right. His wife was dressed in cool white, and her long, blond hair was held back from her face with a band of diamonds. She shimmered in the darkened hall. Her emerald green eyes glittered coldly.

Sigerric stood stiffly to Aelfwyn's right. He was dressed in black and emeralds, the black accentuating the pallor of his tight face. His dark eyes drank in the air of the hate-filled hall, and his thin hand clenched the dagger at his emerald-studded belt.

Havgan nodded to the men at the doors, and the wyrce-jaga was led in to them. The man was pitiful in his fear, his black robe making him seem even paler. His hands twisted around a small, silvery, bejeweled box.

"You were the wyrce-jaga at Maen in Prydyn, five months ago," Havgan began.

"I was," the man said stiffly.

"What is your name?" Aelfwyn interrupted.

"I am called Hild, Lady, son of Hildas, of Winburnan, in Ivelas."

"Why do you ask his name?" Havgan demanded of Aelfwyn, his voice low. "It is nothing to me."

"My father always asked the names of any who came before him. It is what a true ruler would do. You would not know that, of course."

"Of course," Havgan said smoothly. "Being only the son of a fisherman."

"Just so," Aelfwyn said coldly.

"My dearest wife," he said with a smile, "it is unwise to be so very, very sure that I will not have you killed."

"You can't," Aelfwyn said flatly. "Not yet. Not while my father lives. You are a fool to try to frighten me."

He smiled again, a smile to say that she mustn't be too sure. But she was right. And he knew it. And so did she. He turned back to the wyrce-jaga. "And we entrusted you with the testing tool. The one we captured from Cian, the Bard of Prydyn."

The wyrce-jaga swallowed hard. "Yes, lord, you did."

"And yet, since five months ago, this device has caught no

witches."

Havgan did not say what had prompted him to send the wyrce-jaga to Maen with their only testing device in the first place. He would never tell anyone that the prompting that there was something in Maen had come to him in a dream.

"Lord, I have done nothing to the testing device! I swear it. It is only that the witches are too clever, now, to be caught with it. It is only that. I did nothing to it!"

The poor man was getting excited. And Havgan did not want him to do that. Not yet. Not until he told everything. "Of course, wyrce-jaga. Of course that is so."

Hild relaxed slightly. The fool.

"Tell us, then. When was the last witch you caught?"

"Five months ago," Hild said promptly. "In Maen. A child. A little boy. I think his parents were shocked. I do not think they knew. We took the boy to Afalon, to join the other captured witches. And we killed the parents, for daring to breed a witch."

Out of the corner of his eye Havgan saw Arianrod's fist clench. Her knuckles were white. One hand went to her belly. But Havgan could not comfort her now. He did not even want to think too much, now, of what his beloved was. And of what their son would be.

"And the day after that?"

"The day after?" Hild asked.

"Yes, the day after. Did anything unusual happen? Anything at all?"

"Nothing. Just the people going in and out of the city."

"Did you not see a man with dark hair and gray eyes? And with him a woman with black hair and eyes of green?"

"That describes many of the Kymri. How could I possibly—" The wyrce-jaga fell silent.

"Ah," Havgan said. "You have remembered something."

"Just a merchant. And his family. The merchant was in a hurry. Insistent that he and his be tested so they could be on their way. Most Kymri, they hold back. They hate it. But he did not. He seemed to almost be—"

"Looking forward to it."

Arianrod leaned forward. "Did the device leave your hand at any time? Did that merchant touch you at all?"

The wyrce-jaga's face stiffened and he did not answer.

"Wyrce-jaga," Havgan said gently, too gently, "answer the question."

"I will answer no question put to me by a witch!" Hild cried.

"You will answer any question I wish, Hild," Havgan purred. "You will tell me anything."

Sigerric left the dais, drawing his dagger and came to stand behind Hild. "You will answer the question, wyrce-jaga," Sigerric said softly. "Never mind who asks it."

Hild broke into a cold sweat and stubbornly held his tongue. But as Sigerric laid the edge of the blade against the wyrce-jaga's neck, he answered. "Yes! Yes! The merchant, he knocked the device out of my hand!"

"Ah," Arianrod said softly. "And did he pick it up for you? Bring it back to you?"

"Yes," Hild sobbed. "Yes, he did."

"Bring it to me," Arianrod commanded.

Sigerric took the device from the wyrce-jaga's shaking hands and returned to the dais, handing it to Arianrod.

She held the box in her left hand, and inserted her right finger into the opening on its side. The amethyst and topaz in the center of the top of the box glowed. But the other stones—the emerald, the opal, the sapphire, and the pearl—did not.

"The pearl should be glowing to indicate that I am Dewin," Arianrod said to Havgan. "It would, if this were real."

"Gwydion," Havgan breathed.

"Yes," Arianrod agreed. "Many years ago he was there when Arthur, the Prince of Gwynedd, was tested. And the device showed that Arthur had no gifts. But Arthur was, as we know, destined to be High King. The box should have sung for him. But nothing happened."

"Gwydion had a false box made."

"Yes. To show the world that Arthur had no gifts. That Arthur could not be important."

"And kept the device. And switched it, taking the one we had that was real."

"Yes."

"So, this fool lost the real device. He let it be taken from him. Right beneath his nose. The only testing device we had."

"Lord," Hild began as the tears started to stream down his white face. "Lord, the Dreamer is the cleverest witch of all. He has fooled us all for years and years. It is not my fault if—"

"Hild," Havgan said gently as he stood up, Gram in his hands. The naked blade flashed as Havgan descended the dais and came to stand before the wyrce-jaga. "Hild, you are not wise to remind us of our failures."

"Your pardon, Lord," Hild sobbed. "I, I did not mean—"

"No, I'm sure you did not."

"Lord, please—"

But the blade flashed through the air to bury itself in the wyrce-jaga's heart. Gram slid into the man's chest, effortlessly parting flesh. Hild's eyes widened as he stiffened in agony. Havgan kicked Hild off the blade and the wyrce-jaga crumpled at his feet. Gram dripped blood and Havgan cleaned the blade with the wyrce-jaga's robe and then returned to his chair, still holding the unsheathed sword.

Warriors began to carry away Hild's bloody body, and some knelt down on the flagstones to clean up the blood. Just then a warrior, sweat-slicked and panting, sprinted into the hall and flung himself at Havgan's feet.

"Lord," the warrior gasped. "I bring messages."

"Get this man some ale," Aelfwyn snapped, and the ale was instantly brought. She knelt down beside the warrior and made him drink.

"Lord," the warrior said again when he could speak. "I bring news."

"Tell it then," Havgan said quietly.

"Your ships. Your ships are burning. All over the coasts of Kymru they burn. The Cerddorian. They come in the night like the wind, bringing fire. You have not one ship on this island that is whole."

"He told you," Arianrod murmured to Havgan, her face white and set. "He told you he would do this."

"Arthur," Aelfwyn agreed. "That night he came here. He said that if you would not leave, then you must stay and fight. And you refused to leave. And now it is too late."

Sigerric, his dark eyes burning in his thin face, said, "It is not just that he prevents you from leaving. Do you understand that?"

"I do," Havgan said steadily.

"Yes, husband," Aelfwyn said sweetly. "With your ships burned, you cannot send for more warriors from Corania. The High King will fight you. And fight you with the warriors you have to hand, for there will be no more."

"Oh, but there will," Havgan said calmly.

"Impossible," Aelfwyn snapped.

"You are wrong, Aelfwyn," Havgan said with a serene smile. "Again."

Chapter Three

Cadair Idris
Gwytheryn, Kymru
Helygen Mis & Onnen Mis, 500

Suldydd, Calan Morynion—early morning

Dinaswyn ur Morvryn, one-time Dreamer of Kymru, reached the bottom of the stairs and hurried down the third level corridor, her heart beating fast. For Arthur had sent for her and she desperately hoped that the summons she had waited for had come at last.

Mabon, King of the Sun, she prayed, *whom I have served for so long, please. Please, let me this once receive what I ask for. Let me receive what Gwydion promised me so very long ago. It is all that I ask. All that is left to me.*

She stood still for a moment outside the door of the garden room. Surreptitiously she wiped her clammy palms on her black dress. She touched her long, silvery hair, held back from her face by a band of fiery opals. Schooling herself to show nothing of her feelings, her gray eyes hardened and cooled. And then she was ready.

She stepped in the room, taking in her surroundings at a glance. The walls were bathed in gold and the circular room was brilliantly lit from the same unknown light source that lit all of Cadair Idris. Jewels winked from the fronts of the seven doors set at intervals around the chamber. Behind each door, she knew, was a small chamber dedicated to the various gods and goddesses of Kymru. Each door was carved with the symbol for that deity and outlined with the appropriate gems, and next to each door grew that tree associated with the god or goddess. The Stewards said that the golden light helped the trees to stay strong, even without sunlight.

The yew tree, for Annwyn, Lord of Chaos, and the hazel tree for his mate, Aertan, Weaver of Fate, stood beside the door decorated with onyx and bloodstone. The rubies for Y Rhyfelwr, the Warrior Twins, flashed between elder leaves, like blood-red berries. Silvery birch blended with sapphires for Taran of the Winds. The opals for Mabon of the Sun flashed fire between the branches of the rowan.

Ivy twined around the trunk of an alder tree, for Cerridwen, Queen of the Wood and Cerrunnos, Master of the Hunt. Amethysts and topazes glittered between the leaves. Emerald flashed through the leaves of the oak tree for Modron, the Mother. And the delicate leaves of the ash tree shimmered through the soft glow of pearls for Nantsovelta of the Moon, Lady of the Waters.

A jeweled fountain bubbled and splashed as water streamed from it, skipping over stones to feed the roots of the trees. Scattered throughout the chamber were small tables containing musical instruments, games, even an ornate set of tarbell, the Kymric game of logic and skill. The tarbell set itself was the most elaborate Dinaswyn had ever seen. The playing board, with its interlocking squares of black and white, glowed. The carved figures glittered with jewels. The silver dragon, representing the Ardewin, glimmered with pearls. The brown bull of the Archdruid shimmered with emeralds. The black raven of the Dreamers spread its opal-studded wings, and the Master Bard's nightingale glistened with sapphires. The wolf of Prydyn, the hawk of Gwynedd, the horse of Rheged, and the swan of Ederynion were all there. And Arderydd, the eagle of the Brenin flickered with emeralds, pearls, sapphires, and opals.

Arthur was seated at the table with the tarbell set, while Gwydion stood behind Arthur's chair.

Slowly, she approached the High King. Gwydion's gray eyes, so like her own, bore into her. But she only glanced at him. All her attention was focused on Arthur. And he was studying the tarbell board with a frown, and did not look up as she approached.

Her slender fingers reached out and picked up the figurine that glittered with onyx and opals. She gripped the carved raven tightly in her hand and waited.

After a moment, Arthur looked up. The scar on his face glittered palely. He studied her tense shoulders, her arrow-straight posture, her silvery hair and gray, cool eyes. Then he smiled, and held out his hand. She smiled back, slowly, and returned the figurine to him. He nodded for her to sit, and then began. "Gwydion tells me of a promise he made to you long ago."

She nodded, her mouth dry.

"Do you remember it?" he asked softly.

"Yes," she answered her voice steady. "It was some years ago. He wanted me to carry a message to Uthyr, your father. It was a coded letter, telling Uthyr where to meet Gwydion for a journey."

"And the secret journey my father was to take?"

"To see you. For the last time."

"Yes. This is what I have seen," Arthur replied.

"You have seen that?" Dinaswyn asked, startled.

"In the Time-Walk I took," Arthur said smoothly. "The one you and Gwydion and Cariadas helped me to take. For that time I was the Walker-Between-the-Worlds of past and present. And I saw his promise to you."

"We did not see what you saw," Dinaswyn answered. "We only knew that you needed our power. That you needed the Time-Walk."

"And so you gave me what I needed. Because?"

"Because you are the High King. And even the Dreamers bow to you and your need."

"But this thing that I ask you now, this task, is not from my need. It is from yours. From the promise Gwydion made. The promise—"

"To use me," Dinaswyn said fiercely, "that when the fires of testing were upon us, he would use me for a great task. He would help make my life mean something."

"More than it already does?" Gwydion asked harshly, speaking for the first time.

"And what does it mean now?" Dinaswyn shot back, her voice hard and bitter. "What has it meant for so many years? What has it meant since the dreams passed on to you? Do you remember how many years that has been, Gwydion? If you do not, I can assure you, I do."

She rose from her chair and came to stand before Gwydion. Her hands were twisted into the cloth of her skirt, gripping the material hard in her need to make him understand, he who had never understood.

"It was eighteen years ago, nephew. Eighteen years I have not dreamed. Eighteen years since the only thing I ever really had was taken from me. Can you understand what that means? Did you ever even try?"

"Dinaswyn—" Gwydion began.

"No," she said harshly. "You never did. You set me aside and never gave me another thought, except to think that I was a meddlesome old woman. That's all you have thought of me since I taught you all I could so long ago."

"You are wrong."

Arthur's voice, so quiet and yet so powerful, stilled her. She turned away from Gwydion, her brows raised. "How would you—"

"I have seen," Arthur said softly. "Gwydion loves you. More than you could ever know. More, I think, than you would even wish for. He has thought often of you. He knew from his dreams that defeat would come to us. And he sought to keep you apart from it. He sought to keep you safe."

"By shunting me aside?" Dinaswyn asked incredulously.

"Even so," Arthur said.

"For Mabon's sake," Gwydion began, his silvery eyes snapping in irritation, "do you think, nephew, you are qualified to tell anyone how I feel and what I think?"

"I have Walked-Between-the-Worlds, Gwydion ap Awst," Arthur said with a twisted smile. "I am the High King. And I saw and understood much more than any other Walker would, because of what I am. And what I am, you helped make."

"Thanks for the reminder," Gwydion muttered.

"Gwydion," Dinaswyn said hesitantly. She had never been any good at this sort of thing. But she had to try.

"Aunt," Gwydion said, taking her cool hands in his. "You need say nothing. There is nothing to say that either of us could deal with. We are too alike, you and I."

Dinaswyn's smiled was twisted. "So we are. I taught you far too much."

"Only everything I needed to know," he said gently.

For a moment she stood before him, wanting to speak of their misunderstandings, of the wasted years, of everything they had never spoken of. But Gwydion was right. There was nothing they could say to each other now. They were too alike. So she turned to Arthur, once more taking her seat.

"The task, High King. What is it? What would you have me do?"

"Your task, Dinaswyn ur Morvryn, is to journey to the country of Ederynion, to the city of Dinmael. There you are to establish contact with the Cerddorian that are secreted in that city, and bring Queen Elen and her Dewin, Regan ur Corfil, out of captivity."

Dinaswyn's face lit up. This was a formidable task indeed. For Queen Elen and her Dewin were closely guarded, and had been these past four years. This was the task she had waited for, and she was grateful.

"I will leave within the hour," she said eagerly.

"Aunt," Gwydion began reasonably, "the Calan Morynion celebration is later on tonight. Stay for that, and leave the next day."

"No," she said, decisively. "I have waited long enough."

"Aunt—"

"No. High King, have I your leave to depart?"

"You do, Dinaswyn," Arthur said steadily. "Go with the blessings of the Protectors, Cerrunnos and Cerridwen. May they guard you."

"And may the Hunt come to take me, should my spirit be reft from my body," Dinaswyn finished. Then she was gone.

Gwydion turned to Arthur, a frown on his face. But before he could speak, Arthur raised his hand, motioning for silence.

"No, Gwydion," Arthur said calmly. "We will not go through this again. We have already argued enough."

"You send her to her death," Gwydion said harshly.

"As that is something neither one of us has seen in our dreams, I hardly see how you could be so sure."

"All deaths are not seen in the dreams," Gwydion shot back. "You know that."

"So I do. Gwydion, Gwydion, there is nothing else for it, but this. A promise is a promise. And you know that to be true."

"I do," Gwydion growled. "And I know that this is one promise I never, ever, meant to keep."

"Nonetheless—"

"Nonetheless, I do as all true Kymri do. I bow to my High King and his will." Gwydion's bow was curt and sharp, like a slap in the face. As Gwydion strode from the room Arthur's scar reddened, then whitened. He picked up the figure of the raven, the symbol of the Dreamers, and turned it over and over, while the fiery opals glittered silently.

Dinaswyn followed Myrrdin through the dark passageway. The flickering torches sent shadows scurrying across the rough walls. It seemed to her as though they had been traveling through the bowels of the earth forever, though she knew it was really only a quarter league or so. Impatiently she shrugged, adjusting the pack strapped on her back, eager to be in the sunlight and on her way.

"Patience, sister," Myrrdin said calmly. "We're almost there."

"I'm not impatient," she snapped. Knowing Myrrdin knew her well enough to know she was lying made her speak crossly.

Myrrdin chuckled softly. "Oh, no, of course you're not. It's only the most important thing you have been asked to do in years."

"It's the only thing I have been asked to do in years," she retorted.

"Then," Myrrdin said, coming to a halt before a bend in the passageway, "you may begin." He gestured elaborately, bowing, and stepped aside.

The dim light pooled at her feet and she looked up the slight incline. "This takes you to the center of Coed Llachar," Myrrdin said. "From there I assume you will go north."

"Yes," she replied absently. "North for a few leagues to get far enough away from the patrols. Then east across Gwytheryn and make for Sycharth in Ederynion. And there purchase a horse to take me to Dinmael."

"Have you a plan to rescue Elen?" Myrrdin inquired, almost, but not quite, idly.

"Do not fear for me, brother," she said, her eyes drawn to the pale light. "I will not take foolish chances. And, though a Dreamer who no longer dreams, I still have the other talents of the Y Dawnus. These I will use as I see fit. Queen Elen will be freed."

"Confidence, little sister, was never your problem."

She smiled at him and lightly kissed his cheek. "Good-bye, brother," she said and turned away, striding up the passage, not even waiting for his reply. And not turning back for one last look.

But Myrrdin would have said nothing in any case, even if she had spoken to him one last time, for he had caught a glimpse of her eyes before she had turned way. And he saw that she knew the truth—that they would not see each other again on this earth. That their next meeting would be in Gwlad Yr Haf, the Land of Summer, where the dead go to await rebirth and their next turn on the Wheel. Just which one of them would make their way to the Summer Land first, he was not sure. But that his instinct, and hers, was right, he knew without a doubt. They both did.

DINASWYN EMERGED INTO the forest of Coed Llachar. The morning was cold, and her doe skin boots crunched on the snow-covered ground. Bare branches laced overhead and she moved through the forest with care. Her trousers and tunic of white and her white cloak blended with the snow as she silently made her way north.

Overhead a few ravens cawed, fluttering from branch to branch. Two more birds, three more, five more, joined them. Soon an entire flock roosted in the trees, fluttering from branch to branch.

Follow me not, little brothers and sisters, she said in Mind-Speech sternly to the flock. *I am on the High King's business.*

The birds cocked their heads to one side knowingly, and continued to follow. Dinaswyn said nothing, for perhaps they were right. Their fluttering made sufficient noise to distract any of Havgan's patrols from Dinaswyn's slight movements. She Wind-Rode, briefly sending out her awareness, searching for safe passage through the forest. But she encountered no sign of any patrols, neither in the forest nor to the northeast beyond it. Later she would realize what that meant. But now she was only grateful. And she did not send the flock away, for to do so would cause more commotion than she wanted. So she allowed them to follow her, even to the edge of the forest.

Again she Wind-Rode, searching the seemingly empty land before her. But there was nothing to alarm her. Nonetheless, she stepped from the forest cautiously and began to make her way northeast across the plain of Gwytheryn.

Cadair Idris rose majestically from the snow-covered plain. It was lightly dusted with snow, giving it the appearance of a glittering dagger, thrust from the bottom of the earth as a challenge to her enemies.

During the next few hours the ravens followed, leaving the forest, flying overhead as though to scout the way for her. Over and over they wheeled through the sky, circling back, settling on and around the occasional lone tree. They were strangely black against the glittering white snow, as though night had taken shape to roam the earth and sky in the light of day.

After a time she ignored them, becoming used to their fluttering, their cawing, and their restlessness. The sun was directly overhead as she halted near a copse of bare trees. Her raven escort settled in the branches, calling out to one another. She shifted the pack from her back and took out a flask of water, drinking deeply. She rummaged in the pack and came up with a hunk of bread. There was cheese and meat but she would save them for later. For now she merely gnawed at the bread, and let her eyes scan the snow-covered plain. A dark blot to the southeast caught her eye. That could be Caer Duir, the home of the Druids, the traitors.

Yet they were not all traitors, were they? Had not her own son, Aergol, come to Arthur with his allies, pleading (or, rather, demanding—after all, he was her son) that Arthur allow them this chance to redeem themselves? Never had she been prouder of her son than at that moment when he offered his life to Arthur in expiation of what the Druids had done. But Arthur had not taken Aergol's life. And though that was not something that surprised her in the least, she knew that Aergol and his Druids had been deeply shocked. But that was not Arthur's way. And it had not been motivated so much by his mercy as by his sense of expediency. Arthur was not one to waste a good tool, apparently. And this Dinaswyn admired greatly, for compassion was weakness and had no place in this struggle. She understood that Arthur could not afford to be anything but cold and hard. For this is what she was. And what she had taught her nephew, Gwydion, to be. It was the only way.

Yes, Myrrdin had certainly tried to teach the boy different, but, in the end, the child had learned the right lesson. That to succeed, to win, you had to be firm, be unmoved by the desires or suffering or needs of others.

It occurred to her, briefly, that perhaps Arthur had indeed acted out of compassion by choosing her to lead the rescue of Elen. That, perhaps, she had misjudged him. That he had given in to her obvious need to be of service again. But, no, that could not be. He had chosen her for this task because she was the best person for the job. No longer young, but strong in the arts of the Y Dawnus, clever and experienced, whatever she did would neither be foolish nor impulsive.

Indeed, she had never been foolish or impulsive. Perhaps if she had, all those years ago, the man she loved would have turned to her. But she had let him turn to another, never telling him the truth of her heart. Awst had not known when he wed her sister that Dinaswyn was in love with him. She used to think that Awst had never known, had never found out, had gone to his grave in ignorance. But, sometimes, when she looked back at her life, she would not be so sure. Hadn't there been something in his eyes, a few times before the end? She winced away from that thought, hardly able to bear, even after all this time, her memories of his murder at the hands of her sister. Even now she could clearly see the surprise on his dead face as he lay in the pool of bloody water.

She and Gwydion had found him, and had found Gwydion's mother, too, dead by her own hand in that bloody bath. And Dinaswyn's heart had broken then, not only for herself and her loss, but for Gwydion's loss, too. For she had loved—did love—her nephew, pretending in her heart that he was her son—hers and Awst's.

Suddenly the ravens took wing overhead, cawing, complaining. Startled, she looked up, squinting against the glare. To her mind came an image, ill-defined but urgent, an image of two people nearby. But who would be here? She Wind-Rode, finding them easily less than a league away—a man and a woman, each sitting a horse, cantering towards her. The hood of the woman's amber cloak was up, covering her features. The man with her wore a cloak of blood red and his hood, too, was up, obscuring his face.

Hastily she thrust the flask and bread back into her pack and slung it over her shoulders, covering it with her white cloak. She dropped to the ground behind a straggling tree and waited for the man and woman to ride by. By their direction she guessed them to be on their way to Eiodel, Havgan's dark fortress.

The ravens wheeled across the clear, cold sky, flying this way and that, calling and crying.

So intent was she on the two figures that the third one was able to get far too close before she knew of his presence. Sensing something out of kilter, she twisted around at the last moment, foiling his grip on her. She wrenched herself free of his hands and leapt to her feet, pulling her dagger from her belt. The man, whose brown cloak shadowed his identity, did not pull his dagger, contenting himself with spreading his arms and circling around her, preventing her escape.

The two people on horses were getting closer and she knew she had little time left. She threw her dagger in an underhand cast.

The dagger should have gone straight into his belly. Indeed it did, but merely bounced off his body with a clang. The man threw back his hood, his face solemn and intent. The sun flashed off his silvery chain mail. And although she had never met him she knew him from her Wind-Rides. It was Sigerric, Havgan's general. And where Sigerric was, Havgan would not be far behind.

And then she knew who the figure in the red cloak was, who was now cresting the slight rise before her. She whirled, for she knew that capture by this enemy was far worse than anything she could imagine. But Sigerric was upon her before she could even begin to run. He caught her from behind, pinning her arms to her sides. He whipped out his dagger and held it to her neck.

The flock of ravens plummeted from the sky and, for a moment, she thought they would attack. But they did not. They settled thickly on the bare branches of the scrawny trees. Dinaswyn sent a thought to them in Mind-Speech, calling for their aid. But they did not move. Still as shadowy statues, they clustered within the trees, their clever eyes alight.

"Do not struggle, Dinaswyn ur Morvryn," Siggeric said softly, "or you will die."

"I will die in any case, Sigerric of Apuldre," she panted. "Better it should be now than on the island of Afalon with the rest of the Y Dawnus you have managed to capture."

"I do not think that is what Havgan has in mind for you," Sigerric murmured, nodding at the blood-red figure who had now dismounted from his horse and was crunching through the snow to stand before them. "And if I kill you now you will miss the chance to talk with your beloved niece."

"Arianrod," Dinaswyn said bitterly as the figure in the amber cloak dismounted from her horse and came to stand before her. "How very unpleasant to see you again."

"Aunt," Arianrod said neutrally as she pushed the hood back from her face. Her amber eyes gazed at Dinaswyn with no hint of glee, but no hint of sorrow, either.

"It is grateful I am that your mother and father are dead and cannot see that you carry the son of the enemy of Kymru in your belly," Dinaswyn said. "The horror they would feel at what you have done would indeed kill them."

"If you hadn't already done so," Arianrod said bitterly.

"Their blood is not on my hands," Dinaswyn said firmly, just as she had for so many years.

"You sent them to Corania," Arianrod spat. "You dreamed and they went. And they never came back."

"Yes, I dreamed. I do not send the dreams. The gods do. You must take up your grievance with them."

"As you always told me. So I did," Arianrod sneered. "And they care not. So I have found my own way." She gestured towards Havgan, who stood silently, the hood still over his face.

"Dinaswyn ur Morvryn," he said softly. "The Kymri are burning my ships."

"Of course they are, Havgan of Corania," she said. "The High King has told them to. And he told you he would. No one leaves the island. No one comes to it. This is between him and you, now."

"So it is," Havgan agreed, his hood still shadowing his face.

Arianrod stirred restlessly. "Aunt Dinaswyn," she began, "we wish to know . . ."

"Hush, child," Dinaswyn said absently, her eyes trying to pierce the shadow the hood cast over Havgan's features. Something about the tilt of his head, about the way he stood there, something she had never realized those other times when she came across him as she Wind-Rode, distracted her. Something. Something familiar.

Sensing her interest but clearly not understanding why, Havgan at last pulled the hood away from his face. His triumphant grin at capturing his prey should have stung her. Would, perhaps, have frightened her, if she had not at that moment realized the truth of what he was. She gasped, shocked. So that was why, all those years ago, she had dreamed of sending Arianrod's parents across the sea. That was why. For this.

She knew, now, how these three had known she would be here. Havgan had dreamt it. He should have been Dreamer, would have been, had his parents not died in Corania, leaving him stranded there.

And as she realized this truth her eyes widened as she realized just what the child Arianrod carried must be.

Oh, gods, she thought, her mind in chaos. Oh, the Shining Ones could be so cruel. Her eyes fastened on Havgan's amber hawk eyes, and she saw in them an inkling of the truth. He did not know it all, but he guessed some of it. He guessed the truth of where his home really was, but he so obviously did not know that his mistress was his sister. And that the son she carried—

She opened her mouth to speak to the shadow of truth she saw in Havgan's eyes. He must know. He must. It could change everything.

But she was not able to speak, for the burning sensation she suddenly felt in her chest was agony. She looked down, shocked. Havgan's jeweled dagger, rubies clustered at its hilt, protruded from her heart.

He had seen. He had seen she had a truth to tell and he had chosen to kill her for it. Now, at the edge of death, she understood that this was the choice he had made all along. That this is what he always chose to keep the truth at bay.

Blood gushed from her mouth as she sagged forward, falling from Sigerric's hold. Havgan caught her as she threw herself against him. Slowly he let her sink to the snowy ground. The three of them stood over her as she lay on her back in the snow, her blood staining the white crust, seeping through to mingle with the brown earth beneath.

With the last of her strength she reached out an arm to touch Havgan's leg, her eyes fastened on Arianrod. For Arianrod must be told. She must understand what she had done. "Arianllyn," Dinaswyn croaked, her eyes never leaving Arianrod's. "Brychan," she said, her arm reaching toward Havgan.

But she did not see any understanding in Arianrod's eyes. As the darkness began to close in on her she heard Sigerric ask, "Those names. Who are they?"

"My parents," Arianrod said, clearly puzzled. "I don't know—"

"She was reaching out to you, Havgan," Sigerric said softly. "Reaching out to you when she said it. Ah, Havgan, I do not even need to ask why you killed her, do I? You saw she knew something. Just as you saw it in the face of the Ardewin you killed when you first came here. Saw it, I think, in the Master Bard's eyes before you had him murdered. You are always seeing something but you always turn away."

"Enough, Sigerric," Havgan said quietly, looking down at Dinaswyn. "You presume too much."

Sigerric laughed, the sound harsh and bitter, for there was no joy in it. "I presume?"

Dinaswyn whispered one last thing, determined to get them to understand. "Kill," she whispered. "Baby."

But they couldn't hear her. It was too late.

Havgan knelt beside her in the snow. "I will have your body returned to Cadair Idris," he said pleasantly. "And the sorrow it will cause Gwydion ap Awst will be worth all the effort."

She wanted to answer him. She was desperate to tell him the truth. But she could not. The last thing she saw before she died was a bright light coming towards her. And Awst was in the light. And he was smiling, his arms outstretched, happy to see her.

The horns of the Wild Hunt echoed through the clear, cold air as her spirit sprang free from her body. And the ravens took wing, crying in triumph as Cerridwen and Cerrunnos, the Protectors of Kymru, came to take her home.

Calan Morynion—night

RHIANNON STOOD QUIETLY as Elstar stretched her hands over the great, golden bowl of clear, cool water set on the lip of the fountain in the center of Brenin Llys.

Delicate snowdrops, the first, tiny flowers of spring glittered in her dark hair, and in the hair of the other women in the circle who waited for Elstar to begin the celebration of Calan Morynion, the festival dedicated to Nantsovelta, Lady of the Waters, Queen of the Moon.

All the women were dressed in white. Cariadas and Sinend, heirs of the Dreamer and the Archdruid, stood close to each other, fast friends as they had been for many years. Gwen stood between Sinend and Sabrina. The other Druids, Ceindrech and Madryn, those two women who had come in with Aergol, stood calmly, ready to offer the goddess her due. Elstar Ardewin stood between Madryn and Rhiannon. The wives, mothers, and daughters of the family of the Stewards also joined in the celebration. As always they stood quietly, their calm faces giving nothing away.

Elstar's hands hovered above the bowl with its eight white candles floating in the water around a center grouping of three more white candles.

"This is the Wheel of the Year before us," she began. "One candle for each of the eight festivals when we honor the Shining Ones." As she pointed to each candle Sabrina's finely honed Fire-Weaving lit each one. "Alban Awyr," Elstar said smoothly, as the candle was lit by Sabrina's psychokinetic ability, "Calan Llacher, Alban Haf, Calan Olau, Alban Nerth, Calan Gaef, Alban Nos, and Calan Morynion, which we celebrate tonight."

The eight candles, now lit, floated serenely on the surface of the water. Elstar pointed to the three inner candles. "Great goddess of the Moon, Lady of Waters, we honor you." At Elstar's gesture, one of the three candles lit. "Nantsovelta of the Pearls, Lady of the Swans, we honor you." The second candle burst into flame. "Silver Queen of the Night, the Bride of Day, we honor you," she intoned, as the last candle flared up.

"Let the Shining Ones be honored as they gather for the wedding of the Sun and the Moon." As she called out the name of each god or goddess, the women laid a snowdrop on the surface of the water.

"Mabon, King of Fire, Bridegroom to the Moon. Taran, King of the Winds. Modron, Great Mother of All. Annwyn, Lord of Chaos. Aertan, Weaver of Fate. Cerridwen, Queen of the Wood. Cerrunnos, Master of the Hunt. Y Rhyfelwr, Agrona and Camulos, the Warrior Twins. Sirona, Lady of the Stars. Grannos, Star of the North and Healer."

"We honor you," the women said softly in unison.

"With water are we refreshed and cleansed," Elstar went on. "With fire we are purified. Blessings on the marriage of Fire and Water."

At this the eight women began to chant.

"Oh, silver flame of the night,
Enlighten the whole land,
Chief of maidens,
Chief of finest women.

Dark the bitter winter,
Cutting its sharpness.
But Nantsovelta's mantle
Brings spring to Kymru."

Each of the women reached into the water and picked up a lit candle. As they again sang, the door of the hall opened and the men came in, gathering around an unlit pile of ash wood. Arthur was in the forefront, with Gwydion on one side and Aergol on the other. Elidyr Master Bard and his sons Cynfar and Llywelyn were next. Then came Aergol's colleagues, Aldwr and Yrth, as well as Aergol's son, Menw. Myrrdin, Dudod, and Rhodri came in, followed by Rhufon, the Steward of Cadair Idris, and his family—sons, husbands, grandsons of the Cenedl of Caine.

The women joined the men around the wood. Elstar raised her hands. "Now let the Bridegroom, Mabon of the Fires, come to claim his Bride." The women threw their candles into the wood. But before the candles could even begin to flare up, a fiery sun swooped from the ceiling and hovered briefly over the wood, then roared into flames.

"Thank you, Gwydion," Rhiannon murmured calmly. "You really must get over this tendency to be shy about your Fire-Weaving."

Gwydion grinned, a sight that seemed to shock Aergol (and a few others) to the core.

"By the gods," Aergol murmured to Arthur, "he's almost human."

"Sometimes," Arthur murmured back. "It can be a little disconcerting, can't it?"

"Disconcerting? More like impossible."

Arthur merely smiled and took the hands of Aergol and Gwydion at Elstar's signal. The men circled around the crackling bonfire to the right, while the women in the inner circle danced to the left. At Elstar's next signal the women turned around to face the men.

As luck, or something, would have it, Rhiannon turned to the man behind her, and it was Gwydion. He smiled at her, a sight that, even now, knowing all that she knew of him, still had the power to make her heart skip a beat. Sternly, she tried to repress that wayward feeling, but it was no use, and she knew it.

So she smiled back, knowing she was a fool and knowing she could not stop herself from being one. And as his hand reached out and touched hers she shivered. And she thought, for a moment, that he had shivered too, feeling, perhaps, some of what she was feeling. But no, that was impossible. For he did not, he could not, love her. Did not, could not, love any woman. And she knew it. She knew that no wishing on her part could ever change that, could ever change him. He was what he was. She struggled, again, as she often did, to accept that as truth and wish for nothing more.

His hand was warm, and his silvery eyes were alight with something she would have recognized in anyone else. And she could not look away.

"High King of Kymru," a melodious female voice broke in. "High King Arthur, you are summoned."

Rhiannon froze as Gwydion dropped her hand, searching for the source of that voice.

"Arthur," Elstar called. "What is it?"

"High King Arthur, you are summoned," Rhufon said.

"By the gods," Gwydion murmured. "It is the Doors."

Gwydion was right. The voice belonged to the spirit that was Drwys Idris, the Doors of Idris, the Guardian. The spirit of Bloudewedd, a princess of Prydyn and consort of the last High King, had been imprisoned in the Doors hundreds of years ago for her crimes. And she lingered still, serving the cause of the High King, waiting for her spirit to be set free.

"Bloudewedd," Arthur called out. "Why do you summon me?"

"High King, there is a corpse at the Doors," the disembodied voice answered. Though the voice was, as always, neutral, Rhiannon thought she caught a faint undercurrent of sadness.

"A corpse?" Arthur asked, not understanding immediately.

But Rhiannon knew. She knew instantly, and she picked up her skirts and ran for the door. Perhaps she could get there before the others. Perhaps she would have a few moments to compose the body before Gwydion, Aergol, and Myrrdin saw. Even as she thought this, even as she fled down the hall to the Doors, she knew it was a forlorn hope.

"Guardian," she called out as she ran down the hall. "Is it safe to open? To bring the body inside?"

"It is safe, Rhiannon ur Hefeydd," Bloudewedd answered calmly. "The living have gone."

"You saw him bring her," Rhiannon panted.

"I see all who come to the Doors."

"Open, then," Rhiannon commanded. "And let me bring her in."

At the end of the hall a crack of darkness met her eyes as the doors opened slightly into the night. She slowed and stepped through the narrow opening.

Just as she thought, Dinaswyn lay mangled and bloody on the top step. Yet her face was calm, serene, more beautiful than Rhiannon had ever seen her. Havgan's jeweled dagger blossomed from her breast, the blood-soaked rubies glittering darkly in the silvery light of the full moon. Carefully, Rhiannon dragged Dinaswyn's body in through the Doors, and the Doors shut behind her.

Dinaswyn's cloak was twisted beneath her body, and Rhiannon tugged at it, straightening it and covering the dead woman's bloody wound. And that was as much as she had time to do before the rest of them were there. A sound from Gywdion's throat might have been a strangled shout, might have been a sob. Myrrdin slowly knelt beside her, taking her hand, smoothing her silvery hair back from her serene face. Aergol knelt on her other side, his face white to the lips.

"Sister," Myrrdin whispered. "And so you are at peace, at last. Wait for me in the Land of Summer, for I will surely be there soon."

"Mam," Aergol whispered brokenly. "Oh, Mam."

Gwydion took Dinaswyn's hand. "I would have spared you this. But you would not let me." Tears spilled down his face and dropped on the smooth, dead hand of his aunt and teacher. "So much I would have done for you, but you would not let me." Harsh sobs came from his throat, the sobs of a man who never cries, whose control was, at last, breaking.

Rhiannon knelt beside him and took him in her arms. For a wonder he did not pull away, but simply let her hold him as he wept. Knowing what he needed, knowing what they all needed, she began the Death Song of the Kymri.

"In Gwlad Yr Haf, the Land of Summer,
Still they live, still they live.
They shall not be killed, they shall not be wounded.
No fire, no sun, no moon shall burn them.
No lake, no water, no sea shall drown them.
They live in peace, and laugh and sing.
The dead are gone, yet still they live."

As Dinaswyn's body grew colder the song gained in strength, as the rest of them began to sing. The dead were never truly gone, the song reminded those that gathered there. They still lived, beyond the reach of grief and sorrow. Forever.

Chapter Four

Cadair Idris, Gwytheryn,
Caer Siddi, Kingdom of Prydyn, &
Eiodel, Gwythern, Kymru
Onnen Mis, 500

Suldydd, Disglair Wythnos—morning

Arthur stared down at the gaming pieces. The board of alternating dark and light squares glittered and the jeweled figures gleamed in the soft, golden light. Emeralds and sapphires, opals and pearls, rubies, garnets, and diamonds glimmered and winked, as though holding a secret.

As perhaps they do, Arthur thought. For the tarbell game had drawn him from the beginning, from the moment he came into this garden room on the third level of Cadair Idris. And still he did not know why.

His hand reached out to the board to pick up the piece that represented the High King. The human face, set on an eagle's body, was stern and set. Around its neck was the High King's torque, set with an emerald for Modron the Mother, a sapphire for Taran of the Winds, a pearl for Nantsovelta of the Waters, and an opal for Mabon of the Sun. He turned the piece over and over in his palm, as the eagles' wings glittered.

The face of the carved figurine stared back at him. It was a face he recognized. He wondered if anyone else had noticed it.

"Just a game," he whispered to himself. "Just a game."

"More than that, High King."

Arthur started, almost dropping the piece. But he recognized the voice and did not turn around. "You think that the tarbell game is more?" Arthur asked.

"That we are more," Gwydion said quietly.

"Sometimes I don't believe that."

"Are you afraid, nephew?" Gwydion asked.

Arthur turned from the gaming board, his face set. "Yes. Aren't you?"

Gwydion smiled wryly. "Always. But this move we make in the game now, it is the right one."

"Yes," Arthur nodded. "I believe that it is. The Master Smiths have been imprisoned too long."

"And have made far too many collars for the enemy. And now, I must ask you once again—"

"Uncle, we have been through this."

"Then humor me," Gwydion said between gritted teeth. "Go through this with me again. Reconsider. Do not take Aergol and his Druids with us to Caer Siddi."

"You are a fool, Dreamer," Arthur said with a smile as he set the High King's piece back on the board. "You know we can't do this without them."

"I don't trust them. I don't trust any Druid."

"Which is why you are the Dreamer," Arthur said crisply. "And why I am the High King."

"Arthur, you are surely the most—"

"And you, Gwydion, are even worse. Why I ever—"

"Are you two children playing again?" Rhiannon asked from the doorway in acid tones.

"That game, my dear Rhiannon, is never over," Arthur replied.

"Don't I know it," Rhiannon said dryly as she entered the room. She came to stand between the two men, and gazed down at the gaming board. Her slender hand reached out and gently lifted the opal-studded raven that represented the Dreamer. She set the piece down facing the High King's eagle. "I believe you will find that, if they work together, they will win the game."

When neither man replied, she continued. "We are all ready for the journey. Aergol and his remaining Druids wait by the underground tunnel with Sinend and Sabrina. Ceindrech is ready to go to Prince Lludd, and Yrth to King Owein. The last Druid,

Madryn, has volunteered to stay here with Gwen, Dudod, Elstar, and Elidyr."

"And has Gwen calmed down at all at being excluded from this expedition?" Arthur asked.

"Not noticeably, no," Rhiannon replied. "Though she cannot quite hide her glee that she will at last begin her Druid's training under Madryn's guidance. After a fashion."

"She should have begun that long before now," Gwydion pointed out.

"Thank you, Gwydion," Rhiannon said crisply. "As always you are so very quick to point out my little faults."

"I'm not saying anything you don't already know yourself—" Gwydion began.

"Then you are not saying anything that needs to be said," Rhiannon shot back.

"Enough," Arthur said, his tone brooking no argument. For a moment the three of them were silent, their eyes caught by the gaming board and the glittering pieces.

"Are Rhodri and Myrrdin ready to go?" Arthur asked after a moment.

"Packed and ready for their journey north."

"Have they a plan?" Gwydion asked.

"Nothing they will speak of," Rhiannon said. "All Rhodri will say is that it that it is a poor father who will not take the time to properly discipline his son."

"Then Madoc had best take care up in Tegeingl," Arthur said softly. "For when Rhodri says that, he has the coldest eyes of anyone I have ever seen."

"And you sent Cadell to Arberth. Are you sure you know what you are doing there?" Gwydion asked.

Arthur smiled with a hint of bitterness. "As sure as I am of anything I do now."

"It's Ellywen I don't trust," Gwydion said quietly. "I wonder about the wisdom of Cadell going directly to her."

"Since she saved Cadell and Aidan from the Coranians at Arberth she seems to have had a change of heart," Arthur pointed out in a mild tone.

"Her change of heart began when she helped capture Cian," Rhiannon put in. "And the night Anieron died. I, for one, believe in it."

"Why am I not surprised you disagree with me?" Gwydion asked.

"Don't start," Arthur begged. "Change the subject. Please."

"I understand you have allowed Geriant to go to Owein in Rheged to help rescue Enid," Rhiannon said to Arthur. "Do you think that wise?"

Arthur shrugged. "He begged me to be a part of that rescue. So I gave him the permission he needed."

"Geriant might expect too much from the lady," Rhiannon warned.

"As near as I can tell, Geriant expects nothing at all."

"So Rhoram agreed," Rhiannon said.

"He did. You knew he would."

"And our other captive," Gwydion broke in, "will also soon be freed."

Arthur nodded. "As well as sending Ceindrech, I have sent Prince Rhiwallon of Rheged up to Ederynion, to lend his aid to Elen's brother. Prince Lludd, now that he has my permission, will not hesitate to rescue her. It has been very difficult to hold him back this long."

"Only your authority could have done it," Rhiannon said.

"And even that was almost not enough."

"Have they moved their headquarters yet?" Rhiannon asked. "For the gods only know what Llwyd Cilcoed was up to when he ran."

"The move to Ial is complete. If his plan was to capture the Cerddorian he has failed."

"I do not think that was his plan," Gwydion said softly.

"Nor do I," Arthur replied, frowning down at the tarbell board.

"According to Elstar there has been no word of him at all since he escaped from Coed Ddu," Gwydion said.

"True," Arthur said heavily. "It is almost as though he has

vanished off the face of the earth."

"Or as though he had help waiting for him."

"That remains to be seen," Arthur said coolly, "but it would not surprise me."

"Nor me," Gwydion said shortly.

"Have you a plan for rescuing Elen?" Rhiannon asked Arthur.

"Lludd and I have talked through his Bard, Talhearn, and we have managed to come up with an idea or two. They need a Druid to help them, which is why I sent Ceindrech."

"So the freeing of the captives begins," Gwydion said.

"Yes. First, the Master Smiths in Caer Siddi. Next, Queen Elen in Ederynion and Queen Enid in Rheged. It begins."

"And the Y Dawnus in Afalon?" Rhiannon asked. "They suffer under the enaid-dals, the soul-catching collars. They work under the lash of the Coranians and they die every day."

"They are not forgotten," Arthur said. "All captives will be free before Calan Llachar. Before this year is more than six months old, Kymru herself will be free from bondage."

Arthur surveyed the gaming board, then turned to Rhiannon and Gwydion.

"It is time," he said.

Meirigdydd, Tywyllu Wythnos—afternoon

Eighteen days later Gwydion stood on the beach in the commote of Camain. Next to him Arthur sat his horse. Horse and man were so still, so silent, that they seemed to have been carved from stone. Rhiannon and Cariadas stood on the other side of Arthur, their hair, silky dark and red-gold, mingling and tangling in the wind. Llywelyn and Cynfar huddled against the stiff breeze on the other side of Gwydion. Behind them Sabrina, Aergol, Sinend, and Menw, along with the other Druid, Aldwr, stood quietly against the salty wind.

The freshening breeze off the ocean rushed to them, engulfed them, mingled with them, then withdrew, hurrying away on other, unknown errands. Seagulls cried out as though in mourning for something lost. The waves broke on the beach, reaching eagerly for the white sands, then retreated. The water sparkled and shimmered beneath the afternoon sun.

Arthur stirred at last and looked down at Gwydion. "They're coming," he said.

"Yes," Gwydion replied in a clipped tone. "I can Wind-Ride, too."

"Don't be so sour, Gwydion," Rhiannon said crisply.

The warriors crested the dunes. King Rhoram was dressed all in black. On his head was the golden helmet of Prydyn, fashioned like the head of a snarling wolf with emerald eyes. Beside him rode Achren, the captain of his teulu. She, too, was all in black. Her dark hair, braided tightly to her skull, shone with a blue light. The silvery hilts of daggers winked from the tops of her boots.

Twenty of Rhoram's best warriors followed them. They wore tunics of dark green and trousers of black leather, and their hair was braided and bound for battle. They carried bows with quivers of arrows slung across their shoulders, as well as short spears. Their daggers were thrust into their belts.

"High King," Rhoram said, leaping from his horse and bowing his head. Achren and her warriors also dismounted and bowed to Arthur. "You have called for us," Rhoram continued, "and we have come."

"Then you might try showing up when you are supposed to," Gwydion said.

Rhiannon gave an exasperated sigh, but Rhoram sprang to his feet with a bright smile, his blue eyes alight. "Ah, Dreamer. How wonderful to see you!" Rhoram crossed to Gwydion and grasped his arm in a friendly fashion. It finally occurred to Gwydion that he genuinely amused the King of Prydyn. "But we poor warriors, unlike you Y Dawnus, must use more mundane methods to know when others arrive. We have been here since yesterday but we had to hide ourselves within the cliffs. When we saw you ride up, we began our descent. And so the wait."

"And well worth the time," Arthur said. "You are most welcome here."

"Brenin of Kymru, Penerydd of Gwytheryn, we are yours to

command."

"Are the boats ready?"

"They are, High King, as are your warriors. Now, what is this thing you would have us do?"

"We sail to the island of Caer Siddi. And then we will release the Master Smiths of Kymru from their terrible bondage."

"My heart had hoped that the time had come for that. At last, freedom comes to Kymru."

"Yes," Arthur said. "At last."

GRIED AP GORWYS, Master Smith of Gwynedd, stared down at his hands in the fitful light of the guttering torches inside the rude hut. The light flickered over the scars earned in over forty years of practicing his craft. His hands had created oh so many things. He had forged swords and spears and arrow tips for King Uthyr's warriors. He had fashioned necklaces and rings, and vessels of silver and gold for Queen Ygraine. Once he had even secretly made a copy of a testing device for Gwydion ap Awst. He had never told anyone that, not even his wife, dead now these five years. He had kept Gwydion's secret as he had been asked to do. That much he had done for Kymru.

Again he stared at his hands. The guilt was so terrible, the shame so raw, that he thought he might die of it. For his hands had fashioned something else. They had made collars for the Y Dawnus. They had fashioned collar after collar, some so tiny he knew they were destined for the slender necks of children. And as he had made these collars he had wondered on whose neck they would be placed. Would this one be for Gwydion the Dreamer? Would this one be for Neuad the Dewin? Would his one be for the Master Bard? Sometimes he thought he might go mad thinking of it. And now—oh, now he wished he had gone mad. Then maybe he would no longer be aware of what he was doing.

He glanced up from his hands and saw that Siwan of Prydyn was staring over at him, as though she knew what he was thinking. And perhaps she did, for he had often seen torment in her eyes. Aware that someone else was staring at him he turned his head to see Llyenog of Rheged's stern gaze. Across the silent hut Efrei of Ederynion raised his head, his dark eyes unyielding.

So the time had come, then. And he was not sorry that it had.

"We cannot do this any longer," Gried said.

"No," Siwan replied quietly. "We cannot."

"Almost a year we have been doing what we know to be wrong," Llyenog said.

"We have been waiting," Efrei put in. "For rescue."

"But it has not come," Siwan said.

"It is not coming at all," Greid whispered. "Not at all."

"You know what they will do to us when we refuse," Efrei said.

"Why, nothing," Greid said bitterly. "Not to us."

"But to our families," Llyenog said, his eyes sweeping over the sleeping forms of his children and grandchildren.

Slowly Greid replied. "The Coranians cannot hurt them if they are already dead."

There. At last it was said. And he had underestimated his fellow Master Smiths, for not one of them was shocked. Not one of them had even flinched.

"Rescue is not coming," Greid said again. "We must rescue ourselves."

"By dying," Siwan whispered, her hand gently stroking the head of her sleeping husband.

"By dying," Llyenog agreed, his hand hovering over the still form of his eldest son.

"By dying," Efrei said, his dark gaze resting on the tiny shape of his youngest grandson.

"By dying," Greid said thickly through his tear-filled throat as he picked up his sleeping granddaughter. The little girl's golden hair gleamed in the dancing firelight.

"But how?" Efrei whispered in despair. "How?"

"With this," Greid said as he pulled a tiny dagger from beneath his bedroll.

Siwan sucked in her breath. "Where did you get that?"

"I made it," Greid said quietly. "I worked on it a little bit at a time for the last few months. I made it as sharp as it could be made. I made it with love."

"With love," Llyenog said with wonder in his gravelly tone. "Then let us do what we must do."

"With love," Greid whispered as he brought the tiny blade to his sleeping granddaughter's throat.

And it was then that the crows began to scream.

Arthur stood in the dark forest, eyeing the dying campfire in the center of the clearing. One large hut stood still and silent surrounded by four smaller huts. The four smaller huts, Arthur knew, each contained four sleeping Coranian guards. Four more guards currently patrolled the perimeter of the clearing, criss-crossing in a pattern that did not vary. Now that was foolish, he thought. It should never have been a pattern so easily read. He did not know so much of war, but he knew that much.

No sound came from the larger hut where the Master Smiths and their families had been bedded down for the night. Nonetheless, there was something about the mute building that he did not like at all, something that hummed at his nerves in its silence, in its dark stillness, something that gibbered at him to hurry.

At his side two Dewin, Rhiannon and Llywelyn, stirred, their awareness returning from their Wind-Ride to the compound. Rhiannon looked up at him, her wide, green eyes filled with urgency.

"We must hurry, High King," she said urgently.

Llywelyn grasped Arthur's arm. "The Master Smiths have reached an end. They have determined to kill themselves and their families rather than continue."

"Greid fashioned a dagger," Rhiannon put in. "And he prepares to use it."

"Then we must, indeed, hurry. But all is in readiness," Arthur said smoothly. "So let it begin."

He nodded to Gwydion and the Dreamer, along with Cariadas and Cynfar, closed his eyes and reached out to the night crows that had waited here at Arthur's bidding. The crows rose from the branches of the surrounding trees and began to caw. Their sharp screams ripped through the silent night. Dark feathers parted the air with a hollow rush. The pacing guards halted and drew their swords. The sleeping guards in the huts began to stir.

Arthur nodded to his Druids. Aergol, Menw, Aldwr, Sinend, and Sabrina linked hands with him. He closed his eyes and bowed his head. He took their Druid's Fire deep within him. It grew and grew inside, straining to leap from him like a deadly shoot from fallow ground.

Inside him a flame-colored sun rose, dripping hungry fire. He harnessed it, bending it to his will, aiming the power like a lighting bolt, shaping and honing it on the forge of his desire until it gleamed in his mind like a shining blade. And then he struck.

The walls of the small huts burst into flame. Angry tongues of fire shot up into the dark sky, cutting through the air like a scythe bent on gathering a deadly harvest.

The guards burst out of the huts, some men already on fire and attempting to beat out the flames. It was then that Rhoram's warriors burst through the trees and into the clearing. Arthur saw King Rhoram fall on a disoriented guard, almost cutting the man in half with his blade. Achren gleefully ran another guard through with her short spear. As the man fell she plucked a dagger from her boot and threw it in an underhand cast that caught the next running guard in the belly.

Lluched, the Gwarda of Crueddyn, used her bowstring to strangle a hapless guard. Her hair was set in hundreds of tiny braids, fastened at the ends with pieces of brass, and it glowed amber in the fiery light. With a violent wrench she broke the guard's neck and let him fall to the now-blood-soaked earth.

Arrows flew through the clearing to embed themselves in the throats of the guards. Those who were not killed in the first volley were killed with the short spears and daggers of Rhoram's Cerddorian as they leapt into the clearing, shouting out Arthur's name as their battle cry.

Within moments all but one of the guards were dead. The Cerddorian halted at Arthur's signal, standing over the bodies of those they had killed, wiping the blood from their weapons. Achren held her dagger at the throat of the remaining guard. Her dark eyes glittered as she waiting for Arthur's next command. Arthur stepped into the clearing and the fires died down at his glance. The Druids followed him, their faces wet with sweat from the heat of the fires they had given their High King.

Rhiannon and Gwydion stepped into the clearing, followed by Llywelyn, Cynfar, and Cariadas. Rhoram went to the door of the large, still-silent hut. He looked at Arthur, his brows raised. At Arthur's nod, Rhoram opened the door and stepped back.

Gwydion stepped forward then and called out. "Greid ap Gorwys of Gwynedd, Siwan ur Trephin of Prydyn, Llyenog ap Glwys of Rheged, Efrei ap Gwifan of Ederynion. Step forth, at the command of your High King."

Four figures stepped out of the shadowy hut and came to kneel in front of Arthur. The families of the Master Smiths followed, young children whose eyes were still dilated in terror, men and women who held their children tightly with tears in their eyes.

"High King," Gried said slowly. "You have called us and we are here."

"I have called you," Arthur agreed. "For you are mine."

"We offer you our lives as payment."

"As payment?" Arthur asked quietly.

"For what we have done. We beg you to spare our families. That is all we ask, we who have no right to ask anything at all."

"Indeed?" Arthur asked, his brows raised. "Then if you have no right to ask, why do you?"

"But we do have a right," Siwan said flatly. "You owe us a boon, High King of Kymru."

"Do I?"

"You do. For we waited for you," Siwan accused. "We waited. And you did not come."

Greid, Llyenog, and Efrei gasped in horror at Siwan's words. "High King," Gried began, swallowing hard.

"Ah, the Kymri," Arthur interrupted, shaking his head. "Stubborn. Willful. With no respect for their Rulers."

"High King—" Greid began again.

"And always right," Arthur continued. "For I am sorry that

I took so long. She is right. I do owe you a boon. But first I must take care of another matter."

Arthur turned to the last guard. Achren's knife glittered at his throat as Arthur spoke to the trembling Coranian.

"Your name?"

"Edwald," the guard whispered, swallowing hard.

"Edwald, I want you to take a message back to Havgan."

"I will."

"Tell him exactly what happened here tonight. Tell him that High King Arthur, as promised, took the Master Smiths away from him. Tell him that I warn him yet again—leave Kymru, and live. Or stay and die. That is the message."

"I will deliver it as you say," Edwald rasped.

Arthur nodded at Achren. "Take him with you when you go. Let him loose after you return to Prydyn. Give him a horse and food and see him on his way to Eiodel."

"As you command, High King," Achren said.

Arthur turned back to the Master Smiths. "You spoke of me owing you a boon. How then if I offer you this? You return to Gwytheryn with me. In Cadair Idris is a forge the likes of which I have never seen, a forge that surely was made for the fashioning of weapons of war. Which is what Kymru needs now, as she prepares to be free."

"High King," Greid said with tears in his eyes. "You would spare us?"

"I do not spare you. I command of you that you put your talents to my use."

Siwan smiled. "It shall be as you say, High King. We will serve you until the end of our days."

"And may that be long from now."

"As you command, High King," Greid said with the beginnings of a smile on his grizzled face. "As you command."

HAVGAN SAT UP in his bed in Eiodel with a cry. His sweat-slicked skin glimmered in the light of the dying hearth fire. The flickering flames illuminated the shifting shadows, lighting a precious jewel here, a tapestry there, a gleaming goblet, the ruby-red bedspread stitched with golden thread.

A soft hand touched Havgan's shoulder and silken hair of honey-blond whispered across his back.

"My love?" Arianrod murmured. "What is wrong?"

He turned to face her and her amber eyes, so like his own, gleamed with an inner fire as they shimmered in the shifting light.

"A dream," he said past the tightness in his throat. "It was just a dream."

She sat up straight and grasped his shoulders with an urgency he did not understand. "What kind of dream?" she asked.

"What does it matter?"

"What kind of dream?" she asked again, more urgently this time.

He sat back, settling himself against the carved headboard, never taking his eyes from her. "A dream of Caer Siddi. Arthur ap Uthyr and the Dreamer came to the island with his Y Dawnus. Aergol was there, as was Rhiannon and King Rhoram. Others."

"What happened?"

"Arthur harnessed the power of the Druids. He set fire to the huts. He freed the Master Smiths."

"The Master Smiths are free," Arianrod repeated, stunned.

"In my dream only," Havgan said sharply.

"Fool," she said. "You know it was more than a dream."

"I do not know that and neither do you."

Arianrod said in a voice so soft it held a dreamy quality, "You know more than you say. More than you have ever said."

"You dare—"

"Which is why you try to hide the truth. But I can name it."

"Arianrod—"

"I name you Dreamer."

He sat upright, stung. "I have killed others for saying even less than that, Arianrod," he hissed. "Do not forget that."

"I do not forget that," she said, the light in her eyes burning brighter. "And you should not forget that I am not a fool."

He laid his hand on her swollen belly, laid his hand on the

child that grew there. A boy, she had said. His son. "You know what I am," he whispered to her. "For that I will kill you one day."

She smiled slowly. "You have tried. Try again, if you dare."

He grabbed her shoulders and forced her down on her back. He mounted her, and wrapped his hands around her throat. Her silky hair tangled in his fingers. The firelight crawled greedily over her lush, naked body. She reached up her hands and pulled his head down to hers, her full lips opening in a passionate kiss. But instead of kissing him, her mouth darted to his shoulder and she bit him, hard enough to draw salty blood.

He hissed, then covered her mouth with his, tasting the coppery tang of his own blood. He entered her, his sweat-soaked body arching in pleasure. She cried out in ecstasy as he thrust into her again and again. Again she cried out and this time his cry mingled with hers as he spent himself inside her. He fell forward, pinning her underneath him as he struggled to quiet his breathing.

She was his Woman on the Rocks, the Woman of his Dreams, and he would never let her go.

Chapter Five

Cil, Kingdom of Prydyn &
Cadair Idris, Gwytheryn, Kymru
Bedwen Mis, 500

Gwyntdydd, Disglair Wythnos—midmorning

Llwyd Cilcoed made his way cautiously through the rough countryside surrounding the town of Cil. The morning was bright and clear but still cold, for it was late winter. Although snow no longer fell there was frost late into the mornings, and the wind had a cold edge to it as though it still carried the memory of fierce blizzards and icy nights.

He scrambled through copses and thickets and oddly bent trees, staying away from Sarn Iken, the main road, but keeping it in his mind's eye with his clairvoyant gift, never losing sight of it. It would never do to be seen by the Y Dawnus that watched, no doubt, the main road. He knew from the talk around the campfires in Coed Ddu that Elidyr and his wife, Elstar, had finally repaired the damage done to the network of Dewin and Bards when the Coranians had taken Allt Llwyd and caught so many of the Y Dawnus in their net.

Yet there were many places the Y Dawnus could not keep under surveillance, for there were not enough of them—not any more. But he knew that they kept a good watch on the main thoroughfares. And he knew he was a hunted man. Prince Lludd of Ederynion would have sent out the word as quickly a possible. The Prince would be unforgiving should he ever find Llwyd Cilcoed in his path again. For the Prince had always hated him. And Llywd had killed a man that last night in Coed Ddu.

Llywd grimaced at that thought. For though he had not cared in the least about the Cerddorian warrior he had killed he also had not enjoyed it. Llywd had not been trained as a warrior. No, he had, from the moment of his birth, been meant for better things. He had been born Dewin, and was above the dirt and blood and muck that filled the lives of ordinary men. And the feel of the knife as it had slid through the guard's body still had the power to make Llywd feel a trifle ill.

But he did not doubt that he had done what he had to do. He did not doubt that the course he was taking was right and good. For at the end of this path he was taking was a better life for himself. A life he deserved. A life he had always deserved and had while he was the beloved of Queen Olwen. Then he had slept in a comfortable bed. He had eaten well. He had been treated with deference.

He had truly been someone.

But that had changed when the Coranians came. To them he was only a witch, someone to be hunted and killed. So he had hidden for two years as best he could. And when he understood how he could find his way back to a life worthy of him, he had come to Coed Ddu and surrendered himself to the Prince. And he had done what he was told to do for many, many months and waited for his chance. And when the time had come, when he was ready, he left the forest and contacted the one who promised him the life he wanted.

He sensed her long before he saw her with his eyes. She was waiting for him as she said she would be—in a copse just a league east of Cil. She sat on a blanket of fine, white wool. Her honey-blond hair shone like precious gold as it cascaded smoothly down her white, fur-lined cloak. Her cat-shaped amber eyes glowed in the morning sun, which filtered through the trees and fell hungrily on her. Precious stones of amber and topaz dripped from her ears and throat and slender fingers.

The Golden Man treated her well it seemed. And planted a seed in her belly that he sensed before he even saw it with his eyes. There was something about the child that lay within her body. Something he could not put a name to. Something that caused him to shudder momentarily. But something he knew better than to speak of.

He stepped into the clearing and stood quietly as her two Coranian guards roughly searched him. But, knowing better, he had carried no weapons and so there was nothing for them to find. One guard stood behind him, his spear at the ready. The other went to the woman and helped her to her feet, his face expressionless.

"Arianrod ur Brychan," Llywd Cilcoed said with a bow. "You are looking well." He stared pointedly at her belly, then grinned.

Arianrod leisurely looked him up and down from head to toe. "Llwyd Cilcoed," she said neutrally. "You, on the other hand, do not look well at all. I trust your journey was difficult?"

"I was not followed, and not seen," he said sharply, "if that is what you mean."

"That is not what I mean," she said with a malicious smile. "But no matter. You are here and that is what is important."

"Let us be sure we understand each other, Arianrod," he said, "before we get much further. I have agreed to perform a service for the Golden Man. One that he will surely be grateful for."

"Yes. So he will."

"And in return—"

"In return, Llywd Cilcoed, you will be named the Lord of Arystli."

"A title now held by my brother."

"Your brother could call himself King of Ederynion for all that would matter," Arianrod said. "As a Cerddorian he is declared outlaw by the Coranians. At Havgan's orders you will be installed as Lord in Arystli. It is you who shall rule in Ymris. It is your word that shall be as law."

"I will require that I not be surrounded by Coranian watchdogs in Ymris."

"Of course. You will be free to do as you will to whom you will when you will. You will be answerable only to Havgan in matters of defense. Are we in agreement?"

"We are, Arianrod. With one more requirement."

"And that is?"

"That an army of Coranian warriors enters Coed Ddu and ensures that my brother is killed."

"That may be somewhat difficult," Arianrod said with an edge to her throaty voice, "for the Cerddorian are surely no longer in Coed Ddu."

"I will not suffer my brother to live," Llwyd said between gritted teeth.

"Poor Llywd Cilcoed," Arianrod murmured, "didn't your brother counsel the Prince to take your life when you first came to Coed Ddu?"

"He will not live one month beyond the completion of my bargain to the Golden Man."

"It is agreed," Arianrod said with a smile.

"Then I am yours to command," Llwyd said with a smile as false as the one Arianrod wore.

Arianrod took a small glass bottle from the inside pocket of her fur cloak. As she handed it to him the morning light flashed off the bottle, illuminating the milky-white liquid inside.

"Mistletoe," Llywd Cilcoed breathed. "So, that is how you want it."

"That is how Havgan wants it. You are to watch the dose. You must not kill him until he tells us what we want to know."

"And what am I to ask him?"

"We want to know what the High King's plans are. We want to know the secret ways into Cadair Idris. And we want Rhiannon ur Hefeydd."

"With Gwydion as bait."

"A bait she will take."

"You are sure?"

"I am sure."

"I have read of this but have never tried it myself. You are sure it will work?"

"He will be disoriented, unable to focus. Your voice will be the only thing he can hear and understand. Given long enough he will tell you what you want to know." Again Arianrod reached into her cloak and this time she pulled from it something wrapped in a white cloth. With clear distaste she unwrapped it and an enaid-dal spilled across the cloth, lying in her hands with dull, gray menace.

Llywd could not even bring himself to touch it, so much did he loathe the sight of it. He felt a chill creep across the back of his neck and his heart beat faster. Perhaps she had brought him here for another reason. Perhaps they meant to betray him, the way he had betrayed his Prince and his brother, the way he intended to betray the Dreamer. Perhaps—

Arianrod's almond-shaped eyes glowed with malice. "Don't be a fool, Llywd Cilcoed. You are not, and never have been, important enough to capture. It is not you that we are after. And you will not have to touch it," she went on. "These two guards will go with you. One of them will carry it and put it around the Dreamer's neck."

"And just how do you intend to lure him here?" Llwyd asked as she re-wrapped the enaid-dal and handed it to the guard who stood beside her. "He will never leave Cadair Idris for you."

"He is not in Cadair Idris. He is returning there from southern Prydyn. I have seen him on the Wind-Ride."

"How did you know where to look for him?"

"I didn't. I knew only that he was no longer in Cadair Idris. And I knew that only by a feeling. So I left Eiodel and began to journey south. I knew that he had gone that way, but not where he had gone."

"What has he been doing in the south?" Llwyd Cilcoed asked.

"I have not yet been able to determine that," she said crisply, for she would tell no one what Havgan had dreamed about the Master Smiths. "But it is of no matter. What matters is that I have found him and he is coming this way—close enough for me to contact him. I shall Wind-Ride to him tonight. Two days from now he will be close enough for you to take him."

"You don't think he will really trust you?"

"Of course not. But he will agree to meet me nonetheless."

"How can you be so sure?"

"You simply have to know him. And I know him very well indeed."

"So you say, Arianrod."

"Just leave that part to me. Be assured that the Dreamer will meet me outside of Cil. You and the guards be ready to take him."

"I will be ready, Arianrod," Llywd said. "Believe me."

THE SHADOWS LENGTHENED, casting smoky gray cloaks over the chill fields. The sun sank, turning the sky an angry red. At last the sky darkened enough for the scattered stars to spring forth. It was disglair wythnos, and so the full moon rose early in the east, casting its silvery glow over Arianrod as she stood on top of the hill.

The moonlight spilled over her, so bright that she cast a shadow down the hill that faded and mingled with the dark, cold earth. Far off she heard the lonely howl of a wolf as it paid homage to the shining moon.

She felt a momentary chill in spite of the warm cloak she wore, and her hands wrapped protectively over her belly and the child she carried. The only real qualm she felt was that she would not lie in Havgan's arms tonight, nor for a few nights yet. When she had left him in Eiodel, setting forth on this errand, he had not wanted to let her go. He had not said so but she had known.

But she knew how important it was to her lover that Gwydion ap Awst be found and brought to him. And she had not even struggled within her heart against such a task, though for many years the Dreamer had shared her bed. For never had she loved anyone as she loved the Golden Man. Never had a man's soul called to her, wrapped around her, comforted her and stirred her as Havgan's did. Never had a man looked at her with such passion, such longing, and such promise as the son of Hengist.

Never would she feel alone again, as long as Havgan shared her world. And he would continue to do so if she could make Kymru safe for him. And one of the ways to do so would be to capture Gwydion.

So she would do this. Do it for the Golden Man, the other half of her lonely soul.

She closed her eyes and willed her breathing to slow. "Nantsovelta," she murmured, "Lady of the Waters, Queen of the Moon, beloved of the Dewin, be with me as I Ride the Wind." She breathed in slowly and her body felt as though it was made of glowing, silvery light. The pearl in the torque around her neck glowed softly. She spread her arms to the sky, and felt her awareness shoot forth—up and up, and to the south, seeking Gwydion, knowing he and his party were camped for the night less than thirty leagues away.

The glow of the distant campfire guided her as she neared the campsite. She spiraled down, coming to rest just at the edge of the firelight. She remained hidden in the shadows as she scanned the faces of those by the fire.

She saw High King Arthur and knew that the boy had become a man. His clean profile shimmered in the firelight, which played off the scar that ran down one side of his stern face as he stared at the flames in a way that made Arianrod want to shiver. For she sensed a little of the distant presence of Annwyn and Aertan, of Chaos and the Weaver, of Death and Fate, in the way Arthur gazed at the hungry fire.

She saw Aergol, the Archdruid's heir, one of her former lovers, surrounded by four other Druids. So, it was true that Aergol had turned against the Archdruid and offered himself to the High King. That Arthur had not killed the traitorous Druid made her think the boy-turned-man was weak, for she did not understand mercy or wisdom and never would.

She saw Llywelyn and Cynfar, the sons of the Master Bard and the Ardewin. And she saw Cariadas, the Dreamer's heir, and Sinend, Aergol's daughter.

She saw a group of men, women, and children huddled together beside another fire and knew them instantly. So, the High King had indeed freed the Master Smiths of Kymru and their families, just as Havgan had dreamed. Even now the news would be traveling to Eiodel.

She saw Rhiannon, the woman Arianrod had hated from the first moment they had met at Y Ty Dewin so many years ago. The firelight played off Rhiannon's shadowy hair and emerald eyes as she smiled and answered some question of Cariadas'.

It was to Rhiannon that Gwydion's silvery gaze flickered the most, though this was something that she did not seem to notice. The flames played off of Gwydion's handsome, stern face as the Dreamer stared into the fire, as though seeing a future there of which he could not speak. When Rhiannon turned to him for a moment and asked him something, Gwydion's face softened in a way that Arianrod had not even known he was capable of. And the Dreamer smiled at Rhiannon in a way that Arianrod had never seen him smile.

It was a smile very like that she saw on Havgan's face when he looked at her. And for a moment Gwydion and Havgan seemed the same man, two sides of a single, shining blade, one light and golden as the sun and one dark and silvery gray like the moon. And her body standing far, far away at the top of a lonely hill shivered.

Then Gwydion looked up and saw her.

She did not even have to gesture for him to be silent. She did not even have to turn her head and nod at the surrounding trees. She did not even have to gesture with her hands in the language of the Anoeth for him to know that she wanted to speak to him alone.

They had always known each other so well. It was what she had been counting on.

He quietly rose to his feet and walked away from the campfire. The rest did not question his leaving, though Rhiannon shot him a sharp glance that he did not see. And Arthur looked up from the flames with gleaming eyes but did not speak.

She followed Gwydion as he made his way through the trees, stopping some distance away from the campfire where he knew he could not be seen or heard. He turned away from the distant glow and looked for her as she came to stand before him.

Her hands moved, her fingers shaping the Anoeth, the gestures that Dewin used to communicate to others when they Wind-Rode.

Gwydion ap Awst, you look well.

And Gwydion answered her with Mind-Speech. *How it must hurt you to be pleasant to me for even one moment.*

Then we will not continue the pleasantries, if you don't mind. And get down to business.

Ah, yes. Business.

Dinaswyn—

You dare to use her name? Gwydion's Mind-Speech was ragged as his anger and sorrow leapt from his mind to hers.

Havgan killed her. He took his dagger and thrust it through her heart. Her hands faltered then began again. *Dinaswyn sank to the snow and her blood seeped from her. And I knew then—*

You knew what? Gwydion's contempt hit her like a blow. But she had known it would be like this.

Her blood was mine. We were one, and always had been. Oh, Gwydion, if only I had known this when she was alive! For now it is too late.

Too late to save her, yes. Arianrod, what do you want?

To take it back. If only I could.

But you cannot. And I must tell you, I do not believe you for one moment.

I did not think you would.

Then what now? You have found us this night. Can we then expect Havgan's Coranian's to capture us tomorrow?

No. I have left him.

You have not.

I have. I left Eiodel a week ago. Havgan did not see me go. But I believe Elstar knew. I felt someone watching from Cadair Idris. I thought, at the time, that it was you. But I know now that it was not.

Gwydion hesitated. Arianrod almost smiled, for now she had him. He had heard something from Elstar. Had heard, but not quite believed. And now he did.

This child I carry has made me see what I have done, even as Dinaswyn's death did. It is a boy, a son. It is a child that I cannot let Havgan have. I cannot let him twist the boy as he has been twisted. I cannot let the child ever know his father. I cannot let my son leave Kymru. He must stay here, where his heritage is. And if I must pay full price for that, than that is what I will pay.

Still Gwydion did not speak, so she went on.

I saw in your eyes, so long ago, what having a child of your own could do. How it could change everything. And this boy is changing my heart, even as Cariadas changed yours.

She saw, then, the belief beginning in his silvery eyes, though his Mind-Speech was as cool as ever.

What do you expect me to do, Arianrod? Welcome you to Cadair Idris?

No. The most I hope for is your protection. You may send me where you like, as long as I am far from Eiodel. And the Golden Man.

Where are you now?

And she knew that it was as good as done. *I am a few leagues outside of Cil.*

In her mind Gwydion sighed. *Arianrod, you must know that you will not be believed. Arthur will need to be convinced. And I, too, will need more persuading.*

I knew you would. And so I tell you this, and can provide proof. Havgan has plotted with Llwyd Cilcoed to capture you.

Llwyd Cilcoed! Where is that chicken-hearted weasel?

Here with me, near Cil. He does not suspect the truth. He thinks that I am going to lure you here for him to capture.

And how does he intend to do that? I am to tell you that he is here with me. I am to offer him to you, as though I do this without his knowledge. You will meet us and he will collar you, for he has an enaid-dal.

And just how does he intend to collar me?

It is to seem as though I have bound him. His wrists will look as though they are tied. But they will not be. You will think him helpless and turn your back on him to face me.

And where am I to meet you two?

Where you tell us. You are not too far from us now. Llwyd and I will be nearby when you camp two nights from now. You will leave the others to meet us.

And how is he to know that I come alone?

He thinks you will tell no one, for you would wish to bring him to Arthur yourself, for his judgement.

Then I will indeed meet you both near where we will camp two nights from now. And be assured, Arianrod, that I will not come alone.

I did not think you would, Gwydion. Bring whom you wish, it is nothing to me. I ask only one thing of you.

What is that?

That you ensure the safety of my child. For everything I do here, I do for him.

And that, out of all the things she had said that night, was true.

Addiendydd, Disglair Wythnos—early evening

AELFWYN, DAUGHTER OF the Emperor of Corania, Star of Heaven, despised and neglected wife to the Golden Man, smiled to herself as she crossed the almost deserted courtyard of Eiodel.

She knew, finally, that there would be nothing he would keep back from her. Not anymore. Not now that she realized his secret.

For he was in love with her. And she knew it.

Now that she knew she wondered why it had taken so long for her to see. It had come to her unexpectedly, simply, in the quiet manner that the deepest truths make themselves known. She had been at the evening meal and she had put out her hand and picked up her golden goblet of wine and had accidentally brushed his hand as it lay tensely on the table. At the barest contact he had snatched his hand away, curling it into a fist so hard his knuckles had whitened. His breath hitched, then he was still.

And then she had looked up and, for the first time, had truly seen him look at her.

At first she had not known what to do with that knowledge. At that moment she had looked away, uncertain as she rarely was. Worse than not knowing how to use this truth was that she had not known how she felt about it.

She had lain awake most of last night trying to come to a conclusion or two. In the end she could only decide that this meant he was an avenue to that which she desired most. For the rest—for her heart that had begun to stir for the first time in years—she had put that aside deciding it was unimportant for now. If she accomplished what she must, then—perhaps—she could think of it.

The dusky twilight dimmed the diamonds scattered through her blond hair as she mounted the steps leading to Eiodel's battlements. Her white gown whispered across the black stone of the cold fortress as her clear green eyes glittered in the wavering light of the torches set at regular intervals in brackets along the fortress wall.

At last she reached the top and made her way across the flagstones. He would be on the north side, looking at Cadair Idris. As he always did when he came up here.

Overhead the stars began to spring forth in all their jeweled, cold beauty. His back was to her, though she knew he heard her approach. He would know it was she, for his heart would tell him.

"What do you see when you look at the High King's mountain?" she asked.

Sigerric turned and looked down at her. His thin face was carved into bitter lines. But she saw the light in his eyes, limned with starlight.

"My Lady," he said and began to bow.

"Don't bow to me, Sigerric," she said softly. "Never to me."

"Then to who?"

"To my husband, perhaps," she said with an edge to her voice.

Sigerric turned away and looked again on Cadair Idris. His thin, tense hands gripped the top of waist-high stone wall. "To him I have always bowed."

"And always will." Oh so delicately her voice rose at the end of that statement to make it—almost—a question.

"I cannot answer you, Princess," he said, not looking away from the glowing mountain.

"Cannot or will not?"

"Dare not."

"Ah." She said nothing for a while, gazing across the plain at the softly glowing mountain that rose from the bones of the earth. Even from this far off she could make out the jewels that winked and glimmered on the Doors of Cadair Idris. The silence of the night sank into her skin, almost soothing her, almost making her forget that one thing she wanted more than anything in the world. Almost, but not quite.

"Where is she, Sigerric?" she asked quietly, knowing he would answer.

"Gone."

"Yes. But where?" she insisted.

Sigerric turned and looked down at her upturned face. She was not sure how much he saw there, but she knew he saw something of the reason she was here. And she saw him close his eyes to it and she knew that no matter how long it took, no matter what she had to do, he would not prevent her from having what she wanted so badly. But neither would he directly aid her.

"She left to meet another Dewin. They plot to capture Gwydion ap Awst."

"But how?" she gasped, for she had not expected this. "How can they get to him in Cadair Idris?"

"He is not in Cadair Idris. Not any longer."

"How do you know that?"

"I did not know. Nor did Havgan. Arianrod told us that this was so."

"And my husband believed her."

"It is, I think, the truth," he said mildly and turned away from her again to look back across the darkening plain.

"Is Havgan really at Caer Duir?"

"He is. Arianrod told him to leave this to her. He chose now to remind the Archdruid that he is master, because there is nothing to hold him here in Eiodel for now."

"Because she is not here."

"Yes."

"When will she return?"

"When she has done what she set out to do. Most probably a few days from now."

"Bringing the Dreamer with her?"

"No. She will not bring him here, for they seek to use him as bait for Rhiannon. And she could never be lured here."

"Then where?"

"I am not sure of that. I do not know if that has even been decided yet."

"How can Arianrod imagine that she can fool Gwydion ap Awst? The way it has been told to me, she is the last person he would trust."

"That is true. But he does not need to trust her for this to work. She has offered him bait in the form of a renegade Dewin. He will come so he can recapture Llwyd Cilcoed. It will not occur to him, in his arrogance, that he can be taken."

"Surely he is not such a fool."

"Arianrod will meet him and take him to Llwyd Cilcoed. She will have told him that the Dewin will appear to be bound but will not be. She will have told him that the plan is for Llwyd to collar Gwydion while Arianrod distracts him."

"But?" she inquired.

"But there will be more than the two of them in that clearing. There will be twenty Coranian guards as well, well hidden."

"That will never work! I have been told of the Dreamer's powers. He would surely scout out that clearing before he ever went near it. He would see them!"

"They will be well hidden. He will never see them."

"They cannot know when he will do what they call Wind-Riding. He could be leagues away and discover them there."

"Which is why they will have lain in the underbrush for two days, waiting for him. Undetectable, invisible to his Wind-Ride."

"They cannot possibly lay there for two days! They are men."

"They are Coranian soldiers. They will do as they must."

Aelfwyn turned her gaze to the cold sky. The stars glittered like carelessly strewn diamonds on a black coverlet. To the north Cadair Idris glowed softly. To the east the full moon rose, bathing even black Eiodel in silvery beams.

"They will do as they must, Sigerric," Aelfwyn said softly as she fastened her eyes on the Doors of Cadair Idris. "And so will I."

Meriwydd, Disglair Wythnos—early evening

"AGAIN," MADRYN SAID implacably.

Gwen sighed. Every time the Druid told her this she was determined to say no. But, somehow, when Madryn's brown eyes turned on her, she couldn't refuse. So she tried again.

She touched the bracelet of oak that encircled her slim wrist. The dwyvach-breichled, the goddess-bracelet, shone in the soft golden light of the High King's hall. The bracelet of oak, polished to a glowing sheen, was incised with dozens of circles and spirals, all flowing into each other in a manner that seemed impossible for the eye to follow, like a maze that folded into itself and opened out again. Gwen did not understand the patterns, and knew she did not. She wondered if she ever would.

It was galling to fail and fail and fail in these baby steps she was taking. She, who had once Shape-Moved Modron's Cauldron itself from the bottom of the pit in Ogaf Greu now could not move the tiniest pebble. She who had once Shape-Moved the ring of the House of PenAlarch from the fat finger of the Master-wyrce-jaga into a convenient wine jar now could not even nudge the smallest leaf.

She opened her mouth to remind Madryn of the things she had once done, but stopped herself in time. After all, they hadn't made a difference the one time she had mentioned them. Madryn had simply asked her coldly if she could do any of those things now. The silence that answered Madryn's question was answer enough. Gwen had tried to say that if she hadn't had to learn to control her powers she would still have access to them. She had begun to say that she did not need to be taught, she needed to be left alone. She had started to explain that she was a different kind of Druid, one that the Mother herself had blessed, and she did not need to learn lessons for babies.

But Madryn had not answered. Instead, she had simply risen and left the room. Gwen had run after her, frantic, begging her to stay and teach her. But Madryn had gone to her own chambers and shut the door, refusing to open it in spite of all Gwen's pleading.

The next morning Madryn had, without comment, been sitting in the Druid's Alcove off of the High King's golden hall. Gwen had joined her and they had begun her lessons again. That had been weeks ago, just a day after Arthur and the others had left her here while they traveled to Caer Siddi to free the Master Smiths. She had argued with Arthur hard and long about that, for she had wanted to go. But Arthur had said no. He had said that Aergol had insisted that Gwen be taught, saying that it was dangerous to leave her in possession of unpredictable powers.

As her mother had told her so long ago, Aergol explained again. The power of the Druids could not be reached in the same way as the Dewin and the Bards grasped theirs. For them, they must be in a state of relaxation, of meditation, and the crystal triskale of the Dewin and the harp music of the Bards were tools to help put them in that state. Of course, after a time, neither the triskale nor the harp was needed and an experienced Dewin or Bard could simply drop into the necessary state without further thought.

But a Druid could not access the powers of the Mother through relaxation or meditation. It was only through intense concentration that these powers could be touched, held, and used responsibly. For druidic powers could be released in another way—in a highly emotional state, an unstable state of mind—and then the gods and goddesses help those that were in the way of an untrained Druid.

When a Druid was young, their teaching began. When they were little their powers were weak and easily controlled by their teachers. But Gwen was a young woman. And her powers were considerable, though raw and untrained. She was a danger and she knew it. So she tried, even though sometimes it made her angry.

And she had learned to control that anger. For whenever she did begin to get angry Madryn would end the lesson. And once Madryn decided to end it, there was no persuading her otherwise.

Once, and once only, Gwen had been angry enough to lash out at Madryn, hoping to frighten the Druid into continuing the lesson. But when she had pushed out with her powers with all her might, trying to shove Madryn from the alcove and spill her onto the floor she had received a ringing slap both across her face and inside her head. She had reeled from the blow and it had been Gwen who ended up sprawled across the floor.

"You hit me!" Gwen had said, more in astonishment than anger.

"You did it to yourself," Madryn had said calmly as she rose and smoothed her brown and green robe over her hips. The Druid had begun to walk out of the High King's hall.

"Wait!" Gwen had called as she ran after Madryn. "I won't get angry again. I promise. Please."

"No more for the next week," Madryn had said implacably. "I will not try to teach a brat."

"Please—"

"No." Madryn had stopped then and turned back to Gwen. "What will you do now, Gwynhwyfar ap Rhoram var Rhiannon? Will you try to hurt me in your anger?"

"No," Gwen had whispered, hanging her head. "No."

"I will not change my mind," Madryn had gone on. "You will have no lessons for the next week. You will not even try to use your powers. Is that understood?"

And Gwen, tamed at last, had nodded miserably. She did understand. After so long, she finally did. She was a menace if she could not control herself. She was a liability to Kymru. More importantly, she was a liability to Arthur. And that thought had startled her, for she had not known that it was important to her. But it was.

Now, sitting in the Druids' Alcove, with Madryn's eye on her, she rubbed the tips of her fingers across the dwyvach-breichled. The spirals and whorls and circles seemed to move of themselves beneath her fingertips. She closed her eyes and saw the spirals and circles incised in glowing emerald green across the inner darkness. She concentrated, following the patterns, plunging into the maze and finding her way out again.

Her heart quickened as she felt dusty granules of earth brush across her fingers and golden stalks of grain brush across her open palm; she smelled the scent of honeysuckle and newly turned earth; she heard the scampering of a hare through underbrush and sweet birdsong in the whispering trees; she tasted heavy purple grapes and golden apples in the back of her throat.

And then, because she knew she could, because the Mother had come to her, she reached out with her mind and Shape-Moved.

"Open your eyes, Gwenhwyfar," Madryn said softly.

She opened her eyes and looked at Madryn, a question on her

face. Madryn stood and motioned for Gwen to stand. She took Gwen by the shoulders and gently turned her to face the golden room.

And she saw what she had done.

The heavy, golden eagle-shaped throne of the High King stood at the bottom of the steps that led up to the now-empty dais.

"I—" Gwen began.

"You did well. Now, Gwenhwyfar ur Rhoram, Princess of Prydyn, put it back." Madryn said this last as though it would be easy.

And perhaps, Gwen thought, it truly was.

This time she did not close her eyes. She delicately touched her bracelet. The oak felt warm beneath her palm. She breathed in the scent of a spring morning, and concentrated. The golden throne rose in the air and steadily traveled above the jeweled steps, coming to rest gently back on the dais.

"You see?" Madryn asked quietly. "You see now?"

"Yes," Gwen breathed. "Oh, yes. I do see now."

Before Madryn could continue, a melodious voice, which seemed to come from nowhere and everywhere, sounded throughout the glowing hall.

"There is," Bloudewedd's disembodied voice said, "someone at the Door."

Chapter Six

Cadair Idris, Gwytheryn &
Cil, Kingdom of Prydyn, Kymru
Bedwen Mis, 500

Meiriwydd, Disglair Wythnos—early evening

It took her most of the next day to slip away from Eiodel unnoticed.

She had not expected it to take so long, not with Havgan away at Caer Duir. But, somehow, things had continued to get in the way. Situations that demanded her attention had continued to crop up all day, almost as though she was being subtly prevented from leaving the fortress. If that were so, she had certainly underestimated Sigerric. She had thought he would leave her a clear path to do what she had come to Kymru to do, but now she knew he had his own kind of honor she must contend with.

Within those confines—he would neither wholly prevent her nor help her, he would neither wholly desert Havgan nor support him—she could and would work toward her goal. She did not understand Sigerric and knew she did not. She had thought he would help her to free herself from her hated marriage. She had thought him completely disgusted with her husband. But Sigerric was more complex than she had imagined. Men, she had found, were usually relatively simple to understand. There were only two she had met that were not—her husband and his dearest friend.

She dismounted her horse in the gathering twilight. The Doors glowed softly, lighting the now-mended stairs. It was odd how the stairs, once broken and faded, had, one morning after Arthur and the rest of the Kymri returned to Cadair Idris, been made whole and shining. The Coranians in Eiodel had seen no one come out of the mountain, but the stairs had been repaired just the same. Arianrod had said it was the work of Druids, who could Shape-Move, and Havgan had held tightly to his rage while she had said it.

The Doors shimmered as she approached them. She repeated to herself what she had learned. There was dark onyx and bloodstone for Annwyn Lord of Chaos and his mate, Aertan the Weaver. There were emeralds for Modron the Mother and sapphires for her mate, Taran of the Winds. There were opals for Mabon of the Sun and pearls for his mate, Nantsovelta of the Waters. There were rubies for the Warriors Twins, Camulos and Agrona. There were diamonds for Sirona of the Stars and garnets for Grannos the Healer. There were amethysts for Cerridwen and topaz for Cerrunnos, leaders of the Wild Hunt, Protectors of Kymru.

As she came to a stop before the doors the symbol for Arderydd, the High Eagle, formed of all the jewels, blazed abruptly and from somewhere far away she heard the faint sound of hunting horns. She shivered briefly, then raised her hand to knock. But before she could, a voice, which seemed to come from everywhere, from nowhere, spoke softly.

"Not of mother and father,
When I was made
Did my creator create me.
To guard Cadair Idris
For my shame.
A traitoress to Kymru,
And to my lord and king.
The primroses and blossoms of the hill,
The flowers of trees and shrubs,
The flowers of nettles,
All these I have forgotten.
Cursed forever,
I was enchanted by Bran
And became prisoner
Until the end of days."

Her heart was in her throat as she almost stepped back and fled.

"What do you do here, Aelfwyn of Corania?" the voice asked.

"You know my name?"

"I know your name. I know you."

"How could you?"

"How could I not? Why wouldn't one false wife know another?"

"I—I have heard of your tale. And it is not the same as mine."

"Yes," the voice said dryly. "We all think our own tales are different. But I can assure you, Princess of the House of Aelle, by virtue of my greater experience in this world, that we are not different from each other. Not at all."

"I have been told that your dead husband, Lleu Silver-Hand, was a good man. But mine is not. I do not think to betray him because I have fallen in love with another."

"No. I betrayed my husband because I loved another. You betray yours for plain hate. Does that make you better, Princess?"

Aelfwyn swallowed. "I did not come here to be judged by you."

"Think of it," the voice said softly, "as a bonus."

Aelfwyn, determined to go on, ignored the barbed comment. "I came here to speak to the High King."

"You may not enter."

"I tell you, I must speak to him."

"You may not enter," the voice of the Doors went on, implacable, emotionless.

"Then send him out here to me!"

"I do not send the High King. The High King goes where he will."

"I have news of a plot! A plot to capture the Dreamer!"

The voice fell silent. A rare evening breeze ruffled the grasses of the plain. The full moon was beginning to ride the sky, and its silvery beams flooded over the shining steps, bathing the glowing door, turning Aelfwyn's white gown into glowing silver, as though she were sheathed in steel.

"You may not enter here," the Doors repeated at last.

"You fool!" Aelfwyn raged. "You would throw away this chance to save the Dreamer for—"

"For what, Princess?" a voice challenged from behind her.

She whirled around to confront the owner of that voice. A man stood at the top of the steps. Around his neck gleamed a sapphire set within a triangle of silver. He was tall and lean, and his brown hair was streaked with gray. Even in the uncertain moonlight and the softly glowing golden light of the doors she could tell that his eyes were green.

"Who are you?" she demanded, and she held her head high to hide her surprise.

His expressive mouth quirked and his green eyes danced. He bowed briefly, then replied.

"I am the son of Poetry,
Poetry, son of Reflection,
Reflection, son of Meditation,
Meditation, son of Lore,
Lore, son of Research,
Research, son of Knowledge,
Knowledge, son of Intelligence,
Intelligence, son of Comprehension,
Comprehension, son of Wisdom,
Wisdom, son of the gods."

"I see," she said dryly. "Well, that answers that."

"My dear, it is as much an answer as you deserve. But I will tell you my name in spite of that, for all my life I have had a weakness for beautiful women."

She almost smiled, for she felt the effects of his charm in spite of herself.

"I am Dudod ap Cyvarnion var Hunydd. And your husband had my brother, Anieron, killed," the man said softly. But for all its softness the last sentence was said with a tone of such underlying rage and grief, that Aelfwyn was almost afraid.

"I am sorry for your loss," she said formally, not knowing what else to say. "And if you wish revenge on him, you will listen to what I have to say."

"You have news of a plot, the Doors tell us. A plot to capture the Dreamer."

"Yes," she said eagerly. "And I have been told that the Bards of Kymru can put words to wings. If that is so, you may yet save him."

"Tell me of this plot," Dudod said crisply. "And of your price."

"I have no price."

Dudod's expressive brows quirked. "I find that very hard to believe."

"Then I will rephrase. My price is simply that you use this information to keep the Dreamer free. For there is very little else that my husband desires beyond the capture of his false blood brother. And what my husband desires, he shall not have. That, if it can be said to be a price, is mine."

Dudod took a step nearer to her. He looked down on her upturned face and said softly, "It is a pity that the Golden Man would waste the Star of Heaven. For she, diamond hard and diamond bright, might have been warmed at a gentler fire."

For some reason she could not fathom his words brought tears to her eyes. Humiliated and angered by his sympathy, she spoke harshly. "That is none of your affair."

"You are right, Princess," he said quietly. "Very right. So, then, we will move on to other things that are my affair. Tell me of this plot. And when it comes to fruition."

"Unless I am very much mistaken, it comes to fruition tonight."

Dudod, his eyes wide, reached out to her, grabbing her by the arms. "Tell me then," he said swiftly. "Tell me, and I will give my words wings!"

"I wish to speak to the High King. I will tell no other!"

"You will tell me, Aelfwyn of Corania," Dudod said evenly, gripping her shoulders tightly. "And if you do I will let you leave here unharmed."

"The High King—"

"Is not available to you. But rest assured, he will know of this as though you spoke to him yourself."

She hesitated. Though Dudod had not said, she thought it likely that Arthur was not in Cadair Idris. And so she told him of the trap Arianrod had made for the Dreamer.

Dudod released her then and she stumbled back. "Go," the Bard said in a terrible voice. "Go, for you have done what you came to do."

Then Dudod lifted his face to the sky, and flung back his arms. And though Aelfwyn could not hear his cry with her ears, she knew some message sprang desperately from Dudod's mind, speeding across the sky to the distant south.

She only hoped it would be in time.

GWYDION RODE NEXT to Cariadas at the rear of the party as they neared Cil. The gathering dusk shrouded the small group as they lead their horses through the thickening trees toward a small stream where they could camp for the night.

The group that had left Caer Siddi with the Master Smiths in tow was dwindling. After returning to the mainland King Rhoram and Achren had equipped the lone Coranian guard for the journey to Eiodel. The man had looked as though he did not relish the task of carrying Arthur's message. But carry it he would. Rhoram and his teulu had then split off and gone west, heading for the new headquarters set up in Penfro. It would be from Penfro that Rhoram—along with the help of Arthur and the Y Dawnus—would make his bid for the freedom of Prydyn.

Indeed, the Cerddorian throughout Kymru were on the move to gather near the Coranian-held capitals. Prince Lludd in Ederynion was moving toward his new headquarters in Ial. And King Owein and his folk would soon be moving north, to the commote of Maenor Deilo, to be closer to Llwynarth. Queen Morrigan and her people had already moved to Cemais when their hiding place in Mynydd Tawel was compromised. Soon they would move back northeast, to Coed Dulas, to await the signal to take back Tegeingl.

And then let Havgan face the Cerddorian of Kymru, the warriors who had waited for the past years to avenge the deaths of their friends and families and rulers. Then let the Warleader of Corania reap what he had sown.

The Golden Man would have to stand and fight with what he had, for there would be no reinforcements to help him. Havgan's ships had been burnt and the shores of Kymru were watched to ensure that no help from Corania could arrive in time. With Havgan dead the Coranians would no longer be a threat, for it had been the force of Havgan's personality, the force of Havgan's schemes, the force of Havgan's terrible, terrible need that had bound Corania to this venture.

The next step in this deadly game would be to free Queen Elen in Ederynion and Queen Enid in Rheged, for Arthur would not leave these two as hostages in the hands of the Coranians when the war began again in earnest. Even now Ceindrech, Aergol's lover and the mother of his son, was on her way to Ederynion to meet up with Prince Lludd. And King Owein, along with the Druid, Yrth, and a few of his trusted people would soon be on their way to Llwynarth to take Queen Enid back from the enemy.

In Gwynedd, Myrrdin and Rhodri were awaiting their chance to rid Kymru of Rhodri's son, the traitorous King Madoc. And then it would be time to deal with Cathbad, the Archdruid, who would dare to use the ceremony of tarw-casgliad to ensure Havgan's place as ruler of Kymru. For that alone Modron the Mother would surely fry her Archdruid to a crisp. Gwydion was only surprised that she had not done so before this.

Yes, the Kymri were on the move, and plans were reaching fruition. By Calan Llachar, less than three months from now, the gamble would be lost or won. They would either all be dead, or be free.

They reached the stream as twilight surrounded them, and Gwydion and his six companions let their horses dip their heads and drink their fill. There were only six left now of the original group that had rescued the Master Smiths from bondage, for yesterday Arthur had split their party even further. He had sent the

Druids—Aergol, Aldwr, Menw, and Sabrina—ahead to Cadair Idris with the Master Smiths and their families, giving them orders to make their way to the mountain by circling northwest around Llyn Mwyngil. He gave Aergol the leadership of that party, telling him to split the groups even smaller as he saw fit to ensure that they reached Cadair Idris. Arthur had said that it was best to have the Druids protect the Smiths, and perhaps he was right, for these Druids were experienced and capable. Yet Gwydion knew there were other reasons for Arthur to split the party.

He thought he understood why. For, besides Gwydion and Rhiannon, the High King had retained in his party the four young people that would, in the fullness of time, be the High King's Great Ones—Cariadas as his Dreamer, Llywelyn as his Ardewin, Sinend as his Archdruid, and Cynfar as his Master Bard. During this trip Arthur had spoken to these four extensively, getting to know them better, storing in his mind and heart who they were, what they wanted, what—and who—they loved and hated. Gwydion watched him do it and silently applauded the young man. For he saw Arthur examine these four as one might examine a set of tools that one needed for a delicate, prolonged task.

And he saw something more—he saw the seeds of friendship and love sown between these five. And Gwydion would wonder what the years ahead might bring and know that, whatever they brought, his dreams of the future were nearing an end as Mabon of the Sun prepared to welcome another Dreamer.

And he was not sorry, for he was more than ready to hand over the dreams to his daughter. He had been Dreamer of Kymru for almost eighteen years and he had sacrificed a great deal to fulfill his task. Soon he would be able to turn to Rhiannon and beg her to give him the chance to show her how very, very much he loved her. When King Rhoram had been a part of their party Gwydion had watched the two of them and had, finally, discovered something—that he did not need to be jealous of the King of Prydyn. For Rhoram had his eye on another woman now, and Rhiannon knew it and did not care. It had become evident even to Gwydion that Rhoram was in love with the captain of his Cerddorian—and that the captain of his Cerddorian was far too wary to reciprocate. He did not doubt for one moment that Achren would lead Rhoram quite a dance. And that Rhiannon would be smiling all the while.

Ah, Rhiannon. As always he knew exactly where she was without having to check. And he knew she was watching him, without having to raise his head to see. She had been keeping her eye on him closely for the last few days. She was watching him because she knew him too well. She knew he was planning something, but she did not know what. She had no inkling that he had been in contact with Arianrod, but she knew enough to be sure he was planning something of which she would not approve.

Gwydion knew that no one would approve of what he meant to do. For he would spring the trap that Arianrod had thought to capture him with. He was not such a fool as Arianrod apparently thought he was, for he knew better than to fully believe her.

It was unlikely that Arianrod would so easily turn herself and Llywd Cilcoed over to Arthur. That she wanted protection for herself and her child from Havgan he could readily believe. She had always discarded her lovers before they could discard her. And Havgan must be tiring of his pregnant mistress. But Arianrod's price did not seem to be enough. He was sure she had some plan to gain more. Which she would, if she held the life of the Dreamer in her hands. With that she could bargain with Arthur for anything she wanted for herself and her child—guarantees of protection, the comforts of life, whatever she thought she would need.

As surely as he knew his own name he knew that Arianrod was planning to double-cross both Llywd Cilcoed and himself, but he had not yet determined how. He had kept a close eye on her the past few days, surreptitiously Wind-Riding to observe her.

Last night he had Wind-Ridden and found her in a tiny clearing outside of Cil, just where she said she would be. There had been one other in that clearing—Llwyd Cilcoed, the one-time lover of Queen Olwen of Ederynion. Llywd had been staring blankly down at his tied hands. He had been pale and shocked as he huddled on the cold ground, looking over at Arianrod, who had sat smiling on a convenient log, trimming her nails with a gleaming dagger. Gwydion had seen the dull gleam of gray lead around the Dewin's neck and, for a moment, almost pitied the man. He could think of few worse things than to be collared.

He had told Arianrod that he would not come to her alone. But he had, of course, lied. He would do this thing himself. He did not need anyone else's help.

His horse lifted its head and snorted. He led the horse from the stream and fastened the reins to a nearby sapling. That done, he looked up and caught the gleam of Rhiannon's emerald eyes fastened on him as the dusk deepened.

RHIANNON KNEW BETTER than to put any faith at all in the innocent looks of inquiry that Gwydion kept giving her whenever he would raise his head and see her staring at him.

He knew perfectly well why she watched him so closely. He was planning something. And she would not let him get away with whatever foolish action he was contemplating.

She knew him very well by now. Nothing he could say or do would surprise her. Indeed, it did not surprise her at all that, even after all their time together—almost six years—he would not share with her what he was thinking. He might trust her when the occasion seemed to demand it, but he would not think he needed her. Not now and not ever.

But he did need her. Not in the way she used to hope for, for Gwydion's heart was closed and locked and she would not humiliate herself any longer by standing before that door and begging to be let in. It would not open—at least, for her—and that was an end to it.

No, he did not need her as his lover. But he did need her as his partner in this long and deadly game they played with fate. She would have thought that even a man as stubborn and prideful as Gwydion ap Awst would have understood by now that he could not do everything alone. Sometimes she thought he had learned that lesson, but then he would always go back to who he truly was. When he had publicly apologized for his unreasoning anger toward her when she had saved his life at the Storm Tree, she had thought for a brief time that his pride would allow him to at least acknowledge her as a trusted friend. But that had not lasted. None of the times he had been gentle with her—and there were a few—had ever lasted. He would always seem to come to some realization that he had been kind, and would repent of that. Why he did this she truly did not know. She doubted that she ever would.

But she was done with eating her heart out for Gwydion ap Awst, so she no longer cared why he insisted on keeping her and the rest of the world at arm's length.

Of course, she seemed to decide that she was through with him quite a lot. And then he would smile at her and his silvery eyes would glow and her wayward heart would skip a beat. Sometimes, like the time he had danced with her at Alban Awyr in Allt Llwyd, she had seen something in his face that made her heart beat faster. Sometimes she would lay awake and wonder what it would be like if she kissed him and let the passion she knew he had inside loose. And she did know that it was there, for she had felt it that day by the lake in Ederynion when he had forgotten himself long enough to kiss her.

But here she was again thinking about those things when she had vowed to stop thinking of them. For the hopes and dreams she had about being loved by the Dreamer were hollow. And always would be. She determined again, for the thousandth time, to remember that.

And remember that she would. But for now that was not her concern. Her concern was that Gwydion was planning something, thinking something, scheming something. And she would not let him out of her sight until she knew what it was.

GWYDION LOOKED AT Arthur as Llywelyn laid the last log for the fire. He wanted to give Arthur a chance to start the fire if he wished. Arthur returned Gwydion's gaze and nodded to him. Gwydion stretched out his hand and huge, perfectly formed rose-blossoms, made of flames, bloomed over the wood. They floated down and touched the logs and fire burst forth.

"Very pretty, Da," Cariadas said approvingly as she stretched out her hands toward the flames.

"Thank you," Gwydion said gravely, although there was laughter in his eyes. "But it was not I that lit the fire."

"But Arthur nodded to you! I thought he meant that you could do it and not him," Cariadas protested, looking over at the High King.

"I did," Arthur agreed. "But it was not I that lit the fire either."

Sinend, the future Archdruid, looked up from her contemplation of the flames. "I did it," the young woman said firmly.

They were all somewhat surprised, for Sinend rarely said anything, much less in such a firm tone.

"Because?" Arthur asked quietly, although Gwydion did not think Arthur was puzzled.

"Because I am the Archdruid's heir," Sinend said simply. "It is I who should Fire-Weave, for that is a druidic gift."

"One that both the High King and the Dreamer happen to share," Rhiannon said gently.

"Nonetheless, protocol states that, even in the presence of the High King and the Dreamer, the first right of refusal to Fire-Weave belongs to the Archdruid."

"She's right," Cynfar said. "That is the proper protocol."

"And I am happy to bow to that," Arthur said with a smile. "I was not aware of that, for I am just an ignorant shepherd."

"Arthur!" Sinend said, shocked. "You are not an ignorant shepherd. You are High King!"

"I was not offended, Sinend," Arthur replied. "Merely stating a fact."

"My intention, High King," Sinend said earnestly, "was not to belittle you in any way! It was merely to—"

Arthur, smiling at the vehemence in her tone, held up his hand and Sinend fell silent. "Archdruid's heir, that you should point out the proper method of showing respect to the Archdruid pleases me. The responsibility of leading the Druids back from their darkness, begun by your father, will later fall to you. I would not have servile Druids in Kymru. I would have ones that know their worth and their place. Ones that are proud to be what they are, and yet ones that acknowledge their true master. Ones that revere the Mother but serve their High King. And I see, now, that you are a worthy heir of the task to ensure that such Druids are made."

"And," Rhiannon said with a smile, "they were such lovely roses."

Sinend, who had reddened with embarrassment at Arthur's words, smiled shyly at Rhiannon.

"And I know whereof I speak," Rhiannon went on. "I have traveled leagues and leagues and even more leagues with the Dreamer and have seen him start more fires than either one of us could count. And there would be new ways of doing that every day. Honeycomb and wheat fields, and fiery horses and swords and flame-colored waterfalls and I don't know what all."

Gwydion was still as Rhiannon spoke. He knew she was leading up to something. He could tell by the tone of her voice, although he did not think the others were aware of it yet—except, perhaps, for Arthur.

"Of course he would have to light fires," Rhiannon went on, "because he insisted that we camp out every night. Never would he stop at a village or a farmhouse and invoke the Law of Hospitality. Even when we were at peace, he would not do that."

"Why not, Da?" Cariadas asked curiously.

"Yes, why not?" Llywelyn asked, puzzlement in his steady brown eyes.

Gwydion gritted his teeth, knowing that he would not be allowed to answer that question. Knowing that Rhiannon would take it upon herself to do that.

"Oh, because he would never, ever trust anyone—not even the simple people of Kymru. He thought that they might ask him questions. Or perhaps talk about him when he was gone."

"But the Law says people cannot ask questions of travelers who stop at their house for the night," Cynfar protested. "The Kymri would never do that. If we were anywhere near a settlement, we wouldn't be out here in the woods tonight."

"Besides," Rhiannon went on, "he would never want to be beholden to anyone—not even for a meal."

"Rhiannon—" Gwydion began in a dangerous tone.

"A meal does not oblige you," Llywelyn pointed out. "I don't see—"

"Oh, that's just something you have to learn about the Dreamer," Rhiannon said airily. "He does exactly what he wants to do and doesn't care if you don't understand. In fact, he would just as soon you didn't."

"All right, Rhiannon," Gwydion said harshly. "You've had your fun and made your point."

"Have I?" she said swiftly. "Then why don't you and I talk privately for a moment and you can show me that my point has been made."

"By doing what?"

"By telling me the truth."

"Very well," he said abruptly. "Come with me." He got up and strode away from the fire to the edge of the clearing. As he did so he clearly saw Arthur's face. The High King had not spoken a word during Rhiannon's musing-turned-tirade, had not even looked up from his contemplation of the fire. But he looked up now and something in his dark eyes made Gwydion wonder if Arthur didn't know exactly what Gwydion was up to.

Rhiannon rose and furiously stalked over to Gwydion.

"Well?" she demanded her arms crossed. "What have you got to say for yourself?"

"How about 'how dare you talk about me that way?'" he hissed.

"It is the truth. And it is the truth that hurts the most, isn't it?"

"I have had enough—"

"No, it is I who has had enough. You are planning something, Gwydion, and don't bother to deny it."

"I will deny it."

She went on as though he had not spoken. "It is not that which is the most hurtful. It is that even now, even after all this time, you still cannot bring yourself to be honest with me. What more can I possibly do to show you that you can trust me? What more can I do?"

"Rhiannon," he began, appalled to see the sudden gleam of

angry tears in her eyes. "Rhiannon, I do trust you."

"You are a liar, Gwydion, and we both know it," she went on furiously. "How could you say that? You have never trusted me if there was a way around it. Over and over and over again in these past six years I have shown you that you can. But you refuse to. Over and over and over again in these past six years I have hoped that you would see how we could have—"

She broke off as though startled to hear what she was saying.

"How we could have what?" he asked, puzzled.

"Nothing," she muttered. "It was never anything at all. As you have always strained to make so clear to me."

"Rhiannon, what are you—"

"Never mind. Never mind any of it. Keep your secrets. I am done trying to make you see that you don't need to. Done."

She turned and stalked back to the campfire. Gwydion stood frozen at the edge of the clearing as he stared after her. What had she almost said? Could she have possibly meant—? No, she couldn't have.

Arthur raised his head again from the fire and looked Gwydion full in the face. And Gwydion saw pity there. And understanding. And he even thought he saw the knowledge of what Gwydion was about to do, but he would never be sure of that.

And Gwydion, knowing that if he did not go now he would not go, knowing that it was far too late to change who he was, knowing, even, that he was being a proud fool, Shape-Moved, causing a bush on the other side of the clearing to rustle loudly.

And as the others around the fire leapt to their feet, drawing their weapons, he slipped away from the clearing like a ghost, rushing to meet the fate that awaited him in another clearing not far away.

Rhiannon turned to where Gwydion had stood, slipping her dagger back into its sheath. Whatever had rustled the bushes was gone, and the others began to relax, turning to take their seats next to the fire.

Rhiannon's eyes darted around the clearing, but Gwydion was

gone. "That son of a bitch," she said softly.

"What do you suppose it is he is planning?" Arthur asked.

"You knew he was planning something?"

"Of course. Since two nights ago. I could swear he left the camp that night to Wind-Ride."

"But Wind-Ride to who?" she asked. "I believe that too, but who in the world could he have been talking to and what could they have been saying that he would not tell us of it?"

Arthur shook his head. "I don't know. But I tell you that I don't like what is happening here tonight one bit. Something is terribly wrong."

Rhiannon nodded. She knew what Arthur meant. There was a tension in the quiet night that seemed to raze her skin. "I'll Wind-Ride after him. I'll find him, and when I do—"

She cocked her head, breaking off what she was saying. She thought she heard something, a faint cry echoing in her mind. She glanced over at Arthur and saw that he, too, had cocked his head as though straining to hear something.

"What?" she whispered.

"Someone trying to Mind-Speak with us," Arthur said. "From too far away."

"Use Cynfar and Cariadas," she said urgently. "Cynfar is a Bard, and Cariadas can Mind-Speak. Use their powers to help whoever is trying to Speak to us."

Arthur nodded as Cariadas and Cynfar rushed to join Arthur. He took their hands in his own and bowed his head. Rhiannon strained to hear something, opening all her senses as fully as she could. If Arthur could use his power to augment the message that was trying to reach them, she, too, would be able to her it.

For a moment the Mind-Voice quieted, then she could hear it louder, but she could not yet distinguish the words. And then, as Arthur linked their powers of Cynfar and Cariadas, as the High King reached up and out and across Kymru to find the message and the messenger, the words burst upon her brain appallingly clearly.

Warn the Dreamer! It is a trap! Arianrod waits for him with twenty warriors. Warn him! Oh, gods, can anyone hear me? Anyone at all?

No time now to wonder how Dudod had found this out, for she recognized the Mind-Speech of her uncle. No time to reassure him that his warning was heard. There was only a brief moment to wonder how Gwydion could possibly be such a fool before she sent a message straight to him, one she hoped with all her heart it was not too late to send.

GWYDION! IT'S A TRAP! COME BACK!

GWYDION MADE HIS way swiftly through the trees. He knew exactly where Arianrod and Llwyd were. He would go there, thwart whatever transparent plan Arianrod had and return to Arthur and the rest with both traitorous Dewin in tow.

He halted as he neared the clearing. It looked right. Llwyd was still sitting on the ground, to all appearances securely bound, with a collar around his neck. Arianrod was sitting on a log, impatiently tapping her foot.

"Ah, there you are, Gwydion," she called out. "I have been waiting."

"I'm sure you have, Arianrod," Gwydion replied pleasantly from the shelter of the trees.

"Come on, we don't have all night."

When he did not immediately move she laughed. "I see. You think that two poor Dewin could possibly betray the Dreamer. You, Gwydion, are a fool."

"Not as big a fool as you apparently took me for," Gwydion said, still scanning the clearing. "Or did you think I would blithely put myself in your hands?"

"You are not putting yourself in my hands, Gwydion," Arianrod said with a smile. "For I could never hold you and you know it. Did I not already tell you that Llwyd Cilcoed would only appear to be bound? Did that not show my good faith?"

Llwyd gasped as he jumped to his feet. The bonds around his hands slipped to the ground. "You told him that?" the Dewin cried. "What game are you playing?"

"My own, you fool," Arianrod laughed. "When have I ever

played anyone else's?"

Enraged, Llywd leapt at Arianrod and slapped her so hard she screamed and went flying back, falling heavily to the ground. Llwyd did not hesitate, but strode to where she lay. He straddled her swollen belly and wrapped his hands around her throat.

"This is the last time you even think to double-cross me, you bitch," Llwyd hissed. "The last time."

It was as he was leaping into the clearing, as he was knocking Llywd Cilcoed aside from Arianrod's prone body, as he was propelling himself after the Dewin that he heard Rhiannon's Mind-Shout.

GWYDION! IT'S A TRAP! COME BACK!

And it was as he was realizing just what kind of fool he had been that he felt a heavy blow to the back of his head. His eyes caught a glimpse of Llwyd's and Arianrod's smiling faces, of a clearing suddenly filled with Coranian warriors, of the dull gray of a collar, when darkness swallowed him.

Part 2
The Prisoners

The hall is dark tonight,
Without fire, without bed;
I shall weep a while, I shall be silent after.
The hall is dark tonight
Without fire, without candle;
Longing for you comes over me.

Peredur, King of
Rheged
Circa 270

Chapter Seven

Sycharth & Dinmael, Kingdom of Ederynion &
Cadair Idris, Gwytheryn, Kymru
Bedwen Mis, 500

Suldydd, Tywyllu Wythnos—evening

He wandered through the dark wood from place to place, searching desperately for a way back to a world bathed in the golden light of the sun, searching hopelessly for the possibility of living through this dark, cold, eternal night.

Searching helplessly for her.

But she was not there. He knew why. It was because he had left her time and again. And now he had left her for the last time. This time he would never return. He would never again know the light of her smile, the warmth of her spirit, the comfort of her heart.

He would never get out of this darkness. He would never see her again.

He tried to call out with his mind, but there was only silence. He tried to separate his essence from his body and spring up into the sky, but he was earth-bound. He tried to call fire to light the way, but there was only darkness.

He tried to dream, but found only nightmares.

There was no way out. He was trapped. Trapped in the dark. Alone, forever.

"Gwydion," the voice murmured softly. "Gwydion. Answer me."

There was the voice again—the voice that asked questions he should not answer. The voice that asked questions he must not answer.

Oh, but the voice promised so much. The voice promised to show him the way out. The voice promised that he could be with her. If only he would answer.

He was cold and tired, hungry and lonely. He would always be, now. Never again would he know the warmth of life and love. Never again would he behold her beautiful face. Never again.

"Gwydion, it is I, High King Arthur. Now tell me. Tell me the ways into Cadair Idris. Cadair Idris is my home, now. And I must know."

He did not understand why the voice asked him these questions. Arthur knew the secret ways into Cadair Idris. Why should he ask?

"Gwydion, I have forgotten. I have forgotten the way in. I must know. My people await me. They wait for me to lead them into freedom. But I cannot get into the High King's hall. You must help me."

Gwydion shook his head. No, that wasn't right. For Arthur knew the way.

Bewildered and exhausted Gwydion fell to his hands and knees on the forest floor. Strange, but the earth beneath his feet felt like smooth wood. And the leaves that covered the ground made no sound at all as he plunged his hands through them.

He lifted his head and peered into the twilight, into the unforgiving darkness that he wandered in, searching for the owner of that voice. Searching for Arthur, for the boy that he had turned into a High King. But he was alone.

He rose unsteadily to his feet, his fists clenched. He would find a way out of here. He must. He tried to move forward, to thread his way through the dizzying maze of gnarled and darkened trees. Yet the trees themselves always seemed to shift and block his way so that he never left the place he started from.

There was no path. No way out. He would never get out.

"Gwydion, answer me! Answer me and I will lead you out of here and into Cadair Idris itself. Answer!"

But Gwydion shook his head. He could not tell. He should not tell. He must not tell.

"You must tell me, uncle, what I am to do next. Tell me, Dreamer, what is my next move?"

Surely Arthur knew that. Why, Arthur would know that better than anyone else, for Arthur had been directing this game ever since he had survived the Tynged Mawr— ever since he had put the torque around his neck and ascended the throne of Idris and declared himself High King of Kymru.

The voice fell silent when Gwydion did not answer. Gwydion glanced around the darkening wood. How to find a way out? How?

"Rhiannon waits for you, Dreamer," the voice said softly. "She waits for you in Cadair Idris."

Rhiannon! Rhiannon, his love, though he had never told her so. She waited for him?

"She waits for your return. She will not eat or sleep in her grief. She waits for you. You must go there. To her."

Cariad, Gwydion thought. Beloved. Oh, beloved, I am coming to you. Oh, *cariad*, my heart's delight, I am coming.

"Yes, Gwydion," the voice soothed. "That's right. Tell me. Tell me and I will take you to her. Tell me."

He shook his head. He must not. He could not. Not even to see her again.

Someone yanked his hair, forcing his head back. Someone forced his mouth open and poured something down his throat. He tried to spit it up, but someone held his mouth shut, pitching his nose until he swallowed.

"Gwydion," the voice said. "I grow tired of waiting."

Tired. Yes, he was tired. He would never get out of this place. And no promises could make it so. He did not know how he knew that, but he did. He did not remember who spoke to him, but he knew it was not Arthur. He did not remember how he came to the dark wood, but he knew he was lost in it forever.

Lost without her.

Llwyd Cilcoed ground his teeth and stepped back from Gwydion's still form.

He gestured sharply and the two guards that held the Dreamer's chains pulled them tight and secured them again against the wall so that Gwydion hung limply from the chains, his head sunk to his breast. The Dreamer's tunic was crumpled and stained with dirt and blood. His face was bathed in sweat. Around his neck hung a dull, gray collar. At the edge of the collar Gwydion's skin was raw and blistered, for that is what an enaid-dal did when hung around the neck of an Y Dawnus.

Llwyd seated himself back in the chair and thought.

Gwydion was trapped in his own mind, trapped there by the enaid-dal and by the continuous doses of mistletoe he had been given. But even trapped, the Dreamer got away. Llwyd had gained absolutely nothing in the two weeks since he had captured Gwydion.

It had taken a week to get to Sycharth, traveling cautiously to ensure that they were neither watched nor followed. During that week Gwydion had been collared and drugged, but Llywd had been unable to question him with so much activity around them. And the second week was proving as unfruitful as the first, for Gwydion simply refused to answer.

No matter what Llywd promised, no matter who he pretended to be, Gwydion would not answer. The Dreamer hadn't even spoken one word since being captured. Llwyd knew enough about the drug and the collar to know that Gwydion did not know who had captured him, did not even fully realize that he was a prisoner. But Gwydion should have been too confused to keep his secrets, too cold and weary to hold anything back.

But the Dreamer had always been made of stone and ice. He had never behaved like a normal human being. Why would he start now?

Llwyd Cilcoed stared at the nearly unconscious Dreamer. He must think of a way. He must. He had to give Havgan answers to the questions the Golden Man most wanted to know—how to get into Cadair Idris, and what the High King's next moves were in this deadly game.

If Llywd Cilcoed could not give Havgan the answers he sought, then his own life would be forfeit. He would never become Lord of

Arystli. He would never rid the world of his hated brother, Alun. He would never be somebody. He would never be anything more than just another Dewin in Kymru. He would never be more than just a hunted man.

He had to think of a way.

And then he thought of it. And it was so simple that he could scarcely believe it had taken him so long.

He stood and walked to stand before Gwydion. He reached around and gently unclasped the collar. He pulled it from the Dreamer's neck and heard Gwydion sigh in relief as the ability to reach outside his mind began to return.

He gently took Gwydion's battered face in his hands and lifted the Dreamer's head up. Gwydion's gray eyes, dilated until they were almost black, blinked and teared in the smoky light of the torches set in brackets around the walls of the dim, cold cellar.

"She is waiting for your message, Gwydion," Llywd said softly. "Call to her. And she will come to you. Call for her, Dreamer. Call."

Gwydion shook his head to clear it. The voice. The voice said that he could call to Rhiannon. The voice said she was looking for him.

If she found him she could lead him from this wood. This wood called—

"Sycharth," the voice said. "That is what it is called."

Sycharth, Gwydion thought. That is the name of the wood. Yes.

"She must come to you alone, Gwydion. She is the only one you trust. There must be no one else, for they mustn't see you like this. Only Rhiannon is to know. Only her. And she mustn't tell anyone."

Yes. There was no one else. Only her. He would call to her. And she would come and let him out of the darkness. He would call to her.

His beloved.

Rhiannon sat across from Arthur at the small table in the garden room at Cadair Idris. The trees around the perimeter of the room seemed to shiver momentarily as Arthur stirred in his chair and hunched over the tarbell board, frowning in concentration. The fountain laughed as it threw droplets of sparkling water in the fresh, flower-scented air.

The High King's massive torque of emerald and opal, of sapphire and pearl and onyx glittered around Arthur's sinewy neck, bathed in the glowing light that emanated from the golden walls. His long fingers reached forward and curled around the silver dragon with outspread wings. The pearl around the dragon's neck glittered as he shifted the piece forward from its white square to a black one.

Rhiannon stared down at the board, but she did not really see it. All she saw was Gwydion's handsome face and his silvery eyes. She wanted to scream with rage when she thought of him as a prisoner of the Golden Man. Havgan would ensure that Gwydion suffered exquisitely before he killed the Dreamer. He would see to it that Gwydion died and died and died again. He would—

"Gwydion is not at Eiodel, Rhiannon," Arthur said quietly. "Havgan himself does not have him."

"Does that matter?" she asked sharply. "He is still a prisoner."

"Of Llywd Cilcoed. Not of the Golden Man."

"What do you care?" she retorted. "Either way we cannot get to him. Not if we can't find him."

"I told you why we could not rescue him when they first took him."

Rhiannon looked up into Arthur's piercing, dark gaze. The scar on his face whitened momentarily as he returned her stare. She clenched her hands in the folds of her skirt to keep herself from hitting him.

"So you did," she said coldly.

"I could not risk the lives of those with me. They were my Great Ones. I could not pit them against twenty Coranian warriors and two Dewin. The odds were too great."

"You lie," Rhiannon spat. "You do. You are the High King.

You could have taken the powers of any of the Y Dawnus for leagues around. With those powers you could have saved him. But you didn't."

"I couldn't," Arthur said quietly.

"You mean you didn't."

"No," Arthur said evenly. "I mean I couldn't."

She stared at him, for this was not something she had thought of.

"Do you think it so easy to take the powers of the Y Dawnus and shape it whenever I please? Do you?" Arthur asked, his face taut. "Do you think that I can do it on a whim? At a moment's notice? At any time, anytime at all?"

She did not know what to say. For she had thought, perhaps, that it would be easy for the High King.

"It is not easy," he went on, his dark eyes boring into hers as though willing her to understand. "I was tired from the effort to free the Master Smiths. That was the first time I had ever used those powers in battle. When I take those powers to fight I see the faces of the Lord of Chaos and of his mate, the Weaver. It is from them that the power springs and it to them that my spirit must journey. It is to Gwlad Yr Haf that my spirit goes, to the place where they dwell, the home of the dead. Do you think that is easy?"

"I do not think any of it easy, Arthur," she whispered through her tight throat. "None of it has ever been easy. But I thought you could save him."

"But simply chose not to?"

She nodded, unable to speak past the pent up tears in her throat.

"Ah, Rhiannon ur Hefeydd, do you really think so little of me?"

"I think, Arthur, that you are a man who has accepted his fate. And I think you will do what you must do to save Kymru. And I think that does not include saving the life of the man that you hate most."

She stood and walked to the door. Her back was to him as

she neared it so he did not see the expression on her face when she heard the voice in her head.

Rhiannon. Cariad.

She stopped, for the voice was faint. But she knew who it was. She knew, as she knew the beat of her own heart.

Cariad. Beloved. Help me, please.

Where are you?

I am in Sycharth. You must come to me. Only you. I wander in the woods. I am lost. Please. Please, cariad. Please. Help me.

"Rhiannon," Arthur called as he rose from the tarbell game. "Are you all right?"

She turned to face him, her emerald eyes veiled.

"I am fine," she said shortly. She left the room and waited for the door to close behind her. In the faintly glowing corridor she stopped and put her hands to her cold cheeks, her heart beating wildly.

I am coming, she called.

Only you. Only you, cariad, his voice whispered to her heart. *No one else.*

Yes, she answered. *I am coming to you. Alone.*

Llundydd, Tywyllu Wythnos—evening

REGAN SAT IN the Queen's ystafell, a feeling of dread inexplicably settling around her.

On the surface there was nothing out of the ordinary. She and Queen Elen sat near each other, Regan on a chair next to the canopied throne where Elen sat. The pearls set within the canopy of white and sea green glowed softly in the light of the fire on the hearth. The firelight burnished Elen's auburn hair to a reddish sheen. But Elen's blue eyes were cold and frosty. The silver and pearl torque of Ederynion gleamed around her slender neck as she sewed tiny pearls onto a white veil with swift angry stitches, savagely jerking the thread through the delicate silk.

"Elen," Regan began, her own light brown eyes wide with a fear she did not yet understand. "Please."

Elen slowed her stitches but did not look up at her friend. "Dewin," Elen asked softly, "do you, of all people, not understand?"

"You know I do," Regan said just as quietly.

"I doubt it," Elen said dryly.

And Regan began to doubt it, too. She was not a fool, but Elen had always been better at understanding subtleties, at reading between the lines.

Memory of the small incident from this morning nudged at her. She and Elen had risen from the table in the hall after breakfast. And Guthlac, the Master-wyrce-jaga of Ederynion, had not risen when they did. General Talorcan had, of course, done so, as had all the other Coranians at the high table. They always did, at General Talorcan's orders. Even Guthlac always had.

Until this morning.

At the time Regan had noted an expression of triumph on Guthlac's heavy-set face. But she thought it had been triumph only at such a small defiance of the protocol Talorcan had insisted on. She had not understood, until just now, that it had been more than that.

Now she knew where that sense of dread had come from. Guthlac was, at last, making his move. And though Elen might survive it, Regan knew that she herself would not.

And Elen knew it, too.

Regan cleared her throat so she could talk past the lump there. Though she had been a prisoner these last few years, she still loved life. Though she had tried to avoid the truth, she loved Talorcan with all her heart and the thought of dying, of leaving him, brought tears to her eyes. And the thought of leaving Elen all alone among the enemy—well, that was even worse.

"Do you think Guthlac will slaughter me privately? Or have it done publicly in the marketplace?"

"Or send you to Afalon," Elen said in a low voice. "I do not think it is Guthlac's plan to make it quick. He would want Talorcan to suffer, knowing that you are suffering."

"Ah," Regan said quietly. "In Afalon, with an enaid-dal around my neck, dying inch by inch, day by day, with the rest of the Y Dawnus there. Yes, I would suffer. Suffer enough to satisfy even Guthlac." Regan clutched the cloth she had been embroidering. "They say Havgan likes to go there sometimes, to watch the Y Dawnus die in slow agony." She smiled bleakly. "If I see him, I'm sure I can think of a few choice words to say. Is there any message you wish me to give him?"

Elen flung the veil to the floor and flew from her chair, kneeling in front of Regan, her blue eyes blazing. "I will never let them take you. Never."

"Elen, there is nothing you can do."

"Talorcan will never let you go."

"He won't be able to stop it. If Guthlac dares to do this it is because he knows he can. Because Havgan himself has said he could."

"I do what they tell me because by doing so I can keep you alive," Elen said fiercely. "If they think I will not give them trouble—"

"Oh, Elen, you must not. Don't you see? If they take me it is because they do not need you to bend to their will. They will kill you next, if you do not take care."

"They will kill me in any case," Elen said matter-of-factly. "They always meant to do that eventually. What in the world is taking my brother so long?"

"You know better than that, Elen," Regan reproached. "You know Lludd would free you if he could."

"He had better find a way soon," Elen threatened," or I will roast him whole next time I see him."

"He would no anything for you," Regan said. "You know that. I am sure he will find a way to rescue you before they—"

"But not before you are taken," Elen said bitterly. "For he will be too late for that."

"But he will come for you. You have always known that."

"Yes," Elen said as she stood up with her fists clenched. "I have always known that."

"HURRY UP, WILL you?" Angharad exclaimed impatiently.

The Druid sent by High King Arthur looked up at her coldly. "If you think it is so easy, you do it," Ceindrech said.

"I'm not a Shape-Mover."

"No, you are not. But I am. So kindly step back and let me do what I came here to do."

Muttering beneath her breath, Angharad stepped away from where the Druid crouched on the forest floor. The glimmer of torches faintly illuminated the edges of the trapdoor, disguised so cleverly that she could scarcely believe it was there. And to think, neither she nor Prince Lludd had ever known of this secret passageway that led underground from the forest outside the walls of Dinmael to the Queen's ystafell in Caer Dwyr. According to Rhiannon, the passageway actually ended beneath the throne itself.

Of course, Angharad would believe it when she saw it. For Queen Olwen had never told her of such a tunnel. When the Druid, Ceindrech, had shown up at Prince Lludd's camp speaking of such a passageway Angharad had outright called her a liar—an act that had gotten the two women off on the wrong foot. But Angharad had been shocked. She still could not understand why Olwen had never spoken of it.

It was Rhiannon who had told Arthur and Arthur who had informed Ceindrech of the existence of this tunnel. For Rhiannon and Gwen had discovered the tunnel while escaping from Dinmael last year with Queen Elen's ring. It had been General Talorcan himself who had led them to it, saving their lives in the process. Talorcan locked both trap doors and he alone had the key.

Which was why Ceindrech was busy manipulating the lock with her druidic Shape-Moving abilities—for it was hidden from their sight on the inside of the impregnable trap door.

Prince Lludd stood stiffly, his jaw clenched. His brown eyes glittered with impatience but he did not speak.

Next to him stood his cousin, Prince Rhiwallon of Rheged, the younger brother of King Owein. The torchlight glittered on his reddish-gold hair as he fingered the sharp blade of a short sword, a martial light in his blue eyes and a half smile on his handsome face. A likely boy, Angharad thought indulgently, who had been schooled well as a warrior by his father, King Urien. Rhiwallon even had the dead king's bluff good nature and bull-like physique.

Emrys, her lieutenant, stood quietly, his dark eyes never leaving the trap door—unless it was to look at her. Angharad pretended not to notice how often he did so. But she knew full well that Emrys was in love with her. It was truly a shame that she did not return his regard, and never had. So she pretended not to know his feelings for her, treating him as a much-valued fellow warrior and nothing more.

Her heart ached, momentarily, for Amatheon, her dead lover. Sometimes she could be surprised, still, at how fiercely and unexpectedly grief could grip her heart. Resolutely, as she had a thousand times before, she forced her thoughts away from her memories of him.

Talhearn, Lludd's Bard, sat on a nearby log, his legs stretched out before him. He fingered the torque around his thin neck and the sapphire glittered beneath his long fingers. His gray hair shone silver under the starry light, for he sat away from the light of the torches. Behind the Bard stood several warriors, each holding the reins of a horse. Horses and warriors stood rock still, not making a sound.

An audible click got Angharad's attention and the Druid rose smoothly to her feet. She gestured and the trap door slowly rose, the hinges creaking. A dark hole gaped in the forest floor.

"It is done," Ceindrech said coolly, triumph in her dark eyes.

"And the lock at the other end?" Angharad asked.

"Will be much easier," Ceindrech said. "For I will be able to see it, not work blind as I had to with this one."

Angharad grinned. "Good work. I see Arthur sent the right Druid."

"In spite of the opinions of the Archdruid's heir," Ceindrech said with a touch of asperity.

"Aergol did not want you to come?"

"He can be overbearing at times."

"What was his objection?"

"That the mother of his son should not place herself in such danger," Ceindrech sniffed derisively.

Angharad's brow rose. "Indeed?"

"Men can be foolish," Ceindrech said with disdain.

"Foolish we can be," Prince Lludd broke in, "and we can be impatient, too. For I tell you, Druid, I have waited long enough to rescue my sister. I will wait no more."

"For the completion of such a task, I am also impatient," Ceindrech answered. "Come, then, Prince of Ederynion, let us rescue your queen."

Ceindrech went first, dropping lightly through the dark hole to the ground below. Angharad handed one of the torches down to her. Lludd went next, then Rhiwallon. Emrys stepped back to stand with the rest of the warriors. He looked at Angharad with his heart in his eyes, but he said nothing.

At the edge of the hole she turned back to look at Talhearn as she clutched the second torch. "If we are not back within two hours we aren't coming back," she said.

"I know," the Bard replied quietly.

"Tell Arthur to come for Elen himself if we cannot free her."

"I will."

Angharad hesitated for a moment, not certain what she wanted to say. But of course Talhearn said it for her. He always had.

"Go, then," Talhearn said gravely. "The warriors and I wait here for you. Go, brave heart, and free our Queen."

Elen stiffened as she heard the footsteps. She reached for Regan's hand and the Dewin rose from her chair. The two women stood side by side in the center of the room. On the wall behind them the white swan with outstretched wings on a field of sea green shivered, its eyes of pearl gleaming.

The door opened and Guthlac, the Master-wyrce-jaga of Ederynion, strode into the room. His black robe with its tabard of dark green was rucked up over his huge belly. There were food stains on the front of his robe. But at the smile on his fat face and the coldness of his blue eyes Elen's derisive comment died on her lips. For this was indeed a Master-wyrce-jaga in all his power. And the gods help them now.

Iago, her one-time Druid, entered behind Guthlac. His head was bowed so that he need not look her in the eyes. Iago rarely returned her gaze directly, though she knew he watched her all the time.

Behind them came two Coranian guards. The firelight played off their woven byrnies and their helmets shaped like boars' heads glittered in the light of the flames. With them were two wyrce-jagas, their hooded black robes covering them like shadows.

Guthlac clutched a piece of parchment in his greasy hands and did not even bother bowing. "Queen Elen," he began.

"And where is General Talorcan?" Elen interrupted.

This brought Guthlac up short. "General Talorcan?"

"Yes. Surely you remember him—blond hair, green eyes, commander of the Coranian army in Ederynion. That General Talorcan."

"His presence is not necessary," Guthlac said stiffly.

Elen threw back her head and screamed piercingly. Guthlac started and Iago's head came up, his dark eyes wide and shocked. Within moments she heard running footsteps and smiled as Talorcan burst into the room.

"What in the name of Lytir is going on here?" he cried, his sword in his hand.

"That is just what we are preparing to find out, General," Elen said crisply. "I thought you might like to know as well."

"Guthlac, Iago, what are you doing?" Talorcan asked. The fact that the general did not sheathe his sword was not lost on any of those present.

"We are doing our duty, General Talorcan," Guthlac said. "We are doing what you should have done long ago."

"And that is?" Talorcan asked.

"Taking the Dewin to Afalon."

"No, Guthlac, you are not," Talorcan said, his green eyes cold.

"Are you prepared, General, to ignore a direct order from your commander?"

"What order?" Talorcan asked with contempt. "You have no such order. I am in command here."

"That is as it may be—for now. And more is the pity. But I do have an order for Regan ur Corfil. The Dewin is to be collared immediately. She is to be taken from Dinmael tonight and sent to the isle of Afalon. There she is to await the death that all Y Dawnus suffer at the hands of the rightous."

"You lie," Talorcan whispered.

But Elen saw from his face that the General knew Guthlac wasn't lying.

Guthlac smiled and held out the parchment. "I have the order here."

"I will see that order, Master-wyrce-jaga. And may Lytir help you if it is false."

Guthlac handed the order to Talorcan with a flourish. "It is not false."

Everyone was silent as Talorcan read the order. Elen saw from the General's pale countenance that the order was genuine. But she had known that from the beginning. She gripped Regan's hand tightly. The Dewin's hands were cold, but they did not shake. And for that Elen felt dim pride in her friend.

At last Talorcan raised his head. He looked at Regan with love and hopelessness in his eyes. "The order is genuine," he rasped.

Regan moved forward to stand in front of Talorcan. She looked up at him with her heart in her eyes. "I know," she said softly. "And I also know this—that I would not trade the chance to have loved you for anything. I could never say that to you before. But I say it now, here in the shadow of death. I love you, Talorcan of Dere. I will carry you in my heart when I leave this place. When I close my eyes it will be your face I see. Yours will be the face I see in my mind's eye when I breathe my last."

"Regan," Talorcan whispered as he took her hands in his. "Regan, I cannot let you go."

"You must. You have no choice."

Elen felt the tears film her eyes. She was surprised by it, for she did not know when her hatred of Talorcan had fled. But fled it had, and her sorrow at the pain that Talorcan and Regan felt pierced her heart.

It was then that she heard a loud click, as though a key had turned in a lock. And in that moment she knew that what she had longed for had at last come to pass. She sprang past the startled guards and swiftly barred the door.

And just as swiftly the throne itself shot across the floor, sweeping the two wyrce-jagas off their feet and coming to rest with a crash against the opposite wall. Her brother sprang from the now-gaping hole in the floor, followed closely by a bear-like young man. Then came Angharad, followed by a woman dressed in a druidic robe of dark brown.

Before anyone could even speak, Lludd and the other young man rushed the two Coranians by the door and the guards went down in a welter of blood. Angharad leapt across the room and spitted Guthlac with a short spear. The red-haired woman smiled as she twisted the spear in the Master-wyrce-jaga's vitals. Guthlac choked and spat blood, all the while looking at Angharad with shocked eyes as he sank to the ground.

From across the room a heavy platter flew, cracking open the heads of the stunned wyrce-jagas as they struggled to rise. They fell back, dead, as the female Druid smiled in satisfaction.

The young man with the reddish-gold hair whirled around and caught Iago round the neck, whipping his dagger up to press the blade against the Druid's throat. And Angharad flew at Talorcan, her sword drawn.

"No!" Elen screamed as one with Regan. With an almost impossible midair twist Angharad sprang back from Talorcan and whirled to face Elen, her eyes shocked.

"What do you mean, no?" Angharad demanded. "He's a Coranian! More than that, he's the Coranian that killed your mother!"

"I know who he is," Elen cried. "And I don't need to explain myself to you."

"It's nice to see you, too, Elen," Angharad said, her lips twitching.

Before Elen could answer she found herself enveloped in a warm hug.

"Elen," her brother whispered as he held her close. "Elen."

"Lludd," she whispered back as tears streamed down her face. "I knew you'd come some day. I should have known you would be just in time."

Lludd lifted her tear-stained face and kissed her brow. "So you should have," he said with a grin.

"You've grown, little brother," she said with a grin of her own.

Ludd nodded to the female Druid. "This is Ceindrech ur Elwystl. She was sent here by High King Arthur to free you."

The Druid inclined her head to Elen, her eyes proud.

Lludd went on, gesturing to the young man who held a dagger to Iago's throat. "You remember Prince Rhiwallon of Rheged."

"Why, Rhiwallon," Elen exclaimed. "I didn't recognize you, it's been so long."

Rhiwallon grinned and sketched a salute, all the while holding Iago by the throat. His blue eyes lit as he looked at her. "Well met, cousin," he said cheerfully.

Something about Rhiwallon's smile fascinated Elen, making her heart beat faster. She opened her mouth to reply, but Angharad forestalled her.

"And why, my Queen," her captain asked with a gesture of her dagger at Talorcan, "are we not allowed to kill this one?"

"Because he is an honorable man," Elen said. "He is a good man, and does not deserve to die at our hands."

"Then at whose?" Angharad retorted.

Regan took one of Talorcan's hands in hers and faced the others. "This is the man I love," the Dewin said, her voice proud and strong. "I will have him and no other."

Lludd came to stand in front of the General, his hand resting on the pommel of his sheathed dagger. Lludd's brown eyes were calm as he spoke. "General Talorcan, you killed my mother in front of the walls of Dinmael."

Talorcan nodded. "I did. For that was my duty."

"And your duty now?"

Talorcan bowed his head. "My duty is to call for my men. But I cannot."

"No, I did not think you could. For we know of you, General Talorcan. The Kymri know that but for you my sister would perhaps have already been dead. We know that her Dewin certainly would be. We know that many of the people of Dinmael would have met their deaths by now. If not for you."

Talorcan dropped his eyes.

"Are you ashamed?" Lludd asked sternly. "Are you sorry?"

Talorcan raised his tormented face to the Prince, but answered firmly, his green eyes unwavering. "No, I am not sorry. I did what I did out of love of my own country."

"Love for Dere, the country that the Coranians took for their own many, many years ago."

"'Oh, Elmete,'" Talorcan murmured. "'We remember you.'"

"Yes, 'The Lament for Elmete,'" Lludd said. "A sad song you could not bear to have us sing about Kymru."

"Yes," Talorcan whispered. "It was heartbreak enough to hear it sung of my own country."

"We Kymri know you very well, General," Lludd went on. "Better, I think, than you know yourself."

"What do you mean?" Talorcan asked. But something in his green eyes told Elen that he knew perfectly well.

"You are what we call Dewin, what you would call a Walker. And what your people would call Wiccan."

Talorcan stood stock-still, not even bothering to deny it. Elen had thought he would, but she had underestimated him.

"Yes," Talorcan said. "Somehow, I am."

"We know how. Through your mother you are the great-grandson of the last king of Dere. And the royal family of Dere has always been blessed with the gifts. Veleda, the last High Priestess of Corania, was of that line."

"How did you know this?" Talorcan whispered.

"I did not know this," Lludd said quietly. "But High King Arthur did. He charged Ceindrech to tell me this. So that I may convey to you his offer."

"Which is?"

"Which is to come home to your true people. Which is to

proudly be Dewin, and embrace your gifts."

"To forsake my country—"

"For another which welcomes you. And values who and what you are."

The room was silent as Talorcan closed his eyes and bowed his head.

"The blood of Veleda calls to you," Ceindrech said softly. "It calls to you to be what you truly are, to forsake the false chains that were set around you. It calls to you to be free, to be what you were born to be."

"And my family?" Talorcan asked. "What of them?"

"Your younger brother, Torhtmund, can be Eorl of Bernice in your stead," Lludd said. "And Arthur says—"

"Arthur says what?" Talorcan cut in sharply, his green eyes burning.

"Arthur says that you will see your family again. And that he waits for you in Cadair Idris, for he is always grateful to have another Dewin by his side."

"*Cariad*," Regan said softly. "Oh, beloved, say yes."

"And my honor?" Talorcan asked.

It was Elen who answered him, for she knew him well. And she knew the truth of it. "Has been smirched by Havgan himself, and no other. Smirched by the things you have done because of the blood oath. But restored to you, should you renounce the evil that the Golden Man has done and is doing."

"Then you forgive me, Queen of Ederynion?" Talorcan asked. "For the death of your mother?"

"A fair death in battle," Elen said. "There is no shame in it."

"Then High King Arthur has won himself another man to serve him. I will do so with all my heart, with all that I truly am, now that I have the freedom to be what I was born to be." Talorcan turned to Regan. "And you, Regan ur Corfil, I will be your husband if it is your will. And you can teach me the ways of the Dewin."

Regan smiled and her smile was dazzling. "With all my heart, *cariad*."

"And Iago?" Rhiwallon asked, as he still held the Druid. "What of him?"

"Iago," Elen said softly. "What is your will?"

Outside the door they heard shouts and the sound of footsteps coming to the door.

"They were waiting for Guthlac to bring you," Iago said to Regan. "And they have decided that they have been waiting too long."

"How many?" Lludd asked.

"Twenty. But they will alert all the others. You must go. Now."

"And you?"

"I will stay," Iago said, his dark eyes sad. "And hold them off."

"Do you expect us to believe that?" Angharad asked sharply.

"I swear by the love I hold Queen Elen, that I am telling the truth. Go, I tell you. Only a Druid could hold them back long enough for you to get away. The entire army in Dinmael is waiting to smash down that door."

"He is right," Ceindrech said crisply. "Only a Druid could do that. But where one is good, two are better. I, too, will stay to hold them off."

"Ceindrech, no!" Angharad cried. "You will never get away from here alive."

"Yes, I know," Ceindrech said calmly. "But unless I stay behind neither will any of you. Let Iago go, Prince Rhiwallon. He and I will see to it that you all escape."

Rhiwallon looked to Elen for his answer and she nodded. The Prince released Iago and stepped back warily. But Iago merely turned to face the door. He closed his eyes and from outside came a scream. A fiery glow came from beneath the door.

"Good," Ceindrech said. "Hold them back with Druid's Fire. I will find a few objects outside that will make them uncomfortable."

"Ceindrech," Angharad began.

"Go now, all of you," Ceindrech said. "Do not let Iago and me die in vain. Tell Aergol—" Ceindrech hesitated for a moment as the name of her longtime lover left her lips. "Tell him to take care of our son," she went on. "And tell him—tell him that I love him. Tell him that I will wait for him in the Land of Summer."

"I'll tell him," Regan said as she took Talorcan's hand. "I will be sure of it."

"Then go," Ceindrech said. "Go quickly. Queen Elen, we will give our lives to save you. Do not make a mockery of it."

"Regan," Elen said, suddenly. We must take—"

"I know," Regan replied, rushing to the stairs. "I'll get it."

While Regan took the stairs two at a time, Lludd turned to Elen. "What is she getting?"

"Mam's helmet."

"Ah, of course. We couldn't leave without that, could we?"

"Never," Elen answered. Regan rushed down the stairs, a leather bag slung over her shoulder. She patted the bag. "Got it."

"Then go," Ceindrech said again. "Go."

Elen turned to leave, the tears almost blinding her. From far, far away she thought she heard the faintest sound of a hunting horn—of the horns blown by the Wild Hunt when they rode the sky. Prince Rhiwallon offered her his hand to help her and she took it. It was large and strong and warm, and she looked up at him and saw him looking down at her. Lludd waited to follow her and she turned around one last time before descending.

Ceindrech and Iago stood hand in hand, shoulder to shoulder, their eyes closed. From outside the door came screams and curses. Then Iago opened his eyes and looked at her. In his dark eyes, where she had often seen madness, she now saw peace.

"Go, Elen," Iago said. "And know that I was a Queen's man and a Kymri, at the last."

"Yes," Elen whispered. "You are all that. At the last."

And then she was free.

Chapter Eight

Arberth
Kingdom of Prydyn, Kymru
Bedwen Mis, 500

Gwaithdydd, Tywyllu Wythnos—evening

Penda, General of the Coranian forces in Prydyn, sighed inwardly as he mounted the dais and took his seat at the high table in the Great Hall of Caer Tir.

Another meal in the company of those he despised—just another day in Kymru.

If only he was home! Home at the foot of Mount Badon in Mierce. Home, in Lindisfarne with his father and son. Home with his people, the brave and generous folk of Mierce who were themselves crushed beneath the heels of Coranian invaders six generations ago.

Home. Oh, he did miss it so.

Throughout the fire-lit hall his warriors stood at attention, waiting for him to sit before they took their places at the long tables. The Coranian banner shimmered red and gold in the smoky light; the ruby eyes of the boar seemed to gleam maliciously as Penda glanced up at it.

He took his place on the king's left, signaling his warriors to sit and begin their meal. He contented himself with a mere nod at King Erfin.

King Erfin returned Penda's nod calmly but his beady brown eyes were angry. The torchlight glittered off his unruly red hair and the golden circlet that rested on his head. It flickered over the long, jagged scar across his right cheek, a scar put there by King

Rhoram almost three years ago. Erfin tore into his meal with his usual lack of grace and, mercifully, did not even try to converse with Penda.

Efa, Erfin's sister, sitting to her brother's right, leaned forward slightly to catch Penda's eye. She smiled brilliantly at him as the firelight shimmered off her smooth, pale skin. Her large and beautiful brown eyes spoke of seduction but Penda was not interested. He knew that wouldn't matter too much, for Efa had been busy since she came to Arberth sampling what the Coranian warriors had to offer. In fact she had already gone through the garrison like a scythe through wheat. It seemed as though she was ready to begin at the top again.

For he had, of course, taken the lady up on her offer the first time out of sheer curiosity. The few times after that had been the result of pure boredom. After the last time he had sworn to himself that he would never allow himself to sink that low ever again. It was hard to explain just what there was about Efa that was so repellent. She was beautiful, sensual, and good in bed. But there was something about her that made his skin crawl. Perhaps it had to do with the fact that Efa, the one-time Queen of Prydyn, had betrayed her husband and her people, deserting Rhoram and returning to Arberth to share power with her brother, the false King of Prydyn.

For, no matter how much he said otherwise, Penda was fully aware that Erfin was not the true King of Prydyn, and never would be. The true king, Rhoram ap Rhydderch, was still alive, still leading his Kymric warriors in lightning raids against the enemy, still waiting for his chance to take back his throne.

Penda would not admit to anyone how glad he would be to see it happen.

For the thousandth—no, for the millionth—time he cursed the day he had pledged himself to Havgan in the Coranian Brotherhood Ritual. If he had not done that he might, even now, be a happy man. He would surely not be here in this defeated country knowing he himself had a hand in their defeat. He wondered how his friend Talorcan was faring over in Ederynion. He was another one of their band who also regretted this tie to Havgan. Silently

Penda prayed to Lytir that Talorcan was not suffering unbearably. And he spared a thought for another member of the band who he knew was suffering—Sigerric, the man who had once been Havgan's closest friend.

How was it that the three of them had not seen all those years ago who and what Havgan really was? Oh, but they had been young and foolish and dazzled by the powerful personality of the Golden Man. He shook his head, for no amount of regret could change the past. And it was far too late to turn back now.

He passed platters and took food without even knowing what he was eating. He chewed mechanically, and drank a great deal. His eyes skimmed over the others at the table. Whitred of Sceaping, the Byshop of Prydyn in a robe of green and Eamer of Geddingas, Master-wyrce-jaga in his robe of black with a green tabard ate greedily.

His eye came to rest on the figure of Ellywen. She wore her Druid's robe of brown with green trim and sipped daintily and sparingly from a golden goblet chased with emeralds. At the sight of her he became very thoughtful indeed. For Ellywen was not who she had once been. She had changed in the past eight months and Penda was now sure why.

She sat now, done with her meal, calm and self-contained, as always. Her glances to her fellows were cold and contemptuous, also as always. But she no longer wore her brown hair closely braided and pulled tightly back. She wore it loose, held back from her flawless face by a green ribbon. Her gray eyes no longer reminded him of treacherous ice but rather of a misty sky on a spring morning. And, if anyone happened to mention Modron the Mother, the Kymric goddess revered by the Druids, she no longer flinched.

And that told him everything.

Having her followed, as he had for the last month, was almost a mere formality.

Two or three times a week she would go to the marketplace. But she rarely bought anything. She would visit a few stalls and exchange a few words. She usually ended up at the smithy and said a few words to the smith there. She occasionally brought her horse to the smith, who would solemnly examine the horse's hooves. Surely, Penda thought sourly, Ellywen had the best-shod horse in Prydyn.

Thinking of the smith reminded Penda of the news he had heard yesterday. The Master Smiths of Kymru and their families had been rescued. A guard from Caer Siddi had brought the news to Havgan. And the rescuer had been none other than High King Arthur himself. Aided by a number of renegade Druids, as well as by Gwydion, Rhiannon, and King Rhoram's warriors, Arthur had neatly defeated the Coranian garrison.

Penda had also learned that Gwydion had been captured by Arianrod, Havgan's Kymric mistress. Gwydion's current whereabouts were a carefully kept secret. When Penda had heard the news of Gwydion's capture he had felt a sharp stab of grief for the Dreamer and for the woman who loved him. In Corania, when he had first met Gwydion and Rhiannon, Penda had liked them both. He had known them as Guido and Rhea then, and he had counted the two as his friends. Until, of course, he had learned who they really were. Still, he was grieved for them, for they had done what they had done in order to save their people. And that was something Penda understood very well.

A warrior approached the high table and bowed to Penda. "My Lord, the prisoners are here."

"What prisoners?" Erfin demanded. "And why was I not informed?"

"You were not informed because it was not necessary," Penda said absently. "Bring the prisoners to me."

"What prisoners?" Efa asked repeating her brother's question.

"They are a few Kymri from town that I believe to be feeding information to the Cerddorian," Penda answered. "Along with their families."

"Their families?" Ellywen repeated calmly. But her hand tightened on her goblet as she spoke. "What use for that?"

"Such a question," Efa said with contempt. "To get them to talk, of course."

"Of course," Ellywen said softly.

And though Ellywen did not gasp, did not cry out, did not

even move when she saw the prisoners, Penda knew that he had the right people. For Ellywen's face tightened and for a brief moment he saw the truth in her fine, gray eyes.

For the prisoners were none other than the smith himself and the proprietors of the two stalls Ellywen visited most. The three Kymric men held their heads high as they were brought through the hall and up to the dais. Behind them their wives and children followed silently, their faces solemn and still. One of the women carried a small baby in her arms. Another of them held the hands of two little boys. The third, the wife of the smith, led three young girls and two young men, all with their heads held high, pride in their Kymric faces.

For a moment Penda wished he could be anywhere but here as he studied the three families. Then he mentally shook himself. He had a job to do, and he would do it.

"You are accused of being spies for the Cerddorian of Prydyn," Penda began.

"I would be proud to be, were it the truth," the smith interrupted.

"It is the truth," Penda said. "And one that I will not argue with you. Not here. You will all be taken to the cells and held there until you tell me the details that I wish to know. And be advised that we will do whatever we must to learn what we want to know."

The three families merely looked at Penda with contempt in their eyes. But they paled nonetheless. Penda hoped that he would not have to actually hurt these folk for he had not had them brought here in order to hear anything from them. They would tell him nothing and he knew it. No, he had them brought here for a different reason—to trap Ellywen ur Saidi. That was another thing he did not wish to do. But his life was not his own; it had not been his own for many years. His life belonged to the Golden Man and Penda would do what he must do to serve him.

"How dare you take these people prisoner without consulting me!" Erfin began.

But Efa knew better than to let Erfin go on. She laid a hand on her brother's arm and put her finger to her lips. Erfin subsided with a frown, but he subsided nonetheless.

Penda, who had not even glanced over at Erfin, sat quietly. It was harder for him to do this than he had thought. He was not quite sure why—he should be used to doing these kinds of things by now. He looked over at Ellywen. Ellywen was looking back at him with something almost like pity in her eyes. "Take them away," Penda said after a moment.

Guards led the families from the hall as Ellywen gestured for the Coranian minstrel. The minstrel bowed as he reached the high table.

"What is your wish?" the minstrel asked.

"It is my wish that you should play a tune for General Penda," Ellywen said.

The minstrel bowed again. "Anything for my lord."

"Play the 'Lament to Mierce.'"

The minstrel froze, looking at Ellywen with shocked eyes. "I—"

"Do you not wish to have it played, General?" Ellywen asked innocently, turning to Penda. "Do you not wish to hear a song from your homeland?"

Penda gripped the armrests of his chair. He would not let Ellywen know how close to the mark she had come. "If you wish to hear it played it is nothing to me."

"Indeed?" Ellywen said with raised brows. She turned to the minstrel who stood trembling, his face pale. "Then, minstrel, play the song for me."

The minstrel hesitated a moment, then brought the lute up to playing position. He strummed the opening chords of the song that was written hundreds of years ago when the Coranian king, Sigger, killed the King of Mierce, captured and raped the Queen, spitted the baby prince on his deadly spear, and ground all of Mierce beneath his merciless heel.

"The forms of our kinsmen take shape in the silence
In rapture we greet them; in gladness we scan
Old comrades remembered. But they melt into air
With no word of greeting to gladden our hearts.

Then again surges our sorrow upon us;
And grimly we spur our weary souls
Once more to toil under our yoke.

Alas for Mierce, you are no longer.

One by one, proud warriors died
The battlements crumbled, the wine halls burned;
Now joyless and silent the heroes are sleeping
Where the proud host fell by the walls they defended.

Alas for Mierce, you are no longer.

We brood on old legends of battle and bloodshed,
And heavy the mood that troubles our hearts:
Where now is the warrior? Where is the warhorse?
Come to defend us from this heavy yoke.

You are caught forever in the grave's embrace.
Alas for Mierce, you are no longer."

That night, Penda dreamed. And wept as he did so.

His spirit flew high in the darkening sky. Purple clouds, swollen with the brewing storm massed above him. Beneath him he recognized Beranburg, nestled at the foot of Mount Badon and tears came to his eyes. Home. He was home.

Mount Badon rose from the silent earth to pierce the brooding sky. Studded with tall pine from its base to near the top of its jagged peak, the mountain itself seemed to glow and pulse with power in the dim, uncertain light.

He saw orange flames dotting an area on the side of the mountain and flew closer, for his knew that it was the Heiden, the Old Believers, come to the mountain to worship the Old Ones on Galdra Necht, the Night of Magic. This was the time when the Heiden would honor Wuotan One-Eye, the God of Magic.

Wuotan had hung on Irminsul, the World Tree, for nine days. The son of Death and War, he had torn out his own eye to obtain knowledge of the runes.

And on Galdra Necht the Wild Hunt, led by Wuotan and by Holda of the Waters, would ride on the wings of the storm over Mount Badon, and may the gods help those mortals that they found in their path.

His spirit spiraled down and he saw that the Heiden had gathered in a clearing surrounded by tall, heady pines draped in long ribbons of gray and lavender. Torches glittered around the clearing, held by the steady hands of the warriors of the Eorl of Lindisfarne. A rough-hewn altar of stone sat in the middle of the clearing. A drinking horn of silver was set in a polished holder of bone on the left side of the altar while a bowl fashioned from glittering gold sat on the right. At the front of the altar the blade of a long knife glinted in the firelight. Laid across the back was a piece of leather strung with tiny bells. Candles of purple and gray sat at each corner. A banner of gray, worked with the purple rune of Wuotan was draped over the front of the altar. The rune, a circle divided into four quarters, shimmered briefly.

The clearing was filled with those Penda knew from the town of Beranburg, over one hundred folk. His heart ached as his eyes went directly to his young son. Readwyth was ten years old now. The boy's dark blond hair, so like Penda's, glistened in the torchlight. His blue eyes—so like Penda's dead wife's—were shining as he looked up at his grandfather.

Eorl Peada stood quietly, his gray hair braided in hundreds of tiny braids, each braid tied off with a ring of bronze. Peada's dark eyes glittered in the torchlight as the Godia, the Priestess, dressed in a robe of pure white, took her place behind the altar. Next to her stood the Hod, the Sacrificer, in a robe of black, his black hood secured over his face. On his arm he held an eagle, the bird of Wuotan. The bird strained against its bonds but could not break free. The Priestess picked up the string of bells and shook it. The delicate sound floated over the clearing and the crowd fell silent.

"The Dis are with us, the gods have come," the Godia called.

"Wuotan and Donor, Fal and Fro and Logi, Dag and Mani, Saxnot and Tiw."

"Hail to the Dis," the Heiden responded.

"The Disir are with us, the goddesses have come. Nerthus and Freya, Holda and Nehalennia, Sunna and Sif, Natt and the Wyrd."

"Hail to the Disir."

"The Afliae are with us, the powerful ones have come. Hail to Narve, the One that Binds. Hail to Ostara, the Warrior Goddess. Hail to Erce, Gentle Mother. Hail to these, the Afliae."

"Hail to the Afliae."

"This is the night of Wuotan," the Priestess continued. Her blond hair shimmered and her beautiful voice soothed as she effortlessly captured the magic and mystery of the night. "This is the night of Wuotan. Wielder of magic, Wearer of Masks, the Hanged Man."

"Blessed be the Leader of the Hunt," the Heiden called out. As they did so lightning flashed above them. A clap of thunder so huge that some of the people covered their ears boomed across the sky.

The Godia smiled and lifted the drinking horn. "Drink now, ye followers of the old ways. Drink now, ye hidden, ye faithful ones," she called. She took a sip from the massive horn and then passed it around the clearing. When all had sipped and the horn was returned to the altar, she nodded to the black cloaked Sacrificer.

"All hail to Wuotan," the Hod called out. "Lord of Magic, One-Eye, who hung nine days on Irminsul and gained wisdom. Accept our sacrifice." He lifted the eagle high over his head then swiftly broke its neck. He then slit its throat with the ritual knife, catching the blood in the golden bowl and draining it from the still-warm body.

Carefully, reverently, he set the dead eagle down on the altar, then picked up the bowl of blood. He dipped a bundle of oak leaves into the bowl and, walking slowly around the clearing, he sprinkled the blood on the bowed heads of each of the Heiden. At last he returned to the altar and sprinkled blood on the long, silky hair of the priestess. He lifted the bowl and drank the remaining blood then set the bowl back on the altar.

The Priestess lifted her slim hands and called, "Lord of Magic, hear our plea. Give us a message, speak to us with magic." From the cord around her waist she unhooked a white bag made of swan's skin.

For some reason Penda began to feel cold and afraid. He knew this was a dream—how could it not be? And if only a dream, what harm could come to him? So why be afraid? But he was.

At the Priestess' gesture the black-clad Hod reached into the bag and pulled out a rune made of gold. He held the rune high, then laid it on the altar. "He has chosen *Ansuz*," the Godia called. "Choose another."

Again the black figure reached into the bag and pulled out a rune. The Priestess named it. "He has chosen *Chalk*. Choose another."

Something in the man's movements, some dimly recognized pattern made Penda's blood run cold. He did not fully understand why but it was enough to make it difficult to take a breath, enough to bathe him in the sheen of terror.

The shadowy figure chose another rune, which the Priestess then set on the altar. "He has chosen *Beorc*."

The Priestess studied the runes then lifted her head to the Heiden. "The message that the Sacrificer has chosen is not complete. See here. He has chosen *Ansuz*. A good rune, for it means a message from the gods. He has chosen *Chalk*. A difficult rune, for it means barrenness, poison. It is the dead man's rune. The third is *Beorc*, the rune for growth, rebirth, and new life. What has been chosen tonight is a message from the gods. It speaks of a life of sorrow, a living death. Then, finally, of a new life. But how is the new life obtained? That is what is not clear. To determine this, he must chose another."

Once again, the Sacrificer reached into the bag and pulled out a golden rune. As it glittered above his cowled head, the Priestess cried, "It is *Seid*. The rune for the magician, the sorceress. It is only through the witches that a new life will be given to the one who suffers. Through this alone!"

A cold, fierce wind whipped through the pines, moaning and crying. The torches guttered fitfully, bent by the wind. Overhead another flash of white lightening almost blinded the Heiden. They raised their hands over their faces and bowed their heads to the storm—all but Penda, the Godia, and the Hod. These three lifted their faces to the night sky and watched as the storm clouds rushed in over the mountain.

A figure rode across the sky—a dark, hooded shape on a horse as pale as bone. The figure held a spear in its hand and as it raised the spear another flash of lightning tore the night. Following the figure was a woman on a gray horse, dressed in a gown of sea green. Her eyes flashed and changed to the gray of an angry sea. She raised a horn of mother of pearl to her lips and as she blew thunder boomed and rumbled.

Behind these two came a pack of slavering white dogs with eyes of blood red. They rode the sky on the wings of the lightening, baying hungrily. Behind them came skeletal figures, their bony hands gripping the reins as they rode pale horses, and they screamed of despair and madness.

The Wild Hunt has come to Mount Badon on Galdra Necht, Penda thought. And may the gods have mercy on us now. But he was not sure there would be any mercy. At least, not for him. For he knew now, he felt the horror of what he had done.

He had supported the Coranians, those who held his country in bondage. He had not tried to stop the hunting of the Heiden, the believers in the Old Gods, or of the Wiccan, those with psychic gifts akin to the Y Dawnus. Worse yet, he had journeyed to Kymru to crush that land as his own had been crushed, to crush the people, as his own had been, to crush their witches, as the Wiccan were.

The Heiden cried out as the Hunt circled the sky, coming ever closer to the clearing on the mountain. The figure with the spear raised it again and the lightning almost blinded Penda. The figure swooped over the clearing and slowed his horse, coming to rest before the altar. It threw back its hood. His hair and beard were long and gray. A scar twisted up one cheek to disappear into an empty eye socket. In that empty socket lightning brimmed.

The Priestess fell to her knees, her hands raised as she cried, "Wuotan has come, ye Heiden! He has come!"

The Sacrificer stood as though frozen before the one-eyed god. From the sky above the clearing the woman guided her horse to rest next to Wuotan's. Her stormy eyes flashed as the Priestess cried out, "It is Holda, Goddess of the Waters, daughter of Fro and Freya. Ye Heiden, the Wild Hunt has come!"

Still the hooded Sacrificer did not move, standing before Wuotan and Holda as though transfixed. Penda took a step forward to stand next to the Priestess, but no one looked at him. Then Wuotan One-Eye took a step forward and yanked off the Sacrificer's black hood.

And to Penda's horror his own face was revealed. The people in the clearing melted away. The Priestess, the altar, Penda's father and son, they were all gone. He stood alone in a clearing in a forest he did not recognize. He looked down and he was clothed in a black robe.

But Wuotan One-Eye had not disappeared. The God of Magic still sat his bone-white horse and held a black hood in his scarred hands. And Holda, too, had not gone, but sat her gray horse calmly, looking down at Penda.

"Wuotan, I—"

"You betrayed me," the god said. "You betrayed them all." Lightning flashed from Wuotan's empty eye socket and burned the ground at Penda's feet.

"Yes," Penda whispered and bowed his head. "I did. You are right to have your dogs tear me limb from limb, to have your Hunt kill me. I ask only that you do not punish my father, my son, or my people for what I have done. Punish me alone, for I deserve it."

"You knew what you were doing," Holda accused as thunder pealed.

"I did," Penda said.

"And did not stop it."

"No. I did not. My oath—"

"Was no more binding for you than for Gwydion ap Awst."

Penda's head came up. "Gwydion took the Brotherhood Oath with Havgan. And he—"

"Broke it," Wuotan said as lightening flashed. "Think you this was wrong?"

"He gave his word—"

"And you think it is more important to keep your word to a madman than to do what you know to be right?" Wuotan asked.

"I was wrong," Penda whispered. "Wrong. And it is too late to mend it."

"It is not too late," Wuotan said. "Lift your head, Penda of Lindisfarne."

Penda lifted his head and stared at Wuotan and Holda. The figures changed, melted into different figures, figures Penda recognized from the Kymric stories he had heard.

Wuotan's face elongated and darkened. Antlers sprang from his forehead and his eye sockets filled with the gleam of topaz as both eyes changed into the eyes of an owl. The spear in his hand changed to a hunting horn and his muscular, bare chest gleamed in the now-still night as calm starlight bathed the clearing.

Holda's outlines changed and flowed into the figure of a woman with amethyst eyes. Her dark, silky hair hung down to her waist. Her white, knee-length tunic glowed as her horse's hide darkened to black. At her feet white dogs with blood-red eyes gamboled and panted, sniffing at Penda and at the leaves on the forest floor.

"You know what *Seid* means," the woman said, her purple gaze glittering. "You know the way to a new life."

"You know how to find that life," the man said, his topaz eyes flashing. "You know what you must do. Do it, and the new life you were promised becomes true."

"But Wuotan, Holda, where did they—"

"It is all one," said the goddess Cerridwen, Queen of the Wood.

"We are all one," said the god Cerrunnos, Master of the Wild Hunt. "Did you not know?"

"I—" Penda began. But he did not finish. For perhaps he had known. Perhaps he had always known. In any case, he now understood what he must do. He had not known the true meaning of honor. He had not known that it did not always mean keeping one's word. Yes, now he knew the truth.

And the truth set him free.

He woke with a start to pounding on his door. "Stop that noise," he shouted as he sprang from his bed. He knew what he would see when he opened the door. Nor was he wrong.

"You were right, lord," the captain of his guard said, grinning. "The witch tried to rescue the captives. And she had another witch with her. We have captured them both."

"Then," Penda said as he shrugged into a fur-lined cloak and pulled on his boots, "take me to them."

And as he walked down the hallways of Caer Tir he walked confidently and proudly. For the time for indecision had passed. Now he knew what he must do.

For he was free, indeed.

The cell where the prisoners were being held was on the first floor of the northwest watchtower. This tower was on the side of Caer Tir directly over the cliffs leading to the sea. When he had first determined to put the prisoners there his captain had protested, saying that there was surely a passageway from the cells leading to the cliffs. And Penda had agreed that was no doubt true, and his steely gaze had dared his captain to reply. But his captain had known better and had done as he was told.

He entered the tower and turned to face the cells, where the three families that he had detained stood against the bars. The chamber was cold and clammy, the only light coming from a brazier set in the middle of the room, well away from the cells themselves.

In front of the cells Ellywen stood with her hands tied behind her back and two guards on either side of her, her manner icy and calm, but a telltale pulse beat wildly at her slim throat.

A stranger stood next to her, his hands also bound behind him. The man had sandy brown hair and his brown eyes were wide with fear. Penda thought he might know who the man was and, when King Erfin came stumbling in, followed by Efa, he was proved right.

"Cadell!" Erfin cried. "General Penda, it's Cadell, Rhoram's Dewin! How did he come to be here?"

"No doubt, Erfin," Penda said in bored tones, "he came here through one of the secret passages that run through the cliffs." Penda nodded to a gaping hole in the wall. "They meant to rescue the prisoners and take them out through here."

"You knew that this would happen?" Erfin asked, bewildered.

Penda sighed. Erfin had always been immensely stupid. "Of course."

"So, Ellywen," Efa said gleefully as she came to stand before the bound Druid, "I see you must have had a change of heart. And how did my husband persuade you to join him?"

"He didn't, Efa," Ellywen said with contempt. "He didn't even have to try. I simply realized what I was doing was wrong."

"Ha! Wrong!" Efa sneered.

"Yes, wrong. I knew it when I helped to capture Rhoram's Bard. Cian and I had known each other a long time, yet I delivered him into the hands of the Golden Man just the same. The night I heard the death song of the Master Bard was when I knew I could not go on as I had been. That was when I was sickened by my own behavior. That was when I knew that the teachings of the Archdruid were false—false to Kymru, and false to the Mother herself. False to anyone who had the wit to see it. Which I finally did."

"And so you began to help the Cerddorian," Penda said.

Ellywen nodded, for she knew it would be useless to deny it. "I helped Aidan, Rhoram's lieutenant, and Cadell escape from Arberth some months ago and it was then that I truly began to help the Cerddorian. Though I must admit," she went on with a wry look at Cadell, "it took them a while to trust me."

"But they did trust you, eventually," Penda said softly. "And you began to help them in earnest. By passing messages through the likes of these folk." He gestured to the Kymri in the cells.

"No," Ellywen said calmly. "You are wrong about these people. They were merely cover for the real people I was passing messages through."

At that Erfin and Efa began to squabble with Ellywen, for neither the king nor his sister believed the Druid. And that was just what Penda wanted. For he did not believe Ellywen either, and he knew she would lie on that point. And he knew, too, that the ensuing argument would give him the chance he needed, the chance he now knew he had to take to begin the new life the gods had promised him.

Unnoticed by any he leaned forward slightly and murmured in Cadell's ear. "Be ready."

Cadell started, and looked swiftly up at Penda with a mixture of fear, mistrust, and dawning understanding. But the Dewin knew better than to ask questions, and bowed his head quickly, fixing his eyes on the floor.

"Enough!" Penda roared, when the argument had reached a fever pitch. Ellywen, Efa, and Erfin stopped immediately and turned to face him. Penda gestured for the guards to open the cells. "Release the prisoners."

"General!" Erfin cried. "How can you even think such a thing? They are traitors to me!"

"They are not," Penda said calmly as the guards did as he bid. "They are bait. As the quarry has been captured they are useless to me."

"How can you say such a thing?" Efa sputtered as she came to stand before him. "Any half-wit—"

"Lady, you will hold your tongue," Penda interrupted, his eyes glinting dangerously.

Efa's indignation was replaced by fear as she slowly backed away a few steps. Erfin came to her and put his arm around her shoulders. Her beautiful eyes were wide and shocked, for she had never yet experienced Penda at the edge of rage.

Penda turned to look at the released prisoners, and as he turned he caught Cadell's eye. He gave an almost imperceptible nod then stepped forward. But as he stepped forward Cadell cried out and lashed out with his foot, tipping over the brazier. The glowing coals scattered across the floor and Efa shrieked, trying to get out of the way. As she jumped back she fell heavily against Erfin. Erfin and Efa went down, Efa screaming as she landed.

Penda, meanwhile, had already whipped out his dagger and, with one swift, unseen movement in the now almost-dark chamber, cut Cadell's bonds. With a mighty shove he propelled Cadell through the dark opening in the wall and hoped that he had not pushed the Dewin too hard. Before anyone could properly see what he had done he fell back against the group of prisoners and they all went down in a welter of cries and tangled limbs.

It took just a few moments for additional guards to rush in and try to sort them all out. Penda was pulled to his feet, panting, hoping he hadn't overdone his fit of clumsiness. Apparently he hadn't, for even Efa, suspicious as she was, did not accuse him of helping Cadell to escape. In fact, the only person in the room who seemed to suspect what had truly happened was Ellywen herself. And she, of course, did not say a word. She merely looked at him with her fine, gray eyes and without a hint of expression on her beautiful face. But for a moment her mouth had twitched when Penda recovered his balance and brushed at his now-dirty cloak.

"The Dewin has escaped, my lord," his captain said as the man emerged from the tunnel. "It's a regular warren down there with no means to determine which way he went."

"A shame," Ellywen said softly.

"Collar her," Penda said briefly as he gestured for his guards to take the Kymric families to the gate and return them to their homes.

"Yes," Efa said with a smile as Ellywen's face froze and fear and panic shone in her gray eyes. "Collar her."

"Go to bed, Efa," Penda said shortly. "You, too, Erfin. Now."

They left without argument as an enaid-dal was snapped around Ellywen's neck. The Druid paled and tears spilled from her eyes. The guards pushed her into a cell and locked the door. Ellywen sank to the cold, stone floor and bowed her head, her hands still tied behind her back. She moaned softly in horror and despair at what the soul-catcher had done to her. At Penda's sharp gesture the guards stepped away from the cell and back out to the outer door. Penda walked to the cell and wrapped his hands around the bars. He let Ellywen weep for a moment, knowing that she needed to.

"Tomorrow I will have you put on a horse and taken to Afalon," Penda said quietly. "A place, I feel sure, you will never reach."

Ellywen's head came up and she lifted her tear-streaked face in dawning hope.

"I did not let Cadell go for nothing," he said.

Meirigdydd, Tywyllu Wythnos—morning

THE MORNING WAS crisp and cool as Penda emerged from his quarters in Caer Tir. In the courtyard Ellywen sat on a horse, her hands bound to the pommel of the saddle, her face still. For a wonder King Erfin was up early and emerged from the ystafell with a cold smile on his scarred face.

"You are up early, slug," Ellywen said coldly.

"I wouldn't miss your leave-taking for the world," Erfin sneered.

Ellywen leaned down slightly and smiled. "When next I see you Rhoram's sword will do more damage than last time. His sword will be sticking out of your useless guts."

Erfin lifted his hand to strike her, but Penda grabbed it in a vise-like grip. "Leave her be, Erfin," he said sharply.

Ellywen settled back into the saddle, without looking at Penda.

"General," Erfin began, "I am told you are sending only two guards to escort her to Afalon."

"That is correct," Penda said. The fact that the two guards were men that Penda thoroughly disliked was his own business. Ellywen's lids flickered over her sharp, gray eyes when she heard this but she did not speak.

"Then you are a fool," Erfin went on. "You know that Cadell has escaped and has no doubt alerted the Cerddorian. They will try to rescue the Druid."

"I think not," Penda said his tone bored. "She has betrayed them in the past. Surely King Rhoram would never forgive that."

"General, my brother-in-law is all kinds of a fool. He has no doubt already forgiven Ellywen. I tell you, he will rescue her."

He had better, Penda thought.

He was counting on it.

Ellywen kept her eyes closed against the blinding light of the sun. Her head throbbed as the poisonous enaid-dal worked its way through her brain, shutting off the pathways to her gift, slowly poisoning her body. She would die in writhing agony, as the rest of the Y Dawnus did when collared. It would be, she thought coldly, no more than she deserved. Her horse lurched beneath her and she forced herself to open her eyes and raise her head.

Her guards lay face down on the road, Kymric arrows fletched in black and green protruding from their backs. Her eyes narrowed to slits and she could barely focus as a slim hand reached out and grabbed the reins of her horse. She caught a glimpse of dark hair, a slender figure clothed in black riding leathers, a wide mouth quirked in a grin as her bonds were cut and she was pulled from her horse.

Someone unbuckled the collar and flung it away. Pillowed against someone's chest, her head was tipped back and a flask held before her mouth. She swallowed the liquid, knowing that it was a concoction of Penduran's Rose and cool, clean water, the only cure for one who had worn an enaid-dal, the only way to counteract the poisonous needles.

"Ellywen," a voice said, a voice that belonged to the man against whose chest her head rested. She thought she recognized that voice, but she couldn't be sure. Surely he himself would not come and rescue her. Not after what she had done to him.

She squinted up at the man and the sunlight turned his golden hair into a glowing nimbus. His eyes, blue as sapphires, smiled down at her.

"Sire," Ellywen breathed. "Forgive."

"I do, my Druid," Rhoram said with a grin as he helped her to stand. "If I didn't I wouldn't be here."

"Achren," Ellywen said as she focused on the woman who held

the horse's reins. "Achren, you would not kill me before. I beg you, do it now."

"For what cause?" Achren asked, her brow raised.

"For my betrayal of our king."

"Don't be a fool, Ellywen," Achren said. "You have atoned for that betrayal."

"What Achren is trying to say in her inimitable style, is welcome home, Ellywen," Rhoram said.

His smile warmed her as life returned to her brain and body. "King Rhoram, my life is not long enough to atone. But I will do what I can."

"You are free, Ellywen," Rhoram said gently. "Free."

Free? How could one such as she be free? For she had done such terrible things. "My King, I—"

"Free," he repeated as the golden morning bathed her in its light. Far above them the sound of a hunting horn drifted across the sky. A meadow dotted with wildflowers stretched out before her. Red rockrose and bright blue forget-me-nots, yellow globeflowers and tall green grasses bowed as though in reverence under a morning breeze that swirled gentle patterns throughout the grass. Nearby a brook capered and sang, spraying tiny drops of diamonds into the morning. Birds sang overhead and grapevines ran and twisted above the dark, rich earth. Apple trees, covered with delicate, pink blossoms spread their branches to the clear, blue sky.

She breathed in gratefully, closing her eyes then opening them again, alive for the first time in many years to the gifts of the earth.

"By Modron the Mother," Rhoram said softly, "by all the gods in Kymru, Ellywen, you are free."

Chapter Nine

Llwynarth, Kingdom of Rheged &
Cadair Idris, Gwytheryn, Kymru
Bedwen Mis, 500

Meirigdydd, Tywyllu Wythnos—midmorning

Enid ur Urien var Ellirri, Queen of Rheged, made her way through the marketplace in the center of the city of Llwynarth. The morning was crisp and cool as was usual for early spring. Overhead the sun shone, doing its best to thaw earth still cold from winter's frosts. A chill breeze swooped through the city, plucking at her cloak, loosening strands of her hair from the gold and opal fillet that bound it and setting the reddish-gold locks to dancing in the sunlight. Fiery opals flashed at her fingers, her wrists, her throat, as though attempting to warm her.

Her fellow Kymri seemed to melt out of her path, as she made her way through the stalls. Behind her two of her husband's Coranian warriors shadowed her. Later Morcant would make them recite the places she had gone, all that she had said and done and seen. She smiled bitterly, for he would never learn anything from it.

She held her head high as she walked, and the sun illuminated the darkening bruise on her cheekbone. She would not bend her head to hide what King Morcant did to her. She had paid and paid and paid again this past year for her foolishness in ever coming to Llwynarth to be captured and wed against her will. She would not continue to pay the price of shame for what had happened to her. It was her husband that should be ashamed, not she.

When she remembered the girl that she had been when she had first returned to Llwynarth, when she remembered her foolish dream of convincing Bledri, her dead father's Dewin, to return to the forest with her, when she remembered how desperately she had loved him, grief filled her. That girl she had been would never return. The girl blinded by love, the girl who risked all for it, the girl who lost all because of it, was gone. All freshness, all beauty, all love had gone out of her in that moment Bledri had betrayed her, had laughed at her dreams, had given her to Morcant Whledig.

Yes, Bledri had given her to Morcant, but not before he had raped her as she lay helplessly bound in the dark cells beneath her father's fortress. He had done that every night for that first week. And then he and Morcant had determined that she would wed the false king to help bolster his claim to the throne of Rheged. And Bledri had stopped the nightly rapes, for Morcant had decided that he must be sure she was not with child by another man before he wed her.

Since then, Morcant alone had raped her. He gloried in trying to humiliate her, in hurting her, in his endless game of trying to make her scream. But she would not. Not even the slightest sound would pass her lips when he did those unspeakable things to her over and over and over again. She would never give him that satisfaction. Never. At least she had the power to deny him that.

She had one other power in her possession—the power to deny him a child. She regularly took small doses of pennyroyal oil, just enough to ensure that there would be no son for Morcant.

Sometimes, late at night, when she lay bruised and bleeding she would think of Prince Geriant of Prydyn, the man who had truly loved her, who had offered for her hand, the man who she might now be married to if not for her own foolishness. Geriant had been so bright and golden, so true, so loving. But she had turned from him to give her heart to such a creature as Bledri. Even after all this time she could still think of Geriant and weep. But when she did weep, she did it alone, for she would never let either Bledri or Morcant see.

Her blue eyes were cool and alert as she came to a stop at the booth of Menestyr, the cloth merchant. Behind her the two Coranian guards halted. Before she even so much as shared a glance with the merchant the two guards were distracted by a Kymric shepherd and a merchant who had begun arguing in loud voices about the price the merchant should pay for the shepherd's wool. Menestyr must have been warned in advance of her coming today, to have been able to set up the distraction so quickly.

Menestyr bowed to her behind the counter of his stall. Brightly colored piles of cloth were strewn across the counter's wooden surface. Thick curtains covered the entrance to the back of the stall, where he kept additional wares. Menestyr straightened and, as he took in her bruised face, his dark eyes narrowed and his jaw clenched.

"It is of no matter, my old friend," she said, her voice pitched low.

"It is," the merchant murmured. "But I will not distress you further by insisting on that."

She smiled bitterly. "I thank you. My time is short. I can tell you only that tonight Morcant, Bledri, and General Baldred plan to dine alone in the King's ystafell. They have been given orders by the Golden Man to come up with a way to get a message through to the Coranian Empire. Havgan needs Coranian reinforcements and with the shores guarded and his boats burned, he is at his wits end to find a way to get word back to Corania."

"Can you tell us what this plan will be once it is formulated?"

She shook her head as she fingered some cloth of forest green. "I will be locked in my chambers to await my lord's pleasure," she said coldly, almost spitting out the last word. "I won't be able to even get close enough. Nor would Morcant dream of breathing a word of it to me when he comes."

Without really meaning to, she shivered at the thought of Morcant again coming to her bedroom. Surely she should be used to the humiliation, the violence, the helplessness by now. After all, it happened to her almost every night. But suddenly she thought she could bear it no longer. For almost a year she had searched and searched for a way to escape. She had not found it and had contented herself with passing on whatever information she could to Menestyr, who was secretly one of the Cerddorian. It had been a way of helping the brother she had loved and so foolishly betrayed.

But she now felt she could not go on, could not face one more night.

"Lady," Menestyr said urgently as she clutched at the counter and briefly closed her eyes against the pain. "Lady, do not give up. Not now."

"And why not now?" she whispered bitterly as she opened her eyes. Behind her the argument was winding down. Her guards would once again be at her elbow, listening to every word, watching her every move.

"Because you have not yet met my new assistant," Menestyr said unexpectedly.

A hand, sinewy and brown, lifted the curtain behind the stall and a figure stepped out. The man bowed to Enid before she could clearly see his face. As he straightened her guards were once again behind her, watching.

Her breath caught in her throat as the sun shone on the man's brown hair, teasing red highlights from it. The man's blue eyes, so like her own, met hers fearlessly. The lines of despair and grief, so prominent on his face the last time she saw him, had been smoothed away and even in her shock she was glad for him. Then he smiled at her and his smile was dazzling in its warmth, in its welcome, in its promise of a return to home and love and safety.

She nodded at the man, acutely aware of the guards behind her. She could think of nothing to say, and she gripped the counter even harder. But the guards were there, the silence would be too long, so she let go of the counter and inclined her head to the merchant's new assistant. "I am pleased to meet you, sir," she managed to say.

Her brother Owein, the true King of Rheged, replied, "And I am more pleased to meet you than I can say."

One last shout from the arguing shepherd and his opponent caused the guards to briefly look away. And in that moment Owein's lips moved, shaping two words that she had longed to hear during this last, nightmarish year.

"Be ready."

She made her way back to Caer Erias almost in a daze. As she came to the gate she glanced up at the figure incised on it—a rearing, golden stallion with a glittering mane of opals, and fiery opals for eyes. As she passed the sun chose to flash off the opals, making it seem that the mighty horse was looking at her with a challenge in its eyes. Her heart leapt in her breast, though she would never let that show on her smooth, expressionless face. Perhaps the time had truly come. Perhaps Owein really could get her out of here. Oh, if only he could.

She wondered who else had come with him and, still wondering, walked by the stables, her guard following. Servants were cleaning out the stalls and the stable doors were open wide. Sunlight spilled into the stable a few feet, illuminating those who worked near the doors, clearing away old straw and spreading new. The sunlight flashed off the golden hair of one of the men. At that moment the man turned to face the courtyard and their eyes met. The man's blue eyes seared her as her own widened in shock, though she knew better than to halt, even for a moment. The man gave a slight nod, then returned to his work, spreading new hay on the stable floor.

She continued on as though nothing had happened, smoothly gliding past the stables. But her pulse beat wildly in her throat. Hope at last raised its battered and bloodied head and beckoned to her. She held in her mind's eye the memory of the man's face. Geriant had come. He, too, had come at last to set her free.

SHE ENTERED HER chambers. Her guard halted at the bottom of the stairs as she ascended, making her way to her bedroom. The chamber was bright and airy. The furniture was carved from light oak, polished to the sheen of new honey. Thick rugs woven in cream and red were scattered on the floor. Her huge, canopied bed was covered with a cream-colored spread worked in gold thread and opals. She was glad, more than ever, that Morcant always chose to have her brought to his rooms to rape her. In this room, the room that had been her mother's, there were no bad memories. The memories held here were of her family, of spending peaceful evenings with her brothers Elphin and Rhiwallon and Owein, with her mother and father whose love covered them and comforted them. Those days were long gone but still she held them in her heart to warm her and never so much as when in this room.

She shrugged her cloak from her shoulders and hung it from its peg in the wardrobe. As she turned she caught a glimpse of a hated face and gasped.

"You did not spend long in the marketplace," Bledri said. His Dewin's robe of silver and sea green strained over his powerful shoulders. His sandy brown hair glittered in the sunlight but his gray eyes were cold.

Enid haughtily eyed the man who had betrayed her parents, the man who had later betrayed her. Her glance was contemptuous and cool but inside she felt like screaming. What was he doing here? What did he want? Or, worse still, what did he suspect?

"What do you want, Bledri?" she asked, her voice bored.

"Just to talk."

She laughed sharply. "Since when do you want to talk?"

"Why, Enid, you know how much I like spending time with you." His gray eyes crawled over her body, gleaming with the memories of doing as he pleased with her when she was bound in her cell a year ago.

"Bledri, get to the point," she said coldly as she went to sit before her dressing table. She unbound her hair and began to brush it slowly. She knew that Bledri would not dare to touch her, much as he might threaten to. And she wished to torment him, as she was able. It would not be much, but it would be something.

His eyes narrowed as she watched him in the glass. He was not a fool, and he did know her well. "I simply would wish to remind you that this is your prison. And one from which you will never escape."

"Do you think I don't know that?" she asked in a bored tone. But her eyes flashed at him.

"The Master Smiths of Kymru and their families have been freed by High King Arthur and his folk," Bledri went on as though she had not spoken.

"I know that."

"Then know this, too. Queen Elen of Ederynion has escaped from Caer Dwyr."

She gasped, dropping the brush and leaping to her feet, spinning around to face him. "What? She has been freed?"

"Two days ago. A messenger from Dinmael just brought us the news."

"Rescued," Elen breathed. "She was rescued."

"Along with her Dewin, Regan. Prince Lludd and Angharad rescued them. Oh, and your brother, Prince Rhiwallon, was there also."

"Oh," she said softly, as she abruptly sat down again on the stool.

"Apparently Iago and another Druid helped to hold the pursuit off long enough for them to get away. Both the Druids died, of course, but not before the rest of them escaped. General Talorcan went with them."

Her blue eyes filled with tears, though she was smiling. "They got away. They are free."

"As you shall never be, Enid," Bledri said harshly.

She stared at him and did not answer. Did he think her own brother would never come for her? But he had. And Geriant had, too. Soon, very soon, she would be free of this daily torment. Did he think to persuade her otherwise?

"I tell you this, Enid, for this is true. You will never escape here. Never."

"You are so sure?" she asked.

"I am. And I will tell you why. I know you will never escape because I will see you dead first."

She jumped to her feet, her hairbrush clutched in her hand. "How dare you threaten me," she raged, but inside she was cold as death. She knew he meant what he said.

"I will do to you whatever I please."

"I think not," she said swiftly. "For my husband would have something to say about that."

"You husband does not, in truth, rule here, Enid. As I think you know. It is General Baldred and myself that truly do."

"It is General Baldred, I agree. Your word is as nothing, and I think you must surely know that. Are you not one of the hated witches? Do you think that the Coranians will ignore that forever?"

He stepped toward her, snatching the hairbrush from her hands and pinning her arms behind her. His face just inches from her own, he loomed over her, his gray eyes cold and glittering. "Rather than see you free I will see you dead."

"Then kill me now, Bledri. Finish the work you began the night you betrayed me. You killed my heart then. Kill my body. Then shall I truly be free."

He bent his head and kissed the side of her neck. The kiss turned into a bite as his teeth nipped at her. But he knew better than to break the skin and he lifted his head again to kiss her lips. His tongue invaded her, forcing her mouth open. She did not respond, but neither did she struggle, for she knew he would like that.

When he at last released her mouth she hissed, "Take me then, Bledri. Then will I go to Morcant and show him what you have done."

His arms tightened around her then released her. He stepped back all at once and she clutched at the dressing table to keep from falling.

"You will never be free, Enid. Not even if both Morcant and I are dead. You will carry with you all the rest of your life the things we have done to you. You will never again taste joy, for we will be in your memories forever."

He stormed from the room as she slowly sank down to the floor, her face in her hands, the truth of what he said lodging like an arrow in her weary heart.

Owein took a firm hold of the slim rope that snaked down the side of the fortress wall. In the darkness he could not even see the top of the wall he scaled until he was almost upon it. As he reached the top he let go of the rope and hoisted himself up to lie flat across the parapet. He laid still for a moment, catching his breath.

Cautiously, he inched across the top of the wall until he was directly beside the watchtower. Above him the light from the narrow window flickered once, twice, three times. Owein grinned to himself. Geriant and Yrth had indeed done their task.

Loud, raucous laughter sounded from the hall in the middle of the huge courtyard. Someone opened the door of the hall and golden light spilled out and down the steps. Owein crouched, not moving, as three figures made their way down the stairs and to the ystafell. Although the light of the torches in brackets set in intervals around the fortress walls was flickering and uncertain, he knew exactly who the three men were.

Morcant, the self-styled King of Rheged wore a dark red cloak, the color of old blood. The cloak clasped at this throat with a brooch of opal and gold shaped in the figure of a rearing stallion. At the sight of the ornament, an ornament he had often seen around his father's neck, Owein drew his dagger and almost leapt to kill Morcant. But he stopped himself in time, though rage coursed through him, leaving him shaking.

The sea green and silver robe of the man on Morcant's left shimmered briefly in the torchlight. Around the man's powerful neck glowed a torque of pearl set in a silvery pentagon. Again, Owein had to grit his teeth to keep from jumping down and slitting Bledri's throat. For this was the Dewin who had betrayed his parents, ensuring their deaths. And this was the man who Enid had thrown everything away for, the man who had betrayed his sister and sold her into slavery.

The third man Owein knew by reputation. He was dressed in red and gold, the colors of his master. General Baldred's stocky figure walked with authority, for he was the true power in Rheged, and he knew it.

The three men disappeared into the ystafell and Owein breathed a sigh. He glanced up at the window and waved briefly. The light again flickered. Owein gave out a soft hoot, so like an owl's as to be almost indistinguishable, and saw the rope below him pulled taunt.

It took her but a few moments to scale the wall. Her golden

hair was covered and muted by a dark scarf, and her dark eyes danced as she took his hand and allowed him to pull her up next to him. He snatched a kiss, because he simply couldn't help it. Sanon smiled at him, then nodded to the window, her brows raised. He nodded back and motioned for her to pass him and stand beneath the window. As she did so he laced his fingers and lowered his arms. She delicately stepped into the palms of his hands and held onto the wall as he lifted her. Hands reached out of the window and pulled her in.

Again, the rope went taut, and he waited. One by one his companions reached the top of the wall and climbed into the watchtower window—Trystan, his captain, and Teleri his lieutenant, followed by Gwarae Golden-Hair, the Gwarda of Ystlwyf. This last gave him a grin and a jaunty salute as he made his way with Owein's help through the watchtower's window.

Owein coiled the rope, then went to the window. He stowed the rope in the front of his dark tunic, then spit on his hands. He scaled the wall carefully, searching for the handholds he knew were there. As his hands reached the window ledge Trystan and Gwarae reached out and hauled him up the rest of the way.

His eyes met the two men who had been waiting in the tower—Prince Geriant and Yrth, the Druid that High King Arthur had sent to aid them. At their feet sprawled the figures of three guards.

Owein nodded at the still bodies. "Any trouble?" he asked.

"None," Geriant answered briskly.

"I still think that I should have been allowed to—" Teleri began with a frown.

"Enough, Teleri," Owein said. "You know perfectly well why only Geriant and Yrth were allowed to go through the gate earlier today."

"Because the two of them were not well known in Llwynarth," Sanon finished for him. "While the rest of you certainly are. But that was no reason I could not have been allowed in. No one knows me here."

Again, as he had through all the previous arguments, Owein could find no good reason to not have allowed Sanon to do it other than that his heart almost stopped at the thought.

"Enough, sister," Geriant said with a smile. "Or do you truly not know why your husband did not allow you to come with us?"

"Maybe it would be best if someone told me why we are continuing to argue about this?" Gwarae asked. "It's a little late to keep on about it."

"True," Owein agreed with relief. "Teleri, the signal."

Teleri went to the window and strung her bow. Owein knew that her shot had to hit the target true or their escape would be well nigh impossible. But, even in the dark, he had no doubts about Teleri's abilities. The arrow sang softly as it left the bow and sped through the still air. A half league away a light flared and died, then another, from further off still. The last flame flared briefly then sputtered out.

"The signal is sent," Teleri said with satisfaction. "March will be on his way with the horses."

"Truly, Teleri, there is no one like you with a bow and arrow," Gwarae said jauntily. "Why, how long has it been now since you sent an arrow through my heart? I remember the moment I first saw you—"

"Oh, leave off, Gwarae," Teleri said as she slung her bow over her shoulder. "You always do that. You always make a game of me."

"A game of you?" Gwarae asked, his brow raised. "Now what makes you think that this is a game?"

Teleri snorted. "It's always a game with you. Why, if I thought you were ever serious—"

"You'd do what, lieutenant?" Gwarae said swiftly, his green eyes glinting.

"Never you mind," Teleri said sharply.

Owein decided to put a halt to this conversation. The two of them always spoke to each other this way—Gwarae paying Teleri elaborate compliments that she clearly did not take seriously. She thought he was playing an elaborate game with her. And, perhaps, he had been, at first. But lately Owein wondered if it really was a game to Gwarae at all.

But now it was time to free his sister, and he was focused on that alone. "We are ready," he said quietly. "Yrth, you are prepared?"

The old Druid nodded. His gray eyes glittered with anticipation in his weather-beaten face. "I am, King of Rheged."

Once that title had made Owein wince in shame and guilt. But those days were past, smoothed over by the love of his wife. So he smiled instead and nodded at the Druid. Although he had not known Yrth long, he knew that this Druid had been one of the five that had followed Aergol to High King Arthur to offer their allegiance. Yrth had been a highly respected teacher in Caer Duir for many years and, in spite of the fact that the old man was a Druid, Owein had liked him instantly for the wisdom in his eyes and the calmness of his spirit.

At his nod Teleri and Gwarae left the room with Yrth, one in front of and one behind the old Druid.

Owein nodded to Geriant. "Let's go," he said to the man who had loved, who still did love, his captive sister.

Sanon kissed them both lightly then pulled her long dagger from her belt. Trystan pulled out his short sword with a steely hiss. Owein turned at the door for one last look at Sanon. She smiled at him, her heart in her dark eyes.

Teleri led the way, with Yrth behind her and Gwarae last. They made their way silently down the twisting stairs of the guard tower. They reached the bottom and Teleri stood to one side of the door, motioning for Yrth to stand next to her. She nodded to Gwarae and he opened the door a crack. He put his eye to the crack, then stepped back, motioning that the way was clear.

Teleri stepped out first, her bow slung across one shoulder, a long gleaming knife in her hands. The courtyard was quiet as they rushed to their left and took cover behind the silent bathhouse.

She glanced behind her and saw the shadowy forms of Geriant and Owein glide the opposite way, toward the ystafell.

"The fools are all in the hall," Teleri whispered furiously.

Yrth's brow rose at her tone. "I would have thought we wanted it that way," he said quietly.

"Ah, Druid, you simply don't understand this beautiful woman here," Gwarae said with a grin. "If she was still lieutenant here in Caer Erias things would not be so sloppy. Guards would patrol the courtyard, not simply be limited to the towers."

"And every last torch would be lit," Teleri said, still angry. "Why, only every other torch on the walls is lit. Anyone could be up to anything in the courtyard! If I had my way—"

"Which you will again, *cariad*," Gwarae said. "For we will take it all back."

"So we will," Teleri said firmly. Almost as an afterthought, she went on, "And don't call me *cariad*."

"Why, for a moment I thought you were going to let me do that without scolding me," Gwarae quipped. "I almost had hopes."

"You can take your hopes and—"

"Pardon me, Yrth," Gwarae said, turning to the Druid. "But could you hold this?" He snatched the bow from Teleri's hands and handed it to Yrth. Then he reached out and pulled Teleri to him, and fastened his mouth over hers. For a moment, a very brief moment, Teleri struggled. But then she seemed to melt into Gwarae's embrace. After a long, lengthy kiss, Gwarae raised his head. He seemed surprised and shaken but did not loose Teleri from his arms.

Teleri smiled up at him, her gray-green eyes almost soft. "And did you think I would never let you do that?"

"After all this time, I feared so," Gwarae breathed.

"Then why did you try?"

"I assumed you would not kill me here, but wait until later."

"I do have plans for you later," Teleri agreed. "But I don't believe you will object."

"Did you really believe that I have been playing a game with you?" he rasped.

"Of course. That's why it took me so long."

"Teleri ur Brysethach, I love you."

Her breath caught in her throat. At last. At long last. "Gwarae Golden-Hair, I love you."

Gwarae bent his head to kiss her again, but Yrth's hand on his arm stopped him.

"While I enjoy the course of true love as much as anyone, I think you had both best concentrate on the task at hand," Yrth breathed, nodding toward the shadows by the ystafell. From the darkness a white cloth fluttered.

"The signal," Gwarae whispered. "Now, Druid. Now."

Sanon and Trystan halted at the bottom of the watchtower stairs. They took up their places on either side of the open doorway, hidden in the shadows. Sanon squinted toward the bathhouse.

"Why," she said with delight, "I believe that Gwarae has caught his quarry at last."

Trystan glanced over and grinned at the sight of two shadows twined together. "Took long enough," he grumbled, but he smiled faintly as he said it.

"I must say, the timing could be better."

Trystan shrugged. "It happens when it happens."

"Trystan," she began, then stopped.

"Yes, my Queen?" he asked softly.

"Be a friend to Geriant," she said. "My brother might need one very badly."

"Enid will come back to us," Trystan said, for he seemed to understand everything that Sanon did not know how to say. "She'll come back. And Geriant will be whole."

In the shadows behind the ystafell a white cloth fluttered.

"The signal," Sanon breathed. "Now, Druid. Now."

Geriant and Owein stood in the shadows that pooled behind the ystafell. Above them the windows of Enid's rooms were shuttered from the outside, for Morcant always had the shutters closed at night. Wan candlelight flickered fitfully in the cracks between the shutters.

She's in there, Geriant thought, and closed his eyes briefly at her nearness. She was so close to him, after all this time. At last he had come to rescue her, to take her from this place of pain and terror and humiliation into the light of Mabon's bright sun. The time had come, at last.

She was no longer the Enid he had known and loved. He had seen that clearly when he had caught that brief, sweet glimpse of her in the courtyard this afternoon. The girl she had been was dead and gone. The woman that the lovely, spirited, generous girl had become was unknown to him.

He had thought, deep in his heart, that this would be so. And he had thought, deeper still, that perhaps it would matter to him—this change. But it had not. When he had seen her he had known, as he had known from the beginning, that she was the one. She was the woman he was born to love. And if he could not have her, he would have no one.

He pulled a slender coil of rope from his tunic. At one end was a lead weight wrapped in dark cloth. At Owein's nod he slung the weight attached to the rope over his head once, twice, three times, then threw. The rope arched high overhead then began to descend. In its descent it looped around a protruding roof beam just over one of Enid's shuttered windows. The weight wrapped the rope around once, twice, three times. The cloth adequately muffled the sound.

Geriant tugged at the rope and it tensed and held. He nodded to Owein that he was ready.

"Go," Owein breathed.

Geriant wrapped the slack around his upper arm and shoulder. Lightly, quickly, he walked up the wall, hanging on to the rope. When he reached the shutter he put his eye to the crack.

Enid had tears on her face as she paced back and forth across the room. She hugged herself tightly, her jaw clenched hard as though to hold back screams. She was dressed in brown riding leathers and her auburn hair was braided tightly to her skull. Every few moments she impatiently dashed away the tears that continued to fall.

Geriant's heart broke a little more when he saw her in her bravery, her fear, her hope and her despair. Oh, Enid, he thought to himself. I have come. *Cariad*, I have come for you.

Geriant turned to look down at Owein. He gave a nod to indicate Enid was within, and was alone.

Now, Druid, Geriant thought as he turned again back to the window. Now.

At Geriant's signal Owein pulled out a white kerchief from his tunic. He glanced back to his left, to the open door of the watchtower and the hidden forms of Sanon and Trystan that he knew stood there. He looked back, further still, to the dark bathhouse, to where he knew Teleri, Gwarae, and Yrth waited. He turned and looked up at Geriant.

He raised the kerchief and waved it.

Now, Druid, he thought. Now.

Yrth was old, over seventy now. He had served the Mother for almost all of his life, having been brought to Caer Duir when he was only six years old. He had been a student, a journeyman, and a full-fledged Druid. When he was fifty, he had returned to Caer Duir as a teacher of the almanac. His whole life he had been happy and satisfied, serving Modron the Mother with his gifts and skill.

When he had first understood that the Archdruid had plans to once again make the Druids preeminent in Kymru, he had rejoiced. The Mother would again be supreme, as she had been in lost Lynonesse, before ever there were Dreamers or Bards or Dewin. When the Coranians invaded and he understood the price of that preeminence, he was less pleased. But still he had thought that the Mother would bless their efforts. But She had not. The land had given little in the few years since the invasion. The harvests had been scant and the winters had seemed longer and colder. He had doubted still more and, when approached by Aergol, he had been more than ready. At first, when he had determined to follow Aergol and reject all the Cathbad had stood for, he had been afraid that the Mother would take back the gifts she had bestowed on him at birth.

But it was not so. His gift was as strong as ever. And because he had used these gifts for so long, he had no need to concentrate, to finger the dwyvach-breichled, the bracelet of Modron that encircled his wrist. It was not even necessary to close his eyes. But, because he always did so, he briefly touched the emerald set in the golden torque around his neck. Then he reached out with his mind to the stable some hundred feet away.

THE WOODEN BAR that closed the stable doors lifted and hovered briefly, then gently floated to the ground. The doors opened inward. After a few moments, a wisp of smoke floated out of the upper loft. Inside the stable, horses snorted. The smoke became thicker, and the horses began to neigh loudly. The doors of their stalls opened all at once, and the horses screamed as they rushed from the stable. Hungry tongues of fire began to lick their way to the roof as smoke poured off the building.

One of the guards in the east watchtower cried out and another guard came out of the tower, speeding toward the hall at a dead run. He opened the hall doors and shouted. Warriors came boiling out, shouting for water, shouting to watch for enemies, some with blades drawn or spears in their hands, some with tankards of ale and bread in their fists.

From the ystafell General Baldred, King Morcant, and Bledri rushed out of the building to behold the fire.

The courtyard was in chaos, as Owein had intended. He nodded to Geriant and the Prince swiftly unlatched the shutters, throwing them open wide. Enid rushed to the window and Geriant guided her hands to the rope. At his direction she grabbed the rope and jumped from the windowsill. She slid down into Owein's waiting arms.

"Owein," she sobbed as he held her close. "Brother."

"We came for you, Enid. I am so sorry it took so long."

Enid continued to weep as he set her on her feet but she stood straight and steady. "Now what?" she asked.

"To the watchtower," Owein nodded. "Then away from this place. We will go out the tower window with ropes. Then make our way to the west wall where some Cerddorian are ready to help us over. March is waiting on the other side with horses for us all."

"All?"

"You, me, Teleri, Gwarae, Sanon, Trystan, our Druid, and, of course, Geriant."

"Geriant," Enid said softly as she turned to the Prince. "Geriant. Thank you."

Geriant bowed briefly but did not speak. The sheen of tears glittered in his blue eyes, but he smiled at her.

"Come," Owein said. "We must be going."

The three of them ran swiftly to the watchtower, bent low. Sanon and Trystan stood on either side just inside the door, weapons ready.

"Go," Trystan said, nodding to the stairs.

"The others?" Owein asked.

"Upstairs already," Trystan answered.

"Any trouble?" Owein asked.

"Gwarae had to kill a guard who almost blundered right into them," Sanon answered. She nodded toward the bathhouse. Huddled against the wall in the shadows between the fortress wall and the bathhouse lay a darker shadow. "But no one else saw."

Then Trystan looked briefly out the door and what he saw made him grip his sword tighter. "Hurry. General Baldred appears to have seen something he does not like."

Owein glanced out the door. Trystan was right. General Baldred was not looking at the stable, but was eyeing the watchtower instead. Had he perhaps seen the Kymri reenter? It was too dark for him to know who was in the tower, but if he had seen anyone go back in, he would have wondered who it was, since all the Coranians were coming from the buildings, not going into them. Baldred, unnoticed by his companions, pulled his sword and walked quietly toward the tower and the open tower door.

"Go," Trystan said again. "Baldred is mine."

"He is mine," Owein said grimly. "He killed my mam."

"He is mine," Enid said tightly. "He and Bledri and Morcant. They belong to me."

Sanon sighed and pulled her dagger from her belt. Without a word she threw the dagger in a swift, underhand cast. The blade gleamed briefly in the light of the fire as it sped clear and true through the smoke, burying itself in Baldred's gut. The General dropped to his knees, clutching the knife's protruding hilt, then slumped forward to the ground, burying the blade deeper still into his dying body.

Trystan, Owein, and Enid stared at Sanon. "There was no time to argue precedence," Sanon said crisply. "Now, we go."

As they silently made their way from the fortress the far-off strains of a hunting horn—the horn of the Wild Hunt—sounded faintly in their ears.

ARTHUR REACHED OUT to move the raven with the fiery opal eyes across the tarbell game board. But as he touched the piece his hand froze. He cocked his head as though listening to something, something Rhiannon could not make out.

The scar on Arthur's lean face whitened momentarily. Then he looked over at her and smiled. "Enid is free," he said simply.

"Thank the gods," Rhiannon breathed.

The torque of emerald and sapphire, of opal and pearl and onyx, glowed around Arthur's neck in the golden light of the game room. The pieces on the tarbell board glittered and gleamed. Arthur picked up the raven that represented the Dreamer, and moved it forward, placing it in the black square where the Dewin with eyes of pearl had rested. He picked up the Dewin and set it to the side of the board, then looked back at her.

Rhiannon returned his gaze squarely, but she did not really see him. Soon she would be able to leave Cadair Idris, in the dead of the night, to journey to Sycharth. Somewhere in the woods outside the city Gwydion wandered, lost and disoriented, possibly wounded, certainly ill. Her heart ached knowing that he waited for her, weak and bewildered. But she had not been able to leave before tonight, not before Enid's rescue had been completed.

Gwydion had begged for her to come alone, so there would be no witnesses to his weakness and humiliation. And that was so very like him. So very like the man she loved. For she admitted it and was at last determined to live with that truth. She did love

Gwydion ap Awst past all reason, past all logic, past all hope of true happiness. She loved him and she would not leave him to his enemies. Not while she still had breath left in her body.

Arthur's dark gaze made her wonder if he knew exactly what she was thinking. Without a word, for she feared that if she spoke the shaking in her voice might betray her, she rose from the gaming board. It was time to go to her chambers and change for her journey.

"Rhiannon," Arthur said softly as she made her way to the door.

She turned her head to look back at him as the door opened.

"Yes, Arthur?"

His dark eyes glittered. "It's your move."

Chapter Ten

Tegeingl
Kingdom of Gwynedd, Kymru
Bedwen Mis, 500

Merigdydd, Tywyllu Wythnos—morning

"There are strangers in town."

When Madoc did not answer immediately, General Catha continued. "Find them," he said to the King of Gwynedd, as one would order a dog to hunt.

Madoc's cold blue eyes narrowed, but he knew better than to challenge Catha's tone—or his authority. "What do you mean, there are strangers in town? There are always strangers, here and there."

Catha sighed to himself. The morning sun that streamed in through the windows of the ystafell burnished his blond hair to a golden sheen, but his light blue eyes were cold and frosty. His proud, handsome face clearly showed the contempt he had for the man who called himself the King of Gwynedd. For Madoc would have been king of nothing without the Coranians behind him. There were times, Catha thought, when it appeared Madoc forgot that. This was perhaps one of those times.

The floor of the audience chamber was polished to an almost deadly sheen and scattered with beautifully woven rugs in blue and brown. Bright banners stitched with silver and sapphires hung on the walls between the windows. On the canopy over the high-backed chair where Madoc sat a hawk, stitched in silver, spread his wings and his sapphire eyes glared. Catha looked back at the hawk balefully. The hawk had no authority here in Gwynedd. The only authority now was the Coranian boar, sign of Catha's master,

Havgan, the Golden Man, the man who was, essentially, Madoc's master also. For without Havgan, Madoc would be nothing more than a lord in Gwynedd, half-brother of the ruling king.

But King Uthyr was dead, by Catha's own hand, and Madoc had been set in his place to be the ruler of Gwynedd. And besides, Catha thought to himself, Madoc wasn't completely useless. He did have a beautiful daughter, a daughter that figured prominently into Catha's plans. One day soon he would have her, in his bed and bound to him by law. Catha would be the next ruler of Gwynedd, as his reward. In the meantime, he had to suffer Madoc's foolishness. But this state of affairs would not last forever.

"These strangers presented themselves to the wool works as expert dyers, were taken in and put to work," Catha said. "They have been here for almost seven days. I want you to determine who and what they really are."

"What makes you think they aren't exactly who they say they are?" Madoc asked sourly. Clearly he was put out with Catha this morning. And Catha knew why. For when he snapped his fingers Madoc's mistress came running, which is exactly what had happened again last night. And Madoc was still smarting over it.

"There is a whiff of something here I do not like. Find out what it is."

Catha watched Madoc closely as the King of Gwynedd struggled between two courses of action—between pretending he had authority and between knowing that he must do as he was told. One day, Catha thought, Madoc will lose that inner battle and say and do something he should not. On that day Catha would kill him and be done with this nonsense.

But Madoc chose the wiser way, and so lived a little longer. "I will find them myself and question them. What do they look like?"

"They are both old, well past their prime. One of them has a short, gray, beard and dark eyes. The other has hair that is almost all gray, though it was probably something more like your color when he was younger. He has blue eyes and carries himself as though he is the lord of creation."

Madoc paled a little, and his hand shook slightly as he brought his silver and sapphire cup of ale to his lips. Catha's brow rose at that. "What, King of Gwynedd, do you think you know these men?"

Madoc mutely shook his head as he drank.

"You are certain you do not know them?"

"I don't know them," Madoc said shortly. "And, anyway, it is almost time to go."

"Go?" Catha asked as though puzzled. Inside, he smiled.

"On the hunt."

"Oh, didn't I tell you?" he asked lazily as he put on his leather gloves. "You are not going on the hunt this morning."

"Not going?" Madoc rose from his ornate chair, his silver goblet still clutched in his hand.

"You begin your investigation this morning. The rest of us will go on the hunt."

"The rest of us? Including—"

"Including Arday. Your beloved mistress, and mine." Catha grinned. "Nor will your daughter be spared. Tangwen goes with us this morning."

"Tangwen is not—"

"Is not what?" Catha asked sharply, cutting into Madoc's sentence.

"Is—is not—not fond of the hunt."

"But," Catha said with a smile, "I am. And I always catch my quarry. Tangwen had best remember that."

He turned and left the chamber, stepping out into the cool morning. In the courtyard men and dogs and horses wandered in controlled chaos. Arday, the sister of the Lord of Arllechwedd and former Steward to King Uthyr, made her way toward him. Her black hair shone almost blue, like the raven's wing, in the morning light. Her sensual, dark eyes glittered as she slowly walked up to him. In spite of himself his pulse quickened at the sight of her. He had no love, but he did have passion, and Arday flamed that passion effortlessly. He would never be brought down by his desires, but he acknowledged them and fulfilled them as he wished.

Arday smiled slowly as she bowed gracefully to him. She rose and lightly touched his strong, muscled arm with her fingertips. She wore black riding leathers that emphasized every graceful curve of her rich body.

"My lord," she said her voice musical and throaty. "Are you ready?"

"For the hunt?" he asked, as he took her hand and lazily kissed her fingers, his tongue teasing each one slowly.

"For the hunt," she agreed with a throaty laugh. "Where is Madoc?" she purred.

"Staying here."

"Why does he not hunt with us?" Arday asked with a very slight frown above her silky brows.

"Why, will you miss him?"

"Not I," she said softly. "Yet I wonder what mischief he might get up to without you here to watch him."

"He will be about my business. There are two strangers in town—two old men, dyers down at the wool works. I have told him to find out who they are."

"Ah," Arday said. "And he will no doubt obey."

"No doubt." Catha was momentarily distracted from Arday as he saw Tangwen feeding her horse an apple. The golden mare lipped the treat off of Tangwen's delicate palm. The princess was dressed in riding leathers of brown and sapphires glittered in her reddish-gold hair. Arday followed his gaze.

"Do you really think she is the woman for you, General?" Arday asked with a sardonic smile on her face.

Catha grasped Arday's wrist and squeezed. He knew it hurt her, but Arday did not cry out, though a sweat broke out on her brow and her dark eyes widened in pain. "Do not even think to criticize me, Arday," he said softly. He let go her wrist where the bruises of his fingers were already beginning to darken on her white skin. The sight of those bruises excited him and he licked his lips in anticipation.

Arday, gently cradling her wrist smiled again. Her eyes flickered with something that Catha could not fully identify. It might have been contempt. It might have been a dark knowledge. It might have been something else entirely. He did identify it, much later, but by then it was far too late.

TANGWEN UR MADOC bent her eyes to her horse's golden mane, so she wouldn't have to acknowledge that Catha's eyes were on her. The forest of Coed Dulas was dark and silent even in the bright morning. Sunlight managed to pierce the dense branches and pool on the forest floor, illuminating piles of dead leaves and scrawny underbrush. Far ahead dogs coursed along, baying and barking, calling to each other, scenting for prey. She was surrounded by people—Coranian warriors in bright byrnies of woven metal and holding short spears, Kymric huntsmen in muted green and brown, officers of her father's court in soft riding leathers—but, as always, she felt so alone behind her wall of dishonor.

Shame covered her like a mantle, a shame she never got used to enough to ignore. For her father had no business calling himself the King of Gwynedd. The true ruler of Gwynedd was Morrigan ur Uthyr var Ygraine, her dear, bright, generous friend and cousin. For Tangwen, having both won and lost the battle of conflicting loves in her heart, had thrown in her lot with her cousin, abandoning her father to his fate. He didn't know it yet, of course. Very few did—those in Tegeingl who secretly did the bidding of the Cerddorian, Morrigan herself, and, of course, the man who claimed her heart, Bedwyr, Morrigan's lieutenant.

She smiled to herself at the thought of Bedwyr, his fearless brown eyes and the love she thought she sometimes saw there. She did not see him often, for things were far too dangerous for that. But, sometimes, as she went to the marketplace to pass on the information that she learned in her father's fortress, she caught a glimpse of him, standing at one of the stalls or hawking wares of his own. Sometimes she was able to speak to him directly and at those times her heart leapt in her breast, though she would only speak her message. Sometimes she had to content herself with a mere glimpse, a smile, a look. Sometimes she did not even see him for days on end. But she always knew that he was alive, for she would know it in her heart if he were dead, though no words of love had ever been spoken between them. She was too conscious of her father, of who she was and of what she was doing to risk telling Bedwyr the state of her heart. But she thought he must know it. And hoped with all her soul that he might feel the same way. If not now, then some day.

She sensed someone else's eyes on her and looked up to find Arday riding beside her. Her father's mistress smiled at Tangwen, though the smile did not seem to reach the dark eyes. As always, Tangwen found herself confused and uncertain with Arday. For she was convinced that things were not all that they seemed with her father's—and Catha's—mistress. But she did not know what to make of the things she thought she saw. Sometimes she thought Arday took up Catha's attention to deflect it from Tangwen. And sometimes she thought Arday was simply what she seemed—a greedy, sensual, amoral—and clever, woman.

"Princess," Arday said equably. All around them the hunt cantered, people laughing and talking. Up ahead Catha had turned away to say something to one of his officers. The insistent sound of the barking dogs cut across the bright morning.

Tangwen inclined her head but did not answer. She bent her head and fingered the bright jewels in her horses' reins.

"There are two old men, two strangers in Tegeingl. At the wool works," Arday murmured.

Tangwen's head came up swiftly, but she did not turn to Arday, afraid that the older woman would see the truth in her eyes. "And what is that to me?" she asked, feigning puzzlement. For she did know that, indeed, two strangers, sent by High King Arthur, had arrived in Tegeingl. But she did not know who they were. Nor what their mission was.

"I am certain that you would not wish anything to happen to them. And it will, unless you act fast."

"Again, I do not know—"

"Yes you do," Arday said swiftly, quietly. "And it will be up to you to ensure they live long enough to do what they came here to do."

"I tell you—"

"Catha knows that they are here. He does not know who they are, but he is suspicious. He has set your father to discovering these men. Whether or not your father suspects who they really are, I do not know."

"Who they really are?" Tangwen asked softly, turning slightly in the saddle to face Arday.

"Do you not know?" Arday asked, studying Tangwen's face. Whatever she saw there made her smile. "One of them is Myrrdin ap Morvryn, the former Ardewin of Kymru."

"And the other?" Tangwen asked, her heart in her throat, although she could not have said why.

"Ah. The other is Rhodri ap Erddufyl, your grandfather. But I do not think that Madoc will be pleased to see his da."

"Who are you?" Tangwen breathed. "Who are you really?"

"Arday ur Medyr, onetime servant to King Uthyr. Which was always enough for me."

Arday turned her horse and rode off up the line. She reached Catha's side and smiled wickedly at him, resting her hand for a moment on his thigh.

Tangwen turned away, her head in a whirl. Arday's motives were still murky to her. But her information might be true. True or not, she would not take the risk of doing nothing. She would send word to the Cerddorian that the two men High King Arthur had sent were in danger. She would keep her eyes and ears open and hope to hear more.

And she would, if Arday's information was true, perhaps come face to face with her grandfather, the man many had thought dead long ago. It might be that he had come to Tegeingl to help her lift the shame from her family.

If so, she would be ready.

Meirwydd, Tywyllu Wythnos—twilight

MADOC AP RHODRI crouched in the lengthening shadows cast by the open gates of the wool works just outside the city walls. Four Coranian warriors huddled silently beside him, their spears held tight in their competent hands. In twos and threes the Kymri of

Tegeingl left the wool works for the evening, going home to their snug houses within the city walls. Torches glittered in their hands as they made their way home, easily passing Madoc and his hidden warriors by, laughing and talking as though they did not have a care in the world.

It had been three days since Madoc had been set to finding the two old men Catha had told him about. Madoc had not for one moment expected it to take so long. But, somehow, he had kept just missing his chances to catch up with the two men. Every time he had come to the wool works they were not there. They had either just left, or were to arrive momentarily. No one knew where the two old men lived. Some thought they had set up camp in the forest. Some thought they were staying just the other side of the river. Some were sure that they were staying with this man or that one, but no one could quite agree on exactly with whom.

Those times he had chosen to wait for them to come to work had been fruitless. The Kymri around him had gone calmly about their business as he and his guards waited inside the wool works walls. His folk had bowed to him when they passed. They had not smiled or been anything but respectful. But Madoc knew that they were laughing at him. His people had always laughed at him. He had imagined that this would stop when he became their king but it had not.

And each day he became more and more conscious that he was being made a fool of. And each day he had become more and more fearful. For he had thought he recognized the description of one of the old men. He could be wrong—he would give anything if he were—but in his shallow heart he knew that he was not.

His father was here. His da had returned to Tegeingl.

Madoc had thought his father long dead. Twenty-four years ago Rhodri had, at the death of his wife, Queen Rathtyen, rode out of Tegeingl without a word to anyone. Madoc had not seen or heard from him since. He had assumed, he had hoped, that his father was dead.

But even this boon was, apparently, denied him. Nothing, nothing ever went right for him. He had become king of

Gwynedd, but no one listened to him. He had a beautiful daughter, but Tangwen was ashamed of him. And now his da had come back. To do the gods only knew what.

An old man walked out of the gate, a torch burning fitfully in his thin hand. His silvery beard was cut close to his lean face. He wore a tunic and trousers of worn, dark gray wool. He walked slowly, as though tired, his brows knit in thought. He kept his eyes on the ground, not even bothering to look around him as he walked.

At Madoc's gesture, the warriors rose to their feet and they all followed the old man at a discreet distance back to the city. They closed the gap as they shadowed the man through the gates of Tegeingl. Once inside the city, at Madoc's nod, the four warriors sprinted to the old man and bade him halt. For a moment Madoc thought the old man would not stop. But he did.

"What is going on here?" the man demanded as two of the guards grabbed his arms. The third pointed a spear at the man's neck. The fourth tied a length of rope around the old man's thin wrists.

Madoc stepped up to the old man, torch in hand, to examine him. He looked the man over carefully. The man's dark eyes danced in the wavering light of the torch, though his seamed face was solemn.

"Myrrdin," Madoc breathed. "So, it is you."

Myrrdin inclined his head. "Yes, Madoc," he said quietly. "It is I."

"What are you doing here?"

Myrrdin smiled. "You don't really think I am going to tell you that, do you?"

"Oh, I think you will," Madoc smiled back. "There are so many ways of persuading you to talk to us."

"Ah," Myrrdin said soberly. "As unoriginal as ever."

Madoc's fist shot out. The old man's nose began to bleed, but his eyes still laughed. "Do not think to make a game of me, old man," Madoc began.

"But, Madoc, it is so easy. And so fun."

Madoc slapped Myrrdin hard, and the sound cracked through the descending night. He reached out and grabbed Myrrdin's hair, dragging the old man's face up. "I said, do not make a game of me."

"Too late, Madoc," Myrrdin gasped, still laughing. "Far too late for that."

"My lord," the captain said, as he moved to halt Madoc's third swing. "Not here. Back at the fortress."

Almost Madoc ignored that advice. But the captain was right. Here was not the place to interrogate the former Ardewin of Kymru. It was too open, too exposed. And the gods only knew where his father was. At his gesture the guards pushed Myrrdin forward toward Caer Gwynt.

Madoc followed just behind Myrrdin and the last two guards followed behind him. He noticed that the streets were unusually empty. At this time of night there should have been some people still about, making their way home. But there was no one. Lights shone at all the windows, but not one person seemed to be out of doors.

But he had thought that too soon. For just ahead of them a figure stepped out of the shadows and stood in the center of the road. The coppery taste of terror leapt into Madoc's throat as he recognized the figure that now blocked his way.

Rhodri ap Erddufyl, Prince of Prydyn, onetime king of Gwynedd, stood motionless in the center of the street. Torchlight glittered off his silvery hair, still tinged here and there with red-gold. His cold, blue eyes surveyed his son, and obviously did not like what they saw.

They never had.

Myrrdin's nose was bloody but his eyes were keen and steady as he raised his head to look at Rhodri. The four guards halted with their hands on their spears, waiting for orders from Madoc.

But Madoc could not speak past the fear that lay on his heart like lead. For he knew his father. And he knew what his father would do.

"You are not glad to see me, my son?" Rhodri said softly as he took a step forward.

"You!" Madoc breathed at last. "You are alive."

"So I am," Rhodri agreed. "Alive. And here to do my duty."

"Your duty?" Madoc asked weakly.

"Yes. For it is a poor father that does not discipline his son." With a rasp like the distant thunder of a summer storm, Rhodri drew his blade from the scabbard by his side. Starlight and torchlight glittered on the tempered steel.

"Da," Madoc whispered.

"My son," Rhodri said, implacably. "My son. What have you done?"

"I—"

"You betrayed your king."

"The son of my mother and another man! A man you hated!"

"King Uthyr was the rightful ruler of Gwynedd. Your mother proclaimed him so."

"Why not me?" Madoc screamed. "I was the son of lawful marriage!"

"Uthyr was destined from birth to be the ruler of Gwynedd. You knew that from the beginning."

"It wasn't fair," Madoc cried. "It was never fair."

"It is the law," Rhodri said coldly. "The law that the first-born, if not of the Y Dawnus, take the royal torque. Uthyr was tested and proved not to be one of the Gifted. Your mother rightly named him her heir."

"Not fair," Madoc rasped. "Not fair."

"And for that, you killed the true king of Gwynedd."

"It was Catha! General Catha killed him!"

"Because you could not," Rhodri said his words like fire and ice. "You helped the enemy defeat Kymru. And in those battles, your sister and her husband and their son died."

"They were killed by the Coranians in the battles in Rheged. I did not kill them!"

"You aided the enemy. The responsibility of all the Kymric deaths belongs to you. Your hands are stained with Kymric blood; the blood of your sister, Ellirri; the blood of your brother-in-law, Urien; the blood of your nephew, Elphin; the blood of your half-brother, Uthyr. Your hands are red and vile with it. Those of your family that remain alive turn from you. We cast you out, and call you exile."

Rhodri lifted his hand and beckoned. A slight figure detached itself from the shadows and came to stand next to him. Fiery torchlight glittered off of Tangwen's unbound hair, turning it to molten gold. Her blue eyes looked at Madoc squarely, fearlessly, and proudly.

Madoc's breath caught in his throat as he stared at his father and his daughter.

"Your daughter renounces you," Rhodri went on.

Tangwen drew a deep breath and said in a voice that did not shake, "From this moment forward, I have no father. I name you outcast. I name you without kin. I name you exile."

Madoc took a step backward, then halted. So, his daughter had shown her true colors at last. As always, as from the very beginning, he was alone, unloved. And did they think that this would stop him? Did they think that they could do this to him? Did they think he was nothing? They would learn better. And he would rejoice in their pain.

"You can name me anything you please," Madoc shouted. "But I rule here. I rule! Guards, take them!"

The four guards, their spears steady in their hands, stepped forward toward Rhodri and Tangwen. At that moment two more figures detached themselves from the shadows and came to stand on either side of the former king and his grandaughter.

Madoc recognized them both effortlessly. Bedwyr, lieutenant to Uthyr's daughter, Morrigan, clasped a drawn sword in his capable hands. His brown eyes were fearless as he faced the guards. Neuad, Morrigan's Dewin, stood glowing beneath the starlight, her beautiful face cold and implacable, a blade in her hands. The pearl torque of Nantsovelta glittered whitely around her slender neck.

The guards halted, for both Rhodri and Bedwyr stood confident and unyielding. And they knew what a Dewin was capable of.

"Tangwen," Rhodri said to his granddaughter. "Release Myrrdin."

Tangwen, her dagger drawn, stepped forward to do her grandfather's bidding. She kept her face carefully calm, but inside she was exalting. At last. The day had come when she renounced her father and all his terrible works. The day had finally come when honor was once again restored to her family.

She knew the price of restoring honor. She had always known it. When she had first faced this it had broken her heart. How many nights had she wept for what she knew must be done?

Until tonight, when she had come face to face with her grandfather, she had always thought that she must be the one to punish her father. But Rhodri had claimed that honor for himself, and Tangwen had been glad to let him, glad to be spared the final act she had dreaded.

Briefly she remembered the moment earlier this evening that Bedwyr had come to her, telling her that she must gather her things and come with him. She had stared at him, unable to believe that freedom had come for her at last, and Bedwyr had taken his first kiss from her and it had been sweet, so sweet. She had followed Bedwyr as he spirited them to the stables, saddled her horse, and lead her from Caer Gwynt.

Bedwyr had brought her to a small house not far from the fortress. Neuad had been waiting for her. Morrigan's Dewin had greeted her warmly and Tangwen had eagerly asked about her friend. Neuad had told her that Morrigan was well and that Tangwen would see her soon.

"You are getting me out of Tegeingl?" Tangwen had asked. "Why now?"

"Because someone has come for you, to take the honor of your family back, to take you with him."

And she knew, then, that what Arday had told her days before was true. She knew him the instant she saw him. His hair was fading to silver but strands of reddish-gold still shone through. His blue eyes warmed at the sight of her. He had spread his arms and she had, without a moment's hesitation, launched herself into them. Her granda had come for her. At last.

Now she walked forward confidently, knowing that Rhodri, Bedwyr, and Neuad were behind her. She had almost reached Myrrdin when one of the guards sprang into her path. Quick as thought she thrust her dagger beneath his shining spear, burying it into the guard's belly. Hot, coppery blood spilled over her hand. She pulled the blade from the guard's guts as the man went down.

There was a moment—a brief span of time before the others went into action, when everything seemed to stand still. Her father's eyes were wide with fear. Myrrdin's dark eyes shone with pity. The guard's dying moan rattled in his throat.

And she, Tangwen ur Madoc var Bri, shamed daughter of a traitor, soon to be orphaned this night, exalted in the blood that stained her hands. Exalted in the blow she had finally struck for her country. Exalted as she lifted her face to the starry sky, and heard, from far off, the call of hunting horns blowing as the Wild Hunt rode the night.

Madoc gasped as his daughter killed the captain of the guard with a smile on her lovely face. Rhodri, Neuad, and Bedwyr leapt forward, making short work of the remaining three guards. It all seemed to happen so fast, too fast for Madoc to run.

Tangwen cut Myrrdin's bounds with her bloody dagger and the old man turned to Madoc. Quickly Bedwyr, Tangwen, Neuad, and Myrrdin surrounded Madoc, preventing him from fleeing.

In the sudden silence, the sound of Rhodri's boots on the cobblestones as he made his way to stand before his son echoed like the sound of doom. Madoc knew that surely, irrevocably, death stood in front of him. And there would be no reprieve.

Far, far above him he thought he heard a faint sound of hunting horns riding the back of Taran's winds. The cry of a hawk that has sighted its prey rang in his ears. He raised his eyes to the blade that his father lifted high overhead. And though he was a coward, he could not close his eyes, could not look away, as his death descended toward him, glittering silver steel and black blood.

The blade buried itself in his chest. And still he could not take his eyes from his father's face. He sank to his knees, the hilt of his father's sword moving in time to the beat of his dying heart. A night breeze lightly touched his face as if in farewell. He tried to speak, tried to say something of his regret, but it was too late.

Darkness filled his eyes and he blindly fell forward onto the street, his life's blood pooling on the cobblestones.

MYRRDIN KNELT BY Madoc's body, his hand searching for a pulse. He sighed and rose to his feet. "He is dead."

"May Taran's Wind take your soul to Gwlad Yr Haf, my son," Rhodri whispered. "And may it be long and long before you are returned to Kymru."

Tangwen took her grandfather's hand in hers. Rhodri laid his other hand on her bright hair and stroked it.

"What now?" Tangwen asked. "Where do we go?"

"You and your grandfather will go to Queen Morrigan in Cemais. Accompanied by Bedwyr and Neuad," Myrrdin answered.

"Accompanied by Bedwyr," Neuad said firmly to Myrrdin. "For I am accompanying you."

Myrrdin stared at Neuad, his mouth agape. "What do you mean?" he asked weakly.

"I mean, I am not letting you out of my sight. I will go where you go."

Myrrdin noticed that Bedwyr was struggling not to laugh. And that even Rhodri, his old friend, appeared to be grinning.

"By the way," Neuad went on, "exactly where are we going?"

"I am going to Cadair Idris to await Arthur's orders. But you—"

"I," Neuad said, raising her voice slightly, "am going there, too."

"You are not!"

"I am. Do you really think that I am going to let you get away from me again?"

Myrrdin opened his mouth to argue with her, to insist that she stay away from him, to deny that he wished her to do otherwise. But Neuad's blue eyes were on his and what he saw in them made his heart skip a beat.

"Neuad," he said quietly. "You are half my age."

"So what?" she asked.

He wanted to answer her. Wanted to tell her why that was important, but for some reason he was having trouble breathing. And a great deal of difficulty remembering just where the problem lay.

Neuad, her golden hair flowing over her shoulder, stepped forward and took Myrrdin's face in her slender hands. "Kiss me, Myrrdin," she demanded.

His breath caught in his throat. All thoughts of how this was foolish flew from his head as he breathed in the scent of her.

"Don't argue with me, Myrrdin. And don't make me beg," she murmured. "For I am done waiting for you."

And Myrrdin was done waiting, too. He bent his head and fastened his lips on hers. He drank in her sweetness, her beauty, her freshness, and her love. And when he at last lifted his head it was Neuad that was breathless.

"Oh, my," Neuad breathed as she clung to him. "Oh, my, my, my."

Myrrdin smiled down at her. "You told me to have done with waiting. And so I have."

"You have indeed," she said, her eyes bright.

Myrrdin lifted his face to the night sky and cast his thought south. Too far away for another mere Dewin to hear him, he knew that Arthur, he who had the strength of all the Dewin of Kymru, would be able to.

It is done, High King. Madoc is dead at the hand of his father. Princess Tangwen is safe and will go to your sister in Cemais.

And Arthur answered, clear and strong. *Well done, my teacher. Return to Cadair Idris as soon as you can.*

I bring with me another. Myrrdin's Mind-Voice was almost hesitant.

She is welcome.

You—you knew?

I knew she would not wait for you forever. Give my best to Neuad ur Hetwin, who has caught her quarry at last.

Arthur's bright laughter echoed in Myrrdin's head, mingling with the fading sound of hunting horns overhead in the jeweled night sky.

Chapter Eleven

Sycharth, Kingdom of Ederynion &
Eiodel, Gwytheryn, Kymru
Bedwen Mis, 500

Suldydd, Cynyddu Wythnos—early evening

The thin crescent of the waxing moon wavered overhead, obscured by the twisted branches that laced Rhiannon's view of the darkened sky as she made her way through the forest.

Somewhere deep in these woods just outside of Sycharth an owl hooted. Here and there she heard things scurrying in the thick underbrush, although she herself made very little sound as she homed in on the clearing where the man who held her heart waited.

She had seen him on the Wind-Ride, slumped next to a tiny campfire. She had not been able to see his face, for it was sunk on his breast as though far too heavy for him to hold up. But she had known that it was he. Would she not know him anywhere, at any time? Not by her eyes alone, or her Dewin-Sight, but by her spirit, by the leap in her heat she would know him—now and always.

As she swiftly made her way through the woods she thought on all that had happened in Kymru in just the last seven days. For events were moving quickly, now that Arthur had chosen to set them in motion.

Queen Elen of Ederynion had been rescued and, along with Regan, her Dewin, had been safely brought out of Dinmael. Elen and her brother, Prince Lludd, were together again and making the necessary preparations as directed by Arthur. Prince Rhiwallon of Rheged had also been a member of the party to rescue Elen, and he remained with them. Rhiannon guessed that the Prince had fallen victim to Elen's unpredictable charm. General Talorcan had chosen to go with the fleeing queen, for love of Regan. And Rhiannon was glad, for she had known Talorcan since she had met him in Corania, and knew him for what he was. For he was what the Kymri called Dewin, what the Coranians called a witch, and his gifts would never have come to full fruition in Corania. Even now Regan and Talorcan were on their way to Cadair Idris, at Arthur's orders.

In the ensuing melee the two Druids, Ceindrech and Iago, had died, perishing so that the others could escape. Aergol, Ceindrech's lover, had been devastated at the news, as had the couple's son, Menw.

In Prydyn, General Penda had secretly allowed Cadell, King Rhoram's Dewin, to escape Arberth. When Penda discovered that Ellywen, King Rhoram's Druid had been aiding the Cerddorian, he had her collared and sent to Afalon. But he had carefully ensured that only two guards would accompany her. Thus Rhoram and his captain, Achren, had easily rescued Ellywen soon after she had been escorted out of Arberth.

Penda was another man whom Rhiannon had met while in Corania, and she was glad to see evidence that Penda's soul had not yet died under his bondage to the Golden Man. She knew that Penda would, perhaps, pay—and pay dearly—for his actions. Although on the surface nothing could be proven against Penda, Havgan would probably guess the truth.

In Rheged, poor Queen Enid had been rescued from her captivity by her brother, Owein, and her former betrothed, Prince Geriant of Prydyn. The party had escaped the city and made their way to Maenor Deilo, where they waited with the rest of Owein's Cerddorian for Arthur's next orders. In the process of freeing Elen, General Baldred had been killed by Queen Sanon. Rhiannon still marveled that Sanon had done such a thing, for the young girl she had known before the war would never have done so. And the young woman she had been after the war would not have done so either—for Sanon had been incapacitated by grief for her dead betrothed, and Rhiannon had not thought Sanon would ever recover.

But recover she had, and joined her life with Owein, the man who had loved her for so long.

It remained to be seen what would happen to Enid. For Owein's sister had been through torture almost unimaginable at the hands of her husband, Morcant Whledig, the false King of Rheged. It was obvious to everyone that Prince Geriant still loved Enid, but it was anyone's guess what there might be left of the girl he loved.

In Gwynedd, King Madoc was at last dead—at the hands of Rhodri, his own father. Princess Tangwen and Rhodri were even now joining Queen Morrigan in Cemais, accompanied by Bedwyr, Morrigan's lieutenant. And, in a surprise move, Neuad, Morrigan's Dewin, had refused to return to Cemais, insisting on accompanying Myrrdin to Cadair Idris. For Neuad, although half Myrrdin's age, had been in love with the former Ardewin of Kymru for many years and had simply decided that she would no longer be ignored. Myrrdin had been shocked and upset at first, but was, apparently, quickly getting over the embarrassment he had always professed to feel at Neuad's obvious feelings for him.

Soon, very soon, Rhiannon thought, as she neared the clearing she sought, Kymru would once again belong to the Kymri. The Y Dawnus held captive on Afalon would be freed. The Archdruid would be brought down and the Druids would again swear their allegiance to Kymru. Havgan would face Arthur in the final battle. And that was a battle Arthur would win, for Havgan would have only the Coranians he had here in Kymru to help him fight. For Arthur had ensured that no word of the need for reinforcements would be sent to Corania. The coasts of Kymru were watched, and all of Havgan's ships were burned. Arthur would defeat Havgan's Coranians and send any survivors packing.

Again, but from closer this time, an owl hooted in the dark wood. She saw the glow of a tiny campfire and, still moving silently, made her way toward it. From the fringes of the underbrush she surveyed the clearing.

Gwydion lay on the ground next to the fire, his face hidden as it rested on his outstretched arms. The fire cackled and sang, darting this way and that, illuminating him one moment and cloaking him in shadow the next. Gwydion's dark cloak was torn and dirty. His tunic and trousers of black were dusty and stained with old blood.

With tears in her eyes, she entered the clearing and knelt by Gwydion's prone body. She reached out and touched his shoulder, pulling him towards her. He muttered something, then laid still on the cold ground. She put her arms around him and settled his head in her lap, stroking his thick, dark hair. His upturned face, illuminated by the fire, was almost skeletal. Dark circles surrounded his closed, bruised eyelids. Shallow cuts and purple bruises covered his sweat-soaked face. Blisters and reddened, peeling skin surrounded his neck, showing where an enaid-dal had rested. His lips were cracked and blistered. He muttered again, and she cradled his head in her arms, stooping down to kiss his brow.

His eyes opened. His pupils were so dilated that his eyes seemed dark and full of shadows instead of the silvery gaze that she knew so well. He narrowed his eyes as he tried to focus on her face above him.

"Rhiannon," he whispered. "Rhiannon."

"Yes, Gwydion. Yes, I am here," she said softly.

"No," he rasped. "No. Run, Rhiannon. Run. It's a trap."

"Hush," she murmured. "Hush."

"No," he sobbed. "Run. Oh, please, run."

Gwydion had been wondering in and out of his dreams for so long, he was no longer sure what was real and what was not. But when he saw Rhiannon's face hovering above him he understood with horrifying clarity what was about to happen.

He had called her. He had not dreamed that, he now knew. In a drugged haze, in his weakness and confusion, he had Mind-Called to her, had begged her to come to him. Worse yet, he had begged her to come alone.

And she had. Oh, she had. He had thought that the worst had already happened to him. But when he knew that she would be captured, and thought of what they would do to her, he knew that the worst was yet to come.

She must go. She must. But he could not make her understand.

"Please," he whispered. "Please run."

"Hush," she murmured again, stroking his dark, sweat soaked hair. "Hush."

And then he saw it, though he was almost blinded by the bright light of the fire, by his sickness and grief, by his terror for her. He saw movement behind her, and knew that it was far, far too late.

"Run!" he tried to scream. But it came out only in a despairing whisper.

The sound of an axe rasping as it was drawn from its holder seemed very loud in the silent forest. At the sound Rhiannon half-turned to look behind her.

There stood a Coranian warrior, his axe in his hands. The warrior raised the weapon high in the air. In the moment before the axe began its descent, Gwydion tried to push Rhiannon out of the way. But he was too weak, and too slow. Inexplicably she did not move, waiting unflinching for the axe to strike. He did not understand why she simply sat there, looking up as her death suddenly began to speed toward her.

Her green eyes did not even blink as the sound of steel clashing on steel rang throughout the clearing, as the axe that had been coming for her life was deflected by another bright blade that seemed to appear from nowhere. Yet Rhiannon did not appear to be surprised at all.

The sword shimmered in the light of the fire as though made of fire itself. The hilt was an eagle with eyes of bloodstone and wings of onyx. Emerald, pearl, sapphire, and opal flashed and shone. The hand that gripped the hilt was sinewy and brown, with long, tapering fingers.

Gwydion knew that blade—Caladfwlch, Hard Gash, the sword of the High King. And he knew whose hand gripped that blade, and he sobbed in relief.

For Arthur ap Uthyr var Ygraine had come. High King Arthur was here and Rhiannon was saved.

Caladfwlch, which had stopped the Coranian warrior's axe in midair, glittered as Arthur pushed the axe aside and sent the warrior staggering back. At that moment twenty Coranian warriors stepped out from the forest, their axes drawn. And Llwyd Cilcoed, the Dewin who had so enjoyed torturing Gwydion, stepped from the trees, his robe of silver and sea green shimmering, with a smile of anticipation on his face.

But before Gwydion even had time to fear for the lives of these two he loved best, Arthur and Rhiannon, the clearing suddenly seemed full of armed Kymric warriors.

He recognized Queen Elen of Ederynion and her brother, Prince Lludd. He saw Elen's captain, Angharad, and Talhearn, her Bard. He recognized Emrys, Angharad's lieutenant, and Alun Cilcoed, the Lord of Arystli, as well as Prince Rhiwallon of Rheged.

Arthur's blade, indeed the blades of all the Kymri, flashed and sparked as they met the axes of the Coranian warriors. One warrior went down with Queen Elen's sword in his guts. She smiled as she slowly pulled out the blade, then struck him a second time. In the firelight her white tunic glowed as though sheathed in precious pearls.

Prince Lludd cried out in triumph as another Coranian warrior went down beneath his blade. Angharad ducked beneath the vicious swing of an axe, then pulled her dagger from her boot. She half rose, sinking the dagger in the warrior's gut, shearing through the protective byrnie.

Alun Cilcoed, a look of determination on his face, waded through the melee, making straight for his brother, Llwyd Cilcoed.

Talhearn, old as he was, actually sank his blade in the back of the neck of a warrior that had been menacing Emrys. Emrys grinned and briefly saluted the Bard as he whirled, sinking his sword in the spine of another warrior. Prince Rhiwallon was laying about him with his blade, bringing warrior after warrior down.

But nothing matched the deadly grace of Arthur and Caladfwlch as man and blade moved through the clearing, meting out justice to the enemies of Kymru. Warrior after warrior faced them and died, falling at Arthur's feet, blood sinking into the waiting, cold earth.

At last the clearing fell silent. The Kymri—Arthur, Elen, Lludd, Angharad, Talhearn, Emrys, and Rhiwallon halted with their bloody blades in their hands. Alun and Llwyd Cilcoed were nowhere to be seen.

Rhiannon, who had drawn a dagger from her boot and guarded Gwydion as he lay too weak to move, crouched down beside him, helping him to sit up. With a tired sigh he allowed himself to lean on her and her arm tightened around his shoulders.

Two worn, dusty boots intruded on his line of sight as he hung his head, trying to focus. He raised his head carefully, looking up at Arthur, who was looking down at him. Arthur crouched down and laid his hand on Gwydion's shoulder. He looked at Gwydion for what seemed like a long time in the shifting firelight. The old scar on Arthur's lean face whitened and faded.

"Uncle," Arthur said, his mouth twitching in what might have been a smile. "Glad I am to see you again."

"Nephew," Gwydion whispered. "I thought Rhiannon—"

"Had come alone," Arthur finished. He shook his head. "We were behind her the entire time. We did not know if Llywd Cilcoed might be Wind-Riding, and would see us, so we had to remain separate from her and well hidden."

"I called to her. I—I did not mean to do it. I told her to come alone."

"But she did not," Arthur said gently. "She told me all about it after you had Wind-Spoken to her. She knew it was a trap."

"How?" Gwydion asked, turning his head to look at Rhiannon.

Her beautiful green eyes glistened and she smiled slightly. "I will tell you later, Gwydion. For now—"

"For now," Alun Cilcoed said as he reentered the clearing with his brother in tow, "we have justice to satisfy."

Llwyd Cilcoed's robe was torn and dirty, mute evidence that his brother's pursuit had been relentless. Propelled across the clearing by his brother, he was brought before Queen Elen. Alun flung Llywd at Elen's feet then drew his dagger.

"My Queen," Alun said formally. "I bring you my traitorous

brother. I bring you your mother's former lover, the man who ran away when she was threatened and so could offer her no comfort before she died. I bring you the man who killed a member of your Cerddorian in order to escape from Angharad's watchful eye. I bring you the man who consorted with Arianrod to capture the Dreamer. I bring you the man who collared the Dreamer, who drugged him and beat him and forced him to play a part in attempting to capture Rhiannon ur Hefeydd. I bring you the man who thought to take them both to the Golden Man, to certain torture and death at his hands."

Queen Elen, her auburn hair gleaming, her blue eyes cold, looked over at her brother. "Lludd, I understand you would not have Llwyd Cilcoed killed when he was first brought to you."

Lludd nodded, his face grim. "You were the Queen of Ederynion, and I did not wish to take from you the pleasure of condemning him yourself."

"In short, you saved him for me."

"I did."

Elen suddenly smiled. "You did well." She turned to Arthur. "High King, you have the first right of justice here. But I ask a boon."

"Ask it, Queen Elen," Arthur said quietly.

"That you let me dispense your justice to Llywd Cilcoed. For the harm he did my mother, and to us."

"First, I have business with this Dewin." Arthur stepped forward until he stood before Llywd. "Llwyd Cilcoed, by the power given me from Elstar, the Ardewin of Kymru, I declare you outcast." Arthur extended Caladfwlch until the tip of the blade touched the silvery torque of pearl around the Dewin's neck. With one swift motion the blade sheared through the torque. Llwyd cried out as the silver necklace fell to the ground. It lay there, gleaming in the light of the fitful moon.

"You are no longer one of the Dewin of Kymru," Arthur said, his voice suddenly huge and powerful in the darkened forest. "Nantsovelta of the Moon, Lady of the Waters, turns her face from you. You no longer belong to her. Your gifts are taken from you."

In the sky above them a sudden cloud flowed over the waxing moon. From far off came the roar of angry, rushing water. The fresh, salt aroma of the distant sea washed into the clearing then receded. Llwyd arched his back in pain and cried out. Then the night became still once again.

Llwyd Cilcoed's eyes widened with horror. He twitched in his brother's hands and all color drained from his face. "You—how could you do that?" the Dewin cried, his voice breaking. "I can not Wind-Ride, or Life-Read! You have changed me."

"Nantsovelta herself has changed you," Arthur said implacably. "She has cast you out. Thus you are no longer Dewin." Arthur sheathed his blade, then stepped back, bowing his head to Elen. "He is now yours to do with as you see fit."

"No!" Llwyd Cilcoed cried, jumping to his feet. His brother grabbed him by the hair and forced him to tip his head back slightly, exposing his throat.

"Be quiet, brother," Alun hissed. "And do homage to your queen."

"Elen," Llywd gasped. "Elen, we have known each other for so many years. Your mother loved me."

"So she did, Llywd Cilcoed," Elen said coldly. "And you repaid that by running away."

"Please—" Llywd whispered. "Please."

"Queen Elen," Alun suddenly said. "I must now beg you for a boon."

Llwyd, dawning hope on his pale face relaxed a fraction.

"Your boon, Alun Cilcoed?" Elen asked.

"This man is my brother," Alun began.

Llwyd Cilcoed relaxed a little bit more in his brother's grip. Confidence began to replace terror on the Dewin's face.

"So he is," Elen agreed.

"And as such—"

"Yes?" Elen asked.

"As such, he is mine to kill."

"No!" Llywd screamed. "No!"

"Very well, Alun," Elen agreed. "He is yours to kill."

At Elen's nod Alun drew the bright blade across his brother's throat. Llywd's despairing scream became a gurgle as blood bubbled from the mortal wound. Slowly, he sank to the ground as blood spewed down his robe and bathed the silver torque at his feet.

Alun stood over his dead brother, the bright blade in his hand dimmed with blood. "You have destroyed our family honor for the last time, little brother," he whispered. Tears ran down his face and fell on his brother's upturned face. "For the last time."

Arthur put a hand on Alun's shoulder. "Lord of Arystli, your family honor is restored to you."

The faint strains of a hunting horn drifted down to them from the night sky as Alun nodded, dashing away the tears with his sleeve. He bent down and wiped the blade clean on his brother's robe, then sheathed it in his boot top.

Gwydion felt a gray wave of tiredness, of sickness, wash over him. His head spun and he blinked his eyes rapidly, trying to bring the scene before him back into focus. But he could not. He felt blessed oblivion, a surcease from pain coming for him. But before it took him he reached out his hand and laid it gently against Rhiannon's lovely face.

"Thank you," he rasped.

"Rest, Gwydion," she said and her voice followed him down into the darkness. She was with him, and so he was not afraid.

SIGERRIC WAITED ON the battlements of Eiodel, his eyes following the distant torches that came steadily closer across the plain. The man Havgan had been expecting was at last nearing the Golden Man's dark fortress. He would be here in a few moments, and Sigerric would take the man to his friend.

Friend. That he should still think of Havgan as his friend was almost laughable. Indeed, he would have laughed at that if grief had not welled up in him, closing his throat with unshed tears. For the man who, years ago, he had counted his friend was truly dead and gone, the best in him burned in the flames of his hatred and fear, carried away like ashes on the wind.

He thought of the other four men from Corania who had been

friends of Havgan, sworn as blood brothers. Baldred was dead in Rheged at the hands of the Kymri who had snatched Queen Enid from her prison. Catha was alive in Gwynedd, but in disfavor with Havgan for letting that fool, King Madoc, be killed. Penda, too, was alive in Prydyn, but also in disfavor, for Havgan had guessed that Penda had purposely let the Druid, Ellywen, escape.

And Talorcan—ah, that was the biggest blow of all to Havgan. Talorcan had gone with Queen Elen when she escaped from Dinmael. He had given it all up for love of Regan, one of the witches. Yet Sigerric thought there was more to Talorcan's decision then that. He had long suspected that Talorcan himself was Wiccan, though he had never seen his friend work even the smallest iota of magic. But there had always been something about Talorcan that Sigerric thought suspect.

He closed his eyes briefly and sent up a prayer to Lytir that Talorcan would find what he had always been looking for. For, witch or no, Talorcan was his friend. His true friend, and would always be so, though they would likely never lay eyes on each other again.

He stared off to the northeast where even now, many, many leagues away, outside of the city of Sycharth in Ederynion, Gwydion was laying by a campfire, being used as bait for Rhiannon.

He bent his head in sorrow for what would happen next. Rhiannon would be captured and both she and Gwydion would be brought before Havgan. And, for Havgan, all the hideous tortures in the world that could be inflicted on their helpless bodies and minds would barely begin to satisfy him. The plans he had for Gwydion would be grim enough. But Sigerric knew what Havgan would do to Rhiannon. She would die beneath Havgan, naked and bound, his hands taking the last breath from her violated body. Havgan would force Gwydion to watch. And then Gwydion, Havgan's false blood brother, would die slowly, hideously, one piece of his body removed at a time until he was nothing more than a bloody husk. And then, perhaps, if Gwydion were lucky, Havgan would let the Dreamer die.

The torches held in the hands of the select group of Havgan's warriors showed the progress of the small party as it neared the closed gates. Horses tossed their bridles, neighing as they came closer to Havgan's fortress. Overhead the stars glittered and the waxing moon shone brightly, hung in the sky like a sliver of luminescent pearl. Sigerric signaled and the gate was opened.

The small group rode through. Six warriors, gathered in a circle around a seventh rider, dismounted. One warrior helped the seventh rider off his horse. The seventh rider, wrapped in a voluminous cloak, nodded his thanks. The warrior led the cloaked and hooded figure up the stairs to the battlements where Sigerric waited.

"General Sigerric," the warrior said, bending his head low. "I have brought to you the one you sent for."

The figure in the cloak bowed also, then threw back his hood, revealing a wrinkled visage. Scanty gray hair framed his almost toothless old face in wisps. But the old man's eyes were a bright, alert blue.

"Your name?" Sigerric asked.

"I am called Torgar," the old man answered.

"Then, Torgar, my name is Sigerric."

"Sigerric son of Sigefrith, the Alder of Apuldre. I know you, General. There is not a man in Corania who does not."

"Torgar, do you know why you have been brought here?"

"Great lord, I do not. I have done no wrong."

"True. You were not brought here to answer for any wrong. But rather to aid our Bana."

"The Warleader? Havgan the Golden? How could I ever be of aid to one as all-powerful as him?"

"You shall see." Sigerric dismissed the warrior and motioned for Torgar to follow him. The two men made their way across the battlements until they came upon a golden figure at the wall, facing north across the plain, staring out at Cadair Idris, the glowing mountain that soared up from the earth's breast, reaching to the sparkling sky.

Torchlight glittered off of Havgan's golden tunic and shimmered off of the rubies that trimmed his rich clothing. His honey-blond hair glowed in the flames and, as he turned to face them, his amber eyes seemed like the fierce eyes of a hawk that has its prey in its sight at last.

Torgar bowed until he almost touched the ground.

"Rise," Havgan said.

Torgar groaned a little as he straightened and Sigerric sprang to help the old man. "Your pardon, I beg," Torgar said as he rose. "Old bones."

"Yes," Havgan said dryly. "I am sure. Torgar, do you know what we see across the plain here?"

"I have heard tell of this. Cadair Idris."

"It glows in the night, Torgar."

"It does that, lord."

"It is well that it glows, but it must glow for me, Torgar. For me, and no other."

"So it should, lord," Torgar agreed, his old eyes bright. "So it should."

"But it does not."

"Nay, lord. It does not. And what can one such as I do for you to make it so?"

"Torgar, did you know I grew up in a little fishing village?"

"Nay, I did not know that. Whereabouts?" the old man asked curiously.

"The village of Dorfas, on the shores of the Weal of Coran."

"I know that place, lord. Good fishing."

"My mother, Torgar," Havgan said softly, "used to call me her gift from the sea."

"Ah. Yes, they got many 'gifts' in Dorfas," Torgar said comfortably. "Good harvesting there off the rocks, after storms. For many a ship has gone to ground at that place."

For a moment the night seemed to take on an unnatural silence, as though the land of Kymru itself held its breath. Havgan hesitated then shrugged as though throwing off something that weighted him down, some knowledge that he did not wish to have.

"And you, Torgar?" Havgan asked. "Have you always been a sailor?"

"Ah, ever since I was a young lad." Then Torgar recited proudly:

"This did say my mother;

That for me should be brought
A ship and shapely oars,
To share the life of warriors
To stand up in the stem and
Steer the goodly galley,
Hold her to the harbor
And hew down those who meet us."

Torgar shook his head. "I was a young wisp of a boy when I followed Aelle down the River Saefern to take the kingdom of Dere for Corania. Those were great days. And there have been none like them since, until now. The years between now and then I spent fishing in Clastburh, remembering the days of glory and war. And then we heard your call, to destroy the witches of Kymru. I took service in your navy and never once looked back." The old man's eyes were fierce with memory and as he spoke he seemed to stand taller and prouder than before.

"I am reminded, Torgar, of that poem written by Sigerad, the first Archpreost of Lytir. He was sailor in his youth, before his brother proclaimed him head of the new church."

"I know that one, lord," Torgar said excitedly. And then they both recited Sigerad's poem together:

"Now 'tis most like as if we fare in ships
On the ocean flood, over the water cold,
Driving our vessels through the spacious seas
With horses of the deep. A perilous way is this
Of boundless waves, and there are stormy seas
On which we toss her in this feeble world
O'er the deep paths.

Ours was a sorry plight
Until at last we sailed unto the land,
Over the troubled main. Help came to us
That brought us to the haven of Lytir,
That we might know e'en from the vessels deck

Where we must bind with anchorage secure
Our ocean steeds, old stallions of the waves."

They were both silent for a moment. Sigerric said nothing as the two men—one young and golden, the other old and weather-beaten—thought their own thoughts.

"Torgar," Havgan said after a moment. "Ah, Torgar, you are a man after my own heart."

Torgar grinned, a nearly toothless grin. "Great lord, you are a man worth serving. This I tell you true. Lytir himself must admire you."

"Our God may do that, but he surely expects results also," Havgan said coolly. "And I mean to give them to Him."

Torgar's smile faded and his blue eyes became earnest. "In what way can I serve you, lord? Why have you brought me here? What can I do?"

"Torgar, you can do what you do best—sail."

"Where to?"

"Home. To Corania."

Torgar was silent for a moment, his blue eyes serious. "I can sail anywhere I have a mind to, in anything that will float. But how in the name of Lytir can I even get on the sea? First those Cerddorian burned all our boats. Then, when we built new ones, they burned those to a crisp. It is said that the blasted witches have eyes everywhere. The few times ships were built and attempted to leave Kymru they were destroyed utterly—and all on board lost."

"I am fully aware of all that, Torgar," Havgan said sharply.

"Still," Torgar went on, as if he had not really heard Havgan at all. "Still, if I could only get in a boat and get off the island, I could make it."

"In how big a boat?" Havgan asked.

"Oh, not a large one," Torgar said, making vague measurements with his hands. "A rowboat would do, as long as it had a small sail."

"A rowboat!" Sigerric exclaimed. "You would attempt to cross the sea to Corania in a rowboat?"

"Oh," Torgar said easily. "It could be done. Given sufficient water and food. Nothing fancy on the food, now," he said confidentially. "I can't eat the way I used to anymore."

"Really, Havgan," Sigerric sputtered. "You don't mean to listen to this. This is nonsense."

"It's not nonsense," Torgar said indignantly. "And I will prove it to you, if the Warleader gives me a chance."

"I will give you that chance, Torgar," Havgan murmured as he half turned to eye Cadair Idris. "I will indeed."

"Havgan, you are not serious," Sigerric exclaimed.

"When you get across the sea, go to Athelin with this token," Havgan said, ignoring Sigerric completely. He took a ruby ring from his finger and placed it in Torgar's hands. "Show it to the guards at the city gates and they will see to it that you are taken to Aesc, the Emperor's brother. Mind you, you will tell your business to Aesc only. No one else."

"Yes, lord," Torgar said, examining the ring closely.

"And do not, Torgar," Havgan said quietly, "even think of betraying me. You will go to Aesc and tell him what I want. If you do not, if you attempt to cheat me, I will return to Corania just to hunt you down. And I will. Believe that."

Torgar swallowed hard. "I believe that, lord." Then the old sailor drew himself up to his full height, almost able to straighten his old spine. "And there is no need to threaten me," he said with a modicum of dignity. "I will do this for you—and for Lytir, my God."

"See that you do, Torgar," Havgan said softly. "See that you do."

Chapter Twelve

Cadair Idris, Gwytheryn &
Dinmael, Kingdom of Ederynion, Kymru
Eiddew Mis, 500

Addiendydd, Cynyddu Wythnos—morning

As he stepped out of the grim forest and into the golden meadow Gwydion laughed and flung out his hands as he lifted his face to the warming sun.

He danced across the meadow, whirling among the tall, green grasses. Fiery rockrose and lemon-yellow globeflowers, dark blue forget-me-nots and white lily of the valley dotted the emerald plain. The heady aroma of wallflowers and violets scented the clean air. A spring bubbled across the plain, laughing and sparkling, beckoning him. He plunged his hands into the cool, clear water then flung out this arms, spilling droplets onto the grasses where they lay like glittering diamonds.

From far away he heard a hunting horn and he welcomed the sound. He knew whose presence the horn preceeded and he was not afraid.

White hunting dogs with red ears bounded across the plain, baying and gamboling, headed straight for him. Gwydion stood still and let them come. They halted before him and he held out his hand. The lead dog stepped forward and gravely sniffed the offered hand. Then he barked once, twice, three times, and the pack halted, then lay down, panting.

Two horses cantered across the plain. One glistened white as pearl and the other black as onyx. The rider of the white horse sat his mount proudly. Antlers sprung from his forehead. His chest was bare and his breeches were made of deerskin. His leather boots were studded with glittering topaz. His face was quiet, but his topaz owl-eyes glittered and his lips seemed as though they might be ready to curve in a smile.

The rider of the black mount was dressed in a glowing shift of pure white. A silver belt encircled her slim waist. Her dark hair cascaded down her back, held back from her face by a band of amethysts. Her amethyst eyes smiled.

Far overhead an eagle called out fiercely and began to spiral down from the clear, blue sky. The eagle screamed again then swooped down, coming to rest on Gwydion's outstretched arm.

"I greet you, Arderydd, High Eagle of Kymru," Gwydion said gravely as he inclined his head to the huge bird. "And I greet you, also, Cerrunnos, Lord of the Wild Hunt, and Cerridwen, Queen of the Wood."

"Well met, Gwydion ap Awst," Cerridwen said her voice musical and light, like the ringing of tiny, silver bells. "For the first time I could almost believe you are happy to see us."

"For the first time he is happy," Cerrunnos amended, his unblinking owl-like eyes focused on Gwydion.

"You speak truly, Cerrunnos," Gwydion replied. "For the first time in more years than I can remember, I am happy."

"Because?" Cerridwen asked, although Gwydion thought she already knew the answer.

"Because I am free at last. Free from the bondage I put myself in for so many years. Free to love she whom I was always meant to love. I saw it truly, finally, when Llwyd Cilcoed captured me and imprisoned both my body and my mind."

"Yes?" Cerridwen prompted.

"All these years I kept her away from me, saying I did so for my duty. But I was wrong. It was not my duty. I was afraid."

"And your adherence to your duty now?" Cerrunnos asked pointedly.

"Is as strong as it has ever been. I have faithfully performed the tasks that you asked of me so long ago. I protected Arthur from both the traitors in our midst and from the invaders. I journeyed to the land of the enemy, to spy for Kymru. I have journeyed throughout Kymru with the others and helped to find the four Treasures. I brought Arthur to Cadair Idris, along with the Treasures, and prepared him to undergo the Tynged Mawr. Now Arthur is High King of Kymru. My task is not yet done. I know this, for Kymru is still held by the enemy. But the task is nearing its end. And it is only now that I discover it was never a reason to be alone. Only an excuse."

"And so, Gwydion ap Awst var Celemon, you have learned the truth. What will you do now?" Cerridwen asked.

"I will lay my heart at the feet of the woman I love. I will beg her to forgive me for taking so very, very long to bring my heart to her. And then I will do all I know how to do to free Kymru. But, before I die, I will love. And not be afraid."

"Very well met, then, Dreamer," Cerrunnos said. "Very well met, indeed. Then you are ready to return to the world in which you live. Your body lies in Cadair Idris, under the care of she whom you love. She has nursed you these many days. To her you owe your life, for with less expert care you might have died."

"To her I owe everything." Gwydion said simply. "And if she will let me I will spend the rest of my life with her, doing all I can to make her happy."

"Then you are ready to return. Listen, now, for she senses you are going back. Go to her, Dreamer of Kymru," Cerridwen said gently. "And know that our good wishes go to you both."

"And, remember, when we are called next, we will be ready. The Wild Hunt will ride again in defense of Kymru," Cerrunnos said, "when the one who was meant to call us calls. And when the one who is meant to lead us takes his place at our head."

"And who is meant to call you to our aid?" Gwydion asked. "And who is to lead you?"

"They will know when the time comes," Cerrunnos said. He brought the hunting horn to his lips and sounded a note. The challenge rose through the air. The eagle launched itself from Gwydion's arm with a fierce cry and spiraled up into the sky. The dogs bayed and launched themselves into the sky after the eagle.

The white and black horses leapt up after them.

Gwydion watched until the Hunt was no more than specks high overhead. He lifted his head at the sound of his name called across the wind. She called him, he knew. She called him and he would answer.

He opened his eyes slowly. Above him her beautiful face hovered, her green eyes glowing in the soft golden light. The bed he lay in was covered with a spread of red edged in onyx. A banner of a raven with opal eyes shimmered on the far wall. Wardrobes of polished oak lined one wall. Next to his bed was a small table, covered now with bottles and a few golden goblets chased with opals. The door to the chamber was golden and the symbol of the Dreamers was outlined there in fiery opals. He blinked again, and knew that he was in the Dreamer's chambers at Cadair Idris.

"How long?" he whispered.

"Fourteen days in all," she answered as she wrung fresh water from a soft cloth and laid it gently on his forehead. "Four days here from Sycharth and ten days in Cadair Idris."

"It was very bad, then."

"Very bad indeed," she said. "You were suffering from lead poisoning from the collar. For that I have been giving you a tincture of Penduran's Rose, which also helped to reopen the pathways in your brain for your gifts. I believe if you take a few moments to check, you will find that your gifts have fully returned."

He nodded, for he could tell she was right. "And what else?"

"The mistletoe poisoning was the worst. That was what Llywd Cilcoed kept making you drink, to keep you disoriented. I gave you hawthorn to counteract its effects on your heart. And valerian for the convulsions."

"Very efficient," he murmured.

"But for a time, nonetheless, we thought we had lost you." Her lips tightened as her voice wavered slightly and she looked away for a moment, unwilling to meet his eyes.

"Rhiannon," he began.

"But you turned the corner a few days ago," she continued,

wiping his face with the cloth. "And I am doubly glad you woke today, for I predicted you would."

"Did you now?" he asked, his brows quirked. He smiled and she blinked down at him, startled.

"Gwydion, do you know you just smiled?"

"I do," he said, and laughed softly.

She frowned for a moment, clearly puzzled. "I have made you a good broth. And you are to drink every drop," she said and she rose and went to the fire that crackled on the hearth. A small pot hung over the flames on a spit. She swung the spit out over the hearth and ladled the broth into a golden bowl. She brought the bowl back to the bed and sat down again in her chair. She helped him to sit up, propping him up with pillows. Then she spooned the broth into his mouth.

He ate obediently, willing to bide his time and regain at least a measure of his strength. And for all that he had just woken up he did feel almost strong again. The warm, tasty broth made him feel even better.

"I could almost get up," Gwydion said as he swallowed the last bit. "I feel strong enough."

"Then you may get up," Rhiannon said. "But not for long. It won't take much to tire you."

"I am sure you are right," he agreed, and was rewarded with another tiny frown when he did not argue with her. "I am wearing something, aren't I?"

She laughed. "You are wearing a pair of very comfortable breeches."

"Ah. And who dressed me in those?"

"I wish I could say I did, but it was Arthur."

"I wish you could say you did, too," he replied. He flung back the covers and swung his feet to the floor. He rose slowly, but did not feel dizzy. "I feel surprisingly good," he said as he took a few steps.

Rhiannon shadowed him, ready to put out a hand if he fell. For that he almost felt like falling, just to have her hold on to him. And perhaps he would have, if only Cariadas had not chosen that moment to burst into the chamber.

His daughter flew across the room, laughing to see him on his feet, and threw herself in his arms. But he was not as strong as usual, and he tottered back. Rhiannon grabbed his arm to steady him but missed and he and Cariadas ended up on the floor, their fall cushioned by a soft rug woven in red and black.

"Da!" she cried, clutching him around the neck. "Da, you're alive!"

"For the moment," Gwydion croaked, loosening her grip somewhat so he could breathe. He stroked her bright, red-gold hair and tears came to his eyes as she sobbed.

"Oh, Da, we didn't know if you would be all right. Rhiannon kept insisting that you were too stubborn and too mean to die, but I was so afraid."

"Did she?" Gwydion asked as he raised his eyes to Rhiannon over Cariadas' bowed head.

Rhiannon looked back at him steadily. "I certainly did," she said crisply. "Cariadas, dearest, perhaps you would help your da up."

"Oh, Da," Cariadas said, laughing and crying at the same time. "I'm sorry!"

"Don't be," Gwydion said as she helped him to his feet. "It is so wonderful to see you again, I don't mind a bit. I missed you, daughter. Very much."

Cariadas' brows raised at that. "Da, are you feeling all right? I mean—"

"I know what you mean, my dear," Gwydion said gently. "And, yes, I feel very fine indeed." He smiled and Cariadas looked even more shocked.

His daughter turned to Rhiannon, her face anxious. "Are you sure he will be all right? This is all very—"

"Odd," Rhiannon finished for her. "Yes, it certainly is. And, no, I don't know how long this will last."

"For the rest of our lives," Gwydion said softly. "Believe me."

Meirwydd, Cynyddu Wythnos—early evening

Gwydion slept most of that night and a good deal of the next day, waking occasionally to eat. With every passing moment he felt stronger. Cariadas stayed with him, saying Rhiannon needed to rest, as she had hardly left his side at all in the last two weeks.

Toward evening he rose and took the bath they had prepared for him. He luxuriated in the warm water, occasionally humming a tune to himself as he trimmed his dark beard. He toweled himself off and dressed in the clothes they had laid out for him—a tunic and trousers of black with opals at the hem and throat. His hair was held at the nape of his neck with a golden clasp chased with opals. His boots were black leather and opals glittered at the turned-down cuffs. He fastened the Dreamer's torque of gold and opals around his neck then went to the door and opened it.

Rhiannon stood there, her hand out to grasp the door handle. She was dressed in a gown of sea green over a kirtle of white. A girdle of glowing pearls encircled her slim waist. Her dark hair was held back from her face by a band of pearls and her Dewin's torque of silver and pearl was clasped around her slender neck.

For a moment he simply stared at her, drinking in her beauty. Her green eyes softened slightly as she returned his gaze. He crossed to her side and held out his arm, never taking his eyes from hers. She smiled and laid her hand on the crook of his arm.

"Arthur and the rest are waiting in Brenin Llys to welcome you back to the land of the living," she said.

"The only welcome I need is yours," Gwydion said quietly. His quicksilver eyes gazed into her emerald ones. He reached out and gently touched her face, his thumb lightly brushing her lips.

He was about to say—and do—more, much more, but just then Cariadas appeared on the landing. And though he loved his daughter dearly he momentarily wished her leagues away. Cariadas smiled at them both and then took his other arm.

"Arthur is waiting for you," Cariadas said.

"I am surprised he has not come by to see me," Gwydion replied.

"Oh, but he has," Cariadas protested. "He was by your bedside every day until yesterday, when you regained consciousness."

"Was he now?" Gwydion murmured thoughtfully.

To his surprise even descending five levels of stairs did not tire him. When they reached the bottom level Gwydion saw that the golden doors to Brenin Llys, the High King's Hall, were flung open. A soft golden glow emanated through the archway, spilling warm light into the corridor.

He stood for a moment in the archway, Cariadas on one side and Rhiannon on the other. Light played across the glittering walls and pillars sheathed in gleaming gold. Jewels winked from the banners that hung within each of the eight shallow alcoves—azure sapphires and verdant emeralds, glowing pearls and fiery opals. Trees shimmered in each alcove—hawthorn and birch, hazel and rowan, ash and alder, oak and aspen.

In the center of the hall a golden fountain bubbled and laughed, spraying tiny droplets of clear water into the golden air. Next to the fountain the Four Treasures gleamed. At the far end of the hall eight steps led up to a raised dais. Each step was covered with jewels—the first step topaz and the next amethyst, followed by emerald, pearl, ruby, onyx, opal, and sapphire. The throne on the dais was shaped like an eagle, with outstretched wings forming the high back of the golden chair. A tree of yew and another of hazel stood behind the throne.

His first impression was that the hall was filled with people, and that they were all looking at him. For a moment he almost wanted to turn and run, for it seemed like a very long time since he had been around so many people. But a second glance told him that these were all people that he knew. More importantly, he was aware that he was happy to see them again, and—for the first time in his long tenure as Dreamer of Kymru—actually looking forward to greeting them.

He first passed Elidyr and Elstar, the Master Bard and the Ardewin with their two sons, Llywelyn and Cynfar. Elstar stepped forward and softly kissed his cheek, while Elidyr smiled as their two sons sketched a bow. Instead of merely inclining his head as he might have done in the past, Gwydion halted. He softly returned Elstar's kiss, then grasped Elidyr's hand. He briefly touched the shoulders of Llywelyn and Cynfar, these two who would one day be King Arthur's Great Ones.

Next he greeted Aergol and the Druids that clustered around him—Yrth, Aldur, Madryn, and Menw, Aergol's son. Gwydion, remembering something he had been told by Cariadas yesterday, halted for a moment and grasped Aergol's shoulder. "I am so sorry, cousin, about Ceindrech."

Aergol nodded his thanks and his dark eyes shimmered with the sheen of tears. "Thank you, cousin," the Archdruid's heir whispered. "I regret—I am afraid that she did not truly know how much I loved her."

"She knew," Rhiannon said quietly. "For she knew you well, I think."

"I pray to Modron that it is so," Aergol whispered.

Sinend, Aergol's daughter and heir, stood to one side with Sabrina, King Owein of Rheged's Druid. The two women smiled at him as he stopped and pressed a kiss on their hands, bowing low. Next to them the Master Smiths of Kymru and their families clustered together. He hugged Greid, the Master Smith of Gwynedd and an old, old friend. He greeted the other three smiths—Siwan of Prydyn, Llyenog of Rheged, and Efrei of Ederynion, and nodded pleasantly at their spouses and children.

As he neared the throne tears came to his eyes as he recognized Myrrdin standing at the bottom of the stairs. The old man stepped forward and sketched a bow. But Gwydion would have none of that. He grabbed Myrrdin, hugging him so tightly that his uncle protested.

"By the gods, boyo," Myrrdin pretended to gasp. "You'll break these old bones."

"Not such old bones any more, I'll wager," Gwydion grinned as he nodded at Neaud, the beautiful, young Dewin who stood by Myrrdin's side.

Myrrdin blushed but Neuad laughed. "Too, true, Dreamer," Neuad said with a wicked smile.

"He appears to be getting younger by the moment," Gwydion observed. "What an amazing thing."

"Isn't it?" Neuad asked archly.

Dudod, Rhiannon's uncle, stepped forward. Dudod's green eyes sparkled wickedly as he took in Gwydion's appearance, seeming to find something there that amused him. His eyes flickered to Rhiannon's face and back to Gwydion's. "You've changed, Dreamer," Dudod said with delight.

"I have. More than you know, perhaps."

"Oh, probably not. But more than others know."

Gwydion grinned and all those around him, except Dudod, blinked in surprise. "No doubt. And I thank you, Bard, for your warning to Rhiannon the night I was taken. If I had not been so pig-headed, you would surely have saved me."

Dudod's brow rose. "I thank you, Gwydion. I am sorry that I was not in time."

"Not your fault, Dudod. Mine and mine alone."

Next he saw Ellywen, King Rhoram's former Druid. He had expected to see her, for Cariadas had told him of her capture and rescue. But for a moment he blinked in surprise, for she was not at all the same woman he thought he knew. Her rich, brown hair was worn loose around her shoulders, held back from her face by a band of emeralds. Her gray eyes—eyes which Gwydion had always likened to ice—were warm and smiling.

"Gwydion ap Awst," Ellywen said, her voice low and vibrant. "How glad we are to see you freed and healed."

"And to see you free and healed, also, Ellywen," Gwydion said with astonishment.

"Yes, Dreamer, I have been healed of who and what I was. But I am not free. I owe too much for that. I owe amends that I fear I can never truly make. But from now on, I will try."

"The gods forgive us what we are, Ellywen," Gwydion said. "And so we can forgive each other."

"And ourselves?" she asked.

"Ah, perhaps the hardest part of all."

He saw another face he thought he would never see again and smiled. At his gesture Talorcan stepped forward. He gripped the arm of the man who had once been his blood brother. "Talorcan of Dere, I am gladder to see you than I can say."

Talorcan's smile was strained and taut. "I have done what I have done. May my God forgive me."

"Your God created you and all that you are," Gwydion said sincerely. "He did not mean for you to be half a man, but all of what you were made to be."

Talorcan's smile became less strained and more genuine. "Regan is teaching me how to Wind-Ride."

"Dewin you are, Talorcan, and Dewin you shall always be. Your new home is with us and we welcome you." Gwydion bowed low over Regan's hand then smiled at them both. "I am sure Regan is taking very good care of you."

"Oh, I am, Dreamer," Regan said with a smile. "I am indeed."

"Gwydion," Gwen said softly as she came forward. The golden light of the hall shimmered in her golden hair. She smiled, but something was changed in her face. The infatuation he had seen there for so long was gone and he breathed a silent sigh of relief as he pressed a kiss on her hand.

"My mam has done well by you," Gwen said. "You look very nearly recovered."

"Your mam is the only reason I am alive at all," Gwydion answered as he turned briefly to look down at Rhiannon. He took her hand and lifted it to his lips, turning it over to press a kiss on her palm. Rhiannon's eyes darkened to smoky green and the light that Gwydion saw there made his pulse race. For a moment he passionately wished that they were alone. But there would be time for that later. For now, there was still one more person for him to greet.

He turned to face the dais and the man who sat on the golden throne. Gwydion gently disentangled his arm from Rhiannon and ascended the eight steps, never taking his eyes off of Arthur. As he reached the top step Arthur stood. For a moment the two men faced each other, each searching the other's countenance, not speaking. They never really knew which one moved first, for at the same time they each flung their arms open wide and grasped each other, pounding each other on the back and laughing. When they at last pulled back, Gwydion saw tears on Arthur's cheeks and felt his own flowing down his face.

"Uncle," Arthur rasped. "Uncle." The scar on Arthur's face whitened, as it always did when he was moved. "Thank all the gods, you live."

"Thank Rhiannon that I live," Gwydion murmured. "Without her—"

"At least you have learned how to be grateful."

"I have indeed, nephew," Gwydion said quietly. "Grateful to each one of you here, grateful most of all to you and Rhiannon. For she saved my life. And you saved hers at the clearing. I will never forget what I owe to you both."

"And I will never forget what I owe you," Arthur said, indicating the golden hall with a sweep of his hand. "For it is only because of you that we are here in Cadair Idris, that I am High King of Kymru, that we have a chance to free our country. Come, uncle, sit here," Arthur went on, gesturing at a chair that had been set to one side of the throne. "Rhiannon says we must be sure you rest for a few more days."

"Thank you," Gwydion said as he gratefully sank down on the seat.

"My friends," Arthur called, turning to the people that filled the great hall. "Now is our time to welcome those that have recently come to Cadair Idris. I welcome the Master Smiths of Kymru and their families." The folk in the hall applauded as the Smiths briefly bowed. "And glad I am that they are here, for on the fourth level, the level of Y Rhlfwyr, the Warrior Twins, is a forge the likes of which we have never seen. And it is here that the Smiths have labored since their release, forging weapons of war for the Kymri—weapons that will play their part in freeing us from the Coranians.

"And I am glad to welcome among us Talorcan of Dere. For he is Dewin, and we welcome another child of Nantsovelta." The crowd cheered for Talorcan and the Coranian general was obviously both surprised and overwhelmed.

Talorcan stepped forward to face the throne at the top of the dais. "High King of Kymru, I pledge to you my sword and my heart. For you are surely a man to be trusted, unlike the man to whom I previously swore my pledge. And I say to you, in the words of the poem of Queen Hildelinda:

"The covenants of companionship
Shall never be broken.
Death cannot touch us,
I am yours forever."

Arthur inclined his head, then drew his blade, Cadalfwlch. At his gesture Talorcan ascended the dais and knelt before him. Arthur lightly touched Talorcan's left shoulder with the shining blade, saying, "In the name of Annywyn, Lord of Chaos." He then touched Talorcan's right shoulder saying, "and his mate, Aertan the Weaver of Fate." He stepped back, resting the point of Cadalfwch on the golden floor, his hand wrapped around the eagle-hilt. "Rise, Talorcan of Kymru," Arthur said. "For you are my man, now and forever."

Talorcan rose and there were tears in his light green eyes. He bowed briefly, then descended from the dais. He took Regan's hand and lightly kissed her brow, his back straight and proud.

"And we welcome among us Ellywen ur Saidi, the Druid to King Rhoram of Prydyn. Come, Ellywen," Arthur said, as she hesitated.

Ellywen ascended the dais and knelt before Arthur. "High King," she began, "for my crimes—"

"Your crimes are forgiven, Ellywen," Arthur said softly.

"I—"

"Forgiven," he repeated. Gently he touched the blade to her left shoulder, then to her right. "In the name of Annwyn, Lord of Chaos and Aertan the Weaver, you are mine."

Ellywen bowed her head. "Then use me, High King. Use me to take back our land. For this I give my life and more."

"Done," Arthur said, for he was too wise to argue with her. "My friends," he called to those in the hall. "Tonight we shall feast with each other. We shall laugh and talk together. We shall sing songs and play games. Later Gwydion, Rhiannon, and the Druids will come together to talk about the next step in the game—for soon the Archdruid will feel the wrath of Modron the Mother and all the Druids of Kymru will again be one with the rest of the Y

Dawnus. For Cathbad has dared to use the tarw-casglaid to falsely declare Havgan the High King of Kymru."

An angry hiss from those gathered in the hall made him grin. "My sentiments exactly," he said and they laughed. "Come, let us adjourn to the banquet hall." He turned to Gwydion and held out his hand. "Come, uncle," he said quietly. "Come and let us plan together."

Gwydion rose, firmly gripping Arthur's arm. "Your da would have been proud of you, Arthur," he said past the tightness in his throat that was always there when he spoke of his dead half-brother. "How I wish that Uthyr were here to see you."

"How I wish he was, also," Arthur said quietly. "For his loss, and for the loss of those others that we loved, the Golden Man will pay. Be assured of that."

"I am, Arthur. Believe me, I am."

"You are certain?" Arthur asked Aergol intently, his dark eyes sharp.

"I am," Aergol answered. "Havgan will journey to Caer Duir with only Sigerric to keep him company. In this he will respect our tradition of the tarw-casglaid. Cathbad will insist on following the forms—though certainly not the spirit."

Gwydion listened intently to the conversation here in the garden room but left it to Arthur to lead the discussion, as was right and proper now that Arthur was a man.

"Then would this not be our best chance to win this war?" Gwen asked.

"How so?" Rhiannon questioned.

Gwydion noticed that the rest of the Druids gathered in the chamber—Aergol, Sinend, Menw, Yrth, Aldur, Madryn, Ellywen, and Sabrina—tensed, for they knew where Gwen was going with her suggestion, even if Rhiannon did not.

"Why, if Havgan is almost alone, we could kill him then and there," Gwen pointed out.

Rhiannon turned to the Druids gathered there, a shadow of shame in her green eyes. "I apologize for my daughter," she said quietly. "She knows no better."

"What?" Gwen asked. "What do you mean I know no—"

"The fault is not hers," Rhiannon went on, raising her voice over Gwen's. "It is mine. If she had been trained properly she never would have said such a thing."

Aergol glanced at Madryn, Gwen's teacher, with a question in his dark eyes.

Madryn nodded in agreement. "We have not chanced to speak of the ceremony, Archdruid's heir," she said to Aergol's unspoken question. "She does not know."

Gwen flushed, for it was obvious to her that she had committed a dreadful mistake. "I apologize for my ignorance," she said stiffly, rising from her place with a humble bow and dropping her eyes before Aergol's stern gaze. "I ask for your guidance, that I may learn."

Gwydion's brows rose at that, for the Gwen he remembered from not so long ago would have argued, would have accused, would have done anything to put others in the wrong. But this Gwen acknowledged that she had made an error and asked to be put right—though she was not particularly gracious about it. Gwydion guessed that Madryn had learned how to handle her pupil very well.

Aergol held out his hand to Gwen and she crossed the room to kneel before him. "Daughter of Modron, the tarw-casglaid is a ceremony that is sacred to the Mother. The purpose of that ceremony is for the Archdruid to declare a High King. The Archdruid drinks mistletoe, lays on the bull skin, and dreams. The dreams that the Mother sends him are sacred, for she speaks to us all through those dreams."

Gwen nodded solemnly to indicate that she knew this.

"This ceremony is one of the most important ones to the Druids. We revere Modron the Mother with all our hearts. That Cathbad thinks to profane this ceremony by using it to declare Havgan as the High King of Kymru is abhorrent to us."

Again Gwen nodded, her blue eyes wide.

"But how much worse still it would be if we ourselves intended to also profane that ceremony by spilling the blood of our enemy.

For that would not Modron turn her face from us forever? For that would we not lose the gifts she has given us? For that would we not lose our souls, as Cathbad has lost his?"

Aergol gently laid one hand on Gwen's head and stroked her bright hair. "Daughter of Modron, do you now understand how we cannot even think of such a thing? Do you understand how it is that Havgan must walk out of Caer Duir unharmed?"

Gwen nodded solemnly and bowed her head. She then rose and turned to face all the folk gathered there. She looked at each Druid—at Yrth and Aldur, at Madryn and Menw, at Ellywen and Sabrina and Sinend. She looked at Rhiannon and at Gwydion. Lastly she gazed at Arthur. "I humbly beg pardon of each person here. I did not understand, but now I do. I was blinded by my wish for vengeance, and forgot my allegiance to Modron. I ask for the forgiveness of each one of you."

"You are forgiven, Gwenhwyfar ur Rhoram var Rhiannon," Arthur said formally. "Most heartily and readily." As Gwen again took her seat Arthur turned to Gwydion. "Uncle, have you anything to add to our plan?"

"Only one thing," Gwydion said. "I would not be so sure, Aergol, that the Mother requires your death in atonement."

"What do you mean, Dreamer?" Aergol asked in feigned surprise.

But Gwydion was not fooled. He knew what Aergol was secretly planning. And Aergol knew that Gwydion knew. That Arthur was now aware of it was enough for now. "Just keep that thought in mind and do not be too surprised if things turn out differently than you think. For the Mother has a way of surprising us all." Gwydion smiled. "She is, after all, a woman."

At Arthur's gesture of dismissal they all rose, making their way out of the garden room to their own chambers. Gwydion took Rhiannon's arm and they made their way up the stairs. He did not speak, for he was uncertain how to begin. At last they reached the door of his chamber. Rhiannon released his arm and turned to go, but Gwydion put his hand out and stopped her.

"Would you—would you care for a cup of wine?" he asked.

Her brow rose in surprise, but she nodded. "But just for a few moments," she said as she followed him into the chamber. "You should rest."

"Perhaps," he agreed. "Except that I am not in the least bit tired." And that was true. He was far too keyed up to be tired.

He poured wine into two golden goblets chased with opals and handed her a cup. She took it and sat at the edge of the hearth. The firelight cast a glow over her smooth features, and her green eyes sparkled in the light of the dancing flames. He took a seat next to her on the hearth. He took a sip of wine, then set the cup down. With a deep breath, he turned to her and began.

"When you heard me Wind-Speak to you, from my captivity, you said you knew I had not escaped," he said abruptly.

She nodded. "Yes, I knew."

"You knew that I wasn't in my right mind."

"I did indeed."

"How did you know?" he pressed. For he thought that she would say that she knew him too well to be fooled. And that would be his opening to tell her the truth. But she surprised him.

"Because you called me *cariad*," she said with a shrug. "You called me beloved throughout your communication with me. That's how I knew that someone was telling you what to say, that you were still a prisoner. You would never have called me that on your own."

"Oh," he said, for he had not expected that answer. "Oh. Well, as to that—" He broke off for he was unsure how to proceed, and so very afraid.

"Don't be concerned about it, Gwydion," she said, putting the cup down. "There is nothing to explain. I didn't misunderstand for a moment." She rose. "Goodnight."

She turned to go but Gwydion rose and stopped her. "Rhiannon. *Cariad*," he said softly. He reached out and framed her beautiful face with his hands.

Her eyes widened. "What?" she whispered. "What are you—"

"Oh, beloved. Did you not know that I have called you that in my heart for so many, many years?" he asked softly, his thumbs stroking her cheekbones. "Did you never guess?"

"Gwydion," she whispered.

"Oh, my love," he said. "I beg you to forgive me. All these years wasted. But I was afraid."

"Afraid?" she asked.

He guided her back to the hearth and knelt before her, taking her hands in his. He tried to explain to her how it had been with his father and mother. How his mother had done all she could to control his father, making Gwydion's home a battlefield. How his father had rarely come home because of that, how Gwydion had grown up so lonely. And that horror-filled moment when he had discovered their bodies, knowing that his father had died at his mother's hands.

"From that moment I vowed never to fall in love, never to let a woman into my heart," he said. "I vowed that my only love would be my duty as Dreamer. It was the only safe thing to cling to. But then I met you. Remember that first time?"

Rhiannon nodded, but did not speak.

"You and Gwen were living in that cave. And you appeared from behind the waterfall. And, oh, you were so beautiful. My heart—even then I think—knew you. When we searched for Caladfwlch I could barely take my eyes from you. That day on Afalon when Amatheon died and I was so cruel to you still shames me."

"Gwydion—"

"Please, let me speak. When we went to Corania, how often I wanted to take you in my arms, to tell you the truth. But I couldn't. Not there, for I knew that you still loved Rhoram, and I was afraid. And then when we came back here, and I knew you would be seeing him again, I couldn't risk it. I couldn't."

He was almost babbling now in his eagerness to make her understand, in his fear that she would turn away from him if he stopped talking. And all the while he was speaking to her she simply stared at him, her eyes wide and clearly shocked.

"That day by the lake, the day you found the Stone, the day I thought you dead—nothing was worse than that. I wanted to kiss you again so badly, but I couldn't. I was afraid that I would fail in my duty to Kymru if I—even once—let you know the kind of power you truly had over me. And now—"

"And now?" she prompted when he hesitated for a moment.

"And now I know that my fears are meaningless. Now I know that nothing else matters but that I love you so. When I was wandering in my mind, trapped in the dark, I called for you. I knew that you and you alone could save me. I knew that if I ever saw you again I must tell you this truth. And you would make of it what you would. I beg for you not to tell me that it is too late. But if you do, know that I will still love you. I will love you forever, and if you will allow me to, I will spend the rest of my life proving it to you."

He paused, looking into her beautiful eyes. Behind her the flames of the fire leapt higher. "The truth I learned at last is that my love for you did not weaken me. It strengthened me. Without you I could not have done my duty at all. Without you I would not have come back from Corania alive. Without you Caladfwlch would not have been found, nor the Treasures. Without you, Arthur would not be High King. Most of all, without you, I will never smile or laugh again. You are all that I want. All that I need. And I love you so."

He reached out and took her face in his hands. His thumb brushed her lips and he leaned forward to kiss her. Her lips tasted sweet, so sweet that he was dizzy with desire for her. He plunged his hands into her silken hair, delighting in the softness of it. He kissed her with rising passion. At last he released her mouth, murmuring her name, raining kisses on her face and her slender throat until they were both breathless.

"I love you," he whispered, pulling back a little to look into her eyes.

"Convince me," she said. And behind the challenge in her eyes was the promise of things he had barely dared to dream.

"I have always loved you. I always will love you."

"Yes," she murmured. "Yes, love me, Gwydion. Love me. As I love you."

His breath caught in his throat as she said the words he had longed to hear. But he began slowly. He took her hand and brought it to his lips. He kissed her fingers, one by one. Her fingers curved around his mouth and he look up at her. Her green eyes were smokey with desire. His hand found the laces of her gown and he loosened them, baring her shoulders on which he rained tiny kisses. She shivered. He gently pulled down the front of her gown and kissed her silky skin.

He raised his head to look at her. "Rhiannon?" he questioned.

She understood what he wanted to know. She reached out and unfastened the laces of his tunic, then drew off his undershirt. They undressed each other slowly until they stood naked together in front of the fire. He gazed at her, his eyes hot and glowing. He picked her up and carried her to the bed, laying her down on the red coverlet. He bent over her and kissed her again.

"Rhiannon ur Hefeydd var Indeg," he whispered. "I love you." He took her slowly, giving her all of himself, holding nothing back. At the peak of their ecstasy they cried out together and he called out her name.

Then he gathered her in his arms, his heart still beating wildly from his release. "*Cariad*," he whispered as he stroked her hair. "Beloved. Forever."

SIGERRIC STOOD IN the center of the marketplace in Dinmael. Coranian soldiers ringed the perimeter, their axes and spears at the ready, pinning the people of the city within the crowded market. When a certain measure of quiet was obtained, Sigerric began.

"People of Dinmael, be it known that Havgan the Golden, ruler of all Kymru, calls you to task for your complicity in a crime. For not many days ago Queen Elen was spirited away from Caer Dwfr."

Even now the Kymri were defiant, for cheers erupted from the crowd at the mention of Elen's escape.

"It is each one of you who allowed this to happen," Sigerric called out. "For her rescuers could not have entered and left the city without your knowledge and cooperation. And for this you will be punished."

He signaled to one of the lieutenants, and the man nodded. The lieutenant lit his torch and raised it over his head. He swung it from side to side, facing the docks to the southeast, once, twice, three times.

"Even now soldiers are destroying your boats," Sigerric cried.

An angry mutter broke from the people gathered there.

"You have brought this on yourselves," Sigerric went on. "The docks will be destroyed. And so will the marketplace."

At his words smoke from the southeast began to rise into the air. And the soldiers around the marketplace began to move in, pushing the people aside, making for the stalls. They began to tear the stalls down, throwing goods onto the streets, trampling and ruining them.

At first Sigerric thought that the Kymri would rise up against the soldiers and he braced himself. Something he felt in the air told him that everything hung in the balance at that moment. But something, he did not know what, and he did not know from where it came, calmed the crowd. Perhaps it was whispered words of patience. Perhaps it was promises that the destruction would be righted. Perhaps it was remembrance that Cadair Idris glowed again with the coming of the High King, and that Arthur would not suffer his people to remain under the Coranian yoke forever. Perhaps it was the knowledge hidden in their hearts that they would win in the end.

Whatever it was, it prevailed that day. The Coranian solders continued their destructive work unhindered by the people of Dinmael. And if the people did not attempt to stop the destruction neither did they appear to mourn it. No one cried out at the loss of goods. No one tried to save anything. They simply stood quietly, murmuring things amongst themselves, as though the destruction around them was meaningless.

They were right, of course, Sigerric thought. But not for the reason they thought. For the destruction of the marketplace and the docks meant nothing to Sigerric, either. That was not why he was here.

Though the Kymri did not know that. And would not know that until it was far, far too late.

The docks southeast of the city were burned and ruined. Boats drifted in the sea, some half burned, some with holes in their sides and slowly sinking, some simply set adrift. Later the people of the city would swim out to some of these boats and bring them back in for repair. Other boats drifted farther out to sea, riding past the waves that attempted to halt them.

As twilight fell over the sea, one boat, far, far away from shore rocked violently. A man's head appeared from within the boat. The man peered around, making sure he was far from shore. Then he sat up, took the oars from the bottom of the boat, and locked them into place.

The man smoothed back his scanty, gray hair and raised the tiny sail. He then grasped the oars and began to row. He had a long way to go, he knew, to reach the shores of the Coranian Empire. But he could do it, and do it in time. He had assured Lord Havgan that he could, and Torgar knew better than to fail.

He would reach Corania and find the Emperor's brother and give him Havgan's message.

And Corania would then be able to defeat the witches of Kymru once and for all.

Part 3

Day Break

Whence come night and dawn,
Whither the earth is moving on slowly,
The hiding place of night before day.

Taliesin, Fifth
Master Bard
Circa 277

Chapter Thirteen

Eiodel & Cair Duir
Gwytheryn, Kymru
Eiddew Mis, 500

Suldydd, Lleihau Wythnos—midmorning

"You must be out of your mind!" Sigerric cried.

Cathbad, Archdruid of Kymru, stiffened in his chair at the insult. But he attempted to keep his voice even when he replied. "I am not out of my mind. And I must insist that you do this the way I say."

"There is no way," Sigerric went on furiously, "that I am going to let Havgan go to Caer Duir without a guard. No way under the sun." For a moment he wondered why he was still such a fool, why he was still so determined to protect the life of the man he had once called friend—once, but no longer. But he knew why. Loyalty was an integral part of who he was. He had always known that. If only he had had the wit to have been more discriminating on whom he originally bestowed it.

"He must come without his men," Cathbad continued to insist. "The ceremony of tarw-casgliad is sacred to the Druids. Anything which smacks of coercion will compromise the results of the ceremony."

"You are a fine one to talk about compromising the ceremony," Sigerric sneered, unable to bear the smug tone of the Archdruid. "Are you not using it for your own ends?"

Cathbad rose, his face suffused with rage. "I am doing this for the Druids! Not for my own aggrandizement!"

"Ha!" Sigerric cried.

The two men continued to argue with each other in the dim chamber at Eiodel, Havgan's dark fortress. The chamber contained a few slit-like windows, which should have brightened it somewhat as the midmorning sun streamed down. But Havgan's form blocked the light from the north window, as he stood there looking out over the plain to Cadair Idris, the mountain hall of the High King of Kymru, the edifice that was still denied to him.

A fire glowed feebly on the hearth, shifting shadows across the ceiling and walls. Firelight glinted occasionally off the goblets of ruby and gold on the dark oak wood table that stood in the center of the room.

Cathbad's dark eyes, even in the gloom, seemed to Sigerric to give off a mad glow. Sigerric knew that the time had almost come to discard this increasingly erratic tool. After the ceremony, perhaps.

Finally Havgan moved, shifting around to gaze at Sigerric and Cathbad. At his movement both of them fell silent.

"We shall do it as the Archdruid says," Havgan said.

Sigerric was outraged. "What? Go alone? What better time might the Kymri have to kill you than at Caer Duir?"

"You will be surrounded by loyal Druids," Cathbad insisted, his old face almost breaking into a smile at his triumph.

"Don't be a fool, Cathbad," Havgan said smoothly. "Your Druids are anything but loyal."

Cathbad's face darkened. "I must protest—"

"Don't argue with me," Havgan said his tone smooth but his words clipped. "Your own heir has recently gone to Arthur, taking with him your most talented teachers, as well as his own son. Is that not so?"

"It is," Cathbad said, making the admission reluctantly. "But that was only six of my Druids. The rest—"

"Are waiting to see who is the stronger—you or Aergol."

"Say rather, you or Arthur," Sigerric cut in, speaking to Havgan.

"Yes, you are right," Havgan replied, crossing the room to pour a cup of wine. The rubies on the cup glittered in the uncertain light like old blood. "I can tell you now which of us is the stronger. For Cathbad will declare me the true High King in the tarw-casglaid ceremony and I will have a claim to Kymru. The restlessness of the Druids will be stilled. And they will, in turn, still the restlessness of the people."

Sigerric opened his mouth to point out the obvious flaws, but shut it as Havgan raised his amber hawk eyes to him. He saw that Havgan was fully aware that this would not be enough to make him High King of Kymru. The only real way to do that was to defeat the Cerddorian and Arthur utterly on the field of battle. And this was just what Havgan was planning to do—providing the old sailor made it to Corania with Havgan's message. But all this was something that Cathbad had best not know. So Sigerric remained silent.

Havgan turned to Cathbad, and the Archdruid's complexion turned from angry red to fearful white as Havgan's amber gaze pinned him, like the soaring hawk that sights the trembling mouse far below. After a few moments Havgan spoke, very softly. "You will not fail me in this, Archdruid."

"Great Warleader," Cathbad stammered at the glimpse of the future promised in Havgan's predatory eyes should he fail, "I will not."

"Good," Havgan said softly.

Gwaithdydd, Lleihau Wythnos—noon

Cathbad stood in the center of the sacred grove of Nemed Derwen. Hundreds of mighty oaks, the tree sacred to Modron the Mother, planted in circle after widening circle, radiated out from the clearing and lifted their branches to the noonday sun. Cathbad faced west, the direction of the element of earth, but he could still keep an eye on the south, the direction that Havgan and Sigerric would be led through the trees. Even through the shifting oaks he could glimpse the massive, dark standing stone that made up Aelwyd Derwen, the burial mounds of the Archdruids.

Brown-robed Druids lined the perimeter of the clearing. The most senior, those teachers still left at Caer Duir, stood next to him, engrossed in their own tasks. Two of them sharpened their knives. The sounds of the whetstones grated on Cathbad's ears, but he said nothing. One of them tended a pot of boiling water that hung on a spit over a crackling fire. The fourth held a sickle of gold, and the sunlight that pooled in the clearing flashed off the curved blade. The fifth held a white, pristine cloth. All five, like the rest of the Druids around the clearing, had their hoods up, covering the sides of their faces, casting their countenances into impenetrable shadow.

Cathbad was dressed in a robe of rich green trimmed in velvety brown. Around his shoulders was a cape of brown bull hide, fastened with brooches of gold and sparkling emerald. The Archdruid's massive golden torque, glittering with emeralds, was clasped around his thin neck. On his head he wore a tiara of shining gold, studded with the verdant stones.

Even though what he would do here today had been staged in advance, Cathbad was not afraid of offending Modron. For all that he did was with one aim in mind—to increase the power of the Druids in Kymru. And surely Modron would not object to that. Were the Druids not her sons and daughters? Modron would understand and he did not fear that the ceremony—and its preordained conclusion—would enrage his goddess.

Aergol had, of course, disagreed. He had shouted that he would not be a part of such a mockery, such traitorous behavior to the Mother. He had spoken of the sacred nature of the rite, of the responsibility of the Archdruid to dream truly and to declare truly. For the tarw-casglaid was a holy rite, a ceremony to enable the Archdruid to speak to the Mother and hear her will and to dare to use it otherwise was to invite disaster.

Cathbad had, of course, disregarded Aergol's arguments. He had not been particularly surprised a few months ago to discover that Aergol, as well as his son and many of Caer Duir's finest teachers, had fled during the night. Surprised, no, but enraged, yes. Nonetheless, he had determined to go ahead with his plan. For he knew he was right. Havgan had to be High King of Kymru, for whom else but the Coranians would ensure that the other Y Dawnus—the Dewin, the Bards, and the most hated Dreamers—were exterminated, leaving the Druids supreme?

Movement to the south caught his eye and he turned, watching as Havgan and Sigerric were led on foot into the clearing. Havgan was dressed all in gold from head to toe and rubies glinted around his neck, in his ears, on the turned down cuffs of his boots. A cloak of red hung from his shoulders and a band of gold and rubies bound his brow.

Sigerric was dressed in rich brown. Gold glittered around his neck and wrists, flashing in the sun. Havgan was unarmed, as the law required, but Sigerric had defied Cathbad's orders by thrusting a dagger into his belt. By the fierce look in Sigerric's eyes Cathbad knew that to insist on disarming the man would be useless. Better to ignore it.

The two men took the places indicated for them on the south side of the circle. Cathbad again turned west and lifted his arms high. "In the name of Modron, the Great Mother of All, the Goddess of the Earth, Lady of the West, I greet you all. In the name of Modron, Mother of Mabon of the Sun, Mother of Sirona of the Stars, Mother of Cerridwen of the Wild Hunt, Mother of the Druids, I greet you all. In the name of Modron, mate to Taran of the Winds, I greet you all. Oh, mighty Mother-Goddess, we beg for your wisdom. We beg for your guidance. We beg for the gift of a dream, that we may know your will for Kymru. Guide us now, in this the sacred ceremony of tarw-casglaid, as we seek to know your desire. Today I beg you to answer the question on our hearts—who should be proclaimed the High King of Kymru?"

At Cathbad's nod the Druid with the golden sickle left the center of the clearing to stand beneath one of the oak trees. The Druid hooked the shining, curved blade onto a strap of leather that she then hung around her neck. With a mighty leap she began to climb the stately tree. She climbed swiftly, for the oak seemed to welcome her, almost seeming to bend to enable the climber to make her way up the trunk. At last the Druid reached a clump of mistletoe hanging on one of the uppermost branches. The Druid with the white cloth came to stand beneath the clump of mistletoe, spreading the cloth tautly between his hands.

The Druid in the tree unhooked the golden sickle and carefully cut the clump of mistletoe. The mistletoe fell from the branch, landing squarely in the center of the white cloth. The Druid who had caught the mistletoe brought the plant with its milky-white berries to the Druid who was tending the boiling water. Both Druids tore the leaves from the plant and dropped them into the boiling pot. The water took on a greenish hue that seemed to glow faintly. Then they plucked the white, leathery berries and dropped these too, one by one, into the bubbling pot.

At that moment two more Druids led a brown bull into the clearing. The bull, secured by ropes tied to the golden ring in its snout, was docile, for it had been drugged before the ceremony. Its small, brown eyes were glazed and its movements were slightly sluggish.

The Druid who had climbed the tree was now back in the clearing, and she handed Cathbad the golden sickle. Cathbad made his way to stand by the bull. "Oh, Great Mother," he called. "Oh, Modron, Queen of the Earth, guide my hand!" He leapt on the bulls back, grabbing the hair between the ears to steady himself. The bull shifted beneath him, but did not run. With his other hand he brought the golden sickle down to the bull's throat and, in one swift motion, killed the animal.

The bull fell to his knees and Cathbad rolled off to stand to one side. Blood spurted in a fountain from its throat and a Druid caught the liquid in a golden bowl. When the bull fell to its side, dead, the two Druids that had sharpened their knives went to work. Expertly, swiftly, they skinned the bull and cut up the meat, piling it on a golden platter.

Finally, their work was done. The two Druids brought the bull hide to Cathbad and laid it on the ground at his feet. Cathbad sat down on the still-warm and bloody hide. Two more Druids brought the bull's blood in the golden bowl and the bull's meat on a golden platter. Cathbad took the bowl and drank, spilling some blood down his chin and onto his fine robe. He then took meat from the platter and began to eat, chewing on the raw meat and swallowing as much as possible. When he could eat and drink no more, he motioned for the Druids to take the bowl and the platter away.

The Druid who had been tending the concoction of mistletoe poured a portion of the contents of the pot into a large goblet of gold and emerald. She brought the cup to Cathbad and he drank. He drank less than it seemed, for though his throat worked he did not swallow much of the liquid. He took care to let some of it spill down his face. If he had drunk the entire cup, as he was supposed to, the contents would indeed induce hallucinations and he did not want that. He did not need those fevered dreams for the Mother to speak to him. After all, he already knew Modron's will. He set the cup down next to the hide, deliberately spilling some of its contents. The brew sank swiftly into the earth, and it was impossible to tell how much he had drunk, just as he had intended.

"Now will I dream the dreams that Modron sends," he declared, careful to make his voice somewhat sluggish. For the entire dose of mistletoe would have lowered the speed at which his blood coursed through his body and slowed his heart, and therefore his speech. "For the Great Mother of All will surely speak to me, giving the Kymri the guidance that we crave." So saying he lay back on the bloody hide while four Druids wrapped the skin around him. Then each stood over him, two at his head and two at his feet.

At that moment the earth trembled beneath them, ever so slightly. The trees rustled as their roots danced. For a moment Cathbad's nerve almost failed him. For surely Modron herself had indeed come to them. But, after a moment, when the earth again stilled, he took heart. He was doing this for her.

That he was really doing it for himself was a secret he was sure he held inviolate in the deepest recesses of his heart.

And that, he realized later, was his biggest mistake of all.

For a moment Cathbad lay on the hide, his eyes still open, staring up at the oak branches that spread across the blue sky over the clearing. In a moment he would close his eyes and pretend to dream. In a moment he would—

He started, every muscle in his body tensed. For he thought

he saw—something. For a moment it seemed as though the face of one of the four shrouded Druids that surrounded him was the wrong face. It should have been that of Hywel, one of the teachers of the almanac. But, instead, for one moment it seemed to have been Aergol's face. He blinked, looking closer at the Druid above him. But the face was shadowed by the Druid's cowl and the hands tucked into the long sleeves of the Druid's traditional robe. And, any way, that was nonsense. Absolute nonsense. Aergol, his heir, was gone. Aergol has repudiated his master, and would not return.

He knew what it was. He had drunk as little of the mistletoe as possible, but he had still drunk some of the concoction. He had, perhaps, swallowed more than he had thought, bringing on the hallucinations he had been trying to avoid. For it was not possible, not at all possible that Aergol was here.

He closed his eyes and willed his body to relax. He needed to lie here for a few moments, at the very least. For a moment he thought that he again felt the ground tremble very so slightly. For a moment he thought he heard the oak leaves rustling as the trees themselves shivered. For a moment he thought he smelled the scent of ripe apples, of grapevines heavy with purple fruit, of aromatic lilies, of thyme and rosemary, of spring gentian and violets.

Indeed, for a brief moment he thought he heard the cry of an eagle as it soared high in the air somewhere over Caer Duir—over, perhaps, this very clearing.

For a moment he thought he heard a woman's voice calling his name from far away. Something in the woman's tone frightened him. Something in the pitch seemed to promise retribution for some wrong.

Beneath him the ground shook again. Surely enough time had elapsed. It would have to do, for he would not spend one more moment lying on the warm and bloody hide. He would not spend one more moment thinking that the earth beneath him was restlessly awaiting its chance to swallow him. He would not spend one more moment imagining that the Mother herself was coming for him in a fury.

He opened his eyes and the four Druids that had been hovering over him drew back, effectively again hiding their shadowed faces from him. Cathbad sat up and stretched out his hands to the Druids. Two of them moved forward and helped him to his feet.

All around the clearing the Druids moved in closer, standing shoulder to shoulder, their hoods covering their expressions. Havgan and Sigerric stood a few paces to the south of Cathbad. The golden sun that streamed into the clearing lit Havgan's robes until the Warleader seemed to be shrouded in a nimbus of flame.

Cathbad raised his hands and declared in a voice that tried to be firm but shook somewhat, for he was unnerved, "Modron has spoken!"

Not a Druid in the clearing moved. In fact, the entire grove itself seemed to fall silent, waiting for Cathbad's next words.

"I dreamed and dreamed truly," Cathbad continued. "I begged the Mother to tell us her will in the matter of a High King. And she told me that the gods themselves were in full agreement. For the High King of Kymru is to be none other than Havgan, son of Hengist, the Golden Man!"

At his declaration Havgan stepped forward. But, to Cathbad's quickly covered dismay, the Druids were still silent. They stood as statues, and did not react at all.

Cathbad held out his hand to Havgan as he came forward and took it. Cathbad raised the Warleader's hand in the air. "Behold your High King!"

Again, the Druids remained silent. The only sound was the cry of an eagle as it circled over the clearing and what seemed to be the far-off call of a hunting horn. Havgan's triumphant smiled faded and Cathbad turned cold. A cloud covered the sun, darkening the grove and Cathbad shivered.

"Cathbad ap Goreau var Efa, Eleventh Archdruid of Kymru, you are a liar." The man who declared this, one of the four Druids who had surrounded Cathbad as he pretended to sleep, pulled off his hood. In the shadowy clearing the man's dark eyes gleamed with truth and purpose. And Cathbad had recognized the voice, had known who it was even before the man had taken off his hood. And why not? Had he not heard the voice every day for years?

"Aergol," Cathbad said, attempting to keep his voice even, "what do you mean? What do you want here?"

"I mean that you are a liar," Aergol ap Custennin, the Archdruid's heir, said firmly. At his words the other three Druids removed their hoods and Cathbad was horrified to discover himself face to face with Gwydion the Dreamer, with Rhiannon var Hefeydd, and—most frightening of all—with Arthur ap Uthyr.

A faint scar ran down Arthur's lean face, giving it a dangerous cast, and his dark eyes were fixed on Havgan, ignoring Cathbad completely. Cathbad clearly saw the boy's resemblance to his father, Uthyr of Gwynedd. But his eyes belonged to his mother, Ygraine of Ederynion, and in those eyes was the coldest look Cathbad had ever seen.

Havgan returned Arthur's stare, he, too, ignoring Cathbad. The two men faced each other over the abandoned bull's hide, and the air in the clearing seemed to thicken.

All around the clearing the Druids were removing their hoods. And among them Cathbad noted the unwelcome faces of Druids that had previously deserted him. He saw Sabrina, she who was once Druid to the King of Rheged, and the woman's blue eyes were blazing with contempt. He saw Ellywen, once Druid to King Rhoram of Prydyn, and the woman's gray eyes reminded Cathbad of thin ice, the kind that hides swift death beneath its depths. He saw three of the teachers that had left Caer Duir with Aergol—old Yrth, Aldur, and Madryn. He saw a young woman who could be none other than Gwenhwyfar of Prydyn. Then two young people came from the fringes of the clearing to stand on either side of Aergol. They were Aergol's children—Sinend and her half-brother, Menw.

"What are you doing, Aergol?" Cathbad asked evenly. Perhaps he could brazen this out long enough to get the other Druids here to turn the tables on these upstarts.

"I am declaring you unfit to lead the Druids of Kymru. I am declaring you reviled by the Mother. I am declaring that you are no longer the Archdruid of Kymru."

"By whose authority? You cannot do that!" Cathbad raged.

"Oh, but he can," Gwydion said softly.

Cathbad turned on the Dreamer, swift as a snake. "Who are you to say what the Druids can do?" he screamed. Why, oh, why did the other Druids not make a move? Why did they not turn on Aergol and his lackeys?

"Hear me, Druids of Kymru," Aergol cried in a huge voice. "Hear me as I declare the truth—a truth you already know in your hearts. I declare that Cathbad ap Goreau is using the tarw-cas-glaid for his own schemes, as he has used you from the beginning. For listen now as I tell you of a wonder. I have been to Cadair Idris. I have seen the Treasures in the golden hall of Brenin Llys. I have seen Arthur ap Uthyr var Ygraine sitting on the Eagle's throne. I have seen the High King's Torque around his neck and Caladfwlch in his hands!"

At Aergol's words Arthur discarded his Druid's robe. He was dressed in a tunic and trousers of silver trimmed in gold. The jewels in the torque around his neck flared—emerald, sapphire, pearl, opal, and onyx. And Caladfwlch, Arthur's gold and silver sword, sang as Arthur pulled it from its sheath and lifted it to the sky. The blade flared as the sun chose that moment to come from behind the clouds.

All around the clearing the Druids sank to their knees. And Cathbad knew that he had lost.

AERGOL, TAKING IN the prostrate Druids, Cathbad's white face, Havgan's enraged countenance, knew that the game was won. In the next few moments he would do his best to ensure that the Druids would return to their proper allegiance. It was the least he could do before carrying out his final plan.

"Arthur ap Uthyr var Ygraine, High King of Kymru, fount of all justice in the land, I ask for your wisdom now. What shall be done with the traitor, Cathbad ap Goreau var Efa? For he has betrayed the Druids, Kymru, and Modron herself."

Arthur gazed for a moment at Cathbad then replied. "Since he has offended his Goddess, he must die by her hand. Let him suffer the sacrificial death of the Mother."

"No!" Cathbad cried. "No! Not that. I beg you!"

"Yes," Arthur said quietly. "I will not cheat Modron of the agony you deserve."

Cathbad turned to run, but three Druids had already surrounded him. Two held him steady while one tied his hands behind his back. Cathbad began to sob uncontrollably. Aergol stepped forward and unclasped the Archdruid's torque from around Cathbad's neck. At his gesture Gwydion unclasped the brooches that held the Archdruid's cape and took the ceremonial cape from Cathbad's shoulders. Rhiannon stepped forward and divested the former Archdruid of his golden tiara.

"Please Aergol," Cathbad continued to sob as the Archdruid's trappings were stripped from him. "If I must die, do not let me die like this."

"For every moment you spend dying know that you brought that moment with the innocent blood of the Kymri," Aergol said sternly. "Think of the thousands that died at the hands of the Coranians because of you."

"Think," Arthur said softly, "that one of them was my father. See his face before you as you wait for death in misery and terror."

"Think," Gwydion said quietly but implacably, "of my brother. Think on Amatheon, whom you had murdered. Think of him."

"Demand your *galanas* then, for their deaths," Cathbad cried.

"There is no *galanas* high enough to repair that injury," Arthur said quietly.

"Name it!" Cathbad cried again. "I will pay it!"

"Yes," Gwydion said his face hard and cold as stone. "You will."

"Take him," Aergol said to the Druids. Cathbad, still screaming, was dragged from the clearing.

"What manner of death is this?" Sigerric asked, his voice shaking.

"The Death of the Mother is death by her element. Earth," Aergol answered.

"You mean—" Sigerric began, his face sick.

"He will be buried alive, entombed in Aelwyd Derwen, the burial mounds of the Archdruids. He will lie there beneath the stone and earth until he can breathe no longer. Earth will eventually fill his lungs and stop his breath," Aergol explained. "Come, Sigerric, do not be so dismayed. You always disliked him. You knew from the beginning that he was mad."

Sigerric nodded but did not reply.

Aergol turned to Arthur and noted that, once again, Arthur and Havgan were staring at each other, taking each other's measure. Arthur's dark, eagle-like gaze clashed with Havgan's amber hawk eyes as the two enemies scrutinized each other.

"So," Havgan said to Gwydion, not taking his eyes from Arthur. "This is the one you betrayed me for."

"This is the High King of Kymru," Gwydion said evenly. "This is the one I have worked to protect all my life. He is the reason I came to Corania. He is the reason I became part of your household, so I could learn all I could of your plans. I never betrayed your brotherhood bond, for I was never your brother. I was always Arthur's man. Never yours."

"Havgan of Corania," Arthur said, "again I must bid you to leave Kymru. Or, better yet, stay here with us. Send your men back to Corania. Give up this battle for Kymru and gain it another way—by living here peacefully. For there is something in you that belongs here. Something I sense—"

"There is nothing!" Havgan cried. "Nothing! I will not send my warriors away! I will stay and I will crush you!"

Overhead an eagle wheeled in the sky. It now folded its wings and dove into the clearing. Arthur raised his fist and the eagle came to rest on his arm, beating its wings and screaming defiance at Havgan.

"This," Arthur said, nodding his head to the eagle, "is Arderydd, the High Eagle of Kymru. This is the bird that marked my face when I tried to run from my nature, from the truth about myself. Beware, Havgan of Corania, that this does not happen to you."

"I will not yield," Havgan said between gritted teeth. "I will not do other than kill the witches of Kymru as I can."

"So be it," Arthur said.

Sigerric moved up to stand next to Havgan, pulling the dagger from his belt.

"Put up your dagger, Sigerric," Gwydion said. "There will be no more bloodletting here today."

"What do you mean?" Sigerric demanded. "Surely you won't let us walk away from here!"

"But we will," Aergol said softly. "For this is the tarw-casglaid and to spill more blood would profane the Mother. The Druids have offended her enough. We will do so no more." It was hard for him to say, for the Golden Man had personally killed Aergol's mother, and he wanted so badly to pay Havgan back for that. But he knew that he must not. Not now.

"Go," Arthur said, still not taking his eyes from Havgan's. Arderydd sat quietly now on Arthur's arm like a statue. "Go. We will not fight today, Havgan of Corania. But I promise you, the day is coming soon when we will face each other on the field of battle. On that day you will die."

"Brave words from a little boy," Havgan sneered, but Aergol saw the flash of fear in the Golden Man's amber eyes.

"On that day," Arthur said again, softly, "you will die."

With a whirl of his golden cloak Havgan turned and stalked from the clearing. Sigerric had turned to follow, when Gwydion raised a hand to stop him.

"Sigerric," Gwydion said, "stay."

Sigerric halted and turned to face Gwydion. Havgan turned at the edge of the clearing to look back.

"Sigerric," Gwydion pleaded. "Don't follow him. Stay. Stay with us. As Talorcan has chosen to do."

"Stay, Sigerric," Rhiannon said, laying a gentle hand on his arm. "We know you. We know you for who you really are. Stay with us."

"If you know me for who I really am," Sigerric said, gently laying his hand on hers, "then you know I cannot stay." Regretfully Sigerric pulled away from Rhiannon. He turned to face Gwydion. "You should know that I cannot change what I am."

"And that is?" Gwydion asked.

"Friend to Havgan the Golden until the day I die." Sigerric

turned away and joined Havgan at the edge of the clearing. Then the two men were gone.

Aergol turned to the Druids gathered in the clearing. "Cathbad ap Goreau is no longer the Archdruid of Kymru. Now must Arthur ap Uthyr declare who shall lead the Druids." He turned to Arthur, waiting for the High King to do as they had agreed.

But Arthur confounded him. "I declare that Aergol ap Custennin var Dinaswyn is the new Archdruid of Kymru!" Arthur called. At his words the eagle spread its wings, and called out in triumph.

Aergol gasped as the cry went up from the assembled Druids. "High King!" Aergol cried. "This is not what we agreed. You cannot—"

"I can," Arthur replied firmly. "This is my will."

"I cannot accept. You know that I have something I must do instead."

"Do not be so sure, Aergol, that you know what the Mother wills for you," Arthur said.

Aergol shook his head. "I have explained more than once," he insisted. Arthur must understand, he thought. If the High King thought that he could turn Aergol back from his purpose, well, Arthur was sadly mistaken. The Mother would not be mocked.

"Yes, you have explained," Arthur replied. "More than once. But I do not accept it. You are the Archdruid of Kymru. Now do your duty."

Aergol opened his mouth to argue further, but changed his mind. There was more than one way to accomplish what must be done. If Arthur would not allow him to sacrifice himself to the Mother in private, then he would do so in public.

"Then," Aergol called, "I declare that my heir is my eldest child—my daughter, Sinend ur Aergol var Eurgain."

At his gesture Sinend came forward and knelt before him. He placed a gentle hand on her rich, reddish-brown hair. "High King, will you acknowledge my heir?"

"I will," Arthur replied. He too laid a hand on Sinend's head. "I declare that Sinend ur Aergol var Eurgain is the Archdruid's heir."

Sinend rose, her normally pale face suffused with pink. Aergol waited until the acclamations had died down and then he began.

"Know, my fellow Druids, that it is not enough to repent of what we have done. It is not enough to fight now on the side of the Kymri against our true enemy. It is not enough to put the former Archdruid to death. For is there anyone here who still doubts that the Mother is angry with her children for what they have done?"

The Druids fell silent, many of them casting their eyes to the ground. Aergol knew his fellow Druids. He knew that many of them had had doubts for some time. He knew that these doubts and the accompanying guilt were the reason they had been willing to listen when Aergol and his Druids had slipped into Caer Duir a few days ago and begun to talk. He knew that the Druids themselves were fully aware that more was needed, even if Arthur himself did not understand.

"The Mother requires another sacrifice," Aergol declared. "For someone must go to her, and beg for her forgiveness. Someone's soul must journey to her and offer itself up. That someone will be me."

A groan went up from the Druids but as Aergol had known would happen, none of them protested outright. For they all knew too well that he was right. Sinend's face again paled and tears stood in her gray eyes. Menw clenched his fists, but did not move. His dearest friends—Yrth, Aldur, and Madryn—bowed their heads to him.

But the one he expected to protest the most did not. Arthur stood quietly, his hands resting on Caladfwlch's hilt, the point of the sword on the ground between his feet, the eagle on his shoulder. The High King's dark eyes gazed at Aergol, but he said nothing.

"The mistletoe," Aergol said, and Madryn nodded. She went to the Druid who now held the golden sickle, and the Druid gently laid the blade in Madryn's hand. Madryn leapt to the lowest branch of one of the oak trees and swiftly climbed to the top, using the golden sickle to cut off a clump of mistletoe. Below her Aldur caught the plant in the white cloth and carried it to the still-boiling pot over the fire. Aldur plucked the leaves and berries and put them into the water while Yrth stirred the brew.

At Arthur's nod Menw picked up the discarded golden cup and took it to Yrth. After a few moments Yrth poured the concoction into the goblet. It was Sinend who took the cup from the old teacher and brought it to Aergol.

Aergol took the cup, lightly touching his daughter's fingers as he did so, in a brief farewell. He leaned forward and gently kissed his daughter's forehead. Then he lifted the cup over his head. "Modron," he cried, "I am coming to you! Accept my sacrifice! In so doing cleanse the Druids of any taint in your sight. For they are again your loyal sons and daughters. Once again, they are yours!"

He quaffed the drink, pouring the bitter brew down his throat. It burned as it went, spreading through his body. He felt a coldness begin to creep through him. His feet and his hands, then his legs and his arms went cold, then numb. He fell to the bull skin, trembling. He rolled onto his back so that his face would be toward the sky, so that his last sight would be of his son and daughter. Menw and Sinend stood side by side, holding hands, tears streaming down their faces as they watched Aergol's shivering, dying body.

Then Arthur came to stand beside them. Aergol could not read the expression in Arthur dark eyes, for a mist seemed to be coming over his sight. But he heard the High King very well as Arthur crouched down and murmured in Aergol's ear, "Do not be so sure, Archdruid, of what the Mother wants from you. For what man is ever sure of what goes on in the mind of a woman?"

And then the darkness took Aergol far, far away.

He opened his eyes to darkness so thick that he was surprised he could move. Though he could see nothing he could hear, and from the sound his robe made as he rose to his feet he thought he was in a large chamber of some kind.

In the darkness he felt for the smooth oak bracelet on his right arm, running his fingers over the wooden circle. "Great Mother," he whispered. His words reverberated off the unseen walls of the chamber and the echoes of his prayer seemed to mock him. "Great Modron," he murmured again. "Though I am unworthy, I beg for your gift of light, that I might better see the place to which you have brought me."

And, to his wonder and secret delight, when he stretched out his hand and called fire, the fire came. A fountain of flame rose up from what he now saw was the floor of an immense cave. The walls sparkled with milky-white crystal, with veins of gold and silver, with the rough angles of precious gems buried in the surface. In the glow of the fire he carefully examined the walls around him and understood what the Mother wanted. For the cave had no way out. He bowed his head to her will. He had hoped that he might see her, that he might fall to his knees before her, might, with his repentance, secure her forgiveness for his fellow Druids.

But it was not to be. He bowed his head in despair. He had no right to see Modron's face, and ought never to have expected it.

"Not so."

The voice, low and musical, with a hint of light, a hint of laughter, a hint of warmth, flowed over him. His head whipped up and his eyes met the green, cat-like eyes of a woman dressed in the robe of an Archdruid. On her head was the ghost of a golden tiara and on her throat was the specter of the Archdruid's emerald and golden torque. He knew her, though he did not understand how.

"Arywen ur Cadwy var Isabyr," Aergol whispered in awe. "Fifth Archdruid of Kymru. One of the Great Ones of High King Lleu Silver-Hand."

"Well met, Archdruid Aergol," Arywen said, smiling. "Very well met, indeed."

Aergol froze. "I fear, Archdruid Arywen, that we are ill-met."

"How so?"

"Can it be that you do not know what I have done? Surely you do. For some years, I supported Cathbad ap Goreau in his mad scheme to rid Kymru of all other Y Dawnus. When the enemy came, I helped them. I was in the highest of enemy councils. I helped lead my fellow Druids into their destruction."

"And did you not repent of that?" Arywen asked softly.

"Can that change what has happened?"

"Does it need to?"

Aergol fell silent, for that was a question he had not thought to ask himself.

"Archdruid Aergol, your wish to see the Mother is granted. It is for that that I am here."

Arywen stretched out her hand to Aergol. Trembling, Aergol took it. Her hand was smooth and cool, and her fingers were strong as she gripped his hand.

"Lift up your face, Aergol ap Custennin var Dinaswyn," Arywen commanded her voice huge and powerful. "Lift up your face and behold your goddess."

And as Aergol lifted his face and opened his eyes light flooded over him. He was standing in the middle of a sun-warmed apple orchard. The tangy scent of apple skins wafted through the air. Some trees were covered with thousands of pinkish apple blossoms, while others bore the ripe, red fruit itself. Branches, heavy with fruit, bent invitingly before him. Arywen reached out and held her hand beneath a branch. At that moment an apple fell squarely into her palm. She held out the apple to Aergol and he took it, without hesitation. At Arywen's nod he bit into the red fruit. The apple juice, both sweet and tart, spurted into his mouth and down his chin. He ate the apple to its core, reveling in the sweet, firm fruit.

Birds flocked throughout the trees, singing sweetly. Overhead the sky was bright blue, tufted here and there with clouds of fluffy white. At his feet herbs grew in profusion—rosemary and thyme, wild mint, sage and chamomile, vervain, feverfew and valerian. Vines twined throughout the orchard, heavy with rich, purple grapes. Other bushes dotted the orchard—hedges of blackthorn, barberry, and honeysuckle. Golden honeybees hummed as they flew from blossom to blossom.

"Behold, Archdruid, the Mother," Arywen said, gesturing to the place where his back was turned.

Aergol whirled around, appalled. His eyes first took in the cluster of eight men and one woman gathered around a huge throne of oak, flanked by two massive, green-eyed wolves. The nine all wore the green robe, golden tiara, and emerald torque of the Archdruids and Aergol knew that he was seeing the Archdruids of Kymru from Govannon, son of Math, the first Archdruid, to

Morvryn, the Tenth. They looked back at him gravely and Arywen crossed to join them, leaving Aergol standing alone.

Silence descended on the grove as Aergol fought for the courage to raise his eyes to the Mother who sat still as a statue on the oaken throne. The birds fell silent. The bees ceased their humming. The dead Archdruids of Kymru did not move. At last Aergol gathered all of his considerable courage and raised his eyes.

Her mass of thick, silky hair was the color of ripened wheat, strewn with flowers of red and purple, blue and yellow. Her glorious golden mane of hair rippled down her shoulders and spilled to the ground in glowing waves. Her beautiful face glittered with precious stones—emerald and ruby and sapphire. She was clothed in a misty gown of green that undulated and shimmered over her lush body.

Yet he could not meet her eyes, for he was too afraid. He fell to the ground at her feet, weeping. "Great Mother of All," Aergol sobbed, "I offer you my life. Take it, I beg—I, who have no right to ask anything at all. Take it in payment for the debt that the Druids owe to you. Forgive them, I beg."

"And you—do you not ask to be forgiven?" Modron inquired. "Think you that you have done nothing to be forgiven for?" Her voice contained something of the howl of the wolf, something of the song of the nightingale, something of the hardness of the oak, something of the softness of lush, green grasses.

"I do not ask forgiveness for myself, because I do not deserve it," Aergol answered through the tightness in his throat, still not daring to raise his eyes. "I knew even more than the others of Cathbad's plans, and still I went along with them."

"Aergol ap Custennin var Dinaswyn, look at me," Modron commanded. "Look into my eyes." And though Aergol was more afraid of doing so than of anything else—even of dying—he did as he was told. And what he saw there in the depths of her eyes shook him to his very core.

For her eyes—one moment the color of freshly turned earth, another moment the color of green fields, another moment the blue of cornflowers, another the gray of a wolf's pelt—held a warmth that he had not expected, a kindness that he had not prepared for, an understanding he had never before seen in anyone's eyes before.

"Arthur ap Uthyr was right, Aergol," Modron murmured. "For what man would presume to know the mind of a woman? Your sacrifice is unacceptable to me."

Aergol bowed his head again in despair. The Druids were lost, for Modron would not forgive them. I have failed, he thought in misery. Failed.

Modron went on. "I will not take your life, Aergol, for I have work for you to do in Kymru."

Aergol's head shot up in disbelief and Modron smiled. Her smiled warmed him, filled his heart to bursting with joy.

"I will send you back to Kymru. Your task is to give to High King Arthur all that he needs to be victorious over the enemy. Your task is to lead the Druids back to their proper place in Kymru—beside the other Y Dawnus, neither above them nor below them. Your task is to be the Twelfth Archdruid of Kymru and to cleanse the Druids of taint. Will you accept this task?"

"With all my heart," Aergol cried as he sprang to his feet.

"Then go, Aergol ap Custennin, and do as I have bid you. Go."

Arthur stood silently in the grove, Caladfwlch again sheathed by his side. Sinend crouched beside Aergol's cold body, stroking her father's hair back from his face. Menw, tears streaming down his face, rose and stood before Arthur.

"I ask that you will stay for the ceremony, High King," Menw choked out.

"Ceremony?" Arthur asked.

"His burial," Menw clarified. "We must bury him."

"Oh, I wouldn't do that if I were you," Arthur said, gesturing to Aergol's body.

Aergol stirred on the bull's hide. His eyelids fluttered opened and Sinend cried out. Menw stood stock-still, his eyes wide in disbelief, his tears turned to tears of joy. Yrth gave a great shout and the other Druids clustered around Aergol's prone but very much alive body.

"How long?" Aergol rasped, looking up at Arthur.

"Only a few moments," Arthur said.

With his children's help Aergol regained his feet. "How did you know?" Aergol asked Arthur.

Arthur grinned. "I didn't. But I hoped."

"She sent me back. She said that I had work to do for her. She said that the Druids must give you all that you need from us to defeat the enemy."

Arthur nodded. "Then this is what I need. I need your Druids to divide into four groups. Each group will journey to one of the four kingdoms. There they will, at my direction, fight in the final battles to regain our land."

"Then that is what you shall have," Aergol answered. "For we are yours."

Arthur signaled to Gwydion, Rhiannon, and Gwen. "We will return to Cadair Idris. Your Druids must be long gone before Havgan even thinks to return with his warriors at his back. Join us at Cadair Idris as soon as you can."

"It shall be as you say, High King," Aergol answered, bowing.

As Arthur walked from the clearing, followed by Gwydion, Rhiannon, and Gwen, the Druids bowed low. Even the oak trees seemed to bend slightly as he walked by.

He exited the grove and took up the reins of his horse. He mounted and turned to the shadowy stones of Aelwyd Derwen, the burial mounds of the Archdruids. He nodded once, in satisfaction, then turned to go. Cathbad's muffled screams followed them across the sunlit plain, until they went far enough to leave the screams behind.

Chapter Fourteen

Cadair Idris & Eiodel
Gwytheryn, Kymru &
Athelin, Marc of Ivelas, Coranian Empire
Eiddew Mis & Nemonath, 500

Suldydd, Cynyddu Wythnos—midmorning

Rhiannon sat in the High King's reception room at Cadair Idris, patiently waiting for Arthur to begin the council meeting. The walls of the oval room, positioned in the center of the fifth level, the Level of Modron, were decorated with sheets of beaten gold and silver. Bright banners depicting the High Kings of Kymru hung on the wall.

One showed High King Idris during the Battle of Coed Llachar, facing the forces of his rebellious son, Pryderi. The second showed High King Macsen in his final battle against the Coranian oath-breakers that would murder him. The third showed High King Lleu returning in triumph from freeing his cousin, Branwen, from a Coranian prison.

A round, oak table, capable of seating twenty, stood in the center of the room. The honey-colored oak was polished to a high sheen and its surface was carved with a map of Kymru, drawn to scale, showing all four kingdoms and Gwytheryn, with the capitals and other main cities represented.

Here Arthur had gathered his four Great Ones—Gwydion the Dreamer, Elstar Ardewin, Elidyr Master Bard, and Aergol, the Archdruid. Within a few years these four would give place to their heirs, and Arthur would have around him those four Great Ones that had been destined to be wholly his—Cariadas as the Dreamer, Llywelyn for the Dewin, Cynfar for the Bards, and Sinend for the Druids.

But for now the war was still not won, and Arthur continued to work with the Great Ones given him by circumstance. Not that these four did not support Arthur—far from it. But they were fully aware that they were a generation older than the High King, and that they must soon give place to their children. Gwydion, Rhiannon knew, was looking forward to it.

Gwydion caught her eye and smiled at her, his gray eyes alight. That was something few would believe also—Gwydion ap Awst in love. But he was. And she knew it with every fiber of her being. He had left her with no doubts about that. When Gwydion did make up his mind he didn't do things by halves. Never in all her life, even in the first flush of love with Rhoram, had she felt so loved, so cared for, and—above all—so safe.

Yet safe seemed like such an odd thing to feel right now. For events were rushing toward a culmination that was anything but safe, and Arthur prepared now for what would be his last throws of the dice in the gamble to free Kymru.

The last gamble two weeks ago, turning the Druids back to Arthur's side, had succeeded. The thought that Cathbad was at last dead continued to have the power to cheer her. For if there was ever a man who deserved the Death of the Mother, that man had been Cathbad. The only man who might deserve it more would be Havgan himself.

Arthur strode in and took a seat at the table. He nodded to the five of them—the Great Ones and Rhiannon, and then, without preamble, began.

"Aergol?" he asked.

Aergol responded promptly. "All Druids are in position. The Druids at Prydyn are lead by Ellywen, and Madryn leads those at Dinmael. The Druids at Llywarth are lead by Sabrina, and those at Tegeingl by Yrth. Each of these has four seasoned Druids with them for you to draw on. Each remaining city throughout Kymru has at least two Druids ready to assist the Cerddorian as commanded. Here in Gwytheryn Aldur, Sinend, Menw, Gwen, and I are available to you for what other needs you may have. Their loyalty—"

"Has been vouched for," Arthur said smoothly.

"No doubts?" Aergol challenged.

"None. I have touched the minds of each one, and know them to be loyal and true."

Aergol inclined his head. "And ready to serve you. Now and forever."

Arthur nodded. "Excellent. Elstar?"

"We have fewer resources, as you know, than the Druids, for many of the Dewin and Bards are still held captive at Afalon," she began. Aergol stirred in his chair and Elstar turned to him. "Aergol, I do not say this to make you uncomfortable—"

"But because it is the truth," Aergol finished. He smiled bitterly. "I know. It's just that—"

"What's done is done, Aergol," Gwydion broke in. "And if your Druids were not on our side today our plans would be fruitless."

Aergol nodded and subsided. At Arthur's gesture Elstar continued. "In each of the four capitals we have at least two Dewin available that Arthur can tap into for visuals of the battle. In addition, in Cadair Idris now we have Myrrdin, Rhiannon, Neuad, Regan, Talorcan, and Llywelyn to augment you as necessary. All Dewin that formed the informational chain around Kymru are moving into position in the cities closest to their respective areas."

"Good," Arthur said. "Elidyr?"

"Essentially the same report, Arthur," Elidyr said. "The Bards are ready and in position throughout Kymru. And here in Cadair Idris are myself, Dudod, and Cynfar to bolster your efforts as necessary. We are ready."

"Although Cariadas and I are only two, we are also ready to help as needed in any capacity," Gwydion said.

"And the Cerddorian?" Elstar asked.

"Are also ready," Arthur said. He gestured at the map of Kymru carved into the table. "Gwydion?"

"In Prydyn," Gwydion began, "Rhoram's Cerddorian are divided into three sections, each taking one cantref under its command. The Cerddorian led by Marared of Brycheiniog and Dadweir Heavy-Hand are taking the remaining four cantrefs.

Although the Cerddorian are spread somewhat thin we believe it will be enough, as the common folk themselves are armed and ready."

"And in Ederynion?" Arthur prompted.

"The Cerddorian led by Elen and Lludd are in position, divided into the three southern cantrefs. The four northern cantrefs are under the leadership of Drwys Iron-Fist. In Rheged, Owein's Cerddorian have been divided between Amgoed and Ystrad Marchell. Hetwin Silver-Brow is taking Penrhyn and Gwinionydd. Breinol and Gwent are under the leadership of Tyrnon Twrf Liant. Atlantas is taking Malienydd."

"And Gwynedd?" Aergol asked.

"The Cerddorian led by Morrigan have been divided into the four southern cantrefs. Isgowan, the Lady of Arfon, is taking Lleyn, Arfon, and Arllechwedd."

"Excellent," Arthur said crisply. "I believe that we will have enough Y Dawnus to accomplish what we must. The hardest part will be the fog, but with a full compliment of Druids that can be done. We have enough Dewin to fully track the progress of each battle and enough Bards to communicate both between ourselves and with the animals as needed."

Although Arthur spoke with confidence there was a slight chill in the room. For none of them, including Arthur, were quite sure that there would be enough Bards and Dewin, considering that the majority of those still alive were held captive in Afalon.

"Again, Arthur," Elstar said. "I must question your wisdom in putting off the rescue of the Y Dawnus. If we only had them to help us—"

"As he has said before, Elstar," Rhiannon jumped in, "those we rescue on Afalon will not be fit to help with anything for some time. To rescue them now, before we begin the major battles, would only put Havgan on alert long before we need him to be."

"Four hundred Y Dawnus were taken in the death march across Kymru," Arthur said in a hollow tone. "Of those only two hundred made it to Afalon. At least half of those have died, but others have been captured since and brought to that island. So now there are at least one hundred Bards and Dewin that suffer agony every single day. They are collared. And tortured. Starved. Beaten. Do you truly think," he went on, his voice harsh, "that I have forgotten them? Do you think that I have forsaken them?"

"No one thinks that for a moment, Arthur," Gwydion said quietly.

Arthur challenged each of them with his dark gaze, then sat back in his chair, gripping the armrests tightly. "They shall be rescued," he said quietly. "At the proper time. And the proper time is coming soon. Suggestions?"

"I have one," Rhiannon said. "What we need most on Afalon is a diversion. So, how about entertainment for the troops?" she asked.

Gwydion nodded. "Not bad. You and I could—"

"Not you," Rhiannon said.

"Why not me?"

"We need a real Coranian," Rhiannon replied, with a triumphant smile, "to get me in."

"Talorcan," Arthur said.

"What do you mean 'to get you in?'" Gwydion asked in a dangerously quite tone.

"What do you think I mean?" Rhiannon asked, challenging him.

Gwydion rose, his face red with rage. "Are you mad?"

"I am an excellent dancer. You taught me yourself, remember?"

"Of course I remember! And that is exactly why you aren't going to do this!"

"You have to admit that you have never seen anyone do the Dance of Freya as well as I do," Rhiannon pointed out. "And if there was ever a dance guaranteed to create a distraction, it's that one."

"I will not permit it!" Gwydion raged. "Not for one moment!"

"Well, Gwydion, far be it from me to be rude—"

"Ha!" he shouted.

"But I believe it is not your decision to make," Rhiannon finished.

Gwydion whipped around to Arthur, his silvery eyes molten

with rage. But Arthur forestalled him, holding up his hand to quiet the Dreamer. "Enough. She will go," Arthur said. His tone brooked no argument. Even Gwydion recognized that tone and sank back into his seat, though it was clear that he was not finished with the subject.

For a moment they were all silent. Then Aergol spoke. "It would seem, High King, that you plan for the final battle here in Gwytheryn to be near Calan Llachar."

"The battle will be on Calan Llachar," Arthur corrected.

"Then know that this. On Calan Llachar there will be a full eclipse of the sun, as there was eighteen years ago."

"On the day I was born," Arthur finished. "Yes. I know."

ARIANROD CLIMBED THE stairs leading to the battlements. She climbed slowly, for her pregnancy was well advanced and her body was cumbersome and she tired easily. She placed her hand on her belly and the child within her leapt beneath her palm. It would be a boy, she knew. And she had determined his name—Medrawd, which meant "skillful" in her tongue. Havgan said that, in Corania, the name would be Mordred, so that was what he had taken to calling the unborn child. But in her thoughts he was Medrawd, and she longed for the day when she would hold her son in her arms.

Torches flickered in their brackets at intervals along the walls. Overhead the night sky was strewn with stars. The constellation of Brenin's Torque, the cluster of stars strung out as if on a necklace, glowed brightly. Wiber, the Serpent, snaked across the sky.

She halted for a moment on the stairs to catch her breath. Her eye caught the constellation of Dahut. Dahut was the woman who had caused the destruction of Lyonesse, the land that had sunk into the sea. Although Dahut had been beloved of Llyr she had cared nothing for the man who would be the first Dreamer. She had cared only for power and had, in reaching for it, reached too far, thus bringing terrible disaster to her people.

Sometimes Arianrod wondered if she as any better than Dahut. For wasn't Arianrod helping to bring disaster to her people? She helped Havgan in any way she could. She had even stood by while her lover killed her aunt, the woman who had fed and sheltered and—let it be said—loved her. Was she any different than Dahut?

Ah, but one thing at least was different—so different. For Arianrod was in love, and not with power. True, for most of her life she had been. But when she met Havgan the Golden all that changed. For she had fallen in love with the Warleader of Corania. He owned her now—all that she was and all that she could be. She belonged to him completely and did not care that he knew it. Her pride had been the first thing to go, along with her heart.

At last she reached the top of the battlements and made her way to the north side, knowing where he was and what he was doing. She was, of course, right. He was facing north, staring at Cadair Idris. The mountain glowed golden against the darkened sky. Torches glittered over the gold and rubies he wore. His honey-blond hair—so like her own—shimmered in the golden light. He heard her coming and turned to greet her. His amber eyes—so like her own—glowed at the sight of her.

She went to him and laid her hand on his shoulder as he turned back around to the mountain. He did not turn around again, but he did place his hand over hers.

"*Cariad*," she murmured. "Won't you come inside and eat? It is late."

"It is later, perhaps, than anyone thinks."

She knew what he meant, and knew what he needed her to say. And so she did say it, though she did not necessarily believe it. "The sailor will get to Corania with your message. Aesc will send the warriors to you that you ask for. They will come. And come in time."

He whirled to face her. "Do you believe that?" he asked, his hawk-like gaze sharp and gleaming. "Do you truly?"

"I do truly," she answered without hesitation.

"The Druids are lost to us."

"That matters, but not enough. Arthur will use them to try to defeat you, but he will not succeed."

"And why not?" he asked.

"Because you are Havgan the Golden, because you were meant

to rule this land, because you belong here. You belong inside that mountain," she nodded to Cadair Idris. "And inside that mountain you will be. It is meant to be. It is right. And it will happen."

Arianrod took his hand and placed it on her belly. "This is the reason why you will win," she continued. "For our child. For our son. You will win so you may hand him Kymru when he is born. He is meant to have it, to take it as a gift from you. It is for this that he is to be born."

He gazed down at her for a long time, and as he did the expression in his eyes began to change. Fear changed to passion. And anger altered to desire. "I have told you, my love," he said, "that in Corania I was promised that you would be here. Holda, she of the Wild Hunt, told me this. The cards of the wyrd-galdra told me this. They all said that the other half of my soul was here, in Kymru. And they were right."

For a moment she thought her heart would break as joy and fear in equal measure spilled from it. For she loved this man more than she had ever thought possible. And she was so close to losing him, for, if he failed here in Kymru, he would be forced to pay for it with his life. Never had she felt for a man the way she felt about this man. Never had she felt such a kinship, as though he was simply another part of her, two sides of the same coin, two halves of the same whole.

Arianrod smiled slowly as Havgan knelt before her. He kissed her swollen belly through the thin material of her gown and reached up to touch her full breasts that strained against her tawny robe. He slowly loosened the ties of her dress then pulled it off her shoulders. His breath was hot as he teased her with his lips and tongue. She moaned and arched her back against the rough stone.

He pulled her to him, kissing her mouth, her face, her neck, her breasts with such passion that she was dizzy. He yanked up her skirts and then he was inside her and she cried out with pleasure as he took her.

She would not lose him. She would never let him go.

PRINCESS AELFWYN MUTTERED curses beneath her breath as she

reached the stairway leading up to the battlements. Always her husband ended up there, staring over at Cadair Idris, as though the strength of his gaze would accomplish what all other stratagems had not—entry into the hall of the High Kings of Kymru.

He would never get in there, she was convinced. And if he should come close, she would be there to ensure that it did not happen. She cared nothing for the Kymri and their freedom, but she did care that her hated husband would not possess the thing he wanted most.

Starlight and torchlight shimmered over her pristine white gown. Diamonds gleamed within the coils of her blond hair. Her green eyes glittered at the thought of her dearest wish fulfilled—Havgan lying dead at her feet.

So far in her time here she had been able to do very little. She had done her best to keep Arianrod from capturing the Dreamer, but her warning had come too late. She had occasionally been able to get word to Cadair Idris of minor engagements, but nothing much had come of that.

In fact, the most important thing she had done since coming to Kymru was to discover a tool she had never imagined she had—Sigerric of Apuldre. For Sigerric was Havgan's staunchest friend. Loyal to a fault, he continued to serve Havgan, even though he was sickened by many of the things Havgan did.

Even though he was in love with Havgan's wife.

Yes, Sigerric was in love with her—a fact she had discovered not along ago. She could say she had done nothing about that because she was still turning over in her mind how best to use him. And that would be true—within limits. Because the other part of the truth was that knowing Sigerric loved her sometimes had the power to make her heart beat faster, to make her skin flush, to make her shiver.

But that was only sometimes. And, even so, it did not really matter. For Aelfwyn was the daughter of the Emperor and Empress of Corania, and she knew better than to be ruled by her heart.

Once she had lost her heart to someone. She had loved her cousin, Aelbald. And Havgan had killed him in the fight for Bana of the Empire, in the fight for the right to wed her, bed her, and rule Corania through her.

She closed her eyes briefly, for the events of her wedding night with Havgan still had the power to make her feel dizzy with hatred and shame. Never would she endure such treatment at anyone's hands again. Never would she forgive the man who had humiliated her, and so obviously gloried in it.

She shook her head, for these thoughts were useless, and began to climb the stairs. She had some business with her husband. She wanted to ensure that he fully understood that the game was almost up, that Kymru continued to slip through his hands, that it always would.

For the Dreamer had been rescued. Queen Elen of Ederynion had been freed from her captivity, and Talorcan, one of Havgan's most trusted generals had gone with her. Queen Enid of Rheged had been freed and General Baldred had been killed. General Penda in Prydyn had captured a Dewin and a Druid, and had, inexplicably, let them both slip through his fingers. And King Madoc of Gwynedd had died at the hands of his own father.

And just a few short weeks ago, the Druids had turned from him, giving their allegiance to High King Arthur. The Druids had put the Archdruid to death in a pitiless manner. She had heard that Cathbad had screamed from his barrow beneath the earth for three days and had lingered for some days more before finally dying.

Arthur had been able to seal the island, ensuring that no word could come to Corania that Havgan needed additional troops. Arthur was nearing the endgame, nearing the time when the two men would face each other on the field of battle. And that was a day that Aelfwyn longed for, because surely, in such a contest, Arthur would win and Havgan would die.

She neared the top of the stairs and rounded the last corner, and came to a sudden stop. For there, blocking her way, was Sigerric.

Sigerric stood stolidly, his arms crossed over his chest. He wore tunic and trousers of dark brown, and gold glittered at his throat, his wrists, and his ears. He had a golden dagger at his belt and the hilts of two more daggers glittered from the turned-down cuffs of his high boots.

"General," she said, inclining her head as he bowed to her. He straightened, then again crossed his arms over his chest. She stepped forward, knowing he would step aside for her. But she sprang back at the last moment to avoid running into him, for he did not move out of her way.

"Sigerric," she said firmly. "Step aside."

"I regret to inform you that I cannot, Princess," Sigerric replied.

"I wish to speak to my husband."

"Then you must wait," he said firmly.

He had never taken this tone with her before, and she was at a loss on how to proceed. "He is my husband and I will speak to him when I please."

Sigerric sighed. "He is busy, Princess. But he will return to the hall shortly. I would be happy to tell him that you wish to see him then."

"But I wish to see him now," she said sharply.

"Princess, it pains me to deny you anything, but I must."

"What is he so busy doing?" she asked. "Staring out at that mountain?"

Sigerric shrugged, but she knew better.

"Is he alone?"

"Princess—"

"Why must you call me that all the time?" she asked irritably. "I have a name."

He swallowed. "I would not dare to use it, Princess."

"Am I so frightening then?" she asked. "Such a figure of horror that you must be so formal?"

"I think you know what you are to me," he said quietly.

She raised her eyes to look into his. They stood face to face like that, not moving, for a very long moment. And in that moment she became aware that her heart was beating faster, that her pulse was racing, that she wanted him to speak of the things she saw in his eyes.

But the hard side of her, the side that belonged to her mother, came uppermost then. She put aside her longing and reached instead for a tool to use to bring down the man she hated. She would speak to Sigerric of Havgan and all that he had done to her. And Sigerric would kill Havgan for her. He would. He must.

"My husband—" she began.

"Will have my loyalty until the day he dies."

"And me?" she asked bitterly, her hopes dashed. "What will I have?"

"My heart. Forever and ever and ever."

"Then free me," she cried.

"I cannot," he replied, his voice low and sad. "I am what I am. And cannot be anything else."

Movement behind Sigerric caught her eye and she saw Arianrod, her husband's whore, his Kymric witch, coming towards them. Her gown was awry and her hair was loosened and disheveled. There were love bites on her neck and her lips were slightly swollen. She moved slowly, awkward from her pregnancy, but her movements were dreamy, and she smiled to herself the smile of a woman who loved and was loved in return.

That was a smile Aelfwyn had never felt on her own face. And the sight of it enraged her. "So this is what you would keep me from interrupting, Sigerric?" she said harshly. "The sight of my husband rutting with his whore?"

Arianrod smiled, as though Aelfwyn's rage amused her. "Ah, the barren wife. Come to seek out the husband who despises her."

"You speak to the Princess of Corania, Arianrod," Sigerric said softly. "And will show her the respect she deserves."

"Oh, but I do," Arianrod replied. "I give her all the respect she does indeed deserve."

Arianrod grinned, her amber eyes alight, her honey-blond hair tumbling around her shoulders in the flickering torchlight. And, for some reason, Sigerric stiffened, drawing his breath in sharply.

"What is it?" Aelfwyn asked.

But Sigerric shook his head and refused to answer.

WHEN SIGERRIC HAD gazed down at Aelfwyn it had taken all that he had to keep from framing her flawless face with his hands and kissing her. He ached to do it, but he could not. For she was Princess of Corania, daughter to the Emperor. She was the wife of his blood brother. That Havgan did not love her did not matter—Sigerric was simply not capable of betraying his brother like that, no matter how much he longed to do so.

And he did. Oh, he did. More than anyone could ever know, he wished with all his heart that he could take the woman he had loved so dearly for so long into his arms.

But it could not be. It could never be, unless Havgan chose to let Aelfwyn go. But that was something he would never do. For it was only through marriage to Aelfwyn that Havgan would rule Corania. And Havgan would not give up that dream—for anyone or anybody.

And why should he? For he could have both his wife and the throne that came with her as well as his mistress, the woman he loved, the woman who would bear his son.

That was the woman he turned to face when Aelfwyn spoke. And that was when Sigerric saw what he should have seen long ago.

It was, he realized, what Cynan Ardewin had seen. It was what Anieron Master Bard had seen. It was what Dinaswyn, the Dreamer had seen. It was the real reason why those three were dead—dead before they could speak the truth.

Because when Sigerric had looked at Arianrod in the fiery light—she with her amber eyes like Havgan's and her honey-blond hair like Havgan's, she with the same lazy smile he sometimes saw on Havgan's face—he had seen the truth.

Havgan and Arianrod. Two halves of the same whole.

Brother and sister.

Which meant, in turn, that Havgan and Gwydion were cousins, for Sigerric knew full well the story of Arianrod's parents and how they were related to the Dreamer. He saw for the first time how alike Gwydion and Havgan were. But he had been blinded, as had so many, by their differences. Yet Gwydion—black and silver as the moon in the night sky—and Havgan—red and gold as the morning sun—were merely two sides of the same coin.

Havgan was one of the hated witches of Kymru. He was that very thing that he had been trying to destroy.

Horror flooded him as the truth washed over him. But he would never speak of this to Havgan or to anyone else. He could not. Never would he be able to speak such words past the dark revulsion and horrified pity he felt.

For what was the child that Arianrod carried beneath her heart? What kind of child would brother and sister witches produce to the ruin of them all?

Mandeag, Sol 30—noon

BY THE TIME HE reached Athelin he was weak and dizzy from adequate lack of food and rest, but he did not pause for either. His clothes were filthy, salt-encrusted rags. His beard had grown out in tangled, dirty locks. He was thin, almost skeletal. But he did not stop. He could not.

He staggered from the docks, down Lindstrat, ignoring the offers of food, companionship, and easy money—all the lures that were thrown his way as he left the waterfront and entered the city proper.

People strode by him in a hurry, intent on their own business. Lindstrat was dim, crowded on either side by houses whose upper stories hung over the street, cutting off the sun. It was spring and the air was crisp but warming slightly. He passed the house where Havgan had lived before winning the hand of the Princess, but he kept going, for there was nothing for him there.

He crossed Flanstrat and beheld Byrnwiga, the great, dark fortress that belonged to the Warleaders of the Empire. But he did not halt there, either, for the man he sought would not be there.

He turned west, headed toward the place where the man he had been sent to find would surely be. The four great towers of Cynerice Scima soared up to the sky as though attempting to pierce it and wrest it to the earth. The Emperor's palace flashed golden and white in the noonday sun. The building, which rested on an island in the center of the city, seemed to float on the River Saefern, like a vision of heaven come to earth. Downstream to his left he could see the shadow of Waelraest Hlaew, where the bodies of the former Emperors and Empresses of the empire came to rest.

He crossed the bridge to the great east gate of Cynerice Scima and waited his turn to enter. Carts full of victuals, men dressed in fine clothes, soldiers in gleaming silver byrnies, all crowded in and out of the palace. After weeks of having only the sound of the sea for company, he felt disoriented and cowed by the din. But he had a job to do. He had promised.

When he reached the guards they took one look at him and rolled their eyes. The captain gestured sharply for one of the guards to help him on his way out with a foot on his backside. But he was prepared for this. Without a word he fished out the ring he had been given.

The great ruby glittered under the sun like a fistful of blood. The captain froze, taking in the gem, then looked up. "What do you do here, with such a fortune, thief?"

"I am not a thief," he said, with what dignity he could muster.

"What are you then?"

"A messenger."

He gave the name of the man he had been sent to see. For a moment he thought he would still not be let in. But the captain finally nodded to two guards, detailing them to take the old sailor where he wished to go.

"But know this, old man," the captain said, his cold blue eyes pitiless, "if this is a mistake, I will see that you pay for it, not I."

"No mistake," he said. "None at all."

"Go then."

He followed the soldiers into the palace. He hardly dared to breathe once inside, for all the richness of the place took his breath away. Great tapestries, spun in rich colors of green and red, of amber and gold, of blue and purple covered the fine, marble walls.

One showed Wuffa, founder of the Wufmaegth, the second dynasty, killing his wife's brothers as they attempted to rescue their sister from his hated embrace. Another showed Sigger of the Sigmaegth conquering the kingdom of Mierce, killing King Centwine, spitting the king's baby son on a spear, and forcing Queen Cyneburga to become his queen. A third showed Emperor Aelle, founder of the present dynasty, the Aelmaegth, defeating the Dereans, killing King Ingild and watching as Queen Hildelinda threw herself off the tower rather than fall into Coranian hands.

But all that was as nothing to the most beautiful room he had ever seen—the Gulden Hul of the Emperors of Corania. The great, golden roof was held up by eight pillars, carved in the likeness of mighty trees and sheathed in gleaming gold. The floor was covered with tiles of gold and the walls were covered with sheets of beaten gold. Candles filled the hall, making it gleam softly. In the center a huge tree of gold stood, spreading its jewel-covered branches up to the roof. Mechanical, jeweled birds nested in its branches, occasionally singing with the sounds of tinkling bells.

Two golden thrones stood at the north end of the hall on a dais covered with cloth of gold. The Flyflot, the banner of the Emperor, hung on the wall behind the thrones, worked in amethysts and gold.

The Emperor himself was surprisingly small and pale, his fine blond hair falling lankly to his narrow shoulders. His head seemed bent by the weight of the golden diadem, Cyst Eorcanstan, and the huge jewels of amber, emerald, and sapphire that adorned it.

The Empress, by contrast, seemed vitally alive. Athelflead sat on the smaller throne and her rich, brown hair, still untouched by frost, was curled and braided, spilling down her alabaster shoulders.

But at this moment he did not really have eyes for either of them. He was only interested in the man who stood at the bottom of the dais. Prince Aesc, the Emperor's brother, seemed to have all the vitality that his older brother lacked. His powerful shoulders strained against the cloth of his amber tunic. His blond beard was rich and full and his bright, blue eyes glittered with intelligence in his tanned, leathery face.

The guards made their way through the crowd in the hall and he followed. At last they stood before Aesc. The prince raised his brow and looked inquiringly.

Torgar, sailor for Corania for years beyond counting, gave an awkward bow and held out Havgan's ruby ring to the prince.

Aesc took it and it glittered in his palm with a light of its own. "He is well?" the prince asked anxiously.

"He was well when I last saw him. I am Torgar, and he has sent me with a message to you."

"What is his need?"

"Soldiers. In Kymru before the month is out."

"Then," Aesc said, simply, "it shall be done."

Chapter Fifteen

Arberth
Kingdom of Prydyn, Kymru
Eiddew Mis, 500

Llundydd, Cynyddu Wythnos—early morning

At Rhoram's signal Achren extinguished the torch. Velvety darkness descended, so thick here in the heart of the caves that honeycombed the cliffs beneath Caer Tir that Rhoram thought he could almost taste it. He put out his hand and lightly touched Achren's arm. He reached out with his other hand and touched the cave just where the rough wall gave way to smooth stone. He moved forward with one hand on the wall to guide him and the other hand in Achren's to guide her.

After a few feet in the palpable darkness, he halted. He could tell by the feel of the air on his face that the hidden door was just in front of him. He pressed one ear against the almost imperceptible place where the stone door joined the stone wall and listened.

The faintest wisp of sound through the stone told him what he had expected—that the chamber on the other side of the door was not empty. He guessed that there were not many guards there—possibly only one in the makeshift prison General Penda had created on the first floor of Caer Tir's northwest watchtower.

He reached out and lightly touched the spring that would release the catch on the door. He could tell by touch that the catch was still in working order. General Penda had indeed destroyed the secret passage that he had discovered when Ellywen was captured less than a month ago. But he had not looked hard enough—if at all—for yet another door. Rhoram smiled in the darkness, for he had been quite sure that the second door had fooled them all.

He briefly squeezed Achren's hand to indicate she should be ready. Achren released his hand. The faintest steely rasp told him she had drawn her sword.

"Now," he breathed to her then pressed the catch. The door sprang open and he and Achren leapt through.

A lone guard whirled toward them, his axe raised. Quick as thought Achren darted forward, ducking low to let the axe swing pass harmlessly over her and thrusting upward with her blade, burying it in the guard's belly. Rhoram sprang behind the man and put his hand over the dying guard's mouth. The guard sank to the floor without a sound.

A few torches lit the chamber, illuminating the stone walls and empty cells. Achren rose and went to the wooden door leading out into the courtyard. She silently opened the door a crack and looked out. After a few moments she turned back to him.

"No movement in the courtyard," Achren said softly. "And the watch won't change for another hour at least. Time for you to do what you have to do before dawn."

Rhoram silently laid the dead man down full length on the stone floor. He glanced up at her and there was something about this moment, about what they had come here to do, about what awaited the city at dawning, that made him want speak the truth.

Her dark hair was braided tightly to her scalp. She wore a close-fitting tunic of dark green and trousers of black leather as well as worn, black leather boots from which two daggers protruded. As she looked down at him her dark eyes sparkled and her generous mouth grinned at the thought of what this day's work would mean.

And, to him, she was beautiful. More beautiful than any woman he had ever seen. More beautiful to him, truth be told, than Rhiannon had been—and she had been his measure of beauty since he had lost her so many years ago. It had seemed so strange at first, when he realized that he had fallen in love with Achren ur Canhustyr, the woman who had been his captain for so many years. Strange because he had known her for so long. He had fought battles with her, had hunted game with her, had fought the Coranians with her at his side. Had, at the last, fallen in love with her. Or, perhaps, had always been, but only recently realized it.

He had spoken of his feelings for her only once, and she had stopped him then, refusing to take him seriously. So he had bided his time, knowing that she would one day come to believe him. That day was today.

"Do you think to crouch here all day?" she asked acidly when he did not immediately rise.

"I love you," he said simply.

Her eyes widened in surprise as he rose to his feet. "What in the world—" she began to sputter.

"I told you once before, but you didn't believe me," he went on as though she had not spoken. "You didn't think I would just let it go, did you?"

"I thought—and do think—that you don't know what you are saying," she said firmly.

"I won't wait forever, Achren, for you to decide to believe me. And, unlike every other man you have ever met, I don't fear you."

"This is hardly the time or the place to—" she began.

But she was wrong. For this was exactly the time and place. This moment, before he cast the die and risked everything on the throw he was making here this morning. The end of this day would see him either restored to his own hall or dead in it. And it was that knowledge that drove him now as he reached out, pulled her to him, and fastened his lips over hers.

The kiss was sweet, sweeter than he had thought possible. He held her tightly against him, feeling every line and curve of her body against his. Her mouth parted beneath his questing lips and he moaned softly as he held her even tighter.

He kissed her slowly, thoroughly, savoring the taste of her. At last he released her and they were both breathless. "Now do you believe me?" he asked.

"Rhoram," she began.

He released her and crossed the room, softly opening the door. "When you get her bring her to me," he said. "You know where

I will be." Before he stepped out into the night he looked back at her. "Oh, and save my place," he grinned. "Because I'll be back to take up where I left off."

And then he slipped out into the courtyard of Caer Tir. He did not look back.

He crossed the silent courtyard swiftly, melting into the shadows that were cast by the flickering torches set at intervals along the fortress walls. Dense, pale fog covered the sky, cutting off visibility.

The watchtower was only a few feet from the walls of the king's ystafell, so Rhoram did not have far to go to reach his destination. He crept through the narrow alleyway between the back of the ystafell and the walls of Caer Tir until he was directly beneath the second-story window of what used to be his chambers.

He pulled out the weighted, thin rope where he had secured it on his belt. He whirled the weight over his head once, twice, three times, then let it fly. It arched overhead and then snaked down, catching the eave as it did so, wrapping securely around the protruding wood. He pulled down on it to ensure it was fastened tightly. He wrapped the rope around his forearm, then began to climb up the wall.

When he reached the second-story window he pulled his dagger from his belt and deftly flicked the catch. He soundlessly opened the casement outward, then climbed inside.

He knew the room well, so he easily avoided the furniture in the darkened chamber, creeping silently until he stood at the foot of the huge bed. By the light of the stars he barely made out the outline on the coverlet—a wolf's head worked in black on a dark green background. The sleeper's even breathing seemed to make the wolf's head nod back at him, as though the animal bade him go on.

Rhoram softly made his way to the fireplace and stirred the glowing coals, laying a log on top of them. Flames licked at the wood then grew to illuminate the chamber. The sleeper stirred but did not awaken.

Rhoram opened the oaken chest at the foot of the bed and

pulled out the scabbard he saw lying on top. He pulled the blade from the scabbard and tossed the naked blade onto the end of the bed. Then he drew his own sword with a steely hiss.

The sleeper awoke. His red hair was awry; his small piglike eyes widened at the sight of Rhoram and his scar whitened on his face.

"Wake up, Erfin," Rhoram said softly. "Wake up and die."

Erfin, who, for all his cowardice always retained a great deal of cunning sprang to the end of the bed, snatched up the sword, and rolled over the coverlet to the floor in one fluid movement.

Rhoram did not move; he merely watched Erfin. "Did you think I was going to stop you?" he asked softly. "Then you are indeed a fool."

"You are the fool," Erfin snarled. "You should have killed me while I slept."

"I wanted to," Rhoram said in a confidential tone. "I really did. But High King Arthur thought it would be best to kill you in a duel. He felt I would enjoy that more."

"A duel? Did you learn nothing from last time?"

"I learned a great deal. And more since then," Rhoram answered gently. "Now, brother mine, fight me."

"I don't have to fight you," Erfin sneered. "I only have to raise my voice and guards will come running."

"I'm afraid not," Rhoram said apologetically. "For your guards are dead by now."

"Achren," Erfin said flatly.

"Indeed," Rhoram agreed. "You are, nonetheless, welcome to try to summon help. As a matter of fact, I think I might like that."

"Rhoram," Erfin began, licking his lips nervously. "Brother-in-law, remember our common kin. My sister, your wife. By our laws if you kill me you would be guilty of fratricide. The punishment by the gods for that is severe."

"The punishment, Erfin, for betraying one's king is even more so," Rhoram countered. "And by Kymric law she is no longer my wife. For she deserted me and sought to betray me. Therefore you are no longer my brother. Say goodbye to this world, Erfin. For the next awaits you."

Rhoram sprang forward, his sword glittering. Erfin brought up his blade and the fight was joined. The two men fought back and forth across the room, Rhoram raining blows that Erfin barely deflected in time.

"You are slower, Erfin, than last time," Rhoram taunted. "Consorting with the enemy has made you fat."

Erfin did not have the breath to answer, but neither did he stop parrying the blows. But he was so sorely beset by Rhoram that he could not even attempt to do anything other than defend himself. Attack was out of the question.

At last Rhoram tired of baiting the man and determined to make an end. With a swing of his sword he sent Erfin's blade flying across the room. He backed Erfin up against the wall, the point of his blade set against Erfin's chest. A bright bead of blood blossomed on Erfin's white nightshirt.

"Brother," Erfin panted. "I am unarmed. You would kill me now? Without a chance to defend myself?"

"Do you think this some kind of game? You had your chance to defend yourself. And you lost."

"Rhoram—" Erfin began.

But Rhoram did not let him finish. He thrust the blade forward into Erfin's heart. Blood gushed from Erfin's mouth and his astonished eyes widened in pain, then glazed over as he sank to the floor.

Rhoram pulled his blade from Erfin's chest and contemptuously wiped it on Erfin's nightshirt, never taking his gaze off his dying brother-in-law. He smiled as the spirit fled Erfin's eyes, beginning its journey to the Land of Summer. Once there Erfin would be judged by Aertan the Weaver. Rhoram did not doubt that the judgement would be harsh, the penalty severe.

The door of the chamber burst open. A stumbling figure was thrust into the room, landing at Rhoram's feet. The second figure stepped in to the room calmly and closed the door.

"Efa," Rhoram said to the woman who sprawled on the floor where Achren had flung her. "How nice to see you again."

"Rhoram!" Efa exclaimed as she rose shakily to her feet. She wore a night-robe of forest green, embroidered with gold thread. Her rich, red hair was unbound, flowing over her gown in a fiery cascade.

He glanced over at his Captain and smiled. "Any trouble?" he asked.

"Not a bit," Achren replied. "The guards are dead. And so, I see, is Erfin."

"So he is," Rhoram agreed.

Efa, Rhoram's one-time queen, raised her hands to her mouth and gasped as she saw the bloody carcass of her brother. She raised her beautiful, velvety brown eyes to Rhoram and he saw her pull herself back from the hysteria that was rising to the surface. He saw her begin to calculate her effect on him, and how she might be able to use it.

He considered stopping her before she even began, but reconsidered. This might even be better than killing Erfin.

"Rhoram," Efa whispered. "You killed him. Oh, *cariad*, I'm glad you killed him."

"You are glad I killed him," Rhoram repeated.

"Yes. Oh, yes. He held me a virtual prisoner here. Did you really think I had deserted you? Oh, yes, I did think to do it. But just for a time. Just until I was sure you were sorry."

"Sorry?"

"For how badly you treated me. Did you think I didn't know about your other women?"

"Of course I thought you knew," Rhoram said. "You have always known. And never cared."

"Oh, but I did!"

"You cared about being Queen of Prydyn," he said flatly. "That is all you ever cared for."

"Oh, *cariad*, you are wrong. Wrong about me."

He stepped forward and gazed down at Efa for a few moments, long enough for a sensuous smile, for hope, to dawn on that lovely face. At last he spoke. "High King Arthur has commanded me to spare you," he said softly. "If it were not for that you would be dead by now."

"You would kill me? Your wife?"

"You are no longer my wife. And I would indeed kill you—as payment for the lives you took. I have been told of how you used your knowledge of Arberth and its people to betray the Y Dawnus to the Coranians. It is only my duty to my High King that persuades me to let you live."

He signaled to Achren and stepped back. Without a word his captain swiftly and efficiently bound and gagged the former Queen of Prydyn.

"Now we go?" Achren asked.

"Now we go," Rhoram replied.

After binding Efa securely and leaving her in Erfin's rooms, Rhoram and Achren made their way from the ystafell and across the courtyard to the gate, keeping to the shadows. Achren swiftly dispatched the guard at the gate, and the two of them slipped through. Rhoram turned back as they moved out of Caer Tir and into the city. The golden doors gleamed even in the heavy fog. The wolf's head outlined in onyx seemed to shimmer, and the emerald eyes glittered balefully.

The two made their way through the silent, fog-shrouded city. Yet though the city was silent, it was not asleep. Everywhere they passed they saw dark figures melting out of the houses, weapons in hand, their movements masked by the fog that the Druids, under Arthur's direction, were creating. The people of Arberth did not speak as their king passed by but they raised their hands in greeting, and nodded. There were no guards to avoid, for the regular patrols were long dead at the hands of the Kymri. The day they had waited for had come at last, and they had wasted no time.

They passed the place where Nemed Collen, the sacred grove of hazel trees, had once stood. A temple to Lytir brooded uneasily on the hallowed ground. Rhoram let it stand for now. Soon it would be gone. They came to a halt at the east gate. In the distance a wolf howled. Other wolves took up the cry. The fog seemed to thicken.

On the other side of this gate one-third of his Cerddorian

army massed, led by his son, Geriant. Outside of the north gate another third waited, led by his Lieutenant, Aidan. The last third waited outside the southern gate, lead by Lluched, the Gwarda of Creuddyn.

They were ready. At last. To take back what was theirs.

He took Achren's hand in his and kissed her palm. Her hand curved to fit his cheek and he smiled down at her, delighted at this proof of tenderness. She smiled back and nodded. At that moment a wolf howled, breaking the stillness.

Instantly the fog over the city lifted. The huge iron bars that locked the gates shot up into the air and the gates burst open, impelled by the power of the Druids who fought on his side this time. Armed Cerddorian, shouting Rhoram's name, poured into the city.

Geriant strode through the gates, a golden helmet in his hands. He knelt before his father and offered it up to him. Rhoram solemnly took the helmet fashioned in the shape of a wolf's head with emerald eyes. He set it on his head and motioned for his son to rise. Just then a pack of huge, black wolves burst through the gate, mingling freely and fearlessly with the Cerddorian. Their leader, the largest wolf Rhoram had ever seen, halted before him. The wolf's dark eyes glittered in the sudden dawn. Rhoram stretched out his hand and the wolf sniffed it. Then the beast lifted his head and howled again as hundreds of wolves answered the call. Then the animals sprang forward into the city, hunting Coranian prey.

And Rhoram joined them.

NOON FOUND RHORAM seated in the Great Hall. His massive chair, canopied with velvety cloth of forest green and embroidered with gold threads and emeralds, had been brought into the hall from his receiving chamber and set on the dais. Around his neck the torque of the rulers of Prydyn glittered with gold and emeralds. He discarded his helmet and ran a hand through his sweat-soaked golden hair. His blue eyes glittered as he surveyed the hall he had not sat in for almost three years.

The boar's head banner of red and gold had been taken down and his own wolf's head banner had been put back in its place.

The black wolf's head worked on a field of forest green fringed with gold seemed to survey the huge hall with satisfaction as its emerald eyes glittered.

Geriant stood to the right of the massive chair, his sword drawn and ready. His tunic of forest green was streaked with blood, as was Rhoram's, but it was all Coranian blood and he moved freely, satisfying Rhoram that his son had taken no hurt. To his left Achren stood, and her sword was also drawn, her tunic blood splattered. Yet she, too, had come through this day with only minor wounds.

Ellywen stood at the foot of the dais. Although the hem of her Druid's robe was soaked in blood the woman appeared to be as cool and composed as ever. Rhoram's Dewin, Cadell, stood next to Ellywen, his brown eyes calm as he surveyed the hall.

Rhoram's counselor and dearest friend, Dafydd Penfro, stood next to Ellywen. In this battle even Dafydd Penfro, who was not a warrior, had taken part, for he would not be stopped. He now mounted the steps, a brimming cup of wine in his steady hands. Emeralds flashed from the golden goblet as Dafydd knelt before Rhoram, offering the cup.

Rhoram took it and swallowed the contents of the cup in a few gulps. He rose and turned the cup over to show he had drunk it all and his warriors, gathered throughout the hall, cheered.

Arberth was theirs again. Not only Arberth, but all of Prydyn was free. For the Bards had brought him word that Marared, Achren's sister, had been victorious in Brycheiniog. And Dadweir Heavy-Hand had retaken Brychan. Morfydd, the Lady of Elfed, had been released and led her warriors against the enemy, freeing her cantref. Rheu Rhywdd, Lord of Gwarthaf, had also been freed and had retaken his cantref. In Aeron, forces lead by Eisywed of Anhuniog had swept through the cantref, and the enemy had fled before her.

"Bring the prisoners in," Rhoram called out as the cheers died. "Bring them, to receive the king's justice."

At his words he saw Aidan push a man in front of him through the crowd, Aidan's dagger at the man's neck. The man wore a black robe with a tabard of green, now torn and stained. His white-blond hair was sweat-soaked and pressed to his pale scalp. His dark eyes glittered with a mixture of fear and contempt.

When Aidan and his prisoner reached the bottom of the dais Aidan flung the man face forward on the steps, for his hands were bound behind him. The man pulled himself to his knees and looked up at Rhoram with hatred.

"Well, Master-wyrce-jaga," Rhoram said softly. "How does it feel to be a prisoner? Much like, I think, the Y Dawnus you captured and sent to their deaths these past three years."

Eamer of Geddingas, Master-wyrce-jaga of Prydyn, spat at Rhoram's feet. Quick as lightening Achren flew at the man, grabbing him by his hair and pulling his head back to expose his throat. The tip of her dagger dug into his skin and blood welled. She looked up at Rhoram, waiting for his signal.

"Eamer of Corania," he said softly. "I regret that we can only kill you once, for many lives have been lost due to you. It is far too late for you to learn mercy, and I have no intention of attempting to teach you. The 'witches' of Kymru will remember the moment you lost your life with a smile. That gift I can give them. And will."

At Rhoram's nod Achren slit the wyrce-jaga's throat. Blood gushed from his neck as he fell forward. Two warriors stepped up and grabbed the dying man's body, hauling it away from the hall and down the steps to the great bonfire that burned in the center of the courtyard of Caer Tir. Eamer tried to scream but it was impossible with a severed windpipe. The two warriors threw the body in and the fire roared as it reached for the pale flesh.

Back in the hall Dafydd Penfro called out. "Bring in the next prisoner!"

At this Lluched, the Gwarda of Creuddyn, came into the hall, pushing a man before her who was dressed in a stained and rumpled robe of green. The man's dark hair hung lankly on either side of his fat face and his beady eyes were filled with terror.

Lluched halted with the man at the bottom of the steps and forced the man to his knees. She then planted her foot on the small of his back and pushed him forward so that he lay prone.

"Bow before the King of Prydyn, fool," she hissed. Out of the corner of his eyes Rhoram saw Aidan smile fondly at Lluched.

"Whitred of Sceaping, one-time Byshyp of Prydyn, what have you to say to us? For surely you can think of something to say that will make us want to spare you," Rhoram said.

Whitred rose to his knees, looking up at Rhoram, the dawn of hope in his eyes. "Do not kill me, King Rhoram," Whitred begged, his voice shaking. "For I can be of use to you."

"How so?" Rhoram asked, feigning interest.

"I could tell you many things," he said, licking his lips.

"Such as?"

"The location of Coranian soldiers throughout Prydyn, their strength and numbers. Their battle plans. That at least must be worth a great deal."

Rhoram sighed. "Well, it would, Whitred, if it weren't for the fact that these soldiers are all either dead or in retreat to Eiodel."

Whitred gasped and turned even paler.

"Of course, all the wyrce-jaga are dead. Them we will not spare. Do you see, now, Whitred, that your information is useless? Still, you offered it and that is of value. Valuable enough, perhaps, to spare your life."

"You won't regret it," Whitred began, eagerly.

"Except for one thing," Rhoram went on, as though Whitred had not spoken. "My Druid, Ellywen ur Saidi, tells me that you have some very unpleasant habits. Habits that involve young boys of my city."

Whitred's face fell and tears gathered in his eyes.

"So you see, Whitred," Rhoram said in a confidential tone, "I can't possibly let you live. Nor will we kill you as swiftly as we killed Eamer. For these boys will never forget what was done to them. For that you will pay for a long, long time."

At Rhoram's gesture two more warriors grabbed Whitred by the arms, hauling him to his feet. The Byshyp began to blubber as they pulled him through the crowd of warriors, many of whom spat on him in contempt. They pushed him down the steps and into the courtyard. His hands were already bound with iron, and they bound his feet also. With a mighty shout they flung him into the fire. Whitred's screams pierced the noonday sky and the smell of burnt flesh spiraled with the smoke up into the clean air.

At Rhoram's nod Geriant left the dais and brought in the last prisoner. The man walked through the crowd of warriors with his head held high. Chains bound his hands in front of him. His sweat-soaked, dark blond hair framed his pale face but his dark eyes were unafraid as he halted at the bottom of the dais.

"Penda of Lindisfarne," Rhoram said solemnly.

"Rhoram of Prydyn," Penda replied, bowing his head briefly.

Ellywen stepped forward to stand next to Penda. "My King," Ellywen said, bowing. "I beg a boon from you. I, who have no right to beg for anything."

"What would you, Ellywen?" Rhoram asked. Though he had a pretty good idea of what his Druid was going to say.

"I beg that you spare this man's life. For he has spared mine. If not for him I would be in Afalon, dead by now. True, he set a trap for Cadell and I. But then he let Cadell go so that he might warn you that I was taken. And then he sent me to Afalon, with only two warriors for company, knowing that you would rescue me on the way and wishing to make it easier for you. I was able to lead my fellow Druids in the fight for you today only because Penda spared me. Through the strength of the High King we called the fog to hide your movements from the enemy. We unbarred the gates so your army might come into the city. We fought with our gifts today for you and our High King. Although I have no right to ask, for I owe you much, I ask in spite of that. I ask for the life of Penda of Lindisfarne. For he is an honorable man."

Rhoram hesitated, for he, too, wanted to spare Penda. But Penda was one of Havgan's generals and closest friends. To spare him would be, perhaps, foolish.

Do not kill Penda, Arthur's voice sounded in Rhoram's mind. *Send him to Havgan. For I have a message for him to carry.*

"And the message?" Rhoram asked, hiding his astonishment. He had known that Arthur was strong, but he was still shocked to see the proof of it.

Tell him this. Tell him that he must carry a message to Havgan. He must tell the Golden Man to leave Kymru. This will be one of his very last chances to leave our land alive. If Havgan does not leave he will die.

Rhoram turned to Penda. "My High King tells me that you must take a message to Havgan."

"And the message?" Penda asked.

"Leave Kymru or die."

"I will tell him," Penda whispered. "But he will not leave."

"Our High King has made his will known, and we will obey," Rhoram said. At his nod Geriant unbound Penda's hands. "My son will see to it that you are provisioned for your journey and that a fresh horse is given to you. We will send word throughout Kymru that you are to leave our kingdom unmolested and allowed to reach Eiodel."

"My thanks again to you, General Penda," Ellywen said softly, "for my life. I do not know what happened to you in your heart to lead you to do so, but I am grateful."

"It was a dream, Ellywen," Penda said. "A dream I had. In the dream I was freed from my oath to the Golden Man. Wuoton One-Eye himself said it was so. I will remain in Kymru until Havgan either leaves or is dead. If I am still alive by then I will return to my father in Lindisfarne. I will never again hunt the Heiden, for, in truth, I am one of them, as my father is. And I will never run from that truth again."

"The blessings of the Protectors on you, Penda," Ellywen said.

Penda bowed to Ellywen, then to Rhoram. Geriant led him out of the hall and gave him to two Kymric warriors to outfit and send on his way. When Geriant returned and mounted the steps, Rhoram opened his mouth to dismiss the audience. But a female voice called out, stopping him.

"Justice, King of Prydyn," she cried. Lluched made her way through the crowd to stand at the foot of the dais. "I claim justice," she repeated.

Rhoram's brow rose. "And what injustice has been done to you, Lluched, that I might set right?"

Lluched's hair, usually woven in tiny braids and bound with copper beads, was now lose and flowing around her shoulders in a dark cloud of riotous waves. Her large, dark eyes flashed. "One of your warriors has played fast and loose with me," she claimed, "and for that he must pay."

Rhoram's eyes flashed to Aidan. His lieutenant's eyes were wide with apprehension. But his mouth was trying not to curve in a smile.

"This man," Lluched said, gesturing to Aidan, "has promised to wed me but refuses to do so."

"I never promised that," Aidan protested. "Not once."

"It was implied," Lluched said haughtily.

"In what way was it implied?" Aidan cried.

"Every time you kissed me," Lluched replied firmly. "Every time you held me. Every time you sweet-talked me into—"

"No need to get into specifics," Aidan said hastily. "I think we all understand."

"Aidan," Rhoram said, trying desperately not to laugh. "Is this true?"

"It is not."

"You call me a liar?" Lluched cried, her hand going to the dagger at her waist.

"I do," Aidan replied firmly.

"And just how am I lying?" Lluched said.

"You lie by implication," Aidan said. "For you suggest that I do not want to marry you." Aidan walked forward and laid one hand gently on Lluched's flushed cheek. "But I do," he said softly. "I always have. For you were born to be my wife and to you I gave my heart long ago. For I love you, Lluched ur Brathach, as I have never loved any woman. As I never thought to love any woman. And glad I am that you will marry me. For I will never let you go." He bent his head and kissed her slowly, his other hand coming up to plunge into the mass of her dark hair. At last he released her and turned to face Rhoram, his arm around Lluched's waist.

"King Rhoram, I wish you to allow your Druid to marry us."

"Today?" Ellywen asked with a smile.

"Today," Lluched said firmly. "Before he changes his mind."

"You could wait long and long for that, Lluched," Aidan said with a grin. "But today will suit me very well also. For the day Prydyn found her freedom is the day I lost mine. And with no regrets, for in truth I lost my heart's freedom long ago in your dark eyes."

"Then my Druid will indeed marry you both today, as you ask," Rhoram said with a grin of his own. "But she must perform a task for me first."

"Gladly," Ellywen said with a smile. "And what task may I do for you?"

"Another marriage," Rhoram said. He turned to face Achren. "A few months ago you said something to me I have not forgotten. I had told you I loved you. And you did not believe me then. Do you remember what you said?"

Achren's face flushed but she met his eyes fearlessly. "Remind me," she said through gritted teeth.

"You said, 'when once again you reign in Arberth over all Prydyn, when once again fortune favors you so that you may have the choosing of any woman of Kymru, offer again, if you still wish it.' Those were your exact words."

"They were," Achren agreed.

"And so now I offer again, in front of all these witnesses. For I am once again King of Prydyn. Fortune has again favored me, and I do not seek out your heart to salve a wound of mine. I seek out your heart because, without you, nothing is complete. Even this," he said, gesturing to his canopied chair, the wolf's banner, the great hall, "is nothing if you do not share it with me."

"I am a warrior, Rhoram," Achren said quietly. "I was not meant to be a queen."

"As to that, I have plans that I believe you will agree to," Rhoram said. "Plans we shall speak of later. But for now, Achen ur Canhustyr, PenCollen of Prydyn, queen of my heart, I ask for your answer."

"Then, my King, I shall give it to you." Achren drew her sword. The steel rasped loudly in the sudden quiet as she moved to stand before him. "My sword belongs to you and always has." She held the sword out to him with both hands and he took it from her. "My heart, too, belongs to you and always has. Rhoram of Prydyn, I will marry you."

He gasped with delight, for his heart leapt at her words and at the truth he saw in her eyes. He handed her sword to Geriant, then took her in his arms and kissed her thoroughly to the sounds of cheers from their warriors. At last he released her from his embrace, and drew her to the crook of his arm.

"Today I declare that Prydyn is free from the enemy," Rhoram cried. "Tomorrow we begin the muster for the battle in Gwytheryn against the Golden Man himself. I appoint Dafydd Penfro as ruler here until we return from that final battle where Kymru will be freed!"

At his words the warriors cried out, calling out his name and that of High King Arthur. And from somewhere outside the city walls, wolves howled in triumph. For today, Prydyn was free.

Chapter Sixteen

Dinmael
Kingdom of Ederynion, Kymru
Eiddew Mis, 500

Gwaithdydd, Cynyddu Wythnos—early morning

The fog-shrouded city of Dinmael was hushed and still in the dark hour before dawn. Tendrils of mist curled around the silent houses and rose from the emptied streets.

Two figures soundlessly appeared at the top of the city's outer wall. Each figure tossed down one end of a length of rope secured to the jagged stones that topped the wall. Each grasping their ropes, they shinnied down swiftly, coming to rest noiselessly inside the city.

Without a word the two figures made their way down the main street of Sarn Ermyn, easily shrouded from discovery by the fog. They stopped in front of Ty Meirw, the standing stones that guarded the bodies of the rulers of Ederynion. They briefly bowed their heads, and the slighter figure reached out to gently touch the nearest stone, as though in greeting or, possibly, in farewell.

The two walked swiftly on. When they came to the nearest row of houses they separated, each one going to opposite sides of the street. Softly, swiftly, they knocked on each door once, twice, three times. Without waiting for an answer, they then went to the next house and knocked again. At each house doors silently opened, and figures stepped out. Some held swords, while others held spears. Some had helmets on their heads, while others were bareheaded. Yet, though the inhabitants in the street stirred in the mist-shrouded darkness, no candles were lit, and no torches blazed.

Even the dogs, which should have bayed at the sound of knocking at such an hour, were quiet. Stilled by an instinct, or, possibly, by the recognition of what the day would surely bring or, perhaps, by something else all together.

As each silent, armed man or woman emerged from their houses, they raised their hands in greeting to the two that had knocked, then moved out of their houses and into the streets.

And waited.

OUTSIDE THE CITY walls Angharad, PenAethnen of Ederynion, Queen Elen's captain, stood silently before the southern gate, her eyes scanning the misty sky overhead. Her dyed white leather breeches clung to her slender body. She wore a sea-green, close-fitting tunic decorated with the white swan badge of her queen, and her arms were bare. Her red hair was tightly braided and bound to her head. A sword was belted around her waist and daggers gleamed at the cuffs of her leather boots.

Behind her, hundreds of Cerddorian fanned out, waiting silently. She knew that Rhiwallon, the Prince of Rheged, was armed and ready to lead more Cerddorian through the west gate. Alun Cilcoed, the Lord of Arystli, was likewise ready with more warriors outside the northern gate of the city.

To her left a Dewin stood silently, his eyes slightly glazed as he Wind-Rode inside the city. And to her right stood Madryn, one of Aergol's Druids. Madryn's eyes were closed and her hands clenched into fists. Beads of sweat gleamed at her temples, as she and her fellow brown-robed Druids concentrated, linked with High King Arthur, to maintain the heavy fog that masked the Cerddorian's army from Coranian eyes.

Yet though the work was obviously strenuous, Angharad had no fear that the Druids would not be able to fulfill the tasks they must fulfill today. For Madryn's competent air had already reassured Angharad that the Druids would be able to do all that was required.

Talhearn, Queen Elen's Bard, made his way slowly through the ranks of silent warriors. His silver hair was misted with droplets and his shrewd, brown eyes glittered in his weathered face. He did not speak, but he did not need to. He knew better than anyone what this day meant Talhearn had been her friend for a very long time and they had faced danger together many times in the past three years.

The Dewin next to her stirred then blinked rapidly. He turned to Angharad and said quietly, "Queen Elen and Prince Lludd have roused the populace. The Coranians suspect nothing. Everything is ready."

At last the day had come when they would begin to take everything back. Or die trying.

All they needed now was the signal that High King Arthur had promised.

Angharad nodded and continued to scan the milky-white sky. Emrys, her lieutenant, made his way to her.

"Angharad, I must speak with you," he said quietly.

"Can't it wait?" she asked absently, still eyeing the silent sky.

"No, captain, it cannot," Emrys replied, an edge to his voice she had never heard before.

Jolted by his tone she turned to him. His handsome face was stern and set. His dark eyes were fastened on hers. His face had a pale cast to it and his mouth twitched as though he was in some sort of pain.

"What is it, then?" she asked, alarmed.

Emrys took a deep breath. "Today we go into battle. And today, I know, I am to die."

"Nonsense, Emrys," she said irritably. She was astonished that Emrys would interrupt such an important moment with such patent foolishness. She did not for one minute believe that what he said was true.

"It is not nonsense," Emrys replied firmly. "It is the truth. I have dreamed it."

"Are you a Dreamer, then, that you should know the future?" she asked acidly.

But Emrys continued, as though she had not even spoken. "And so the time has come to speak other truths to you. Truths that you never wished to hear from me."

"Emrys—" she began sternly. But Emrys would not be stopped. Would not, she saw, be reasoned with.

"No, Angharad. You cannot stop me from saying what must be said. For I love you, *cariad.* I have loved you for years beyond counting. I loved you when I was only a warrior in Queen Olwen's teulu. I loved you when you chose me to be your lieutenant. I have loved you these past years when we have lived hand to mouth, hunted by the Coranians. I have loved you every day, have longed for you every moment. And have never told you so. For I knew it would be useless."

She opened her mouth to tell him to please—for the love of all the gods—please stop this. For she wished to hear none of it. Had, indeed, successfully avoided this for longer than she had ever thought possible. For she had thought that, someday, Emrys feelings would change. But they had not.

And she could not help him. She did not love him, and would not pretend as though she did. Or that she ever would. Amatheon, Gwydion's murdered brother, had once held her heart for a brief time. But though he was gone now, her heart had not yet wholly returned to her. She didn't know if it ever would. Deep inside anger began to stir, born of guilt and of her bitter loss, that Emrys should choose this moment to distract her from the momentous task at hand. She would tell him so, right this moment. She would—

Effortlessly, as Talhearn did everything, the Bard caught her eye. The tiny shake of his head, the pity in his eyes, warned her to be silent and let Emrys finish.

And so she would. But when this battle was over she would have a new lieutenant.

"For," Emrys said, continuing on, "you never wanted to hear it. You never wanted to acknowledge that I loved you. And you knew." His tone was not accusatory. Only certain, knowing he was right beyond the shadow of doubt.

"What would you have me do, Emrys?" she asked between gritted teeth, for she was becoming very, very angry now. "Would you have me lie to you?"

Emrys shook his head. "No. For then you would not be the woman I love. You are not a liar and never could be. I want only one thing. Only one little thing today as I stand in the shadow of death."

"And that is?" she asked.

"A kiss," he said simply.

She stared at him, scarcely able to credit what she had heard. He thought to trick her into kissing him with some stupid story that he would die today? Did he think her a fool? "Emrys ap Naw," she said sternly, "you are impertinent. You have a job to do here, and I expect you to do it. Return to your warriors. Now."

Emrys paled even further and remained rooted to the spot. For a moment she thought he would not obey her. But Talhearn stepped forward and laid a hand on Emrys' shoulder. Emrys swallowed hard, but Angharad would not relent. At last Emrys saluted and turned away, swallowed up by the mist.

"You did what you had to do," Talhearn said, for he knew Angharad well. "Let it go."

She suddenly heard the rush of huge wings beating against the sky overhead. A flash of brilliant white in the fog, a drift of white feathers, the fierce call of an angry swan, and she knew they had come at last.

The signal: the signal High King Arthur had promised had come. In that moment the fog rolled away, lifted completely as though it had never been. The sky was stained red by the rising sun as though a battle had already taken place in the heavens overhead. Hundreds of white swans, with their mighty wings spread wide, dove down from the now-clear sky into the city.

Angharad brought her horn to her lips and blew.

And the Druids brought the gates down.

The fighting inside Caer Dwfr, the fortress of the rulers of Ederynion, was the fiercest. For all that long morning the Cerddorian had been driving the Coranians back, and those enemy warriors who had been able to had escaped into the gleaming white citadel.

All morning Angharad had kept the queen in her sight as Elen cut through the Coranians like a scythe through wheat. Elen's white leather tunic and trousers were blood splattered, but the blood was Coranian blood and she moved easily through the melee. She wore the silver and pearl helm of the rulers of Ederynion that was fashioned in the shape of a swan with outstretched wings, and it gleamed in the daylight as the sun reached its apex.

Angharad had last seen that helm on Queen Olwen's brow the day she had been killed by the invading Coranian force. Today Angharad had no intention of burying another queen, so she stuck with Elen like a burr.

And Emrys stuck to Angharad like bark to a tree, tirelessly guarding her back all morning. In spite of herself Angharad was touched, for she had thought that after their last interview Emrys would stay out of her sight. But he had stuck doggedly behind her throughout the battle.

Smoke billowed into the sky from the southwest portion of the city, for Elen had commanded that the temple to Lytir, built over what had once been the sacred grove of aspen trees, Nemed Aethnen, be burned to the ground. Overhead, flashes of white shone through the smoke as the swans continued to attack the enemy. Their fierce screams blended with the ringing sound of blade on blade and the moans of dying warriors.

As they neared the citadel, ready to bring this day's grisly work to its conclusion, the separate bands of Cerddorian began to catch sight of each other, meeting finally before the closed doors of Caer Dwfr.

Alun Cilcoed, who had led the forces in the northern quarter, hailed them. He appeared to be unwounded and still had a good number of warriors with him. Prince Lludd, too, appeared just then from the east, for he had led a great many of the townsfolk to push the Coranians from the docks and into the sea. His arm was bandaged, but his grin and jaunty salute convinced Angharad that his wound was not serious.

It was Rhiwallon's arrival that caused Angharad the most amusement, for, when the Prince of Rheged, who had led his forces through the western quarter, caught sight of Elen, he threw whatever discretion he had (and it was never very much) to the winds and rushed to the queen. Without so much as a by your leave he picked her up in his strong arms and swung her around, whooping exuberantly.

To no one's surprise—except, perhaps, to Elen's—Elen did not reprimand Rhiwallon. She simply demanded to be put down. But her tone was not as commanding as usual and there appeared to be a smile in it. Lludd caught Angharad's eye and grinned.

Then the swans gathered in the sky above and hovered over the citadel, their fierce cries cutting through the rising smoke. Elen eyed the closed gate of Caer Dwfr. The silver gate shimmered so that the image of the swan, outlined in pearls with emerald eyes, seemed to shiver as though anxious to launch itself into the sky to join the others.

"Madryn," Elen called, and the Druid appeared instantly at Elen's elbow.

"What is your will, Queen Elen?" the Druid asked, as the other four Druids Madryn had brought with her crowded around.

"That you should open the gate of Caer Dwfr," Elen replied, "so that the last of the men who killed my mother shall die."

Madryn bowed her head. "It shall be done, then." The five Druids lifted their faces to the gate and closed their eyes. The gate began to shiver slightly, and then to groan as the will of the Druids focused on it. The outstretched wings of the incised swan almost seemed to spread even wider, as though straining to break the bods that kept it from the firmament.

It almost seemed to Angharad as though the swan itself cried out fiercely in triumph as the gate burst open. At Elen's battle cry the Cerddorian poured into the stronghold, calling out fiercely to the enemy to fight. Overhead the swans folded in their tremendous wings and dove, arrowing into the courtyard and attacking the Coranian warriors who had taken shelter there.

The fighting in the courtyard was the fiercest Angharad had ever known. For the Coranians were cornered, and losing. And they knew it. They fought like madmen, to kill as many Kymri they could until they, themselves, were killed. Fighting was hand to hand, for the quarters were too close for bowmen to do any good.

It was when Angharad had plunged her sword into what seemed like the hundredth Coranian that it happened. Elen was to her right and somewhat ahead. Angharad never knew what impelled Elen to look back at that moment, but something did.

"Angharad!" Elen cried. "Look out!"

Angharad whirled. Yet as she turned she knew, somehow, that she would be too late.

And she was.

But she did not die that day. For Emrys was on time.

He leapt forward, using his body as a living shield between Angharad and the blade that the Coranian warrior had thrust at her back. The sword plunged into Emrys and he stiffened as his chest parted beneath the gleaming blade. The Coranian withdrew his weapon and blood poured from both Emrys' wound and his mouth as he went down.

Angharad screamed in rage and raised her sword, leaping forward over Emrys prone body and plunging the blade into the Coranians' guts. Hot blood poured over her hand as she twisted the blade, making sure the Coranian suffered the maximum of agony before he died. He slumped down and she contemptuously pulled the weapon out and let him fall.

She whirled around again and knelt down beside Emrys, taking his dying body in her arms. She sensed Lludd behind her, guarding her back. And she saw Elen kneel on Emrys' other side. The queen laid a suddenly gentle hand on Emrys' brow, stroking his hair back from his face. Elen gestured for one of the Dewin to attend to Emrys. The Dewin knelt down beside him and laid her hands on the wound. She closed her eyes and Life-Read. After a brief moment she opened her eyes and looked at Elen. The Dewin shook her head.

"Go, then," Elen said quietly, "to those who need your services." The Dewin bowed and left.

Emrys looked up at them and tried to speak. But Angharad hushed him. "Hush," she murmured, as she cradled his head against her breast. "Hush, you mustn't try to talk. Save your strength."

But Emrys knew—of course he did—that he did not need to save his strength. And she knew it, too.

"Angharad," he whispered, raising one bloody hand to touch her tear-streamed face. "Did I not tell you what would happen today? Did I not say?"

"You told me," she agreed. "You said. Oh, Emrys, I am sorry I didn't believe you. Sorry that I became your death."

"You who were always my life could never be my death. It was not you who killed me, but the Coranian."

Her tears fell on his upturned face, but she made no move to wipe them away. Blood flowed from his mouth, but his dark eyes were clear and steady as he gazed up at her.

"Emrys ap Naw, I owe you a kiss," she said steadily. "And I always pay my debts." She bent down and kissed his bloody mouth, slowly, lingering, knowing somehow that he had always dreamed of it that way. When she at last released his lips from hers she drew back and looked down at him again. His eyes were beginning to cloud, but his mouth smiled up at her. With a small sigh he was gone.

Angharad stroked his hair then gently laid his head on the ground. She rose, gripping her sword, and Elen rose with her, standing on Emrys' other side. Angharad knew her mouth was bloody but she did not wipe the blood away. It belonged to Emrys. She had sent him to his death, no matter what anyone else said. She would not wipe away the proof of what she had done.

Elen's blue eyes were rimed with tears, but her face was stern and set. She looked at Angharad and did not say anything about the blood lining her captain's mouth. And Angharad saw that Elen fully understood and would not cheapen this moment by protesting.

Angharad looked at Lludd, and the Prince's brown eyes gazed steadily back. He, too, said nothing, but his eyes said he understood it all.

Then the three of them turned away as one from Emrys' body, and began to kill. They did not shout war cries, but killed silently, implacably, with deadly earnest. Their blades rose and fell, rose and fell again as they cut through the remaining Coranian warriors, showing no mercy as they finished taking back what had once been theirs.

And that was how they mourned for their friend in the only way open to them on that long, bloody day.

Elen sat on the great, canopied chair of silver and pearl that had been her mother's, surveying the Cerddorian packed before her in the Great Hall. Her swan helm was still on her head, her auburn hair braided and tucked under the helmet. Her white tunic and trousers were stained with blood and smoke, but she had refused to change them yet, knowing in her heart that it was too soon to wash away the blood from this day. The ornate pearl-studded silver torque of Ederynion hung around her slender neck, gleaming softly.

When she had last seen this hall the red and gold boar banner of the Warleader had hung over the dais. But that banner had been pulled down and burned. The white banner of the swan, outlined in silver and pearls with emerald eyes, once again hung on the wall.

The Bards had already shared the greatest of this day's news with her—Ederynion was free. In the four northern cantrefs, the Cerddorian under Drwst Iron-Fist had been victorious, freeing the cantref of Dinan. Mechain had been freed under the leadership of Sima, Emrys' sister. Cilyddas, the Lady of Rhwny, had led the forces that took back her cantref. Meilwen, the Lady of Cydewain, had escaped and retaken her cantref. The cantref of Penllyn was freed under the leadership of Llawra of Cynllaith, sister of Susanna, Queen Morrigan's Bard. In Arystli, Angharad's sister Eiodar had led her forces to victory.

All that the Coranians had taken was returned to them. Elen thought that, perhaps, her mother was watching this day. Watching with pride and a smile on her lovely face. Watching with pride not only in Elen, but also in her son, Lludd, whom she had not valued. But Elen did, and always had, from the very beginning. And Lludd had returned that loyalty tenfold, continuing to fight on against the enemy even when she had been captured, then coming for her and setting her free.

Now Lludd stood on her right and his tunic and trousers of sea green were stained and blood splattered. His left arm was in a sling, but he had so far refused medical attention, saying his hurt was not great. Elen made a mental note to ensure a Dewin gave him a Life-Reading before the day was done.

Rhiwallon, King Owein's younger brother, stood on her left. She had not invited him to, he had simply done it, mounting the dais and standing by her chair as though it was the most natural thing in the world. It should have made Elen uneasy to recognize that it did, indeed, feel natural. But she simply accepted his presence and let herself be warmed by it.

Her captain, Angharad, stood at the bottom of the dais, her sword drawn, the point resting on the stone floor. Angharad's mouth was still faintly stained with Emrys' blood. Much as she wished to, Elen would not order Angharad to wash off that blood.

Talhearn stood at Angharad's elbow, his quiet presence doing more for Angharad than any words.

Elen nodded to Angharad, and Angharad nodded to a Kymric warrior who stood just beside the entrance to the Great Hall. The warrior called out, and a prisoner was brought in.

The Byshop's robe was torn and bloodstained, and his hands were tied behind his back. His graying blond hair was matted with sweat. He had belted a sword around his waist, but the scabbard was now empty. It had been Cuthwine who had rallied the Coranians to fight, for he had been the only one with authority left in the citadel. For General Talorcan had thrown in his lot with the Kymri when Elen had been rescued. And Guthlac, the Masterwyrce-jaga, had been killed that same night. That had happened little less than a month ago, and Havgan had not had the opportunity to put someone else in command.

The two warriors that escorted Cuthwine through the hall and to the bottom of the dais now stepped back at Angharad's gesture. Elen's captain quietly told Cuthwine to sink to his knees before Elen, and the Byshop did. He inclined his head briefly to her, then remained kneeling. His blue eyes gazed up at her stoically as he waited to hear his fate.

Elen knew Cuthwine of Cyncacestir very well from her years of captivity. The Byshop had been neither a particularly bad man, nor a particularly good one. He was simply a Coranian, who believed that, in bringing the word of his God, Lytir, he was doing what his God required of him. And he had not been overly squeamish about how he had attempted to convert the Kymri, for he had been sure that, for the good of their souls, he should be harsh when necessary. Yet he had been polite to Elen, giving her a certain amount of deference as nominal ruler of Ederynion. And he had never overtly threatened her Dewin, Regan, although he had certainly thought of her as one of the witches that needed to be carefully watched and controlled.

Yet for all that, he had not been cruel, only misguided, and she almost did not want to have him put to death.

Then don't.

The voice in her head startled her, even as she recognized it. Intellectually she knew that the High King had that kind of power to Mind-Speak from such a tremendous distance. But it was another thing altogether to hear him so clearly.

"What would you have me do, High King?" she asked.

He is to take a message to Havgan for me. This message I believe you know.

Elen nodded, for she did, indeed, know the message. She rose to stand at the top of the stairs of the dais. She looked briefly down at her victorious warriors gathered in the Great Hall. Her heart felt full to overflowing as they gazed steadily back at her, as her hall once again housed the warriors of Ederynion, not of Corania.

Her gaze came to rest on the Byshop who still knelt at the bottom of the stairs. "Cuthwine of Cyncacestir, I had thought to kill you today. But High King Arthur has a task for you."

"I regret I cannot do his bidding, Queen Elen," Cuthwine said softly. "For my loyalty is to my church. And to the Warleader."

"This task does not conflict with that loyalty, Cuthwine," Elen said.

"Then tell me."

"High King Arthur wishes you to go to the Warleader. You

are to say to Havgan the Golden that he must leave Kymru. He must leave Kymru, or die. This is the message the High King wishes you to give your Bana. Will you do so?"

"I will do so, Queen of Ederynion," Cuthwine said. "But I will do so in an attempt to spare my Warleader's life, rather than because your High King wills it."

"It does not matter why you do so, as long as you do it," Elen said crisply. "But I do understand that you are a man who is loyal to what he believes in. It is an admirable trait. But one that does not, I fear, bring you much joy."

"Joy is for another world, Elen," Cuthwine said, his tone almost regretful.

"It is for this one, Byshop," Elen said. "And for all of them. Did you not know?"

Cuthwine shook his head in disbelief. "I will not bandy words with you. But I must warn you, Elen. Havgan is not defeated. Today you have turned him out of Dinmael, but you have not beaten him."

"Oh, but we have," Elen said softly. "For not only is Dinmael freed, but all of Ederynion. And not only Ederynion, but Prydyn also, for Arberth was retaken yesterday. General Penda is even now on his way to Havgan with the same message you will carry."

"Does your High King really think to persuade Havgan to run away?"

"He does not. He only hopes."

"Then he will be doomed to disappointment, I fear. For Havgan will never run."

"Then he will die," Elen said.

"We shall see, Queen of Ederynion."

At her nod a warrior led the Byshop from the hall and began preparations for his journey.

Elen rose and stood at the edge of the dais, looking out onto the sea of faces gathered in the hall. Lludd and Rhiwallon stepped forward with her, flanking her.

"Today," she said, lifting her arms, "Ederynion is free!"

The warriors cheered until she gestured for silence. "Tomorrow we begin to muster for another great battle—the last one in this long game. We will go to join the High King on the fields of Gwytheryn."

She gestured to Alun Cilcoed, who stood at the foot of the dais. Surprised, the Lord of Arystli came to stand before her. "Alun Cilcoed, loyal and true, I appoint you ruler here in Dinmael until I return."

"Elen," he gasped.

"I know I ask a great deal of you, my friend," she said quietly. "I know you want to join us. But I must have someone my people trust to guide them. Will you say yes?"

"I will do as you will, my Queen," Alun replied, bowing his head. "You will return to a Dinmael that will have been cleansed of the Coranian taint."

Elen smiled. "Of course," she said. "For now we are free."

Chapter Seventeen

Tegeingl
Kingdom of Gwynedd, Kymru
Eiddew Mis, 500

Meirgdydd, Cynyddu Wythnos—early morning

Arday ur Medyr, mistress to General Catha of Corania and one-time mistress to the now dead King Madoc of Gwynedd, opened her dark eyes, instantly awake when she heard the call.

Arday.

She sat up in bed cautiously, careful not to wake Catha. He slept with his back to her, his breathing even. The hawk worked in silver threads and brown silk on the coverlet of dark blue seemed to flutter in the dull light of the glowing embers on the hearth. She had shared this bed many times before, but with King Madoc. But now Madoc was dead at the hands of his own father. And Catha, who had ruled Gwynedd in all but name for the last few years, had moved into Madoc's room, the room that had once belonged to King Uthyr.

Arday.

She could not answer, for she was not a Bard. But she knew that Susanna would know that her call was heard.

It has begun.

Arday smiled and glanced out the window. Thick fog pressed against the glass. Silently she got out of bed, cautiously pulling her long, dark hair out of Catha's sleeping grasp. She put on her robe, fastening the red, velvet garment around her waist. Not taking her eyes from Catha's still form, she gently ran her hands beneath the feather-stuffed mattress and pulled out a long gleaming dagger.

For a moment she stood on the other side of the bed, eyeing Catha's muscular back, contemplating. But, in the end, she decided to carry out her original plan. Family honor was more important than killing Catha just now. Catha's turn would come. And come, no doubt, at the hands of Morrigan, King Uthyr's daughter. A just punishment, she thought, for it had been Catha who had killed Uthyr. She would not steal that away from Morrigan, the queen whom Arday had worked in secret for so long to bring back.

She knew that Susanna had awakened her so that Arday could get to safety before the attack began. But she had business to take care of first. She felt that the gods were with her, for the man she must now see had come to Tegeingl just a few days ago. There would be no need for her to hunt him down, and no chance that another might steal her vengeance from her.

She crept from the room, noiselessly opening then closing the door behind her. She made her way silently down the dark corridor, halting at the door of the chamber she sought. Catha had allowed the man to stay in what had once been Queen Ygraine's chamber, saying that he was an honored guest. Her lip had curled at that, but she was glad now, for that meant she had not had to go far to find him. She briefly closed her eyes as she steeled herself. She must do what she must do. And may the gods accept the sacrifice.

She silently opened the door and slipped inside. He lay on his back, deep asleep, linens in a tangle around his sweat-soaked body. So, he had been having nightmares. That was good. For he deserved all of them and then some.

She crept to the bed then called his name. He needed to understand why, or it would mean nothing.

"Menwaed," she whispered. "Wake up."

Her brother stirred and opened his eyes. "Arday?" he asked, his voice blurred with sleep. "What are you doing here?"

Without another word she thrust her dagger into his heart. He gasped, his hands flying up to close on hers around the hilt of the dagger in his chest. His dark eyes were wide with shock and pain as he looked up at her, his back arching in agony.

Her eyes were limned with tears, but her face was stern as she looked down at him, her hands, covered with his warm blood, still on the hilt of the dagger that impaled him. "You were Lord of Arllechwedd, Menwaed," she whispered. "Your duty was to fight by King Uthyr's side. But you betrayed him, for Madoc and the Coranians."

Menwaed looked up at her in disbelief, even as his blood soaked the mattress, even as the light began to fade from his eyes. She twisted the hilt of the dagger and he stiffened with the added pain.

"You should never have done that, brother," she said gently. "You ruined our family honor. I was only too eager to put things right when Anieron Master Bard asked me to. For the past years I have been his source of information, gleaning for him what I could from both Madoc and Catha. Helping to keep Princess Tangwen safe. Doing whatever I could to aid the Cerddorian and ensure Queen Morrigan returns to her rightful place in Caer Gwynt. Did you really think I would betray my people? Did you really think I was like you?"

But Menwaed did not answer, for his spirit had fled his dead body. Arday thought that he would have a bad time of it in Gwlad Yr Haf, the Land of Summer. For surely Aertan the Weaver would ensure that Menwaed paid dearly for his crimes.

She had waited a long time for this day. She was looking forward to welcoming Queen Morrigan to the Great Hall.

But when she heard the door open behind her, she knew that was not to be.

Morrigan waited patiently—though that was a struggle, for it was not really in her nature—for her Bard, Susanna, to finish Mind-Speaking. Although Susanna's eyes were opened, they were slightly glazed, so Morrigan knew she must wait a little while longer.

Mist swirled and eddied as the Cerddorian silently took their places before the closed gates of Tegeingl. The Dewin had already informed her that her lieutenant, Bedwyr, was in position at the western gate, while Duach, Lord of Dunoding, was in position at the southern gate. Morrigan, along with her captain, Cai, was now ready at the eastern gate.

She briefly touched the helm on her head, fashioned in silver and sapphire like a hawk with spread wings. Her father had given it to her mother the day he had sent Ygraine away from Tegeingl. He had also given her the ornate torque of silver and sapphire that now hung around Morrigan's slender neck.

Morrigan was dressed in a tunic and trousers of dark blue, with a brown leather belt and high, brown leather boots. The scabbard of her sword was fastened to her belt, and the hilts of two daggers showed at the cuffs of her boots. Her auburn hair had been tightly braided to her scalp and bound beneath her helm.

On the other side of Susanna stood Yrth, one of the Druids that had been sent here by Aergol. Yrth's seamed face was calm and his eyes were open, but sweat beaded his brow at the effort he was making, for he, along with four other Druids, was linked with her brother, Arthur, making the fog that seemed to rise from the grass at their feet.

Slightly to the right of Susanna stood Cai, Morrigan's captain. Cai held a hunting horn in his hands as he scanned the sky above them. Yet, as often as he eyed the sky, his dark brown gaze went to Susanna's flawless face. The love and fear Morrigan saw in Cai's eyes was so intense she could barely watch. For Morrigan knew that he loved the Bard, but he was afraid to tell her so. For it had been here, at the last battle in Tegeingl, that Cai had lost his wife and son, and the pain of that had marked him forever. His fear of being hurt that way again was just as strong as his love for Susanna. Perhaps, Morrigan thought, it always would be.

At last Susanna turned to Morrigan, her blue eyes sparkling. "Our spy has been awakened. She knows we are here."

"Now will you tell me who it is?" Morrigan asked, somewhat acidly.

"Her secret was shared with me by Anieron Master Bard, and passed on to Elidyr Master Bard and so to High King Arthur, your brother. And without their permission, I have not been able to tell you," Susanna said mildly. "But now Arthur says that I may tell you who it is. It is Arday, your father's former steward."

"Arday!" Morrigan cried softly. "I can't believe it. Why, she has been Madoc's mistress—and Catha's—for years."

"And, therefore, in a perfect position to hear the things that we must know," Susanna pointed out. "I would have thought that Tangwen, at least, would have suspected her, for Arday did much to save Tangwen from Catha's desires."

Morrigan eyed her childhood friend, who had been standing on her left. "Well, Tangwen?" Morrigan asked. "Did you suspect Arday?"

"In truth, Morrigan, I did not," Tangwen replied softly. "Though I was aware that, once or twice, she helped me steer clear of Catha." A slight shiver seemed to go through Tangwen as she said that.

Prince Rhodri stood on Tangwen's left, and at his granddaughter's tone he briefly put a hand on her shoulder. He balefully eyed the fog, his hand on the hilt of his sword. His once red-gold hair was silvery now, but his blue eyes were as alert as ever. Since he had killed his son, Madoc, Rhodri had become more personable, less defensive, and Morrigan had come to know him a little better. And she now trusted him a great deal.

The fog eddied before her as a figure moved through it, coming to stand by her shoulder. Morrigan's mother was dressed in brown leather tunic and trousers and her auburn hair, touched by frost, was tightly braided and tucked beneath a simple helmet. Ygraine's dark eyes, cool and watchful as always, scanned the sky, though Morrigan knew she would not be able to see anything through the fog.

"Susanna," Morrigan said, "please ensure that the other Bards tell our warriors to spare Arday. I want her brought to me unharmed, so that I may give her my thanks."

"I will, my Queen," Susanna said and began to do Morrigan's bidding.

Morrigan put an arm on her mother's slim shoulders. She knew her mother was thinking of the last time she had been in Tegeingl. It had been the day that Uthyr had sent her away, knowing that the enemy would soon be at the gates, knowing that his death was near. Although this day meant much to Morrigan she knew how much this day also meant to her mother.

And then she heard it. The sound of hundreds upon hundreds of wings beating the air above. The fog swirled as the air over Tegeingl stirred.

The signal that Arthur had promised. It had come.

"Cai, blow the horn!" Morrigan called.

And Cai brought the horn to his lips and blew. At this the fog blew away, showing a clear dawn. Above them hundreds of hawks flew, their fierce cries vying with the cry of the hunting horn.

Yrth lifted his hands and threw back his head to the sky. And with a mighty shout, the gates of Tegeingl came crashing down.

CATHA'S EYES OPENED the moment Arday stepped out into the corridor, softly closing the door to their room after her. He wondered just whom she was thinking of visiting in the middle of the night. Some Coranian warrior, perhaps, who had caught her eye? Perhaps she thought he would not mind, for he had shared her with Madoc for the past few years. But he did mind. Madoc was gone. Arday was his and his alone. He would not share her. When he tired of her, he would discard her without a second thought. But share her? No. Not any more.

He went to the door, quietly opening it a crack. He was just in time to see her enter the queen's chamber. So, she was going to see her brother. But why? Were they both in league against him? Plotting, perhaps, to take the throne of Gwynedd? If they were, they would both learn better.

He took a moment to pull on trousers and his boots. He picked up his dagger and crossed to the door. The embers of the dying fire glowed, lighting his blond hair, his cold, blue eyes, and his handsome, cruel face.

He reached the door to the queen's chambers, where the Lord of Arllechwedd slept. He was not prepared for the sight that reached his eyes when he opened the door.

Menwaed was dead and the mattress was drenched in his blood. Arday's dagger protruded from her brother's chest. She whirled around as she heard the door open, her hand pulling the bloody dagger from Menwaed's body.

Catha stood in the doorway for a moment, taking it all in. Arday stood in a semi-crouch next to the bed, her dagger ready. He almost smiled. For this would be a moment he would savor for years. He stepped into the room, closing the door behind him.

"So," he said softly. "All this time. It was you."

"It was," she replied. "You are, I believe, surprised."

"I admit that I am," he said, stepping nearer. "I knew someone was giving information to the Cerddorian. Not too much. Not enough to pinpoint the source. But enough to cause some upsets. A caravan attacked here, a secret raid gone wrong there. Just enough. You were clever. But not, my dear, clever enough. For now you are well and truly caught. Do you think that I will let you live?"

"Do you think that you will survive this day?" she asked.

"What do you mean?"

She gestured to the window where a white mist pressed heavily. "Did you not notice? A very heavy fog—so unusual for this time of year. And dawn just a few moments away."

"What are you saying?" he demanded, stepping still closer.

"You know what I am saying," she answered, shaking her long, dark hair back from her face, taking a fresh hold of her dagger. "Today is the end for you. Surely you didn't think that you could hold back Morrigan forever?"

"If she is here as you say, then today will be the day she dies. I killed her father. I can kill her."

"I think not," Arday said, a smile on her beautiful face. "For her brother, High King Arthur, directs this battle from afar. He is stronger than you can even imagine. Today will be your deathday."

"And yours," he cried as he leapt forward.

Arday lifted her dagger but he was too quick for her. He grabbed her wrist and twisted. With a cry she let go of the dagger. He pulled her to him, feeling her lush body through her red robe full length against his. He bent his head and kissed her, forcing her mouth open.

It was when he felt her change in his grip, when he knew that she hoped to use his passion against him, when he knew she thought she might live, that he struck. He plunged the knife between her beautiful breasts and into her heart.

He should have seen shock in her dark eyes. He should have seen terror. He should have seen the knowledge of her defeat. But instead he saw a smile. Saw her sureness that today he would die. Saw clearly that, in the end, he was the one defeated.

And then the light in her eyes died and she went limp in his arms. He dropped her heavily to the floor, like a broken toy he no longer wanted. He opened his mouth to call for the guards, but the call died on his lips. For that was the moment he heard the fierce cries of hundreds of hawks, and then the call of a hunting horn. Then crash after crash as what he knew to be the gates of Tegeingl came down.

THREE HOURS LATER Morrigan stood outside the closed gates of Caer Gwynt. The streets outside the fortress was full of Cerddorian and townsfolk, all with Coranian blood on their weapons, all waiting for the last act to begin. A pall of smoke hung over the city from the burning temple of Lytir, which stood on what had once been the sacred grove of alders. Nemed Gwernen would rise again, Morrigan had vowed, when she had ordered the temple burned.

Overhead the sky was thick with hawks, and their fierce cries mingled with the scattered sounds of battle as the Kymric warriors quashed the few pockets of Coranian resistance left. Most of the enemy still left alive had retreated inside Caer Gwynt.

Cai, who had not once left her side during the bloody morning, stood on her right. And Prince Rhodri, who had also been near her all day, was on her left. Behind her Susanna, Ygraine, and Tangwen stood, their weapons ready. Bedwyr suddenly pushed through the crowd and bowed before her, but not before reassuring himself that Tangwen was unharmed. Then Duach also came to stand before her. Her father's former Doorkeeper grinned and bowed.

Gwyhar, Susanna's son, ran up. "Queen Morrigan," he said formally, his Bard's voice carrying, "I bring you great news.

Tegeingl is again ours. All other resistance is finished."

"Then only Caer Gwynt, the Fortress of the Winds, remains," Susanna said.

"What are your orders, my Queen?" Cai asked.

The silver door of the fortress glowed in the noonday sun. The figure of the hawk with outstretched wings, outlined in glowing sapphires, shimmered brightly. Overhead, the largest hawk she had ever seen spiraled down from the sky straight for her. Knowing what she must do, she stood still as the hawk landed on her shoulder. The bird's claws dug into the leather of her tunic, but she did not move. She was Morrigan, daughter of Gwynedd, daughter of the hawk, and she would not flinch.

The hawk turned to look her full in the face and Morrigan returned the bird's stare. The hawk's bright, blue eyes glowed like sapphires and its fierce cry rang in her ears. Yes, she thought. Now it ends. Her own fortress was closed against her and she stood in the street outside the doors like a beggar. "Yrth!" she cried furiously.

The old Druid seemed to materialize at her elbow. "Yes, Queen Morrigan?" he asked, his voice calm.

"Bring those doors down!"

"As you wish," he bowed. Four other Druids in their brown robes gathered before the doors, behind Yrth.

After a moment the door began to shiver. Then it burst open with a mighty crash. The hawk on Morrigan's shoulder screamed again and launched itself into the air. With another cry it led the hawks over the wall and into the courtyard.

With a cry of her own Morrigan led her warriors into the now-opened fortress. With cool efficiency, in spite of her rage, she began to kill the Coranian warriors that were massed in the courtyard. One after the other she killed them, aided by Rhodri and Cai, who refused to move an inch from her side.

Out of the corner of her eye she saw her mother plunge her sword into the chest of a Coranian warrior. And she saw one of her mother's rare smiles light her face. Bedwyr stuck close to Tangwen as the two sliced their way through the courtyard.

"Morrigan," Susanna called.

Morrigan looked over at her Bard. Susanna was standing in the doorway of the ystafell, her face pale. Gwyhar, her son, was at her shoulder, guarding her closely from harm.

"Arday is dead!" Susanna called.

Morrigan briefly closed her eyes. She had so wanted to reward Arday for the years of service. But someone had gotten to her first. And she knew who it was, as surely as if she had been there.

It was at that moment that she caught sight of General Catha through the press. His blond hair was soaked in sweat. Blood splattered his golden tunic. His axe flashed in the sun as he skewered a Kymric warrior.

As if he sensed her gaze he raised his head and looked at her across the courtyard. A cruel smile came to his handsome face and he held the axe before him and gave her a mocking bow.

But she needed no such invitation, no encouragement to meet him in battle. For this was the man who had killed her father. This was the man who had sent hundreds of Cerddorian to their deaths. This was the man who had held all of Gwynedd in his cruel grasp for so long.

This was the man who would die today.

She supposed he was not afraid of her, for her knew her to be no more than sixteen years of age. But she knew that, in all the ways that counted, she was no longer a girl. She was a warrior of Gwynedd. She was her father's daughter. She was the PenHebog, the Head of the Hawk. And she would not fail.

She stalked across the courtyard in fury and warriors of both armies seemed to melt from her path. She was vaguely aware that both Cai and Rhodri stayed with her and that her mother, too, followed closely behind her.

She and Catha came to a halt in front of each other. Both held their weapons firmly in their hands.

"So, daughter of Uthyr, you have come to me," Catha said, smiling. "I will do to you what I did to him."

"I think not, General," Morrigan said, her voice clear and calm. "For the time has come for you to pay for your crimes."

"Ha! You are a girl."

"No," Morrigan said grimly. "I am justice."

Without another word they began. His axe and her sword clashed so hard that sparks flew. The air between seemed to be woven of metal as their blades flickered in and out, as each sought to get through the others' defenses.

For Morrigan it was as though every movement that anyone made in that suddenly still morning was unnaturally clear. She seemed to be aware of everything around her. She knew that her mother stood stiff and unmoving, and that Susanna had her arm around Ygraine's shoulders. She was aware that Bedwyr and Tangwen stood close together, their hands clasped. She was aware that Cai and Rhodri were watching grimly, forcing themselves to stand back from the fray, leaving this to her.

She wondered briefly if her father was watching from the Land of Summer. She wondered if he knew that she was fighting his enemy here today. She wondered if he was proud of her.

The battle between the two of them went on and on. Her arm was getting tired and she kept wiping sweat from her brow. But the strength of Catha's blows were also lessening, and he, too, wiped sweat from his face.

Then Catha leapt forward, his axe swinging viciously at her knees. She jumped in the air, allowing the blade to pass beneath her. As she came down to earth her ankle twisted beneath her and she stumbled. She recovered only just in time, rolling out of the way of the descending axe. She leapt back to her feet, panting.

Knowing that the time had come, she cried her father's name and pressed her attack, beating him back with the onslaught of her repeated blows. But he recovered quicker than she had thought he would. He raised his axe and it began to descend more swiftly than she thought possible. She might have died then—would, surely, have—but the sudden harsh scream of a hawk and the beating of wings distracted Catha from fully completing the blow. He ducked to avoid the huge bird, and his stroke went wild, which was all that Morrigan needed. Her blade knocked his axe from his hand. Without hesitation, she plunged her sword into his chest with both hands.

Blood spilled from the wound and from Catha's mouth as he sank to his knees, his hands clutching the sword that protruded from his heart. She stood in front of him, her hands still on the hilt as he stared up at her with shocked eyes.

"This is for my father," she hissed, and she twisted the blade.

He cried out in agony and his cold, blue eyes shone with hatred.

"And this is for my mother's pain," she said, as she twisted it again.

"And this is for Arday," she whispered, as she again twisted the blade in Catha's dying heart.

And then Catha sank fully to the ground, sliding off her blade. She stood over him and watched his spirit flee, defeated.

And then the hawk, the huge hawk that had cried out, cried out again in triumph and shot up into the sky.

MORRIGAN SAT IN her father's chair on the dais in the Great Hall. The boar banner of Corania had been taken down and burned, and the banner that now hung on the wall behind her was the banner of the Rulers of Gwynedd. The banner showed a hawk with outstretched wings worked in blue on brown silk, outlined in silver with sapphire eyes.

Rhodri and Cai both stood stolidly on either side of her chair, neither one giving any indication that they would ever stop shadowing her. She hoped that, eventually, she could persuade them to leave her alone, but she was touched by their obvious devotion.

Rhodri kept his eye on his granddaughter, Tangwen, as she stood with Morrigan's lieutenant, Bedwyr. Rhodri did not seem at all displeased at this, and he almost even smiled.

Cai, on the other hand, kept looking over at Susanna. But just when she would sense his eyes on her and turn to look at him, he would look away. Men, Morrigan thought with a hint of exasperation. They were so silly.

Her mother, who could not be persuaded to mount the dais, stood proudly at the foot of the stairs. Ygraine's dark eyes held triumph at once again being back in the hall she had ruled for so long. But there was pain in her eyes, too, that Uthyr could not be here to witness this moment.

Susanna and her son, Gwyhar, stood on either side of Ygraine. Gwyhar kept looking up at Cai, as though waiting for something. Morrigan had a pretty good idea what that was, but privately thought Gwyhar would wait a long time for Cai to say what he should have been said a long time ago.

Morrigan gripped the armrests of the massive, canopied chair. She was Queen of Gwynedd. She ruled, not just here in newly freed Tegeingl, but throughout Gwynedd. For the past few days had seen success in every cantref. In Llyn, Lady Gildasa, Tangwen's aunt, had been rescued and she and her son, Ydeer, had led the Cerddorian and common folk to victory against the Coranians. In Arfon, Lady Isagwyn who had led the Cerddorian in Coed Arllech for the past two years had also won her battle.

In Dunoding Dywel, Gwarda of Ardudwy had been victorious. He had begged hard to have that chance, for his brother was Bledri, the Dewin in Rheged who had betrayed his people to the enemy, and Dywel was always eager to prove himself. In Eryi, Lord Ciawn had escaped his prison, and freed his cantref. In Rhufonoig no lord or gwarda had been left who was not in league with the enemy, so Morrigan had dispatched Cynwas Cwryfager, the Gwarda of Aberffraw, to lead the Cerddorian there. And he had done so successfully, ensuring that Nerthus and Saranhon, the traitorous gwarda there, had been killed.

In Arllechwedd, Teregund ap Moren had also been victorious. Menwaed, the Lord of Arllechwedd, was dead, and at his sister's own hand as they had discovered earlier. Morrigan had ordered that Menwaed's body be burned without ceremony. And she had seen to it that Arday's body had been treated with reverence and readied for burial. Tomorrow she would be present when Arday was buried in Bryn Celli Ddu, for her father's former steward deserved all honor.

Of course, all this had only been able to happen because of Arthur, her brother. He had dispatched the Y Dawnus throughout Kymru, and had used his powers as High King to ensure victory throughout. Without Arthur they never would have won back their own.

She gestured for the prisoner to be brought in. Very few Coranians were still left alive at this point. Cai himself had killed the Master-wyrce-jaga in battle, and she had given orders before the battle had even begun that not one wyrce-jaga was to be left alive. And those orders had been faithfully followed. Most of the common Coranian soldiers had elected to fight unto the death, and she was not sorry, for she would have been loath to give quarter. But she had seen to it that a very important Coranian was spared, for her brother had told her to do so.

The prisoner was brought in. His hands were tied behind his back. His priests' robe with the tabard of green was torn and dirty. But the prisoner held his head high and made his way without resistance through the crowd of Cerddorian gathered in the hall. At last he was made to halt at the bottom of the dais.

Morrigan leaned forward. "You are Ecgfrith of Deorby, self-styled Byshop of Gwynedd?"

"I am Ecgfrith of Deorby. I was sent here by my ArchPreost to be the Byshop of Gwynedd."

"And do you wish to have your life spared today?" she asked.

"All my life I have faithfully served my God. Should He want me to die today, I will. Should He wish me spared, I will be. You must do as He sees fit."

"Indeed?" Morrigan asked, her brows raised. For a moment she reconsidered what she was going to do, for though she was sure he was sincere, he sounded very pompous about the whole thing. But in the end she let it go. After all, Ecgfrith was only being loyal to his God, even if he was such a pain about it.

"I have a message for you to take to your Warleader," she said. "It is a message from High King Arthur. Will you take that message?"

"I will," Ecgfrith said.

For a moment she hesitated. The message was surely useless. Havgan would never—

Yes, sister, I am sure about this.

She smiled at the sound of the voice in her head, for it was so comforting to hear her brother's voice, to know that the two of them, together, had avenged their father this day.

"The message, Ecgfrith, is that Havgan must leave Kymru. If he leaves, he will live. If he stays, he will die. This is the message."

"I will carry it, Queen Morrigan," Ecgfrith said. "But I do not believe Havgan will leave."

"Neither do I," Morrigan agreed. "Nonetheless, that is the message." She gestured to the two men guarding the Byshop. "Let him rest today, and send him on his way tomorrow, with a fresh horse and supplies."

The guards bowed and took their prisoner away.

Rhodri stepped up from his place beside her and bowed to her. "Queen Morrigan, I beg to give you news."

"News?" Morrigan asked blankly. "What sort of news?"

"News that my granddaughter, Tangwen of Rhufonoig, is to be married." Rhodri gestured and Tangwen and Bedwyr came to the bottom of the dais, holding hands. They bowed to her. Tangwen was blushing, but she was smiling and Bedwyr was grinning from ear to ear.

"Tangwen ur Madoc var Bri," Morrigan inquired solemnly, though she too had a smile on her face, "do you truly wish to wed Bedwyr ap Bedrawd?"

"I do," Tangwen answered, blushing still further.

"Then I, too, will announce some news of my own," Morrigan went on. "As the former Lord of Rhufonoig, Madoc ap Rhodri, is dead, a new ruler must be found for that cantref. And you are my choice. Lady of Rhufonoig, will you swear fealty to me?"

Tangwen's jaw dropped in surprise. Laughing, Bedwyr pushed her up the steps, for she seemed too shocked to believe what she had heard. Tangwen knelt before Morrigan, tears streaming down her face.

Morrigan drew her sword and lightly touched Tangwen's left shoulder with the blade, then her right. "In the name of Taran of the Winds, you are mine."

Well done, sister.

As the Cerddorian applauded first Tangwen's engagement then her elevation to Lady, all of Cai's attention was focused on the beautiful face of the woman he so loved. Susanna watched Tangwen and Bedwyr with tears in her eyes, remembering, perhaps, her lover, Griffi, who had been King Uthyr's Druid. Griffi had died the day King Uthyr had, died defending his king. Died, indeed, only a few days after Cai's wife and son had died.

Their deaths, the deaths of Nest and Garanwyn, still haunted him. For he had so loved them; they had been his world. And when they died so much of Cai had died also. So much that it had taken him a long time to realize that he was even capable of loving again. And by the time he realized that, it was far too late to change it. For he had fallen in love with Susanna and he could not fall out of love with her, try as he might.

And he had tried, because he hadn't wanted to love her. He had been too afraid. But there was no going back. His heart simply refused to come back to him. And when he saw the happiness on Tangwen's and Bedwyr's faces, he had thought that, for one brief moment, such happiness might be possible for him again.

It is.

Cai knew that voice. It was the voice of the son of the man he had served so faithfully. It was the voice of the High King of Kymru.

Your fears make you foolish, Cai. Be strong. Be brave. Be true.

Be true, Cai thought. Why had he never thought of it that way before? Be true. And his truth was Susanna. As if in a dream he walked forward, past Tangwen, who was rising to her feet, now Lady of Rhufonoig. Past Morrigan, who was sheathing her sword. Down the steps and past Ygraine, whose dark eyes glinted as she guessed what he was going to do. Past Gwyhar, Susanna's son, whose face tightened with unspoken hope. And up to Susanna.

"Susanna ur Erim, Y Dawnus of Kymru, Bard to Queen Morrigan of Gwynedd, will you take me as your husband?"

Gwyhar gave out a whoop of joy. Bedwyr shouted in glee. Ygraine actually smiled. Morrigan grinned.

But Susanna stood as though rooted to the spot, her beautiful blue eyes misted with tears.

"Susanna?" he asked, uncertainly. "I—I know I am not the best man you have ever known. But I do love you truly. Will you—will you at least think about it?"

"Will I think about it?" she cried with a smile, tears spilling down her face. "You foolish man, I have thought of little else. Yes, Cai ap Cynyr, I will marry you."

And he took her in his arms and kissed her as he had so longed to do, and it was even sweeter than he had ever imagined. His heart gave a little sigh, for he was home at last.

MORRIGAN COULDN'T SEEM to stop smiling. That Tangwen and Bedwyr were so happy, that Cai had, at last, shown how brave he truly was, touched her. She walked to the edge of the dais and stood looking down at the Cerddorian massed there. She lifted her hands. "Today I declare that Gwynedd is free!" The roar from her warriors was almost deafening.

"Tomorrow we begin muster for the final battle in Gwytheryn. I appoint Rhodri ap Erddufyl, he who was once King of Gwynedd, to rule until I return."

The roar that accompanied this announcement was almost as deafening. Rhodri's jaw dropped, for he had not expected this. Tears came to his blue eyes, and he knelt before her.

"I will do as you wish, Queen Morrigan, in expiation for my son. I will not fail you."

"I never though you would, Prince Rhodri," Morrigan murmured. "I never thought you would."

Chapter Eighteen

Llwynarth
Kingdom of Rheged, Kymru
Eiddew Mis, 500

Gwyntdydd, Cynuddu Wythnos—early morning

Enid ur Urien, sometime Queen of Rheged, stood quietly outside the gates of Llwynarth. Dense fog shrouded the city, turning those warriors that surrounded her into ghostlike figures.

Very substantial ghosts, she amended. More substantial than she, for they were whole, and prepared to fight to take back what was once theirs. And she? Well, she was not whole and would not, perhaps, ever be. Morcant and Bledri had seen to that. As for fighting—well, that was another thing she could not do. For all her strength had been sapped out of her during those long nights in a cell beneath the fortress where she had once lived. During those nights when Bledri would come to her, nights when he would strip her and play with her, and force her to do things she still could not think about without shame.

But those were nothing to the nights with her husband, Morcant. For Morcant gloried in pain and had spent his nights trying to force her to cry out, violating her in ways she had not even dreamed were possible.

The only thing she could say about that was that she had kept her silence during those endless hours in hell. In that small way she had measured her victory. It was the only victory she had, the only one she would ever have.

For though her desecrated body had at last been rescued, the rest of her was still in prison. Every night since she was rescued from Caer Erias she woke up in a cold sweat, her heart pounding, certain that Morcant or Bledri was just outside her tent. But she would lock her screams in her throat and had never told anyone of those fears. Nonetheless, she thought they knew. She was certain that her brother, Owein, did. And she thought his wife, Sanon, was also aware of it. They saw it, perhaps, in her drawn face, in the purplish cast beneath her eyes that spoke of sleepless hours in the still of the night.

And Geriant would have known, had he been here. Geriant had always known her, better than anyone ever had. But he had returned to Prydyn to aid his father. He had come for her, rescued her, then left her.

She remembered clearly the day he had left her. He had come to her tent and asked her to walk with him. She had not wanted to leave her tent, the only sanctuary she had, but she had wanted even less to have a man—any man—enter that tent. She thought, perhaps, that Geriant had known that very well.

They had walked away from the clearing in Coed Addien where her brother and his Cerddorian made their plans to recapture Rheged. They had walked in silence beneath the trees for a while. Then Geriant had stopped and turned to face her.

"I am leaving tomorrow, Enid," Geriant had said quietly.

Her jolt of dismay had taken her by surprise. But she had betrayed nothing of it.

"I go to join my da," Geriant had gone on, in spite of her silence. "It will soon be time for us to free Prydyn, and I must be with him."

"Of course," she had said, for it was clear she must say something.

"I would stay if I could."

"It is best that you don't."

"No?" His blue eyes, blazing in intensity, had caught hers. Somehow she tore her gaze away and looked down at the leaf-covered ground.

"Enid," he had said, reaching out to touch her face.

But she had leapt back, her hand, of its own volition, grasping the dagger at her belt.

Slowly, Geriant had lowered his hand, his eyes bleak. "I see," he had said quietly.

"I don't think you do!" she had replied harshly.

"Oh, I think I do."

And he had. Of course. Hadn't he always?

"Goodbye, Enid. My dearest love."

Then he had turned and left her, his shoulders bowed but his steps firm and purposeful.

That had been some days ago. Almost before she knew it the day had come when Owein, with the power of the High King at his back, would gamble all. According to the Dewin, the people in the city were ready and armed, awaiting the signal soon to come. And the Cerddorian massed silently outside the gates, their movements hidden by the fog generated by the Druids through the power of High King Arthur, who was far away in Cadair Idris.

The five Druids, lead by Owein's Druid, Sabrina, stood still as statues, their eyes closed, their fists clenched, their brown robes barely moving with their shallow breaths. And the Cerddorian stood just as silently, their swords and spears ready. The Cerddorian at the north gate were led by Gwarae Golden-Hair, while those at the east waited with Trystan, Owein's captain, at their head. Teleri, Owein's lieutenant, led the forces at the west gate while Owein and his wife Sanon would lead those at the south gate where Enid now stood.

The fog swirled and eddied as one figure came to stand next to her. Without even looking at him, she spoke, her voice muted and hushed. "This is your day, brother."

"Our day," Owein replied quietly.

She shook her head. "It is yours. Today you take back what you lost."

"And you?"

She turned to him, a bitter smile on her face. His red tunic was muted in the fog, giving it the sheen of old blood. Opals and gold flashed from the torque of Rheged clasped around his neck. On his head he wore the helm she had last seen her father wear.

The helmet was made of gold, fashioned like the head of a fierce stallion. The horse's eyes were fiery opals which shone even in the fog with a light all their own.

She, too, was dressed for battle, wearing a stiff leather tunic of white and breeches of red. Her white leather boots reach to mid-calf and her auburn hair was braided tightly to her scalp. She was armed with a short sword and knives tucked into the top of her boots. Yet for all that, she would not fight this day. Would not fight again, ever. She was only dressed as a warrior due to Owein's insistence, only here at his firm bidding. She would do this much for him and no more. And nothing at all for herself.

Owein's blue eyes searched hers and dimmed at what he saw there.

"What I have lost cannot be returned to me," she said.

"Not if you will not fight to take it back," Owein replied.

"A lecture from you, brother?" she asked, turning back to look at the fog-shrouded city walls.

Owein shook his head. "Never. But still it seems to me, little sister, that you are a prisoner of your own choosing. If that is not true then why will you not fight today for Kymru's freedom? Or for your own?"

"I will not fight because I cannot fight. I do not have the strength. It is one of the many things they took from me."

"It is not the strength you lack. It is the will."

"So it is," she agreed mildly. "Leave me be, brother, for there is no help for me."

"By your choice."

She turned to him, her eyes blazing. "Much you know of it," she hissed. "You who have never been helpless before such depravity, you who have never had to endure what I endured while keeping your screams locked in your throat. And all because I was a fool. Well, I have paid for that foolishness. And I will keep paying until the debt is done."

"The debt is paid, Enid," Owein said quietly. "Paid in full."

"Just leave me be, Owein. I will stay here, outside the gates, and wait for word of your victory. And when it comes I will leave this place and return, alone, to Coed Addien. I will build a small house there in the woods, and you and Sanon will visit me once a year, and bring your children with you. I will exclaim how they have grown, and congratulate you on your brood, your loving wife, on the opal torque clasped around your neck. You will pester me, at the end of each visit, to come to the city. You will, in your heart, think to yourself that I live alone because I like to suffer. You will think I could have the choice to be free, but will not take it. In your heart you will blame me for how uncomfortable I will make you feel. But you will let me do this. Because you know there is no other way for me."

Owein smiled unexpectedly and Enid blinked. "You seem to be very sure of the future, sister," he said. "At one time I thought I knew what mine would be, too. I thought that I would never marry, I thought that I would never see Caer Erias again, I thought that I would die in bitterness and sorrow. But I was wrong. For Sanon, the love of my heart, is now my wife. And I will see Caer Erias again in a matter of moments. And if I die this day it will not be with either bitterness or sorrow. It will be with gratitude for the happiness I was granted, even if only for a brief time."

The fog swirled again and Sanon, Enid's sister-in-law, laid a hand on Owein's arm. Her golden hair, so like her brother Geriant's, gleamed. Her dark eyes were fastened on her husband, her gaze trusting and strong.

Sanon opened her mouth to speak, but Enid shushed her. "I hear it," she said.

The others stood still, straining to hear.

"I think you must be mistaken, Enid," Sanon began, then she stopped as she, too, heard what Enid had heard.

A faint rumbling emanated from the south. Beneath their feet the ground began to shake, trembling with the news of what was rushing toward them. The rumbling grew louder.

"At my signal, Sabrina," Owein said to his Druid. And though Sabrina did not open her eyes, she nodded.

The rumbling was massive now, though the cause was still hidden by the enshrouding fog. As one the warriors moved back from the gate.

"Now," Owein called, and Sabrina and her four Druids opened their eyes and raised their faces to the sky. In that moment the fog disappeared, gone as though it had never been. And Owein and his warriors turned to face the south horizon, to see what they knew they would see.

Wild horses crested the horizon, pouring down the hills and toward the city. Horses white as snow, horses black as night, horses golden as the sun, horses brown as newly turned earth raced across the meadow, their eyes fierce.

"Sabrina!" Owein called, and at his command Sabrina and her Druids raised their fists to the sky. And as they did so the gates opened with a crash.

The lead stallion, his golden coat glistening, his fiery gaze on Owein, halted for a moment before the king. The stallion reared and neighed fiercely. And Owein grabbed the horse's mane and leapt onto the animal's back. The horse neighed again and whirled to the gate, leading the herd into the city.

The Cerddorian poured in the gates after the horses. Sanon, with Owein's name on her lips, sprang forward through the gate.

But Enid stayed where she was, holding her ground.

The Cerddorian, led by Owein, streamed into the city, mingling freely with the wild herd. The horses pounded down the streets, nimbly avoiding the townsfolk who were even now spilling from their houses, weapons in their hands.

A contingent of Coranian warriors, obviously just awakened from a sound sleep, emerged from one of the houses. One of the horses neighed fiercely and sprang toward the warriors, followed by other horses who had caught their scent. The warriors cried out and turned to flee back into the house, but found their way barred by armed townsfolk. They turned back, looking for another way out, but it was too late. The horses reared, striking at the Coranians with their hooves. The men went down in a heap, their heads split open, their bones crushed, their blood spilling onto the cobbled road.

Owein smiled as he clung to the golden stallion's back. The first blow had gone to the horses. And that was as it should be in the country of Rheged. His smile faded as he saw the Temple of Lytir, erected on what had once been the sacred ground of Nemed Draenenwen, the grove of hawthorn trees where the people of Llwynarth had celebrated their festivals, where the queens of Rheged had gone to bear their children. Owein himself and his brothers and sister had all been born there, beneath the branches of the once-sheltering trees. At this time of year the grove should have been white with the clusters of delicate flowers that should have studded the tree branches. But the trees were gone, uprooted and burned when the Coranians built the huge, wooden temple to their God.

The temple loomed before him, silent and forbidding in the early morning light. It was made of a series of sloping roofs of different heights, grouped around a large, square tower. A walkway ran around the building, enclosed by a low wall and topped by an arcade. The gables were carved with an array of beasts—boars and dragons, horses and eagles, serpents and hinds. Steps led up to the huge, double doors of the main entrance.

Owein urged the stallion forward and the horse leapt up the stairs to the closed doors. Outside the doors two torches were lit, set in iron brackets against the wall. He grabbed one of the torches and leapt from the stallion's back. He thrust against the doors and entered the building. This was the place where his sister had been forced to wed Morcant. This was the place dedicated to the Coranian's jealous god. This would be the place that must be destroyed. Today.

He raced down the nave and touched the torch to the white and gold banner of Lytir that lay on the stone altar. The cloth ignited, as though eager to be cleansed by the fire. He backed away, lighting pew after wooden pew. The interior began to fill with smoke, crackling wildly as the hungry fire consumed its prey. He reached the doors and flung the torch down the aisle, whirling around and out again down the stairs.

The stallion was waiting for him at the bottom of the steps, his eyes glowing in the light of the fire. The animal neighed, calling out his challenge. He rose on his hind legs, his forelegs kicking out to the sky. Owein leapt back onto the horse's back and gave his own cry, calling out his challenge to his warriors and the townsfolk gathered there.

"Forward Kymri! Fight the enemy and take back what was ours! I charge you with this in the name of my murdered father, King Urien; in the name of my murdered mother, Queen Ellirri, in the name of my murdered brother, Prince Elphin!"

His wife, Sanon, ran to him, her sword already red with Coranian blood, her dark eyes fierce and glowing. He reached out his hand and pulled her behind him onto the stallion's back.

The horse leapt forward, making for Caer Erias, the fortress where he knew Morcant and Bledri huddled, hatching pathetic schemes to spare their lives.

But they would not be spared. For Owein had a debt to collect. And he would not rest until that was paid.

A FEW HOURS later Owein and his warriors had secured the southwest quadrant of the city and were advancing the last few feet to Caer Erias, the fortress of the rulers of Rheged. Trystan came riding up, with his lieutenant, Teleri, right behind him.

Trystan dismounted and came to stand before Owein. His tunic and trousers were torn and bloody, but he moved easily, and Owein concluded that the blood belonged to now-dead Coranians. Trystan gave Owein a jaunty salute. "My King, your city is secured. All quadrants are once again under Kymric control."

"And the wyrce-jaga were given no quarter, as you ordered," Teleri said. The diminutive lieutenant smiled and her gray-green eyes were bright.

"She says that with such relish, doesn't she?" Gwarae Golden-Hair asked as he, too, rode up. "It's one of her nicer traits." He dismounted and grabbed Teleri around the waist, and kissed her exuberantly.

"What are your orders, my King?" Sabrina asked quietly as she led the other four brown-robed Druids to stand before Owein.

Trystan stepped forward toward Sabrina but was halted by the arrival of Esyllt, Owein's Bard. She flung herself into Trystan's arms. "You are safe!" she breathed.

Trystan put his arms around Esyllt, for if he had not done so he would have fallen. He gave Sabrina a pleading look, but the Druid turned away and again addressed Owein.

"My King?"

The horse's head, etched on the closed, golden gate of Caer Erias, glittered in the noonday sun. The opals scattered throughout the horse's mane danced in the fierce light.

"Bring the gate down, Sabrina," Owein said quietly. "Bring the gate down, and may the Shining Ones soon have the task of dealing with Morcant's black soul."

Sabrina nodded and turned toward the gate. She and the other four Druids raised their faces to the sky, their eyes closed.

"Arthur," Sabrina whispered. "High King, send us your aid." The Druids instantly stiffened, feeling the power of the High King uniting them, guiding them, knitting them together to bring their power together as one. The gate shook, then burst open. As it did, Owein's golden stallion reared high, his deadly hooves beating the air. Then the animal leapt forward and was through the gate, screaming his challenge to the Coranians.

Owein and his people followed, bursting into the courtyard. Coranians lined the perimeter, their weapons ready, and the fight began afresh.

Owein saw Sanon swing her blade and a Coranian went down in a welter of blood. Teleri, Trystan, Gwarae, and the rest engaged the enemy, Owein's name on their lips as they shouted their war cries.

And then Owein saw him. The man he had wanted to kill for so long. Morcant was pressed against the side of the stable, obviously looking for his chance to take a horse and flee. His black hair and dark eyes flashed like shadows beneath the golden sun as he crept forward. His sword was in his right hand, while a sack was clutched in his left. The bag, no doubt, contained whatever treasures Morcant had managed to gather up before the fortress was overrun.

"Morcant!" Owein cried, as he sprinted toward the man who had betrayed Rheged. "You are a dead man!"

Morcant whirled to face Owein. He threw the sack on the ground and brought his blade up, just in time to deflect Owein's blow.

And so the fight began. Their blades sang as they clashed. The swords moved so swiftly that the blades seemed blurred, trailing fire. Suddenly Owein felt a pain in his right leg, just below the knee. A dagger was protruding from his calf and he staggered.

"Finish it, Morcant," Bledri called out from just behind Owein, for it was he that had thrown the dagger. "Kill him!"

Morcant raised his blade as Owein went down on one knee. Owein tried to bring his sword up in time, but he knew he would be too late. Morcant was going to kill him. His family had once again been betrayed at the hands of Bledri, his father's false Dewin. Owein heard his wife cry out his name, but he knew she was too far away to help him. It was over for him. His only comfort was in knowing that though he would die today the Kymri had won this battle.

He made his peace with fate in that moment and so, when the blade came out of nowhere and deflected Morcant's killing blow, he felt only a dull surprise. He stared at the blade, then focused on the hand that held it. It was a slim, white hand that held the hilt so competently. So, she had come after all.

He looked to his right and saw that Bledri had been disarmed and was held securely by Gwarae. The gwarda's blade was pressed against the Dewin's throat while Trystan and Sanon stood on either side, holding Bledri's arms tightly.

Enid smiled as she thrust her blade forward, forcing Morcant to withdraw his and step back. "Husband," she said formally. "You seem surprised to see me."

Morcant licked his lips, his face ashen. "I did not think to see you in a place where decent people gather," he said stiffly.

Her brows quirked as she smiled slowly. "You think I am not decent?"

"You know what you are," he hissed.

"The things you and Bledri did to me do not make me dirty," Enid said softly. "They make you dirty. Foul. Polluted. Poor, poor excuses for men."

Owein smiled, for that was what he had been trying to tell her for so long. Enid saw his smile and smiled back. It had been so long since he had seen a smile on his sister's face that he almost wept for the joy of it.

"High King Arthur spoke to me," Enid went on, "as I waited outside the city. I had thought, husband, never to enter Llwynarth again, never to return to the place of my humiliation. I did, indeed, feel the shame you think I should feel. But no more. For the High King Wind-Spoke to me and he said many things, but none so profound as the last thing. He said that, at the last, it is up to a prisoner to escape his own chains. He said that we can all be prisoners of our past. Or we can escape it. And that the choice is up to us."

Enid smiled again, but this time at Morcant. And this smile was so very different than her first. For this one held a promise of death in it. Morcant saw it clearly and shivered, even as he gripped his blade tightly.

"So you see, husband," Enid said gently, "I chose." In a flash she raised her blade and leapt forward. The blade glowed like fire as it dove past Morcant's defense and parted his chest, eagerly drinking his blood.

Owein mounted the dais in the Great Hall and took his seat upon his father's throne, a massive chair with a canopy of red and white brocade stitched with opals. The Coranian banner had been torn down and replaced with the banner of Rheged depicting the head of a golden horse with opals in its shining mane.

The hall was packed with Owein's warriors, all laughing and talking, drinking ale and telling stories of the battle. On Owein's right stood what had been Queen Ellirri's chair. Sanon occupied that chair and Owein reached for her hand and kissed her palm. Sanon's face glowed and she smiled at him, her golden hair unbound and flowing down her slender shoulders, framing her beautiful face.

Enid mounted the dais and took her place standing to Owein's left. She moved with the same grace she always had but now she held her head high and walked proudly.

Truly, Owein thought, she was indeed free.

As was all of Rheged. For he had just received word from his Dewin that their plans had gone well throughout the kingdom. In Penrhyn the forces led by Anynnas ur Menw, sister of King Rhoram's Bard, had been successful. In Gwinionydd Hetwin Silver-Brow and his son, Cynedyr the Wild, had routed the Coranians. In Ystrad Marchell Teleri's brother, Brys, had rescued Lord Rhun and the two had led their warriors to victory. In Maelienydd Lady Atlantas, Trystan's sister, had defeated the enemy and in Breinol warriors led by Feina, Gwarda of Llannerch, were victorious. Lastly, in Gwent forces led by Tyrnon Twryf Liant had freed the cantref.

His beloved Rheged was now free and his throat ached at the thought. For he had not dared to hope for this day. Not until love had come into his life.

At the bottom of the dais stood Sabrina. Owein's Druid stood quietly in her robe of brown and green. Her dark hair was pulled back from her flawless face and her blue eyes were serene. Across from her stood Esyllt, Owein's Bard. Her robes of blue and white set off her white skin and her blue eyes flickered continually to Trystan.

Trystan and Teleri approached the dais and bowed. "King Owein," Teleri called, "I am pleased to report that all the wyrce-jaga have been killed. Not one is left alive in Llwynarth." At this the warriors cheered, for the black-robed witch hunters had been much hated.

"Even better, Teleri herself has rid the world of the Master-wyrce-jaga, Saebald," Trystan said with a smile.

"That's my girl," Gwarae said as he went to Teleri and took her hand. He picked her up and mounted the dais, setting her on her feet in front of Owein. "My King," he said with a grin, "it is only right that you be the first to greet my wife."

"You got married?" Sanon asked with delight. "When?"

"Just now," Teleri replied, smiling. "Sabrina married us. I didn't think it a good idea to give Gwarae time to change his mind."

"Ha!" Gwarae said. "I've only been begging her to do this for weeks."

"My congratulations to you both," Owein said heartily. "We just have a few more things to take care of, and we will celebrate." He motioned for Trystan to bring in the prisoner. At Trystan's nod two warriors marched in Byshop Oswy. The man's green robe was torn and dusty and his fair hair, turning to gray, was disheveled. His hands were tied behind his back, but he walked calmly and stood quietly at the bottom of the dais. At Owein's nod Trystan escorted the Byshop to stand before Owein.

"Byshop Oswy of Gwyrin," Owein said, "your life has been spared today."

The Byshop said nothing, merely looking at Owein, waiting for what would come.

"Spared by the wish of High King Arthur. Spared so that you may take a message to the Golden Man."

"And the message?" Oswy asked.

Owein hesitated, for he knew that the message was useless.

Nonetheless, Owein, you must give it.

Owein was startled to hear Arthur's voice so clearly. And he was awed, for though he had witnessed the power of the High King today, he still could scarcely believe that Arthur could Wind-Speak from so far away.

"The message, Oswy," Owein answered, "is that Havgan must leave Kymru. If he does not leave, he will die."

"I will deliver that message, but I do not think Havgan will care for it."

"Havgan will soon be hearing a great many things he does not care for," Owein said. "He will soon learn that Prydyn slipped from his grasp three days ago. And that he lost Ederynion two days since. And that Gwynedd slipped from his grasp yesterday. And he has lost Rheged today. Small, rag-tag bands of what is left of his army are attempting to make their way to his stronghold in Eiodel, but very few, I think, will get there. And no wryce-jaga are alive to go to him, for them we slew with no quarter—in the same way they killed our Y Dawnus." At Owein's signal two warriors led the now-pale Byshop away.

Owein's next task would be more satisfying to him, he was sure. He nodded to Trystan and his captain signaled to the warrior at the door. Within moments they brought in Bledri. Next to him Owein heard Enid suck in her breath at the sight of him.

The traitorous Dewin walked slowly, his head down. His silver and green robes were dirty where Gwarae had flung him to the ground after Morcant was killed. His sandy blond hair had come undone from its pearl clasp and hung loosely around his powerful shoulders. As he came to stand at the bottom of the dais he raised his gray eyes to Owein. Although Bledri had known there would be no quarter, he had, perhaps, still hoped. When he saw the martial light in Owein's dark eyes he knew that this last hope was denied him.

Owein glanced over at Enid and saw that his sister's face was still and pitiless. Owein thought nothing would give him more satisfaction than the words he would say next. But he was wrong.

"Bledri ap Gwyn, for your crimes you are to be—"

No.

The single word had been uttered in the heads of all the Kymri gathered here. It echoed in their minds, implacable, unquestionable, final.

"High King—" Owein began, "this cannot be."

No. You may not put Bledri to death.

Enraged, Trystan stepped forward, his sword drawn from its sheath and murder in his bright green eyes.

"No!" Enid cried, moving swiftly to stand before Trystan. "The High King's word is to be obeyed."

Slowly Trystan lowered his raised sword, returned it to its sheath, and stepped back.

Bledri ap Gwyn, one-time Dewin of Kymru, I pronounce a doom on you today. A doom that has been given to me by Cariadas ur Gwydion, the Dreamer's heir, who has dreamed well and true. You are to be exiled Beyond the Ninth Wave. You will be set in a boat with no oars, sails, or rudder. You will be given a knife and fresh water. The boat will be set adrift on the open sea. And the Shining Ones alone know why they require this.

"Will you not kill me now, King of Rheged?" Bledri rapsed. For Bledri knew as well as the rest that exile Beyond the Ninth Wave was nothing more than an extended death sentence. He would die on the ocean, alone, of starvation and thirst. It would be a long death. "Think, Owein, of what I have done to you and yours. I betrayed your mother and father, giving out to the forces of Amgoed that they were not to come to their rescue. I served Morcant, another traitor. And even worse, I raped your sister as she stood bound in the cells beneath Caer Erias. I raped her not once, but several times, each time more brutal than the last."

"No, Trystan!" Owein cried as the captain leapt forward. "Can't you see it's what he wants?" And indeed, Bledri was smiling as he thought Trystan would kill him. But Bledri's smile faded as Trystan stopped in his tracks.

"Don't you see how the Ninth Wave is worse?" Owein asked Trystan quietly. Trystan nodded thoughtfully, then took his hand from his sword hilt.

"Captain Trystan," Owein said sternly, "you are to escort Bledri to the shores of Ystrad Marchell. There you are to see to it that High King Arthur's orders are carried out."

Trystan bowed and moved forward to lead Bledri away, but stopped when Esyllt spoke.

"King Owein," Esyllt said, her voice low and musical, "I request permission to accompany Trystan. A representative of the Y Dawnus should witness the exile."

Sabrina's blue eyes flashed in contempt at this, but the Druid looked away, only to look back, wide-eyed, when Trystan responded before Owein could speak.

"I agree, my King," Trystan said firmly. "One of the Y Dawnus should indeed witness this."

Esyllt's widening smile faded as Trystan went on. "But that Y Dawnus should be Sabrina ur Dadweir."

Esyllt's face mirrored the shock she felt. "Trystan—"

"Sabrina," Trystan repeated. "And no one else."

It was in that moment that March, Esyllt's long-suffering husband stepped forward. "King Owein, I ask for witnesses."

"Witnesses to what, March?" Owein asked, puzzled.

"Witnesses to the fact that, on Calan Llachar, my marriage to Esyllt ur Maelwys will be dissolved."

"Witnessed!" Teleri called out.

"Witnessed!" Enid cried.

Esyllt, faced with repudiation by both her lover and her husband, stood rooted to the floor for several seconds. Then, with immense dignity, she walked from the hall. She did not look back. Which perhaps was just as well, for, if she had, she would have seen Trystan look at Sabrina with his heart in his eyes, and Sabrina's answering smile.

Owein rose and faced the crowd. "I declare today that Rheged is free!" His Cerddorian roared, whistled and stomped their approval. "Tomorrow we begin the muster of Rheged. We march, in a very brief time, for the final battle against the Golden Man."

Sanon rose and came to stand beside him, her hand on his shoulder. Owein turned and gestured for Enid to join them. His sister walked forward, her head held high. "While I am gone I will leave Enid PenMarch to rule Rheged." This time the roar of approval was almost deafening. Enid's blue eyes filled with tears, but she smiled at the acclimation and nodded her head.

Today, indeed, we all are free, Owein thought quietly.

Indeed.

Chapter Nineteen

Afalon
Gwytheryn, Kymru
Eiddew Mis, 500

Meriwydd, Cynyddu Wythnos—early evening

The stars sprang forth, glittering brightly as the sky darkened overhead. It would be hours before the moon rose, so no other light vied with the diamond-hard starlight that pooled over the shadowy plain. Even the steady glow of Cadair Idris could not be seen. For the mountain was a day's march away from the shores of Llyn Mwyngil, where Arthur and his companions now lay concealed in the tall grasses at the edge of the lake. A faint breeze stirred the grasses, but the night maintained its silence, holding its secrets closely.

The dark hulk of Afalon lay silently in the center of the lake, giving out nothing, asking for nothing, inviolate, in spite of the fact that the Coranians had invaded its shores. Arthur could just make out faint pricks of torchlight on the east shore of the isle, pinpointing the compound where his Y Dawnus were held captive.

Arthur, remembering that this was the place where the last High King, Lleu Silver-Hand, fell in battle, shivered for a moment. Lleu had lain here in the grasses, somehow clinging to life, knowing, perhaps, that his dear friend, Bran, would come to him and hear his last words. Knowing, somehow, that Bran would never have let him die alone.

Silently he glanced around at the men and women with him, safely hidden from sight of the lone Coranian guard who paced the docks just half a league north of them. Gwydion hovered at

Arthur's right, simmering silently and refusing to even acknowledge Rhiannon's presence. Rhiannon, wrapped in a voluminous black cloak, was to Arthur's left, supremely indifferent to Gwydion's simmering rage.

Talorcan and Regan huddled closely together, hands clasped. Myrrdin, with Neuad at his side, lay next to Dudod. Dudod's green eyes were bright as he studied his old friend's expression—a curious blend of contentment and anxiety that apparently amused the Bard to no end.

The Druids—Aergol, Menw, Aldur, and Sinend—huddled tightly together, conserving their strength for the heavy demands Arthur would soon make on them.

Elstar, Elidyr, and their sons, Cynfar and Llywelyn, were together next to Cariadas, who lay on Gwydion's right. The Dreamer's heir watched the isle silently, her silvery eyes alight and ready.

Last of all Arthur turned his eyes to Gwen, who lay quietly next to her mother. The starlight turned her golden hair to silver. Sensing his gaze she turned her head toward him, but he looked away quickly, unwilling to let her know how aware he was of her, now and always.

Hidden deep in the grasses behind them lay sixteen large row-boats. These boats had been fashioned by the steward, Rhufon, and his family. It had been Rhufon's eldest son, Tybion, who had led them through the maze of underground passages that ran all the way from Cadair Idris to the shores of Llyn Mwyngil. Tybion waited alone now at the cave entrance less than half a league away to guide them all back later tonight. All of them who were still alive, at any rate.

If Arthur's plans went as expected, Tybion would guide more than one hundred people back to Cadair Idris. The journey back would take some time, for the people that would be with them were ill and tired and some of them were near death. He hoped that the flasks of Penduran's Rose would be enough to help them reach the safety of Cadair Idris, enough to help them begin to heal.

For he was done with waiting. Tonight was the night when he took the captive Y Dawnus on Afalon back from Havgan's clutches. Tonight was the night when they would be freed, their collars would be removed, and they would be led back to the safe haven of Cadair Idris.

For Arthur had come for them at last.

A slight breeze ruffled his hair. From somewhere nearby a night owl called. The stars shone coldly, bathing them in silvery light. And the torchlight on Afalon beckoned.

It was time.

"Rhiannon, Talorcan," Arthur whispered.

Talorcan rose cautiously, and Regan stood, also. Queen Elen's Dewin lifted her face to her Coranian lover and kissed his lips in farewell.

Talorcan clasped her hands in his. "Death cannot touch us," he murmured, speaking Queen Hildelinda of Dere's last words to her husband. "I am yours forever." He turned away before she could reply.

Rhiannon rose and joined Talorcan. Gwydion did not speak.

"We will be watching," Arthur said, rising also. "May the Shining Ones be with you."

"And with you," Rhiannon said. She glanced down at Gwydion, but he turned away. "With all of you."

But Rhiannon and Talorcan hadn't gone but a few steps toward the dock before Gwydion silently rose and took Rhiannon's arm, spinning her around to face him. "You will come back to me," he rasped. "You will come back to me or—"

Rhiannon's lips twitched. "Or you'll kill me?"

"Or worse," he said grimly. Without another word he took her into his arms and kissed her long and deeply, as though he had all the time in the world. At last, he let her go and sank down again in the grass. Rhiannon smiled down at him, and then she and Talorcan walked away.

Gwydion lay silently next to Arthur as the two moved away down the shore. At last Gwydion murmured a line from an old Kymric song. "I have loved you. Is there any help for me?"

Arthur remained silent. If he could have reassured his uncle, he would have. But reassurances would be hollow, and they both knew it. He would not lie. Rhiannon and Talorcan might very well die tonight. They might all very well die tonight.

RHIANNON AND TALORCAN neared the dock.

"Wait here," Talorcan said. "I want to deal with this one alone."

Rhiannon hesitated momentarily, but then gestured him to go ahead, clearly puzzled, but willing to let him do this himself.

Talorcan went forward, hailing the lone soldier standing on the dock. "Warrior," Talorcan called. "I look for passage."

"Passage you shall not have," the Coranian warrior replied, "unless you have cause." The silver mesh of the soldier's byrnie reached to midthigh. He carried a spear and a round shield marked with the boar of the Coranian Warleader. His blond hair spilled out from under the helmet and hung lankly around his thin shoulders. Talorcan doubted that the guard was any older than eighteen years.

"What business do you have there?" the young guard demanded, false bravado in his voice.

"You truly do not know?" Talorcan asked softly.

At his tone the guard took a closer look at Talorcan. Suddenly, he stiffened.

"I see you recognize me, boy," Talorcan said, still speaking quietly.

"General Talorcan!" The young guard backed slowly away. "You who betrayed us."

"I never betrayed you," Talorcan murmured. "Never." Quick as lightening he pulled his dagger and threw it so swiftly that the blade was a mere blur. It plunged into the guard's neck and the dying man fell onto the dock. Talorcan pulled out the dagger and kicked the now-dead body off the dock and into the water.

"A little severe, don't you think?" Rhiannon asked as she came up to join him.

Talorcan shrugged. "One less for Arthur to deal with."

"Ah." Rhiannon went to the lone boat tied up at the dock and climbed in, gesturing for Talorcan to join her. He grabbed the oars as she pushed the boat away from the dock.

They both sat quietly in the boat, each with their own thoughts, as Talorcan rowed steadily toward the island. The soft splash of the oars cutting through the silent, dark water was the only sound. The distant torchlight from the island grew brighter. Torches lined the dock. The shadowy hulk of buildings beyond the dock was illuminated by the light of a large bonfire in the center of the compound. Distant shadows moved near the dock, indicating that the guards were alert.

Talorcan slowed the boat as they neared the isle, looking at Rhiannon with what seemed perhaps to be pity in his green eyes.

"Are you ready?" he asked.

She nodded. "I'm ready."

"Then there is just one more thing." He whipped the enaid-dal from the inside pocket of his cloak. Before she could even move he had it around her throat.

He almost hesitated when he heard her moan of despair as her psychic powers were snuffed out, as a candle is blown out by the wind. But he was a soldier. He had done many things he hadn't liked before. Things for Havgan that he hadn't wanted to do.

This would be just one more thing.

Talorcan shouted. "Hoy, there, soldiers. You have visitors!"

Ten guards, dressed in various states of slovenliness, materialized on the dock. Two held the boat while Talorcan stood, grabbing Rhiannon's arm. He hauled her from the boat, flinging her out onto the dock. Two soldiers, not quite sure what was happening, nonetheless reached out and grabbed her arms, hauling her to her feet and holding her securely.

A large, fat warrior stepped forward. Stubble covered the lower half of his face and his blue eyes were bloodshot. "My name is Sigald, and I am the commander here. What is all this?" he demanded of Talorcan.

"This," Talorcan gestured to Rhiannon, "is my prisoner."

Rhiannon, her green eyes blazing, her neck already beginning to blister from the enaid-dal, spat at Talorcan. "You pig!" she cried.

"My companion does not care much for me," Talorcan said with a twisted grin. "She thought she knew me. But she did not. Tell me, gentlemen, do you?"

Sigald looked closely at Talorcan, his blue eyes narrowed. "You will tell me right now or I will—" he broke off, staring at Talorcan. "General!"

"Yes, General Talorcan," he said dryly. "Traitor to Havgan. Or so the story goes."

"You mean—" Sigald asked, comprehension dawning on his face.

"Yes, I mean just that," Talorcan said. "I mean that this is a little something that Havgan and I cooked up between us. The only way to get them."

"The Kymric witches, you fooled them!"

"I did. And many years I worked at it, too. A plan long in the making. But come to fruition at last." He gestured to Rhiannon, who was now pale and silent. "I bring you the first of many. Next to come will be Arthur himself. And saving the best for last—the Dreamer. Before tomorrow is out Havgan will behold the Dreamer in the dungeons of Eiodel."

"Then by all means, General Talorcan," Sigald said, "welcome to our island. It isn't much, but we call it hell. For the Y Dawnus, at any rate."

He turned, gesturing for Talorcan to follow him. Rhiannon followed, dragged forward by her two guards. As they walked off the dock and onto the shore of Afalon, Talorcan sensed something that made his heart quake. As his feet touched the isle he felt something, something powerful and angry; something that was done waiting. Something, he did not know exactly what, that almost frightened him with its intensity.

He could not, he would not, let these men know what he felt. He had struggled far too long against this thing that was inside him to let it betray him now.

A large, roughly timbered hall loomed on their left as they entered the open gate of the compound. To his right three whipping posts were set up. The posts were covered with blood. Two black-robed wyrce-jaga were removing a man from one of the posts.

"Dead?" the first one asked.

"Not yet," the second one said. "We'll give him a few days to heal up and then be at him again."

"Well, he'll never call us names again after this," the first one said with a grin.

"Don't count on it. This one's been trouble ever since he got here. He was the very first of the witches to be collared, and yet he's still alive."

Talorcan guessed that this must be Cian, one-time Bard to King Rhoram. Cian, along with his testing device, had been captured by Rhoram's Druid, Ellywen, and taken to Eiodel. He had been the last Kymri to see Anieron Master Bard alive. And he had been among the first to be brought to Afalon.

Talorcan glanced over at Rhiannon, for he knew that Cian was an old friend of hers. She took in Cian's scarred body, his bloody back, his skeletal frame, and her eyes hardened to emerald. But Talorcan saw the flicker of fear cross her face.

Cian opened his eyes. His gaze traveled slowly over them until he saw Rhiannon. They looked at each other steadily. At the last Cian was the one to turn away, unable to bear the sight of Rhiannon with a collar around her neck.

A long, low hut in the center of the compound drew his eye away from the half-dead Bard. The stench from the hut was almost unbelievable. Through the barred windows he saw pale, skeletal limbs and lusterless eyes gazing out. Each of the people penned there wore a collar of dull, gray lead. Hopelessness and despair emanated from the hut. Some of the people were children, their dull eyes huge in their ashen faces.

To the right was another hut, this one apparently for housing wyrce-jaga, for they spilled from the hut as he came near. They bowed briefly as the recognized him, but did not speak. Their eyes gleamed as they saw Rhiannon.

A pack of dogs came rushing up, barking and growling at the sight of Rhiannon. Sigald roared for the dogs to heel and they did, abruptly. Sigald, his face red with temper, cuffed the lead dog. The animal yelped but did not give ground. He growled and, for a moment, Talorcan wondered if the dog might not leap for Sigald's throat. But, for now, at least, the dog backed away slowly, acknowledging Sigald as his master.

A kennel for the dogs, a well, and the guard's quarters completed the compound. In the center, just outside the wyrce-jaga's quarters, a large bonfire roared.

"Welcome to Afalon," Sigald grinned. "Who exactly is your prisoner?"

"Gentlemen," Talorcan said to the guards and to the wyrce-jaga. "I give you Rhiannon ur Heyvedd. The woman who journeyed to Corania and, under false pretences, entered our Warleader's house. She ate his bread, she slept beneath his roof, and then she betrayed him."

"Betrayed him!" Rhiannon exclaimed with contempt. "How could I betray an enemy?"

"He thought you a loyal servant," Talorcan replied. "But you were little better than a snake in the grass, waiting for your chance to harm him. I can only marvel that you never killed him. For you surely would have if you could have."

"You are right there, traitor," she spat. "If I could have I would have. And if I had known what you had in mind, I would have killed you."

"But you did not," Talorcan said smoothly. "And so you and the others, you welcomed me into your halls. As we had done to you."

One of the wyrce-jaga stepped forward then, his dark eyes fastened on Rhiannon. "I know who you are, witch. Lord Sledda wanted you brought before him. He wanted that more than anything."

"Too bad he is dead," Rhiannon sneered. "Dead at the hands of High King Arthur, the one whom I serve."

The wyrce-jaga slapped her across the face so hard that she spun and fell to the ground. Instantly she was on her feet, spinning back to face him, her face defiant, blood trickling from her lip.

"Now, now, wyrce-jaga," Talorcan chided. "Havgan will be displeased if you do too much damage before he has his chance."

The wyrce-jaga paled and stepped back.

"A pity," Sigald said. "We could use her here. We take the witch-women, but it isn't the same. They have no spirit. The new ones are good for a while, but then the collars take their energy—they don't even scream after the first few times."

"It is indeed a pity," Talorcan went on. "This one is particularly interesting. I used to watch her do the Dance to Freya in Corania and I still dream about it."

At that Sigald tore his gaze from Rhiannon and looked at Talorcan, a light in his bloodshot eyes. "Freya's Dance?"

"Oh, yes," Talorcan said absently.

"Really?"

"Like you've never seen."

"That so?" another guard asked.

"Turn your bones to water."

Sigald turned back to look Rhiannon up and down. "Take her cloak off," he ordered. Rhiannon's two guards tore her cloak from her. She was wearing a cream-colored shift under a gown of dark green.

"Take the gown off," Sigald ordered.

"I can do it myself," Rhiannon said, between gritted teeth.

At Sigald's gesture the two guards stepped back. Rhiannon took off her outer gown and threw it on the ground. Her shift reached to mid-calf and she bent down to take off her shoes. She straightened up and looked at Sigald, Talorcan, all of the men gathered there with contempt in her eyes.

"Shall I dance for you?" she asked, her tone cold and even. "Is that what you want?"

Sigald glanced at Talorcan. Talorcan shrugged.

"We'll have to take the collar off," Sigald ventured.

"What could she do with all of us here?" Talorcan asked.

Sigald grinned. "Boys," he said to his men, "looks like we'll have a little fun tonight."

They gathered in a semi-circle around the bonfire, the soldiers and the wyrce-jaga. Talorcan and Sigald had places of honor in the front. At Sigald's nod, one of the guards took Rhiannon's collar off. As he did so she sighed and closed her eyes briefly, bowing her head for a moment. At last she raised her head and came to stand between the men and the fire.

The fire played greedily over her shift, over her skin, over her pale and set face, outlining the contours of her lovely body for all the men to see. The firelight shifted, illuminating the lust-filled faces of the men gathered there.

The captive Y Dawnus who had been gazing out from their filthy hut at the scene turned away as the drumbeat began, knowing where this would lead, unwilling to look at the humiliation of one of their own.

Rhiannon raised her hands above her head, her face lifted to the starry sky. Behind her the fire blazed up, roaring for a moment as though in anger. A wind whipped through the compound, stirring up the hard-packed sand, making the flames dance this way and that. The men, women, and children in the hut stirred at that, sensing, perhaps, something, even though the collars had deadened their psychic senses. Some of them raised their heads and looked at each other, a slight, fragile hope stealing into their dull and lifeless eyes. Beneath their feet the earth trembled slightly, shifting for a moment like the movements of a restless sleeper on the edge of waking.

Rhiannon stood quite still for a moment, firelight and starlight playing around her body. And then she began to dance. She twisted her body slowly, her arms spread wide, swaying toward the men as though she longed for them. Slowly, to the beat of the drum, she drew back, then again leaned forward, her arms extended. The gaze of every last man there was fastened hungrily on her.

Which was why, when the fog settled thickly around the island, cutting off their view of the lake, they didn't even notice.

Sixteen boats made their way silently across the fog-enshrouded lake. Each boat was piloted by one of Arthur's companions, and they followed each other closely. Arthur, piloting the lead boat, Wind-Spoke to Gwydion, whose boat was just behind.

Looks like it's going according to plan.

Yes, Gwydion replied sourly. *If your plan is to have a pack of slavering, disgusting, Coranian dogs staring at Rhiannon with lust and bestiality in their piglike eyes.*

It is.

Stupid plan.

Arthur almost smiled.

But Gwydion went on. *You should have brought warriors with you.*

I have told you more than once, Arthur said with a hint of impatience in his Mind-Voice, *why I did not. Y Dawnus take care of their own.*

Foolish, Gwydion snorted.

Wind-Ride with me, uncle, Arthur said suddenly, even as the boats were nearing the dock. *I have a feeling that I don't like.*

Without another word Gwydion's and Arthur's awareness flew ahead, focusing on the scene by the bonfire. What they saw there made the body Gwydion left in the boat cry out in anguish.

Oh, Annwyn, Lord of Chaos, Arthur breathed. Oh, Aertan, Weaver of Fate. Spare them. Spare Rhiannon, and by doing so spare Gwydion. Spare these two who have done so much for me.

Gwydion, alerted by Arthur's tone, Wind-Rode swiftly to see Rhiannon dancing by the bonfire. He was in time to see the captain lurch forward and grab Rhiannon, throwing her to the ground and pulling up her shift. He was in time to see Talorcan leap to his feet and throw himself at the captain and see the two men rolling on the ground, each trying to get the upper hand. He was in time to see a wyrce-jaga leap forward toward the two men with murder in his eyes and a dagger in his hand.

But he was not in time to stop it when the knife flew toward Talorcan's unprotected back. Nor was he there to stop it when Rhiannon threw herself in front of Talorcan. He was not there to stop the knife from sinking into her chest, just below her heart. He was not there to stop the blood from spurting forth beneath her fingers as she laid her hand against the wound and sank to the ground.

The best he was able to do was the call the dogs from their

kennel. But it was, of course, far too late.

Arthur, seeing what was happening through horrified psychic eyes called for his companions to hurry. They brought their boats to shore and leapt from them onto the sand, running for the compound. Arthur was in the lead but Gwydion was right behind him.

As he ran Arthur gathered to him the powers of his Bards—Dudod, Elidyr, and Cynfar—and flung his call to the north, where he knew the ravens were waiting, for he had sensed them earlier that day. And they came, instantly. In an unexpected boon, Ardeyrdd himself led the flock. The huge eagle cried out fiercely as it led the ravens straight into the compound. The birds cried out in reply, then dove, covering the guards and the wyrce-jaga, beginning their dreadful feeding.

The Coranians screamed and tried to beat off the birds, but there were far too many. The dogs, called by Gwydion, were already a part of the fray. They growled and barked, going for the throats of the guards and wyrce-jaga, hamstringing them from behind, fighting in tandem with the ravens to kill the Coranians.

The only two bodies by the bonfire not covered with birds or bloodied by dogs were Talorcan's and Rhiannon's. Talorcan held Rhiannon in his arms, blood flowing through the hand that he pressed on her wound, his face tight and pale.

Arthur barked a silent order to the animals and they backed away from the Coranian bodies. He reached out for the power of the Druids. And the power was there. He took in the flames, the fire from Aergol, Menw, Sinend and Aldur. With terrible concentration he focused the heat on the Coranians. He lifted his hands to the sky and called out. "Annwyn! Aertan! Aid me!"

The bodies burst into blue and orange flames. Some of the men that were still alive screamed, and tried to roll on the ground to put the fire out. But the blue-tinged Druid's Fire burned on and on.

Beside him Gwydion and Cariadas added their Dreamer's powers and they, too, called on the flames, burning the wyrce-jaga and remaining guards to nothing more than smoldering bones and ash.

When the screams ended Arthur lowered his hands. Cariadas and Gwydion raced forward to where Rhiannon lay. Gwydion pushed Talorcan aside and took Rhiannon in his arms. Arthur walked up more slowly, and he had to turn his gaze away from the look in his uncle's eyes as he gazed down at Rhiannon's still, white face.

Elstar knelt on the ground next to Rhiannon. She laid her hands on Rhiannon's wound and closed her eyes. They were all silent as they waited for Elstar's Life-Reading. Cariadas stood behind her father, resting her hands on his shoulders, never taking her eyes from Rhiannon. Talorcan turned away with tears streaming down his thin face, blundering almost blindly into Regan's waiting arms.

At Arthur's nod, the rest of them turned away and went to the hut where the Y Dawnus were kept. One by one they helped the people to stand and exit their prison. Some crawled out on their own, hope sitting oddly on their thin, pinched faces.

At last, just when Arthur could hardly bear it any longer, Elstar looked up. "She is alive. And will remain so if we can get her back to Cadair Idris quickly." She reached for her pack and took out some dried herbs, gesturing for Cariadas to fetch some water.

Gwydion's silvery eyes filled with tears. At that moment Rhiannon opened her eyes and looked up at him.

"Sorry," she whispered.

"Don't be ridiculous," Gwydion said harshly.

Rhiannon tried to smile, but it faded quickly. "Sweet-talker."

Gwydion tried to smile, too, but the pain and fear in his eyes was too great. "You are going to be fine. I won't let you leave me. Ever."

"And I don't want to go."

Elstar, who had been hurriedly binding the wound with the blackberry and chamomile leaves she had taken from her pack, looked over at Gwydion. "No more talking," she said sternly. "She needs to save her strength."

Gwydion nodded, but did not move.

"Arthur," Elstar said crisply, "your people need you."

Arthur turned and saw his captive Y Dawnus slowly making

their way from the hut and out into the open air. He drew Caladfwlch from its scabbard. The blade rang as he did so with a clear, pure note. As he walked by the now-silent dogs the lead dog rose and followed him across the compound, his dark eyes bright.

The first one Arthur saw was Cian, his skeletal frame supported by Gwen and Menw. Cian's green eyes glinted at Arthur as he raised his head with a mighty effort.

"You came," the Bard whispered.

"I did," Arthur replied. "I came as soon as I could."

"Soon enough for them," Cian said, inclining his head a fraction to the rest of the Y Dawnus gathered behind him. "Not for me, I think."

"I disagree," Arthur said, laying his sword against the man's thin neck. "I think there is still plenty of time for you." With one swift movement the blade sheared through the enaid-dal and the necklace fell from Cian's neck onto the ground. Cian looked down at it, shuddering. He raised his head to the sky.

"I can feel it," Cian said, wonder in his voice. "Taran has returned to me. His gift lives in me again."

"Drink, my friend, of Penduran's Rose," Arthur said, gesturing for Gwen to hand him her flask. "Drink, and live again."

Cian drank a mouthful of the concoction and smiled. "Yes," he said his voice stronger. "Yes."

One by one Caladfwlch cut off the hateful necklaces. One by one the sick and weary Y Dawnus drank Penduran's Rose. One by one they were helped up and led to the boats.

There were a few that Arthur recognized. Most notably, the five Y Dawnus that he had briefly met when on the quest for the Treasures—the five who had been prisoners in Gwynedd, who had recognized him and his companions but who had given nothing away.

The two Bards, Elivri and Maredudd, as well as three Dewin, Morwen,Trephin, and the young girl whose name he did not know all recognized him.

"What is your name?" Arthur asked, as he sheared the collar off her neck.

"Morgan Tud," she whispered.

"Morgan Tud, you are free," he said.

Morewen and Elivri had smiled weakly as he had sheared off their collars. Trephin had sighed in relief and briefly closed his eyes as he sipped Penduran's Rose. And Maredudd still had the presence of mind to greet his old friend, Dudod.

"Took you long enough," Maredudd snorted as he drank.

Dudod's eyes were full of pity that he knew better than to give voice to. "You are right, my friend," he said quietly. "I took my own sweet time, didn't I?"

"Probably warming some widow's bed," croaked Trephin.

"Very likely," Morwen said dryly. "Because some things never change."

Elivri, a huge bruise on her cheekbone, rasped, "I think I shall write a song about it."

Dudod smiled. "Make it a good one, then," he said softly.

"All my songs are good ones."

At last, when all was ready, Gwydion picked up Rhiannon and cradled her close to his heart. Assisted by Elstar he settled her into his boat, along with ten other Y Dawnus. At Arthur's signal the boats began their return journey across the lake.

At last the only boat left was Arthur's. Seven Y Dawnus, including Cian and Morgan Tud, sat in the boat, waiting quietly for him.

Arthur held out his arm and Arderydd flew to him, coming to rest on his forearm. The bird's talons sank into Arthur's skin, but the High King did not flinch. Why should he? Arderydd had already marked him more than once. The eagle had given Arthur the scar on his face. And more. Much, much more.

Tell them, old friend, he murmured to the silent eagle. *Tell them that I did what they asked me to do. Tell the Wild Hunt that soon I shall call them to me, to help rid the land of all Coranians.*

The eagle fixed him with its silvery eyes then launched itself into the air. The bird circled above Arthur once, twice, three times, then, with a loud, triumphant cry, flew north.

The lead dog came up to Arthur and sat on his haunches, his brown eyes steady and waiting, but too proud to plead.

But Arthur knew. He nodded at the animal. The dog leapt

up and barked joyfully. He ran straight into the lake and began to swim, the other dogs following.

Arthur smiled. It looked like he might have found a new friend.

To the east the sky began to pale, heralding the return of the sun. By the time the day dawned, Arthur wanted Havgan to see his signal and know that the High King had taken the Y Dawnus back. He wanted Havgan to know that yet another piece of Kymru had fallen through his clutches.

Soon, Havgan would be receiving the messengers sent to him after the battles for the four kingdoms. Soon the four men Arthur had chosen would come to Havgan at Eiodel and tell him of the Coranian defeats. Although Afalon had been the last to be freed, Havgan would learn of this first. It would be another three or four days before Ecgfrith of Gwynedd and Oswy of Rheged reached Eiodel. And it would be another four or five days before Cuthwine arrived from Ederynion. And it would take a few days more for Penda to arrive from Prydyn.

These four men would each bear Havgan the news that the four kingdoms were no longer his. And they would give Havgan Arthur's message—to leave Kymru or die.

But it would be this first message that would be most important. Arthur wanted Havgan to know as soon as possible about Afalon.

Which was why, before he left the island, the entire Coranian compound was burning with Druid's Fire, cleansing Afalon of the Coranian taint. Thick, black smoke billowed up into the air, sending a message to Havgan.

The Y Dawnus were free.

Leave or die.

Part 4

The Final Battle

It is fitting to rise up against them,
We expect no hesitant uprising;
The edges of swords,
The points of spears,
It is right to ply them gladly.

High King Idris
Circa 128

Chapter Twenty

Ystrad Marchell, Kingdom of Rheged,
Eiodel & Cadair Idris, Gwytheryn
Gwernan Mis, 500

Gwyntdydd, Disglair Wythnos—morning

Prince Aesc of Corania stood at the prow of his ship, letting the clean wind wash over him. The huge, carved figurehead, fashioned like the head of a snarling boar with blood red, ruby eyes, jutted forward toward the nearing shore as though hungry and anxious to feed. Misty green land loomed just ahead, rising from the sea like a beautiful woman rising at dawn. Behind him over one hundred ships followed, their sails of red and gold filling out in the freshening breeze.

Aesc had not thought that Kymru would be so beautiful.

Now he understood why his ancestors had always longed to have it for their own. And he understood a little better why Havgan wanted it so. And understood better still why his nephew by marriage refused to admit he couldn't hold this land.

Beautiful though this land was, it was important to Havgan in a way Aesc still did not fully understand. But he had not needed to understand it to support it. He had long supported Havgan's bid for power against the wishes of his sister-in-law. He had seen strength in the fisherman's son long ago. Strength that Aesc knew his Empire needed, strength he knew his brother did not have, and never would. Havgan, through his marriage to Aelfwyn, would one day be Emperor of Corania. Because of that he would soon need to leave Kymru and return to the Empire. Aesc was eager to subdue this land, allowing Havgan to do just that.

It was because of this that he had complied with Havgan's request, delivered just one month ago by the old sailor who had escaped Kymru with the news. It seemed that there was a young Kymric man, a man known as Arthur ap Uthyr, who had challenged Havgan. This man was able to harness the power of the Kymric witches in such a way that communication between Kymru and the Empire had effectively been cut off. Havgan had known that a final battle was coming and needed reinforcements.

Aesc had gathered a force as quickly as he could. His need for haste resulted in a force of only eight thousand. Even that had been a struggle to get, for there were many Coranian lords who saw no profit in the subjugation of Kymru. He wondered if there would ever be enough warriors to subdue this proud land. Something in the inviting but mysterious land he saw before him made him decide there would not.

He had originally thought that his sister-in-law would have attempted to prevent him from gathering these men to aid Havgan. But Athelflead had not. She was not, Aesc thought, sorry to see him go. There had never been any love lost between them. The Empress had charged Aesc to determine that her daughter, Aelfwyn, was well. And then she had turned her back on the venture. No doubt she hoped that neither Aesc nor Havgan would return.

His brother had merely given his blessing in the vague, preoccupied way he had. Athelred always did that. The Emperor was far more comfortable on his knees, petitioning Lytir for various things than ruling the Empire. Aesc sometimes wondered if Lytir ever wearied of Athelred's devotion.

In fact, the only one who had tried to prevent Aesc from coming was his sister, Aesthryth. She had argued long and hard with him, saying that he should let the Kymri be. He thought that, perhaps, she wanted Havgan to fail. Which was why, Aesc thought, she had urged Aelfwyn to join Havgan in Kymru. Aesc had always sensed that she was afraid of Havgan, but he had never known why. There were, to tell the truth, things about his sister that he had never understood. Things, indeed, that he had tried hard not to understand. For she had a way of knowing about things that were to happen, a way of sensing things that others did not. Indeed, he would have been afraid of her if he didn't love her so much.

"Almost there, great lord."

Jarred from his reverie, Aesc turned to look at his companion. The old sailor's scanty, gray hair tossed wildly in the wind. His almost toothless mouth was grinning and his blue eyes sparkled in his seamed, weathered face.

"Yes, almost there, Torgar," Aesc said absently. "After we land it should take us ten days to reach Havgan in Eiodel. From what I hear of the witches, they will know we are here much sooner than that."

"And think, perhaps, to attack us."

"I think not. We are too big a host for them to risk a pitched battle before they are ready. I think we will make it to Eiodel alive and intact."

After that, they would see.

Addiendydd, Lleihau Wythnos—afternoon

SIGERRIC SLOWLY CLIMBED the stone steps up to the battlements of Eiodel. Overhead the sun shone, but it seemed to do little to warm him. A slight breeze played in the air, tugging at his cloak and ruffling his light brown hair, playing over his too-thin face as though trying to get his attention. But his attention was focused on other things, focused on the news that the last few weeks had brought.

Kymru was slipping through Havgan's hands. As Sigerric had always known it would. As, indeed, it always had. Only now even Havgan could not deny that.

Two weeks ago black smoke had stained the sky over Afalon. When Havgan and Sigerric had arrived to investigate, they had found the entire island deserted. The camp where the Y Dawnus had been held and tortured was destroyed. The huts, the whipping post, all of it had been cleansed with fire. The bones and ashes of the Coranian guards had littered the compound. Havgan had not said a word as they rode back to Eiodel. And Sigerric had known better than to speak the thought they were both having.

Arthur had taken back the Y Dawnus when he was ready. Just

as he always said he would.

Three days later, Ecgfrith, Byshop of Gwynedd, had rode into Eiodel, staggered from his horse, and fallen at Havgan's feet, exhausted. He had gasped out his message—Gwynedd had fallen from Coranian control. Queen Morrigan herself had killed General Catha. And her captain, Cai, had killed Wulfhere, the Master-wyrce-jaga, in battle. Indeed, while some Coranian warriors had been spared and were now returning to Eiodel, no wyrce-jagas had been left alive.

It had taken a few moments for Ecgfrith to gather what courage he had left and give Havgan the other message, the message given him by Morrigan, passed on from her brother, Arthur ap Uthyr himself.

Leave or die.

To everyone's surprise, Havgan had not flown into a rage at this. He had simply told his servants to take care of Ecgfrith. Then he had left the hall, grabbed a spear from one of his soldiers and gone straight to Cadair Idris. He had said nothing, merely looked up at the closed Doors. Then he had plunged the spear into the ground at the foot of the stairs and stalked away.

He had said one thing and one thing only to Sigerric on the walk back. He had said, "I will not leave."

As though, Sigerric had thought, he needed Havgan to tell him that. He had always known that Havgan would never, never leave Kymru—alive.

Two days later Oswy, the Byshop of Rheged, had come to Eiodel, carrying his message. Rheged had fallen. Queen Enid had killed Morcant Wheldig. The Dewin, Bledri, had been exiled, put in a small boat and cast adrift in the sea. Saebald, the Master-wyrce-jaga, had been killed in battle by Teleri, King Owein's lieutenant. All the wyrce-jaga had been killed.

And Havgan was to leave or die.

Again, Havgan had taken a spear and marched to Cadair Idris. Again, he plunged the spear into the ground next to the first. Then he had walked away.

Five days after that Cuthwine, Byshop of Ederynion, had

come to Eiodel with the news that Ederynion was once again in Kymric hands.

And that Havgan was to leave or die.

And now a third spear stood before the steps of Cadair Idris.

Sigerric reached the top of the battlements. Havgan stood looking out at Cadair Idris. He did not turn around when Sigerric joined him at the wall. Sun flashed off of Havgan's golden cloak and ruby rings. But his face was bleak, his amber hawk eyes were hooded as he gazed at the mountain.

"I believe the messenger from Prydyn will be here today," Sigerric said. "Whoever was sent from Arberth would have the longest way to come."

"I suppose Penda is dead."

"Yes," Sigerric replied sadly past the lump in his throat. "I suppose he is."

Havgan was silent, staring out at Cadair Idris.

Sigerric gestured to the Coranian warriors camped outside of Eiodel. "They have been coming here for the last two weeks. I do not think we will get more."

"I don't suppose we will."

"I calculate we will likely get twelve thousand, all told," Sigerric went on.

"Very likely," Havgan replied.

"The count of the Kymri at Llyn Mwyngil is twelve thousand. In terms of numbers of men, we appear to be evenly matched."

"Yes."

"But you know as well as I that Arthur has the Y Dawnus with him. We have heard of what they did under Arthur's direction. I do not know if we can withstand that."

But Havgan did not answer.

Sigerric tried again. "And we have seen no wyrce-jagas come. I believe that they are all dead. Except for the few still left at the bardic college, Neuadd Gorsedd. But they seem to be sparing the preosts. Most of them are returning to Eadwig at Y Ty Dewin."

"A boon," Havgan said dryly, then lapsed back into brooding silence.

Sigerric quieted. Cadair Idris gleamed, golden and silver beneath the sun. Wildflowers dotted the plain—bright blue forget-me-nots and yellow corydalis waved in the light breeze. Primroses and golden globeflowers nodded. White alyssum and red rockrose twined around the steps of Cadir Idris.

"Havgan—" Sigerric began.

"You would truly dare?" Havgan asked quietly. "I am surprised. Even coming from you."

"Who else should it come from but me?" Sigerric asked, his throat tight.

"Arianrod. It comes from her."

"Yes. For she loves you as I do. Please—"

But Sigerric did not finish his sentence for a distant shout made him look to the northwest. Havgan, too, turned and saw the rider approaching.

"The messenger from Prydyn," Havgan said, narrowing his eyes against the sun.

"Yes. It would seem so. I will tell the servants to give the poor man something to drink. Come with me and hear—" Sigerric gasped, grasping Havgan's arm. "I think, I think it's—"

"I do, too," Havgan said slowly, not taking his eyes off of the rider.

"Arthur spared him," Sigerric said, almost in awe. "Come on!" Sigerric leapt for the stairs, not even looking to see if Havgan was behind him. He rushed down the steps and into the courtyard, arriving just as the rider entered the fortress. He pushed through the warriors gathered there and ran to the rider, catching the man even as he fell from his horse.

"Penda," Sigerric rasped. "Penda, you're alive."

Penda's dark blond hair was sweat-soaked and his brown eyes were dull with weariness. But he smiled weakly up at Sigerric. "After a fashion," he croaked.

Sigerric called for ale. A brimming cup was thrust in his hands and he put the cup to Penda's lips.

"Havgan?" Penda asked after taking a swallow.

"Right behind me," Sigerric assured him. He looked over

and saw that Havgan had descended much more slowly, and was just now entering the bustling courtyard. Havgan walked with a measured pace to Penda and slowly knelt down beside his blood-brother.

"Penda," Havgan said quietly. "You are alive."

"I am," Penda said.

"Why?"

"I was asked to give you a message. We have lost Prydyn. The Master-wyrce-jaga, Eamer, as well as Byshop Whitred, were executed by King Rhoram."

"I ask you again, Penda, why are you alive?" Havgan repeated his amber eyes glittering coldly.

"I told you. Rhoram spared me. To give you a message."

"Speak the rest of it, Penda," Sigerric said sadly, "although we know what it is. We have heard it from the other three kingdoms already."

Penda's brown eyes were wary as he looked up at Havgan. "I deliver this message to you because I gave my word. It is not a message I wish to give."

"Speak it," Havgan said coldly.

"Arthur ap Uthyr says that you must leave Kymru or die."

Havgan stood up, stepping back from his friends. Sigerric helped Penda up and the two men stood, facing Havgan.

"I ask you again, Penda, son of Peada, why are you alive?"

Shocked, Sigerric answered. "You heard him. He was spared to give you a message."

"Catha was not spared," Havgan said. "And Baldred was killed some time ago. Talorcan has deserted me for the enemy. What about you, Penda?"

Penda drew away from Sigerric and squared his shoulders, confronting Havgan. "Do you dare to question my loyalty to our oath? Do you dare?"

"Yes I dare," Havgan shouted. "Why are you alive? What did you do for them that they let you go?"

Penda lunged at Havgan and the two men went down. They rolled on the ground like dogs, snarling. Sigerric snapped a command

and several warriors pulled the two men apart. They held Penda securely but were afraid to do the same with Havgan. So it was Sigerric that held Havgan back.

"How dare you!" Penda panted, rage in every line of his exhausted face. "I gave up everything for you! My father, my son, my very soul! It was bad in Corania, with your obsession to persecute the Heiden and the Wiccan. Innocents fell beneath your bloody blade. But then I followed you to Kymru! Followed you here because I had promised. And here it was worse—infinitely worse. For these people had done nothing to you—nothing except to live in a land that you wanted. And I helped you. I helped you and their blood will always be on my hands! A thousand lifetimes would not be enough to change that."

"You should not be alive," Havgan said, fury making his amber eyes gleam like a deadly knife's edge. "If you truly were on my side, you would be dead."

"Your side!" Penda spat. "I am your blood brother. And it shames me to say that I am on your side. But say it I will. I took an oath. And this is an oath I shall not break. I will fight for you against the Kymri when they come for you. But that will be the last time I stand by your side. For in that battle one of us will die. In that battle, one way or the other, I will be released from you!"

Suddenly thunder pealed out, though there was no cloud in the sky.

Tears filled Sigerric's eyes at Penda's words, at the look on Havgan's white face.

"Kymru herself witnesses my vow," Penda said bitterly. "One way or the other, I will be free."

EVENING DESCENDED ON Eiodel, adding its own shadows to the dark fortress. Arianrod stood alone at the battlements, looking out onto the velvety dark plain. Cadair Idris rose from the shadows, gleaming silver under the light of the distant stars.

Arianrod's honey-blond hair was wrapped loosely in a linen band. She wore a simple, shapeless shift of creamy linen and a cloak of rich brown, for it was late spring and the nights were still cool. She laid a hand on her swollen belly, and felt the child leap beneath her fingers. She pressed a little harder in an attempt to be closer to her unborn son. She had a longing to hold him, a need to hold on to what she loved.

For everything, everything else was slipping away.

After the first few messages had come she had begged Havgan to leave Kymru. She had promised to leave Kymru with him, if he wished. She had promised to stay behind, if that was what he wanted. She had even promised that he could take their son and turn his back on her. Anything—anything he wanted. If only he would save his own life and leave Kymru far behind.

But he always refused. And she understood at last that no amount of pleading would change his mind. And she understood what he needed from her. He needed her to believe in him. He needed her to tell him that he would defeat his enemies. He needed her to look into his amber eyes, so like her own, and tell him that she would never turn her face from him.

And so she had. For she would do anything for him. Anything at all.

For the past week she had been Wind-Riding, scouring Kymru as far as she could to give him any information she could find. Her abilities would let her see only twenty leagues away. It should have enabled her to see up to thirty, but her pregnancy was affecting her range. Nonetheless, twenty had been enough, so far, to tell him what he needed to know.

She had seen that the Kymri were staging on the shores of Llyn Mwyngil. Soon, she knew, they would begin to march toward Eiodel. When Arthur was ready. She was surprised he hadn't struck before this. But she thought she knew what he was waiting for. For the festival of Calan Llachar was only two days away. And this year, as there had been on the day Arthur was born eighteen years ago, there would be a total eclipse of the sun.

That would be the day Arthur would strike. That would be the day Havgan died.

She closed her eyes as tears spilled from them, flowing down her pale, strained face. She was glad Havgan was not here to see that. He and the others were even now in the hall, sitting down to the evening meal. But she was not ready to join him. Not yet. Not while she was weeping.

To distract herself she began to Wind-Ride. She would not go to the west to once again see the campfires of the Kymri. She had seen that enough over the last week.

So she Rode to the east. She expected nothing, so she was even more stunned by what she saw.

HAVGAN SAT AT the table on the dais of the hall, resplendent in a golden tunic and ruby-red cloak. The fire pit in the middle of the hall shimmered golden and red, the smoke rising to the high rafters. The ruby eyes of the boar on Havgan's golden banner glittered in the shifting firelight.

He sipped his wine sparingly from a golden goblet, all the while eyeing the warriors gathered for the evening meal. It was important now, as never before, that they see him here confident and strong. So he nodded gravely to his captains, and kept his countenance calm and impassive. He spoke to Sigerric and even to Penda in even, measured tones.

As always, he ignored Aelfwyn.

His wife's green eyes sparkled maliciously as she surveyed her husband. She knew that his situation was desperate. She knew that he would never run from the coming battle. She knew—or hoped, at least—that he would die.

But in that, as in all else, he was determined to disappoint her, for there was still time. Still time for Torgar to have delivered his message to Prince Aesc. Still time for Aesc to have brought his men to Kymru.

He knew in his heart that this had indeed happened, even though he could tell no one. He had not even told Arianrod of his dreams for the last week. In those dreams a herd of boars touched the shores of Kymru, heading straight for Eiodel like a dark arrow. He knew that he should not be having these dreams. And so, as he had done his whole life, he turned away from the message that had been trying to reach him for so long. And he did not acknowledge the truth, truth that was as close to him as his shadow, as it had always been.

He had no dreams, he insisted to himself. Only hopes.

Suddenly he saw Arianrod hurrying toward him through the hall, her amber eyes alight, a smile on her beautiful face. She rushed through the crowd and leapt up the steps to the dais. Havgan rose as she neared him and she curtsied deeply.

"My lord Havgan," she said, in a clear, carrying tone, "I bring you great news."

"Rise, then, my heart, and say your news," Havgan said, coming around the table and putting out his hands to help her to her feet.

"Reinforcements," she said crisply, "have arrived."

"What have you seen?" Sigerric asked, rising to his feet as the warriors in the hall fell silent to hear her reply.

"Campfires, two days east of Eiodel. Over eight thousand Coranian warriors flying the banners of Prince Aesc. They come to aid you, my lord. To ensure your victory."

The tumult was incredible, as the warriors began to cheer. Havgan smiled, though he had known all along that this was true.

"Havgan," Sigerric said urgently, in a low tone. "If she saw them tonight you can be sure that Arthur saw them many days ago."

"No doubt," Havgan replied.

"Then why has he not changed his plans?" Penda asked. "For we know that he has only twelve thousand. With these reinforcements we are now twenty thousand. And still he thinks to pit his forces against ours? Why? What does he know that we do not?"

But before Havgan could answer a heart-rending wail sounded out, echoing through the halls of Eiodel. Men paled at the sound and their hands went automatically to their weapons. Aelfwyn, perhaps not even realizing it, reached out and gripped Sigerric's hand. The color drained completely out of Arianrod's face and she clutched Havgan's arm, her eyes wide with fear.

"What is it?" he asked her, for he could tell from her face that she knew.

"The Washer at the Ford," she whispered.

"What is this Washer at the Ford?" Sigerric asked.

"She is death. War. Blood and sorrow," Arianrod answered, struggling to keep her voice steady.

"You have seen her before," Havgan said.

"Yes. Once, before you came, I stood with Gwydion, Rhiannon, and Dinaswyn and we watched her show us of the sorrow to come. She comes to you now, my love, to tell you of what will be."

"Then let us go to her," Havgan said quietly. "Show us."

Havgan, Sigerric, Penda, and Aelwfyn followed Arianrod out of Eiodel and across the darkened plain. At Havgan's command his warriors stayed where they were, for he did not think he wanted them to see this sight.

They followed the sound toward Cadair Idris. Havgan and Arianrod were in the lead, and he slowed his steps to match hers, careful that she did not fall. Behind him Sigerric escorted Aelfwyn, who still had not let go of his hand. Penda brought up the rear.

As they neared the mountain they saw a red glow began to take shape in the middle of the plain. The glowing ruby-colored light seemed to be shining out of the ground itself. At Aelfwyn's gasp Havgan looked beyond the light and saw the Arthur himself, flanked by Gwydion and Rhiannon, who had emerged from Cadair Idris and were also making their way to the light. He noticed that Rhiannon walked slowly and carefully, and that Gwydion's arm hovered near hers as though ready to catch her if she stumbled.

The three came to stand on the fringes of the glow, while Havgan and his people stood on the opposite side. They eyed each other cautiously, but did not move.

A darker red shimmer began to coalesce inside the glow. They could make out the figure of a woman with long, blood-spattered golden hair. A raven perched on her thin shoulder, its eyes glowing ruby red. She lifted her grief-stricken face to the sky and wailed. The sound cut through their hearts like a knife. A river of blood gathered at her feet and she plunged her hands into the scarlet liquid. She lifted her cupped, blood-filled hands out of the river and to the sky, still crying out. Then she poured the blood over her head and let it flow down her face like tears.

"She is called Gwrach Y Rhibyn," Rhiannon said quietly.

"She tells us that death is coming for you," Gwydion said, his silver eyes glittering at Havgan.

"She tells us that death is coming for both Coranian and Kymri alike," Havgan replied. "And you know it, Dreamer." He turned to Rhiannon. "You are injured, Dewin."

"I was," Rhiannon admitted, "on Afalon."

"There were," Gwydion said, "none left alive afterwards to tell you." His keen, silvery eyes studied Havgan as he went on. "Talorcan helped us. Without him, we could not have done it."

Sigerric and Penda exchanged a glance. Although they did not speak it was clear in their faces that they were glad to hear news of their friend. But Havgan did not respond at all, merely looking over at Arthur, studying his enemy.

"Havgan, son of Hengist," Arthur said, "I have given you my message over and over. Why are you still here?"

"I will never leave Kymru. It is you, son of Uthyr, who will die. Not I."

"In two days it will be Calan Llachar. That is the day of my birth, eighteen years ago," Arthur said. "That is the day when we will battle for Kymru."

"Agreed," Havgan said. "You know, of course, that my reinforcements have arrived."

"I do," Arthur replied. "And it makes no difference."

"False bravado, Arthur ap Uthyr, will not save your life."

"Nor will turning away from the truth save yours," Arthur said. "I challenge you to single combat to take place at dawn on Calan Llachar before our armies."

"Done," Havgan replied.

The Washer at the Ford gave a final scream and then began to fade away, the red light getting weaker, leaving a crimson afterimage in the mind's eye. Arthur, Gwydion, and Rhiannon turned to go but Gwydion stopped and turned back to face Havgan.

"Havgan," Gwydion said, "don't do this."

"There speaks my false brother," Havgan said bitterly.

"He won't listen," Sigerric said sadly.

"I know," Gwydion said quietly. "He never has."

GWYDION SAT ON a rug before the hearth as the golden fire crackled and danced. The firelight in the Dreamer's chamber in Cadair Idris played off of the banner of a raven with opal eyes that hung on one of the walls. Gwydion sipped wine slowly from a golden goblet chased with opals as he thought about the events of the evening.

They had been in the garden room when they had heard the cry of the Washer at the Ford. They had not expected it and had certainly not expected to see Havgan.

And he had tried, once again, to get Havgan to leave, to find a way to spare the life of his deadly enemy. He honestly did not understand what continued to compel him to do that. But something did.

He rolled the goblet gently between his hands, thinking. The Kymric forces from the four kingdoms had been gathering at Llyn Mwyngil for the last few weeks. Tomorrow they would march halfway to Eiodel in preparation for the final battle two days from now.

And it would be final. If they lost the battle, Kymru was lost. There would be no second chance. When they had discovered over a week ago that Coranian reinforcements were on their way, his heart had contracted in fear. For though it was true that the Y Dawnus they had rescued from Avalon were doing well, and that most of them had fully recovered from their ordeal, the Kymri were still badly outnumbered.

But he had not said anything to Arthur, had not urged the High King to wait for another time.

For he knew as well as Arthur that Calan Llachar was the day. And there would be no turning back. That was the day when everything could be won—or lost. He did not know which it would be, for he had been given no dreams. The Shining Ones were conspicuously silent. Perhaps they, themselves, did not even know.

A hand appeared on his shoulder and a sweet voice whispered in his ear. "Come to bed, *cariad*."

He reached up and took her hand, bringing it to his lips and kissing her palm. He thought of how he had nearly lost her just a few short weeks ago. She was steadily recovering, recovering well enough to have some roaring arguments with him about her health. Tonight he would hold her in his arms and lay awake for as long as he could. He wanted to savor that. Because he did not know how much more time they would have. Eventually, he would fall asleep. It would not matter if he did, for he would not dream. The Shining Ones had no dreams to send.

But in this, he was wrong.

He was a black raven, with glittering, opal eyes. Cadair Idris stood to the north, its Doors glowing golden in the fading light as the moon slowly cast a shadow across the sun. To the south stood the dark fortress of Eiodel, gleaming like onyx in the uncertain light.

Behind him ranged a band of wolves with emerald eyes, brown hawks with tailfeathers of sapphire blue, fierce white horses with golden manes, and pearl-white swans with glittering wings. Beside him ranged silver dragons, brown bulls, and blue nightingales.

And before him was a massive eagle with a torque around its proud neck. The pearl, emerald, opal, sapphire, and onyx of the torque gleamed brightly beneath the darkening sky.

Facing the eagle a huge, golden boar waited with eyes of ruby red. And behind the boar ranged a mass of boars, the herd fanning out across the plain.

And the raven understood that there were too many, far too many boars. He understood that it was hopeless. And he wanted to turn away. But something made him look up. And what he saw hovering in the sky made him cry out.

For to the north, over Cadair Idris the Wild Hunt massed. The white dogs of Annwyn barked and capered, anxious for the hunt. The warriors of the hunt sat their horses, rock steady in the dimming sky.

The raven knew that if the Kymric hunt did not come to their aid then Kymru was lost. So he called out for the Hunt, but they did not move from their place in the sky. He called out again, pleading. But still they would not move.

And he called out a third time in pain, in anguish, knowing

that his land was lost.

And so he awoke with his own despairing cries sounding in his ears.

SHE POUNDED FRANTICALLY on the chamber door. Rhiannon opened the door so suddenly that she almost fell into the room. She was weeping and she moved into her father's waiting arms blindly. He held her, saying nothing. She could tell that he knew. And she wondered if he had guessed that this would happen now.

The room seemed to be filling rapidly. Raising her head from her da's shoulder she saw Arthur, Gwen, Elstar, and Elidyr rush into the room. She saw Sinend, Aergol, Cynfar, and Dudod. She saw Myrrdin and Neuad. And then she saw the one she sought. Llywelyn's gaze steadied her, and her tense shoulders relaxed a fraction.

"Uncle?" Arthur asked.

"Tonight I have had a dream," Gwydion said, his tone carrying to all in the chamber.

"Tell us," Arthur urged.

"That I cannot do," Gwydion said. "For it is no longer my place."

Gwydion reached up and unclasped the torque of gold and opals from his neck. Solemnly he put it around Cariadas' neck, and fastened the clasp. The torque was warm, resting easily, so naturally against her skin.

Gwydion stepped back and bowed to her. The rest of those in the chamber did likewise. She looked up into her da's silvery eyes and saw the love there, and the sorrow, too. Sorrow for what had come to her. Sorrow for the burden that was now hers to carry.

"I had a dream," Cariadas, the new Dreamer of Kymru, said.

Chapter Twenty-one

Llyn Mwyngil & Cadair Idris,
Gwytheryn
Gwernan Mis, 500

Meriwydd, Lleihau Wythnos—morning

Owein woke with Sanon cradled in his arms. The walls of their tent rippled slightly as a light breeze rose from Afalon and shifted over the lake of Llyn Mwyngil onto the shore where the Kymri camped.

Today they would march along Sarn Ermyn across Gwytheryn to mass before Cadair Idris and Eiodel. Tomorrow they would fight. Tomorrow would be the last throw of the dice in the game of freedom. Tomorrow, some of those he loved would undoubtedly die. If the Shining Ones were kind, his wife would not be one of these. For if they took her, his heart would die as it had once before when his mother, his father, and his brother were killed. Sanon's love had brought him back to life after that. If he lost her tomorrow he did not think anyone or anything would ever bring him back.

Sanon stirred in his arms as if sensing his thoughts. Her dark eyes opened and she looked up at him. She smiled slowly and lifted her face for his kiss.

He could have done more than kiss her—much more—if his brother had not chosen that very moment to want to speak to him.

"Owein?" Rhiwallon inquired from just outside the tent. "Are you awake?"

With a rueful look beneath the blanket he answered, "I certainly appear to be."

"I must speak with you."

Sanon laughed briefly as Owein's sigh. "There will be time for that later, Owein," she said.

"Promise?"

"Oh, my, yes."

He rose and dressed quickly in a tunic and trousers of red and white. He pulled on his boots and left the tent, securely closing the tent flap behind him.

He greeted his younger brother then held out his hands to the campfire to warm them. The mornings were chilly here by the lake.

His lieutenant, Teleri, and her new husband, Gwarae Golden-Hair, also stood next to the fire. Gwarae stood behind Teleri, his arms wrapped around her tiny waist, her head just resting on the curve of his shoulder.

"Trystan?" Owein asked.

"Seeing if Sabrina is awake," Teleri said.

"And, if not, seeing what he might be able to do to wake her," Gwarae added, with a grin.

"Esyllt won't like that," Owein warned.

Teleri snorted. "And who cares about that?"

"Her husband, I suppose," Owein replied, with a shrug.

"He cares about it less than he used to," Teleri said. "If you recall, March has declared that his divorce will be final on Calan Llachar."

Owein would have answered that, but Sanon chose to come out of the tent just then and Trystan and Sabrina also joined them at the campfire. Owein's captain and his Druid were holding hands, and their eyes were bright.

"Owein," Rhiwallon said in an urgent tone. "I must speak with you."

"Of course," Owein replied. "I am sorry, brother. What do you want to speak to me about?"

Rhiwallon blushed and cleared his throat. "Well, I—"

"He wants to fight alongside Elen of Ederynion tomorrow," Trystan said.

"To ensure that no harm comes to her," Sanon went on.

"Because he loves her," Teleri put in.

"And thinks about her every waking moment," Gwarae continued.

"And can't live without her," Sabrina finished.

"Really?" Owein asked Rhiwallon.

Rhiwallon blushed even redder, but stood his ground. "Thank you all," he said, between gritted teeth. "It's nice to have friends."

"Isn't it?" Sanon asked lightly.

Owein took pity on his brother. "Rhiwallon, if you wish to fight with Elen tomorrow, you may."

"Thank you," Rhiwallon said, gratefully, his color subsiding.

"Well, don't just stand there," Teleri scolded. "Go tell Elen."

Rhiwallon blushed again, and left, heading east to where the Ederynions were camped.

"I, too, must meet with someone before we march today," Owein said. "I had best be off."

"Who do you go to see?" Sabrina asked.

"Geriant of Prydyn."

Trystan's brows raised in surprise.

"Enid," Owein said.

"Ah," Trystan replied.

RHORAM OPENED HIS eyes to find Achren looking back at him, her face inches from his own. His arms tightened around her slender body and he pulled her to him, reveling in the feel of her warm skin against his.

It was a timeless moment. A moment he had looked forward to for so long. For he had loved her dearly, long before he knew it. He had—

The elbow she dug in his gut took the wind out of him, and halted any romantic thoughts for some time. She rose from their bedroll, swiftly donning her customary black leather tunic and trousers.

"What did you do that for?" he wheezed.

"There is no time for what you had in mind, Rhoram," she

replied, crisply, braiding her long, dark hair. "We march today."

"But not right this minute," he grumbled as he, too, rose and began to dress.

"Always you think of your own pleasure," she said.

"And yours."

She turned to him and grinned, her dark eyes sparkling. "Well, there is that."

He grinned back. "There certainly is." She left the tent before he did, kissing him passionately then slipping from his arms to ensure that their teulu was making the proper preparations to march.

Rhoram lifted the tent flap and stepped outside. The day was clear and cool. Overhead the blue sky gleamed, and the sun sparkled on the morning dew. A light breeze blew off of the lake and stirred the long grass on the shore.

Tents stood on the shore, stretching out as far as Rhoram could see. The Kymri had been mustering here for the past few weeks. Gwynedd was camped to the north, with Prydyn to the west, Ederynion to the east and Rheged to the south. All told he estimated that they were twelve thousand strong. And due to fight tomorrow against more than twenty thousand Coranians, for Havgan's eight thousand reinforcements were only one day away from Eiodel. Rhoram shook his head at that thought. The Kymri would be badly outnumbered. But there was no turning back now. They did not need Arthur to tell them that. The moment their Bards had given them the news that the Coranians had landed, the rulers of Kymru knew that the battle would go on as planned. Calan Llachar, Arthur's birthday, the day of a total eclipse of the sun, would be the day. It had been meant to be that day since the beginning of time, and the Kymri were too wise to argue with fate.

Geriant, the sun glinting off his golden hair, squatted by the campfire, warming his hands. Rhoram put a hand on his son's shoulder and smiled, letting no hint of his thoughts show through. Geriant looked up and smiled back, but briefly.

Rhoram knew what had been ailing his son since he had returned from rescuing Princess Enid. Geriant had told Rhoram everything about his leave-taking from her. Countless times since then Rhoram had tried to tell his son things might change. He had told Geriant over and over that Enid would heal. But Rhoram wondered if that was true. For she might not ever really come back from the dark places she had been.

"Aidan and Lluched went with Achren to ensure Prydyn's ready to march as soon as possible," Geriant said.

"My King?" a voice asked, uncertain, tentative.

Rhoram turned to see a tall, thin man standing before him. The man's brown hair was touched with frost. His green eyes spoke of pain long endured, and triumphed over. Though the man had changed greatly, Rhoram did not need to see the sapphire torque around the man's neck to know who this was.

"Cian," Rhoram breathed, opening his arms to welcome back his Bard. "Cian."

Cian stepped forward and the two men embraced. Both men were unashamedly weeping. Rhoram could scarcely believe it. Cian, who had been taken by the Coranians and imprisoned in Eiodel for so long; Cian, the last Kymri to see the Master Bard alive; Cian, who had been taken to Afalon, suffering terribly under the whips of the wyrce-jaga; Cian, who had been rescued by High King Arthur and taken to Cadair Idris to heal; Cian, his Bard, had returned to him. At last.

The two men stepped back from each other, but Rhoram still gripped the Bard's forearms lightly. "Thank the gods you are still alive."

"The High King gave me permission to join you for the battle. You will need a Bard to relay his messages to you."

"I need you by my side now and always."

"And that is where I shall be, now and always. Arthur says I am to tell you that the package you sent to Cadair Idris arrived safely."

"A shame," Rhoram said, with a grin.

"I thought so, too," Cian said, with a grin of his own on his thin, worn face.

"Rhoram?"

Rhoram turned to see Owein of Rheged bow briefly. He

bowed back to his son-in-law. "All is well with you, Owein? And Sanon?"

"All is well with us," Owein replied. He nodded toward Geriant. "I have come to speak with your son."

"Then speak your piece," Rhoram said, sweeping his arm toward Geriant, who rose at Owein's words.

"Prince Geriant," Owein began, "I have a message for you from my sister."

"From Enid?" Geriant asked in surprise.

"She's the only sister I have," Owein replied, smothering a smile.

"And she sends me a message?" Geriant asked again, astonishment on his handsome face.

"She does," Owein said.

"Really?" Geriant asked.

"Honestly, Geriant," Rhoram broke in, "at this rate we will never hear the message."

Owein, still struggling to smother his smile, bravely went on. "My sister said to give this to you." He reached inside his tunic and pulled out a silk scarf, woven in the red and white colors of Rheged. "She asks that you might wear it into battle, and, perhaps, think of her."

Geriant took the scarf, holding it gingerly, as though it might break. "Da?" he asked.

Rhoram stepped forward and tied the scarf around Geriant's upper right arm. His son's golden hair and blue eyes flashed in the sunlight as he stood straight and proud. "I am honored to wear this token from your sister," Geriant said rather formally to Owein. "And I thank you for giving it to me."

"She is better, Geriant," Owein said. "Much better, since she herself killed Morcant."

"Though Arthur let Bledri live," Geriant said bitterness in his tone.

"He exiled Bledri Beyond the Ninth Wave. The death that is in store for the Dewin is a very hard one," Owein said gravely.

"Would that I, myself, had been able to give him one even

harder."

"You must content yourself with the battle tomorrow. I don't doubt that there will be many opportunities to kill the enemy."

"No doubt," Geriant said, grimly. "No doubt at all."

Elen exited her tent and eyed the clear sky. It would be a beautiful, crisp spring day, perfect for marching. She knew as well as anyone what the odds were against them, but she was eager to come to grips with the enemy, for the years of waiting lay heavily on her. In those years she had been a captive in her own home, forced to wait for rescue. It still galled her, the helplessness of that time. And so she looked forward to tomorrow's battle, even though she knew that likely some of those she loved would die. But surely the Shining Ones would spare her brother. And they would spare one other, who was dear to her heart.

"Elen?"

She turned at the sound of her name on his lips, her heart beating wildly. "Good morning, Rhiwallon."

The Prince of Rheged smiled at her. His broad shoulders strained at his red and white tunic as he sketched a bow. His red-gold hair glowed like fire, and his blue eyes were warm.

He opened his mouth to speak just when Lludd, Angharard, and Talhearn joined them at the campfire.

Lludd kissed his sister and greeted Rhiwallon. "We will be ready to march within the hour, as the High King has commanded," Lludd reported.

Wishing her brother, her captain, and her Bard at the bottom of the sea, Elen replied coolly. "Excellent."

Lludd's eyes widened in surprise, then narrowed as he eyed his sister. But comprehension dawned swiftly, and, lips twitching, he turned to Angharad. "I believe we should guarantee that my statement will be true. Let's go ensure that all will be ready."

Angharad, whose temper was even shorter since Emrys' death, answered irritably. "We just did that. Don't be ridiculous."

But Talhearn, his wise brown eyes dancing, disagreed. "Now Angharad, how could the Queen's teulu possibly get ready without you there to harass them?"

Angharad snorted. "They know what they are doing."

Exasperated, Lludd elbowed the captain. But Angharad was in no mood for subtleties. She rounded on Lludd. "What?" she demanded.

Talhearn, who had been trying not to smile, gave up at that point and began to laugh. Lludd ruefully shrugged his shoulders and Elen sighed. Rhiwallon, clearly giving up on the idea of a private conversation, cleared his throat and opened his mouth.

But the Prince was once again forced to wait, for at that moment Talorcan and Regan exited their tent and joined them at the campfire. The former Coranian general smiled at his companions as he greeted them. Elen was struck by his easy manner, quite a change from the man she had known for the past few years. For the Talorcan she had known had been a tormented man—hating the bonds that held him yet unable to break them. But all that had changed. He would fight with the Dewin tomorrow, under Arthur's direction. And from the look in his clear, green eyes, he was ready.

Now, if she could only get rid of them all, Rhiwallon might say what he came here to say. But she had underestimated the Prince, for he had clearly decided to take the plunge in spite of their audience.

"Queen Elen," he began his tone somewhat formal, "I spoke with my brother this morning."

He stopped. Clearly she was expected to say something. "Yes?" she prompted.

"He has given me permission to fight by your side tomorrow." His fresh, bright face turned red as he said it. But he did say it.

Elen blushed in her turn, something she rarely did. Though the blush embarrassed her, it seemed to hearten Rhiwallon and his color subsided. For a moment she did not know what to say. The silence spun out so long, that Rhiwallon's smile began to fade. That's when Lludd elbowed her, causing her to take an involuntary step toward Rhiwallon. The Prince reached out to catch her as she fell against him, and he held her briefly before gently setting her back on her feet.

Elen cleared her throat. "I would be honored to have you by my side."

Rhiwallon grinned, relieved. He took her hand and imprinted a kiss on her palm. He bowed briefly then left to join his brother for the day's march.

"Very smooth, sister," Lludd said with a grin.

Elen, without taking her eyes off of Rhiwallon's retreating figure said crisply, "Don't you think there is someone you need to see this morning, too?"

Morrigan stood by her campfire staring out across Lake Mwyngil. She could just make out traces of the blackened, scarred encampment on Afalon. This had been the place where the Y Dawnus had been held captive, up until just a few weeks ago. This had been the place her brother had destroyed, cleansing it with Druid's Fire.

Already it seemed the signs of burning were being replaced by fresh growth. Birch trees, with their silvery white bark and drooping branches mingled with tall ash trees, their large, dark green leaves tossing in the breeze.

Surely, she thought, they were closer to the old encampment than they had been the day before. But then, Afalon had always been a strange, enchanted place. A breeze rippled the clear, blue water as she listened quietly to Susanna.

"Legend says that when Bran found the High King right here on the shore, Lleu was still alive," the Bard said. "He begged Bran to spare the High Queen, though she had betrayed him."

"Why did he do that?" Morrigan asked.

"He loved her," Cai said as he gazed at Susanna. She smiled back at him, her blue eyes alight.

Gwyhar, Susanna's son, smiled at the look in his stepfather's eyes. Even Ygraine's frosty expression melted a little at the tone in Cai's voice, as though remembering the love she and Uthyr had once shared. Bedwyr and Tangwen, newly married, also smiled.

Morrigan sighed inwardly. There seemed to be a great many

people in love these days. She was happy that her friends were happy, but it seemed to her that they were easily distracted. And they had serious business to do.

"Any word from my brother this morning?" she asked Susanna, to get the conversation back to business. She would hear the story of Bran and Lleu another time.

"He asked me to greet you. And to tell you that he requires Gwyhar to stand with the Y Dawnus tomorrow."

Then her mother spoke. "I, too, will join Arthur tomorrow. He has asked me to arm him."

Morrigan's eyes filled briefly with tears at the pride in her mother's voice, for she knew what it meant to Ygraine to have been asked to do that. And she did not begrudge her mother that task. Still, she felt a little deflated that both Gwyhar and Ygraine would not be with her tomorrow.

But that feeling was forgotten swiftly when she heard her name.

"Good morning, Morrigan," Lludd, the Prince of Ederynion, said.

ARTHUR SAT IN Taran's Tower, the chamber at the uppermost level of Cadair Idris. Sunlight streamed through the clear glasslike ceiling, illuminating the silvery walls. Diamonds on the walls, representing the stars over Kymru, glittered brightly. A few small tables and some comfortable chairs completed the furnishings. Arthur sat in one chair, frowning down at the black and white squares of the tarbell board.

The game had once been in the garden room, a room Arthur loved. But since the wounded Y Dawnus had been rescued from Afalon and brought here to Cadair Idris, they spent a great deal of time in the garden room as they regained both their psychic and physical strength. That room, which held a small fountain as well as shrubs, flowers, and trees, soothed them. So he had given the room over to them and moved the tarbell set up here to this chamber.

As from the beginning, the tarbell game fascinated him. He had found that he had a knack for this game of strategy, an ability to plan many moves ahead, keeping his eye on the goal—to capture the opposing side's High King. But there was something else about these particular pieces that drew him. Something he had noticed about them from the beginning. Something that, if other people had noticed, no one had mentioned.

He heard the door open. He did not have to turn around to know who it was. Gwydion took a seat opposite Arthur. After a moment he reached out and moved the raven-shaped Dreamer's piece diagonally across two squares.

Arthur reached out and moved the High Queen to that square, taking the Dreamer's piece off the board. "You sacrificed the Dreamer," Arthur pointed out. "Why?"

Surprisingly, Gwydion grinned. "There's more than one."

"And how is Cariadas today?" Arthur asked.

"A little subdued, actually," Gwydion replied, his smile fading a little.

"Overwhelmed?"

"She's young."

Arthur snorted. "She and I are about the same age."

"So very true," Gwydion murmured.

Suddenly, Arthur laughed. "Yes, I too, am young. But it is my time now."

"So it is," Gwydion agreed. "Are you ready?"

"Almost."

Gwydion's brows raised in surprise. "What do you mean by almost?"

"There is one thing yet to do before tomorrow. And for that I need both Dreamers."

"What do you intend?"

"I intend to Walk-Between-the-Worlds."

"Where do you need to go?"

"I need to go to Gwlad Yr Haf."

"To the Summer Land to speak with the dead? Why?"

"To be honest, uncle, I do not know. I know only that I am drawn to go there. I hope that once I am there, I will understand something that I do not understand now. I only know that there is something I do not know. Something that I need to know if we are to achieve victory tomorrow."

"Unlikely as that is." Gwydion snorted.

"It is unlikely," Arthur agreed. "But it is the only chance we will get."

"Very well. Cariadas and I will return here this evening."

At that the door opened again. Gwen stood framed in the doorway. She wore a tunic of black leather with the wolf-badge of Prydyn sewn to the front. Her blond hair was braided tightly and wound around her head. She carried a metal helmet and her expression was defiant.

Gwydion rose and went to the door. He bowed briefly to Gwen. His silver eyes danced as he took in her outfit and Arthur's face. But he left without a word.

Gwen entered the room and came to stand before Arthur. "I am leaving today," she said abruptly.

"I see."

"To join my father when he nears Cadair Idris."

"Yes."

"I insist that I be able to fight by his side tomorrow."

"Yes, you would."

"I would what?" she snapped.

"Insist. It wouldn't matter to you that I need you here."

"For what?" she snorted.

"To join the Druids. Battle is the hardest on them. I need as many as I can get."

"You won't miss me, then. I am not trained."

"You are not, perhaps, as well trained as some," Arthur replied evenly. "But Madryn has taught you well these past few months. More than that, you are strong—very strong—in your gift. Stronger than you realize."

For a brief moment uncertainty flickered in her beautiful eyes. "Really?"

"Really." He lowered his eyes beneath her gaze to stare back down at the tarbell board. For looking at her made him want to say all the things he knew he should not say. Not yet, at any rate.

Not until—not unless—he won the battle tomorrow. His eyes rested on the face of the tarbell High Queen and he reached out and took the piece in his hands.

"You don't need me here," she said.

"I do," he answered.

"I don't believe you," Gwen said after a moment of silence.

"I don't suppose you do," he said quietly. "To believe me might take some measure of understanding. And you have none."

He expected her to be enraged by that. He expected to have a brief fight with her now that would end with her leaving in a rage. He expected to feel better after that, to feel less like he was risking the loss of something dearer to him than life. But she remained silent. At last he looked up. She was staring down at the piece in his hand, a strange expression on her face.

"I understand more than you think, High King," she said quietly. She reached out her hand and he gently handed her the piece. She held it up, studying it intently. "Or did you really think I hadn't noticed?"

He did not know what to say to that, so he remained silent. She handed the piece back. "I will stay." She left the room before he could reply.

He held the piece in his hand, staring down at the exquisite, carved face, the face that was the image of hers. After a moment, he smiled. She would stay.

The stars wheeled overhead, glittering coldly in the darkened sky. Starlight streamed into the chamber, vying with the low glow of the smoldering fire in the brazier. Rhiannon and Gwen, both with scarves tied over their noses and mouths, slowly fed the fire using wet, green saplings.

Smoke filled the room, dimming the starlight, dimming Arthur's vision. Although he knew Gwydion lay on the floor to his right and Cariadas lay on the floor to his left, he could no longer see them.

It was time. He closed his eyes, and waited.

He stood by a well on the isle of Afalon. Gwydion and Cariadas stood with him, looking down into the clear water. Without even having to ask, Arthur knew that this was the place where Caladfwlch, the sword of the High Kings, had rested for so long. And he knew that this was where Gwydion's brother, Amatheon, had died. Even all these years later Arthur could still see the echo of grief in his uncle's eyes. The sound of wings caused him to look up and he saw that the surrounding trees were filled with ravens. They made no other sound, and their strange silence filled his head.

"They are your escort to the Otherworld," Gwydion said quietly.

"And they will ensure your return," Cariadas said. She held out three black raven's feathers. Arthur took them, stowing them inside his tunic. "Keep these with you on your journey," she went on. "When you are ready to return, take them in your hand, then call us. We will be waiting."

"What must I do?" Arthur asked his uncle.

But it was Cariadas who answered. "Look into the well."

And so he looked, but he could see only his own reflection. The scar on his face whitened, and his dark eyes gazed back up at him. The water, still and silent, began to glow with a silvery light. He reached down and put his hand into the water. And that was when he felt another hand grasp his. And pull him down.

When he opened his eyes he was laying in a meadow. His clothes were dry. The long grasses bent beneath a gentle wind and he thought he heard the faint sound of a hunting horn. Overhead the sky was clear and the sun shone down warmly. He leapt to his feet. Before him stood a massive door of stone set incongruously in the center of the meadow. He walked all around the door, trying to see where it led. But he could not, for it was just a door standing by itself. At last he reached out to open the door when a low growl stopped him. Involuntarily he stepped back.

The hound was huge, almost the size of the door itself. It was white, like the hounds of Annwyn, and its eyes were blood red. But Arthur knew the dog's name. And he knew the dog's purpose. And he knew that the dog would let him by.

"Heel, Dormath," he said to the hound that guarded the door to Gwlad Yr Haf. "I have come to speak to your master and mistress. They have called me."

The hound raised his head to the sky and bayed. The mournful howl sounded out across the meadow, echoing again and again across the plain. But the dog stepped back from the door. Tentatively Arthur reached out and grasped the round, iron ring. He pulled with all his strength. Slowly the door opened. He could see nothing but velvety darkness. Taking a deep breath, he stepped through, to the Otherworld.

In the center of the garden, there was a fountain fed by five glittering streams. The streams played over rocks and the splash of the fountain sounded joyfully. Delicate lily of the valley, impossibly blue forget-me-nots, and shy violets lined the streams. Beds of green moss glowed emerald, lit by lemony yellow globeflowers and sweet, white alyssum.

At first Arthur had thought he was alone. With a start he saw that a man sat on the rim of the golden fountain, his head bowed. The man raised his head as Arthur came to stand before him.

"Da!" Arthur exclaimed in a strangled whisper. "Oh, Da."

Uthyr ap Rathtyen var Awst rose and bowed to his son.

"Da, don't bow to me."

"I do not bow to you, my son. I bow to the High King of Kymru." But then Uthyr smiled. Arthur hurled himself into his father's arms and they held each other tightly, neither of them willing to let go.

At last they reluctantly parted, stepping back to look at each other. Uthyr looked much as he had when Arthur had last seen him, but the lines of strain and care were gone. His face glowed with pride as he looked at Arthur.

"My son," Uthyr said, "you look tired."

"I suppose I do," Arthur said past he lump in his throat. "There is much happening in Kymru."

"Is there?" Uthyr asked. "But now you are here, and I can tell by the life in your eyes that you are not dead. What, then, is your need?"

"I must see Aertan and Annwyn."

"You seek the Weaver and the Lord of Chaos? That is something few of the living dare, or even the dead desire."

"Yes, I know. But the need is great."

"Then your courage must be, also. Come, I will take you to them."

He took his father's hand and the fountain, the streams, the garden melted away. Suddenly a huge wheel began to take shape before his eyes. It appeared to be made of fire and water, of earth and air. Streams of golden fire twined with silvery water as the wheel spun. Green grass mingled with cool breezes. Sunny days twisted with ropes of lighting sped by. Silvery moonlight and golden sunlight were knotted together in an intricate pattern that the mind could not grasp. The wheel spun sometimes slowly, sometimes so fast it was merely a blur. A great rushing sound filled his ears as the wheel spun. Behind the wheel he saw planets moving in an intricate dance, stars wheeling after them, and meteors leaving trails of fire as they rushed by.

Suddenly, the wheel stopped spinning. Silence descended.

"What do you want here, Arthur ap Uthyr var Ygraine?" a voice asked. The voice seemed to be made of bloodstains and grief, of twisting shadows and the coppery taste of fear.

"Annwyn, Lord of Chaos, I do not know."

"Not a promising beginning, High King," another voice said. This voice sounded like the twists of pitiless fate, of unexpected mercy, of long, beautiful summer days and sudden, wrenching loss.

"Aertan, Weaver of Fate, you know why I am here, even if I do not."

By the quality of the silence he knew that if they had chosen to show themselves he would have seen a sparkle in Aertan's bloodstone eyes, he would have seen a glow in the onyx darkness of Annwyn's.

Uthyr, who up to now had been silent, at last chose to speak. "Guardians of Gwlad Yr Haf, I beg you to listen to my son. I beg that you will give him the aid that he asks."

"If he knows what to ask for he shall receive it," Annywn said.

"Yes," said Aertan. "If he knows."

And though Aertan and Annwyn still chose not to show themselves, Arthur saw that crowds of people were coming up to stand beside the wheel. He had never met many of them, yet he knew them. He saw Anieron Master Bard and Cynan Ardewin. He saw Queen Olwen of Ederynion and her husband, Kilwch. He saw King Urien and Queen Ellirri of Rheged. With a gasp he recognized the four Great Ones of Lleu Silver-Hand. He even recognized Lleu himself, who stood with Macsen and Idris, the other High Kings of Kymru.

And then he saw them. And he knew, even as he did, that they were the ones he had come for. And he wondered why it had taken him so long to understand, why it had taken all of them so long to see.

"I ask for the release of two souls," Arthur said.

And then the wheel began to spin again.

Chapter Twenty-two

Gwytheryn, Kymru
Gwernan Mis, 500

Calan Llachar—morning

The false twilight descended silently over the two armies as the sky slowly darkened. The landscape turned to gray as the moon's approaching shadow leached the colors from the terrain and from the two armies that confronted each other.

Arthur stood with Caladfwlch in his hand, the point of his sword just touching the earth of Kymru, silently drawing power from the land itself as he waited. His silvery cloak streamed out behind him in the freshening breeze and his tunic and trousers were black. He wore a helmet of silver and gold fashioned like an eagle's head and the massive High King's torque lay around his throat. The huge emerald, pearl, opal, and sapphire glittered in the uncertain light, while the onyx in the center remained opaque, gleaming darkly, as though guarding a mystery.

Cariadas, the new Dreamer of Kymru, stood on Arthur's right, with a cloak of black raven's feathers around her slim shoulders. The opal Dreamer's torque encircled her neck like a ring of golden fire and her silvery eyes flickered as she surveyed the opposing army.

Gwen stood next to Cariadas. On her head she wore the wolf's helmet of Prydyn, and she held a short spear. Though she would use her druidic gifts today against the enemy, she had claimed a place next to Arthur rather than with the rest of the Y Dawnus. Her blue eyes were fierce and cold as she eyed the enemy, daring them to approach.

Gwydion and Rhiannon stood to Arthur's left. Gwydion wore a plain, black robe trimmed in red and he held a spear. Rhiannon wore her Dewin's robe of green and silver, and carried a bow and arrow. They stood close together, their shoulders just touching, hands clasped. Their eyes—silver and emerald—glittered in the uncertain light, but their faces were carefully still.

Arthur's mother, Ygraine, stood behind her son, flanked by Rhufon, Steward of Cadair Idris, and Rhufon's son, Tybion. Ygraine's eyes were cool as the sky continued to darken, and her face betrayed nothing of her fears.

Behind them the Y Dawnus—the Bards, Druids, and Dewin of Kymru—gathered. Elidyr Master Bard was dressed in blue and white, a cloak of songbird feathers around his shoulders, sapphires glittering around his neck. His youngest son, Cynfar, stood with him, as did his father, Dudod. Most of the Bards, however, were scattered throughout Arthur's army, for ease of issuing his commands to the army's leaders.

The Dewin, led by Elstar, stood next to the Bards. Pearls glowed at Elstar's throat and a cloak of swan's feathers streamed out behind her in the breeze. Elstar's oldest son, Llywelyn, stood next to her, his eyes fastened on Cariadas. Among the Dewin gathered with them were Myrrdin and Talorcan. Both Neuad and Regan were stationed with the army, for their medical skills would be needed, as would the skills they possessed to enable Arthur to see every inch of the entire battlefield.

The Druids massed behind their leader, Aergol. He wore a cloak of bull's hide fastened to his shoulders and glowing emeralds around his strong neck. Aergol's daughter and son, Sinend and Menw, stood to the right of their father, while Ellywen and Sabrina stood to his left. Behind them streamed hundreds of Druids in brown robes. They stood silently, husbanding their strength, for they knew that Arthur's demands on them would be heavy, and they were determined to do all that they could, determined to use this moment to erase the shame of once siding with Kymru's enemy.

Cynedyr the Wild, son of Hetwin Silver-Brow of Rheged, and

his warriors ringed the Y Dawnus, their task to protect them from attack. Cynedyr's golden hair streamed out behind him as he and his warriors ringed the perimeter of the Y Dawnus.

The forces of Gwynedd stood on the far right flank of the Kymric army. Morrigan, with Cai on her right and Bedwyr on her left, sat her horse quietly. Around her head was the helm of Gwynedd, shaped like a hawk with sapphire eyes. Her Bard, Susanna, sat her horse behind her, ready to relay Arthur's orders. Morrigan's three thousand mounted warriors in blue and brown were armed and ready.

Next to them massed the army of Prydyn. King Rhoram, with Achren on his right and Aidan on his left sat his black horse proudly. He wore a golden helmet fashioned like a wolf's head. The wolf's emerald eyes surveyed the battlefield, flashing in the flickering light as though eager to engage the enemy. Rhoram's son, Geriant, sat his horse next to Cian, Rhoram's Bard. Behind them three thousand warriors in black and green waited for the signal to begin this last, desperate battle.

On the far left flank the army of Ederynion waited. Queen Elen wore a helmet of silver, shaped like the upswept wings of a swan. Angharad was on her right, while Prince Rhiwallon and Prince Lludd were on her left. Her Bard, Talhearn, sat his horse patiently, his dark eyes alight in his seamed, weathered face. Behind them streamed Ederynion's warriors in sea green and white, sitting rock steady on their horses.

To their right the forces of Rheged were gathered. Owein, wearing a horse-shaped helmet with glowing eyes of opal, sat unmoving on his golden horse. Flanked by Trystan and Sanon on his left and Teleri and Gwarae on his right, he silently surveyed the Coranian army. Esyllt, his Bard, was behind him. Three thousand warriors waited behind them, dressed in the red and white of Rheged, their weapons ready.

Ravens ringed the trees of Calan Llachar to the north, while wolves waited in the shadows of the wood for the word from the High King—for today even the animals of Kymru would fight for freedom.

Cadair Idris rose at the back of the Kymric army. The mountain glowed in the false twilight, like a pinnacle of hope rising from a dark wave of despair. The golden doors gleamed, the jewels impossibly bright in the fading, silvery light.

It was time.

Caladfwlch felt warm in Arthur's hand. The gold and silver sword seemed to glow slightly as the moon's shadow approached. He thought of the moment this morning, when his mother had clasped the sword's scabbard around his waist.

"Thus do I arm my son, for his great battle," she had said, intoning the formal words. But he had heard the pride, and the grief, beneath those words, and he had gently laid his hand on his mother's arm. She had looked up at him then, her dark eyes unreadable.

"They tell me that I have the look of my father," he had said. "And I could not tell if that was true, for his face was blurred in my mind's eye. Yet now I know that this is indeed true. For I have seen him."

Her breath had caught in her throat at his words. Her dark eyes had lit with an inner fire and she demanded, somewhat fiercely, "How?"

"In Gwlad Yr Haf. He was my guide there."

She had dropped her head and looked away. He had guessed that her eyes had been filled with tears she hadn't wanted him to see. So he answered the question she hadn't asked. "He spoke of you."

Her head had risen at that, but she still had not turned around to face him.

"He said that the life he had in Kymru with you was more than he had ever hoped for. He said that you made everything worthwhile. He said that he knew without asking that you were keeping your promise to him. What was that promise?"

She had turned back to him then, her eyes sparkling with tears she had been too proud to let fall. "I promised to live beyond his death. I promised to take care of our daughter. And to do what I could to ensure that my son ruled Kymru."

Arthur had nodded. "A promise you kept."

"So I have, my son."

A voice jarred him, bringing him back to the present.

". . . too many."

"What?" Arthur asked Gwen. She had whispered the words to Cariadas, but he had heard them, nonetheless.

Gwen, caught, squared her shoulders and turned to face Arthur. "I said, they are too many. Twenty thousand to our twelve. It's hopeless and you know it. Even the Y Dawnus cannot tip those scales."

Cabal, the hound that had followed him back from Afalon, raised his head to look up at his master. Arthur laid his hand on the dog's head. "They don't need to," he said.

OPPOSITE THE KYMRIC army the Coranian army massed, black Eiodel at their back. Sigerric and Penda stood at the forefront of the army, flanking Havgan, while Prince Aesc stood behind him.

Havgan was resplendent in red and gold. His golden cloak whipped about him in the wind, his bright hair streaming behind him. His amber eyes glowed as he took in the opposing army, a half smile on his handsome face.

Arianrod and Aelfwyn stood on the battlements of Eiodel. Arch-Byshop Eadwig stood with them while hundreds of preosts of Lytir filled the dark fortress. Havgan had recalled all of them from Y Ty Dewin for he had wanted all his people gathered to watch this battle. He had also recalled the remaining wyrce-jaga from Neuadd Gorsedd. They stood in a tight knot before the gates of Eiodel, their black robes contrasting with their pale faces. They knew that the Kymri had killed every wyrce-jaga in the four kingdoms, and they could expect no quarter.

Havgan knew, of course, that both the preosts and the wyrce-jaga would be shocked at what he meant to do today. But he cared nothing for that.

Behind Havgan twenty thousand Coranian warriors waited. Unlike the Kymri, they were not mounted. They wore metal byrnies that reached down to mid-thigh and carried shields and axes. Their faces were fierce and the light of battle was in their eyes.

"I can see Talorcan," Sigerric said, squinting into the mass of Dawnus.

Havgan did not bother to look, for he had seen Talorcan the moment he had neared the Kymric army.

"He looks happy," Penda said, envy in his voice.

"He looks free," Sigerric replied.

"If either of you wish to join the Kymri, you are welcome to do it," Havgan said serenely. For he had known these two men a long time. And he knew exactly what they would and would not do. Today they would fight with everything they had to ensure a Coranian victory. Tomorrow would be another matter.

His day had come. His whole life had been leading up to this moment. Everything that had ever happened to him, every move that he had ever made had brought him here, facing Arthur ap Uthyr, with Eiodel at his back and Cadair Idris before him.

Today was the day he would be made High King of Kymru. Today was the day that Drwys Idris would acknowledge him, and allow him to enter. For that was how it had been meant to be from the beginning. He knew that now.

He looked behind him, to the battlements of Eiodel. His eyes passed over his wife, Aelfwyn, and Eadwig, his Arch-Byshop, going directly to the love of his heart, Arianrod. Her tawny hair was muted in the fading light, but he knew that her amber eyes were bright, fixed on him. She raised her hand to him as a sudden gust of wind blew her gown tightly to her body, illuminating her pregnancy. She carried a son beneath her heart. His son. He would win the world for that child, and hand it to him.

Absently he fingered the prayer beads he held in his hand. In Corania they called it the *kranzlein*, the little wreath. The beads of white, red, and orange, of yellow, green, blue, and violet, flashed beneath his restless fingers. The *kranzlein* had been in his hands the night that his father had died. And the night the former Bana had been consumed by fire. The *kranzlein* had helped him to focus his prayers. He had always thought that it had been Lytir who had heard them and chosen to answer.

But now he knew better.

It was time. He could feel it singing in his bones. Now.

IT WAS TIME, Arthur thought. He could feel it singing in his blood. Now.

He turned to Rhiannon. "Call them," he said quietly.

Rhiannon lifted her hands to the darkening sky. Her voice suddenly huge and powerful, she cried out. "Cerridwen and Cerrunnos, Protectors of Kymru, come to me! Hounds of Annwyn, come to me! Wild Hunt of Kymru, I call you in this the hour of our need!"

Suddenly the air was filled with the sound of horns. The sound echoed across the darkening sky. The horizon to the west glowed brighter and brighter as something approached. Then the Hunt burst into their sight, bringing a silvery light with them. The white Hounds of Annwyn with blood-red eyes bayed as they gamboled overhead, mingling with the mounted warriors of the Hunt.

Cerrunnos and Cerridwen, the Protectors of Kymri, led the Hunt. Cerrunnos rode a horse as white and shining as the moon, while Cerridwen rode a steed as dark as a night shadow. Cerrunnos' owl eyes and antlered forehead gleamed and Cerridwen's amythest eyes surveyed the battlefield below without pity.

Just behind them rode three figures that made the Kymric army gasp. Each figure wore a shadowy torque around his neck, a replica of the torque Arthur wore. They each carried a ghostly sword, exactly like the one Arthur held. And each one wore a flickering helmet of gold and silver, fashioned like that of an eagle, on his proud head. The Kymri below recognized these legendary figures as the former High Kings of Kymru—Idris, Macsen, and Lleu Silver-Hand.

The warriors of the host streamed out behind them, waiting silently, spread out across the darkening sky, their faces stern, their eyes bright and pitiless as diamonds, and mounted on horses of moonlight and midnight, of starlight and shadow. Silvery spears and shining swords were clasped in their hands as they confronted the Coranian army below.

The sight of the Wild Hunt heartened the Kymri. Today,

against all odds, they would stand and face the enemy, and those that died that day would find a welcome from those above them.

The Hunt had come from Gwlad Yr Haf, to fight for Kymru.

THE CORANIANS CRIED out when the Wild Hunt filled the sky. The yellow-robed preosts began to chant prayers to Lytir. The black-robed wyrce-jaga joined in. Sigerric, Penda, and Aesc gripped their weapons tighter, all three of them emitting a ragged gasp of shock. But Havgan had not moved. For he had known of this, he had dreamt it, and he was not afraid.

He drew the *kranzlein* through his restless fingers, never taking his eyes off the eastern horizon. Once he would have prayed to Lytir when he held the beads, but now he knew better. He would not call on Lytir, the supposed One God. For that God was powerless. He would call on the one who had brought him here. The one who had guided his life from the beginning, just as the wyrd-galdra cards had told him years ago. He had not listened then. But things had changed. He was listening now.

He bowed his head, staring at the beads, saying the words in his mind.

I hung on the windy tree, hung for night full nine; With the spear I was wounded; On the tree whose roots no one can know.

"Havgan," Sigerric said, putting his hand on Havgan's shoulder. "What are you doing?"

But he did not answer. He stared down at the beads and he moved them from hand to hand, the beads now shimmering in the uncertain, dimming light.

I hung on the windy tree, hung for night full nine; With the spear I was wounded; On the tree whose roots no one can know.

"Havgan," Penda said desperately, "their Hunt is above us! The men are terrified."

But Havgan did not answer.

I hung on the windy tree, hung for night full nine; With the spear I was wounded; On the tree whose roots no one can know.

The beads began to glow brighter. To the east, a wan, golden light appeared on the horizon. From far, far away thunder sounded faintly. Sweat beaded Havgan's brow. They had told him, once that they would not come across the sea. But Havgan knew they would come to him.

I hung on the windy tree, hung for night full nine; With the spear I was wounded; On the tree whose roots no one can know.

The golden light grew, and thunder rumbled. Then lighting split the sky. And suddenly they were there.

Sigerric gasped. "Havgan, what have you done?"

"What I was born to do," he said calmly.

Overhead the Coranian Wild Hunt massed in the sky above dark Eiodel. In the forefront of the Hunt Wuotan One-Eye sat on his horse. Lighting flashed as he lifted his spear. Next to him Holda, Lady of the Waters, raised her tawny head. Her sea-green eyes glowed brightly and as she sounded her horn thunder cried out, shaking the ground. Behind them dead warriors sat their wraith-like horses, madness in their eyes and weapons in their ghostly hands. White dogs with ruby eyes capered and leapt, ready for battle. And here and there throughout the hunt fierce Valkyries raised their snow-pale heads, waiting for their chance to descend to the battlefield and begin the dreadful harvest of the souls that they craved.

CARIADAS TURNED TO Arthur, a hint of desperation in her silvery eyes, though she kept her voice steady. "Havgan has called his own Wild Hunt. Our Hunt will not tip the scales in our favor now. The boon you asked Aertan and Annwyn for is useless."

Surprisingly, Arthur smiled. "But that was not what I asked for."

Motioning for Gwydion and Rhiannon to follow him, he stepped out onto the battlefield, walking toward the Golden Man of Corania, going to meet his destiny.

"OH, HAVGAN," SIGERRIC murmured, "oh, my heart's brother."

"Oh, my one-time friend," Penda breathed, "what have you done?"

Havgan turned to his two generals, his amber eyes serene.

"Did you not know? Did you not see? It was Wuotan all along. It was he that raised me from a mere fisherman's son to be a part of the highest councils in the land. It was he that sent me to Kymru, to find the truth."

Havgan stepped forward then to meet Arthur. He held his golden head high as Sigerric and Penda followed him. He did not appear to hear Sigerric's next comment.

"Oh, Havgan," Siggeric said sadly, "I think it was something else entirely that sent you here."

THEY MET IN THE center of the battlefield. Unlit torches were set in the ground at regular intervals, ringing the perimeter. Arthur, dressed in silver and black and flanked by Gwydion and Rhiannon, faced Havgan, who glowed in red and gold, Sigerric and Penda beside him.

Gwydion clenched his fists as he stared at Havgan. Overhead the western sky darkened, illuminated only by the silvery light emanating from the Kymric Wild Hunt. The sun narrowed to a fiery crescent as the surrounding sky darkened to violet. To the east the sky was lighter, and the Coranian Wild Hunt glowed with a golden light.

And it was there, in the path of the moon's shadow, that Gwydion began to understand what he knew he should have seen all along. He had caught glimpses of it before throughout the years, but he had not understood. He began to get the faintest glimmering of what had made him save Havgan's life in Corania, of what had made him both love and hate his one time blood-brother, of what the battle in his heart had truly meant. For he saw at last, in the coming darkness, as the moon leached away Havgan's red and gold, what had been hidden from his mind's eye for so long.

"In Kymric, Havgan means 'Summershine,'" Arthur said, unexpectedly.

"Son of Uthyr," Havgan replied, "today you will die."

"Son of—" Arthur stopped as though he had spoken too soon. "Tell me, what has made you run so long and hard from the truth?

Why?"

"I run from the truth no longer. There is magic in me. There always was. And it was Wuotan One-Eye who put it there. He has brought me here, to rule you. Your Hunt is useless. And your army is outnumbered. Bow to me, and you will live."

"The truth you think you know is false. Still you are running."

"I see what there is to see."

"No. If you have magic, where did it come from? If you were drawn here, why? Your answers to those questions are wrong."

"They are not. The truth is here, in me. The truth is in the eyes of my beloved Arianrod. The truth is in my dreams. The truth is in Cadair Idris, which will be mine before the day is over. That is the truth."

"You twist the truth. You always have. I would spare you, if I could."

"I do not want or need your pity, son of Uthyr. You may keep it. Everything else, you will lose." Havgan turned to Gwydion, his amber eyes gleaming in the violet light. "And you, false blood brother, I will kill you today."

"Oh, Havgan," Gwydion said, his throat tight with unshed tears, with unspeakable sorrow, "I beg you—"

"You beg me? You beg me for what? For your life? For the life of the boy beside you? For the life of the woman you love? Beg me, my traitorous blood brother. It will get you nothing, but it will please me."

But Gwydion did not answer him. Instead he turned his gaze to Sigerric and Penda. "One-time brothers, you have followed Havgan against your hearts, against your wills, against your very souls. Follow him no longer. Be free."

"Free?" Sigerric asked with a twisted smile. "I am what I am. That is all I will ever be."

"And you, Penda?" Gwydion pressed. "Is it too late for you?"

Penda gazed not at Gwydion, but at Arthur. The High King's dark eyes gleamed and his scar whitened briefly as Penda answered. "If I survive this battle I will return to my native Mierce, to my home in the shadow of Mount Badon. And never do battle again."

Arthur smiled. "I do not think, Penda of Mierce, that will be your fate should you return home."

"Perhaps not, High King."

"Enough," Havgan said quietly. "Arthur ap Uthyr, your business is with me."

"So it is. 'Shall this not be a fair day of freedom,' Havgan?" Arthur asked, quoting from Anieron's last song. "'Silence will be your portion, and you will taste death.' You remember those words, don't you?"

Havgan smiled. "Anieron died by my hand."

"But was freed from you before he died. Enough, Havgan. Have done. It is time to face the truth." Arthur turned to the sky, and raised his hand to the Kymric Hunt. Cerridwen and Cerrunnos nodded, and motioned for two figures to detach themselves and ride forward across the sky.

The first figure was a man, with eyes of glowing amber. The second was a woman, with tawny hair. They rode down together, their shadowy horses alighting beside Arthur as Gwydion and Rhiannon stepped back—the woman on Arthur's right, the man on Arthur's left.

"Havgan, this is the shade of Brychan ap Cynfan, brother to Gwydion's father, Awst."

The man's handsome face was stern, but there was pity in his amber eyes as he stared at Havgan. Havgan stared back at the man, his expression carefully still, a spark of recognition, swiftly quenched, in his eyes.

"And this," Arthur went on, gesturing to the woman, "is the ghost of Arianllyn ur Darun. She was sister to Indeg, Rhiannon's mother."

The woman's tawny hair streamed out behind her in the breeze. Her eyes filled with tears as she gazed down at Havgan. Havgan gasped as the women's hair was lifted by the wind, recognition no longer held at bay.

And now Gwydion fully understood what Arthur had seen in Gwlad Yr Haf. And he knew what Arthur had asked for. Pain stabbed his heart, an ache so fierce he could barely breathe. Rhiannon reached out and took his hand in hers, giving him the strength he needed, as she always had. Strength enough not to look away, as he longed to do but to fully see what he must see.

Arthur went on, his voice implacable but his dark eyes lustrous with pity. "These two were the parents of Arianrod, your lover."

As though against his will, Havgan turned briefly to gaze back at Arianrod. She had one hand to her mouth, her other hand on her belly. The woman lifted her hand to Arianrod, despair written on her beautiful features. The man covered his eyes and turned away from the sight of his pregnant daughter.

And as Havgan turned back around to face them, Gwydion saw that he understood, at last.

"When Arianrod was only a very little girl, our Dreamer, Dinaswyn, had a dream," Arthur said quietly. "The dream told her that Brychan and Arianllyn were to go to Corania. And so they went, leaving their little daughter behind. They arrived in Athelin and stayed there for almost a year, as Dinaswyn had told them to do. Finally, they embarked on a ship to go home. But the ship was caught in a sudden storm. Brychan was drowned when the ship went down. But Arianllyn was not. She barely made it alive to shore. There she made her way to the hut of a fisherman. His name was Hengist. And there she gave birth to a son, named him, then died."

Havgan went white to the lips. On the dark battlements Arianrod screamed in despair and dropped to her knees, sobbing in anguish and misery, in horror and shame.

Arthur waited a moment, his features struggling with something else. Gwydion saw that Arthur had another thing to say and he was afraid he knew exactly what it was.

"Havgan ap Brychan var Arianllyn," Arthur said solemnly, "you were born to be the Dreamer of Kymru."

Havgan swiftly raised his eyes to Gwydion. Golden-amber met silver-gray as the two men stared at each other.

"When the Shining Ones saw that you were to be raised in Corania they sent a new Dreamer to Kymru in your place. Gwydion ap Awst was born soon after you were."

"This is what you learned in Gwlad Yr Haf?" Gwydion asked Arthur in a strangled voice.

"This is what I learned," Arthur answered.

"Which is why you would tell us nothing when you came back."

"Yes."

"Your Shining Ones are cruel," Sigerric said, white-faced.

"They do not arrange our fate," Arthur said. "They merely strengthen us to meet it."

Havgan turned away from Gwydion and looked again at the ghostly figures of his mother and father.

"My son, my son," Arianllyn said with tears in her voice.

"What have you done?" Brychan asked, his amber eyes flashing.

"You left me!" Havgan cried out, rage and anguish in his cry. "You left me!"

"We sent for you," Arianllyn said quietly.

"Time and again," Brychan said.

"We sent you a dream, a dream of me, looking out to sea to the west," Arianllyn went on. "So that you would know to go across the sea, to return to Kymru."

"I sent you to the vallas, who told you that you had what the Coranians would call 'magic' inside you," Brychan went on. "Who warned you against turning away from it."

"The wyrd-galdra told you what you were," Arianllyn said. "But you would not listen."

"He has never listened," Sigerric whispered. "Never."

"But he was told," Brychan said, his voice implacable. "The day you came to Y Ty Dewin and saw Cynan Ardewin on the steps. He recognized you. You saw it in his eyes. So you killed him. But he whispered a word to you before he died, didn't he? He said, 'nephew.' But because you did not want to hear, you did not hear. Because you did not want to know, you did not know."

"Wasn't that the real reason you broke Anieron Master Bard's hands?" Arianllyn said, her voice soft but relentless. "You saw the truth in his eyes and had to ensure he could communicate to no one. And then there was the day you met Dinaswyn the Dreamer. She tried to tell you. But you killed her before she could speak. You would not hear, you would not listen."

"I am not listening now!" Havgan cried. "You left me all alone! And now look what has been done! Do you know whose child your daughter carries? She carries the child of her brother! She carries my child! You let this happen! I will not listen to you, for you left me!"

"Then there is nothing more to say to you, Havgan ap Brychan var Arianllyn," Brychan said, "except for this. We will continue to wait for you, as we have waited for so long. Know that if your soul is parted from your body this day, it will not go to Gwlad Yr Haf alone. We will stay, and wait for you, and never leave you alone again."

"Never again," Arianllyn said, tears in her voice. "And when the time comes to take your sister home, we will do it together. Neither of you will ever be alone again."

Arianllyn turned to Eiodel and reached out a hand to Arianrod, in farewell. Brychan also raised his hand in salute to his daughter. Then he and Arianllyn turned to go, riding up back into the darkening, violet sky to rejoin the Hunt.

Darkness spread in the west, rising up above the horizon, showing a strange, yellow twilight beneath. High above, the moon continued to move before the sun, cutting off the sunlight, casting its shadow below. The crescent sun turned silvery white in surrender, as though trying to emulate the moon.

Gwydion, tears streaming down his drawn face, stepped forward. He lifted his hands and called out, his voice strong and sure. "Today Arthur ap Uthyr var Ygraine, champion of Kymru, calls for single combat with Havgan ap Brychan var Arianllyn."

Havgan's amber eyes blazed at the name, but he did not challenge it. Nor did he turn to the battlements when Arianrod moaned in anguish. He did not take his amber gaze from Arthur, nor did Arthur take his gaze away from Havgan.

"Today," Gwydion went on, "the High King of Kymru will do

battle with the Golden Man. And from this battle the fate of Kymru will be decided. Step forward, then, champions, and do battle."

Arthur stepped forward with Caladfwlch in his hand, while Gwydion and Rhiannon stepped back. Havgan, his sword, Grum, in his hand, stepped forward, as Sigerric and Penda retreated. Havgan's golden sword with the ruby hilt glittered even as the sunlight died overhead. The torches sprang to life, lit by Druid's Fire, to illuminate the battle between the two men. They would fight with their swords only, no shields or other weapons.

Arthur raised Caldafwlch and the bluish torchlight ran greedily over the silver blade. Havgan raised golden Grum. The two swords clashed, the sound ringing over the land and up into the dark sky. Sparks flashed as the blades met.

The last fight for Kymru had begun.

Gwydion forced himself to stand still as the two men fought. A wind rose, keening in his ears like a lost soul. His heart ached and his mind whirled with the news that Havgan was to have been the Dreamer. What would Gwydion himself have done if he had been left alone in a strange land? Would he have done better than his cousin? He suddenly pitied Havgan with all his heart. Who could blame the Golden Man for the things he had done?

"He would not listen, Gwydion," Rhiannon said quietly.

She had known what he was thinking. She always did.

"But—"

"That was his choice. That was the choice he made from the beginning. That was the choice that brought him here."

"I know," Gwydion said sadly. "I know."

Havgan swung his sword with all the rage he had in his heart. Each time he did Caladfwlch met and absorbed the blow. But that would not last, Havgan thought. Arthur was just a boy. Havgan was a man, and Arthur would tire long before Havgan did.

Even as Havgan concentrated on the battle his mind was in turmoil. He should have been the Dreamer. Because he had been deserted, left alone, stranded in a strange country, Gwydion had taken his place. Gwydion, his heart's brother, was all that Havgan should have been. No wonder he had loved Gwydion. And no wonder the Dreamer's betrayal had cut him to the heart.

Quickly he glanced over at Gwydion. And for the first time he saw what few others had seen—that he and Gwydion looked enough alike to be twins. He had never seen it—few had. What had blinded him? What had blinded them all?

He gritted his teeth and swung Grum again and again. The reflection of blue-tinged Druid's Fire crawled greedily up the golden blade as he fought to keep Caladfwlch from coming too close, from drinking his blood.

As Arthur struck back again and again Havgan felt as though the boy was no longer holding a sword, but rather cruel fate itself fought against him. All his life fate had hammered at him, seeking to shape him, drive him, crush him. But he would not let it. He would make his own fate. He would fashion his own truth. He always had.

Overhead, the sun's light was completely blotted out by the moon. The only light coming from the sky was from the two Hunts, silver and gold, as they waited silently for the outcome of the combat below. The moon's shadow thickened; the torches around the perimeter of the battle flickered feebly against the darkness, whipped mercilessly by the moaning wind.

Yes, he had fashioned his own truth.

And it had been wrong.

The thought jarred him, but did not stop him from parrying Caldfwlch's relentless blows. He remembered the wyrd-galdra reading he had had—the same reading three times those years ago in Corania when he was planning to invade Kymru. He remembered the card for Holda of the Waters, symbol of hidden influences. He remembered the Hanged Man, Wuotan, god of Magic and Wisdom. He remembered the card for Fal, god of Light, the guide. That card had always stood for what he was most afraid of. And then there had been the card for Narve, god of Death. And that had stood for what he most longed for. It hadn't meant death, really. It had meant ultimate change, transformation, and renewal.

It had all been true. And that truth was what he had run from. Time and again.

Yes, he had run from the truth. He had run so long and so far it had brought him here, to the place that was his real home. But he had not come home the way he should have. He had come home with blood on his hands and rage in his heart. He had come to Kymru and found love—with his sister. What kind of child did she carry beneath her heart? What would come of a mating with a brother Dreamer and a sister Dewin?

He had brought death and tears to Kymru, to his home. He had killed Cynan, Anieron, and Dinaswyn because they had held the truth in their eyes. He had razed his home, striving for mastery over it rather than to live in it. So peace had been denied him.

They had sent messages to him from across the void that separated the living from the dead. They had tried to tell him, but he had not listened.

No, he had not listened. All his life he had refused to do so. And now his final choice was on him. He could continue not to listen, he could pretend not to know. Or he could change everything. It was late, indeed, to change.

But not too late—he was listening now. He had wanted to doubt Arthur's word—that Brychan and Arianllyn were his parents. But he had known—oh, he had known—from the moment he saw them who they were.

When he had looked into his father's keen, amber eyes he had known. When the wind had lifted his mother's tawny hair, he had known. He had known the full truth then from the singing in his blood, from the tingling in his bones, from the warmth in his lonely heart, that they had returned to him. At last.

The time for doubting his eyes, for turning away, was past.

He knew that it was time to pay the price for all the times he had not listened. And he was willing to pay it, if only it would grant him the peace that had always been denied him.

They said they would never leave him alone again. He wondered if they would keep their promise.

And knew it was time to find out.

Arthur raised Caldfwlch for another blow. The sword left a silvery afterimage as it raced through the darkened air, heading straight for Havgan's heart. It was at that moment that Grum should have met Caldfwlch, halting the sword's deadly path.

But Grum did not.

GWYDION SAW IT in Havgan's eyes, saw the decision made, saw what would happen far, far too late to change it. He cried out, even as Havgan dropped Grum, even as he deliberately took Caladfwlch's silvery blade into his heart.

Gwydion raced forward, catching Havgan, breaking his fall. He sat on the ground, cradling Havgan's golden head on his lap. He took off Havgan's helmet, flinging the golden boar's head as far away as he could.

Havgan's amber eyes looked up at Gwydion even as the Golden Man's blood raced from his body, soaking into the earth of Kymru, joining at last the land he had longed for all his life.

"They said they would not leave me alone," Havgan whispered. "Do you believe that? Do you believe they will come for me?"

"I do," Gwydion said steadily.

"In spite of all that I have done?"

"In spite of all that you have done."

A cry from the battlements sounded out over the dark plain as Arianrod threw her head back to the sky and screamed out her grief to the silent sky.

"Take care of her," Havgan rasped.

"She will be free to go where she will," Arthur promised as he knelt next to the dying man. "I swear it."

Overhead the west brightened while the east darkened as the moon fled from the sun. Beads of light began to form, even as the golden light from the Coranian Hunt began to fade. Valkyries and skeletal warriors paled and faded. But Wuotan and Holda did not. The God of Magic and the Lady of the Waters rode forward toward the Kymric hunt, meeting Cerrunnos and Cerridwen halfway across the sky. The four figures blurred and merged, until only two figures—Cerrunnos and Cerridwen—were left.

"They were one," Havgan gasped. "All the time."

"Yes," Arthur agreed. "It is all one. And always has been."

Brychan and Arianllyn once again detached themselves from the Hunt, riding away to the western horizon. There they stopped, even as Havgan's amber eyes widened, even as his breath ceased. Between them a third rider formed in a flash of gold and rubies. The third rider lifted his hand in farewell then turned to go. Then the three of them disappeared into the brightening west.

SIGERRIC RAISED THE battle horn to his lips even as Gwydion reached out and closed Havgan's eyes.

Penda grasped Sigerric's wrist. "What are you doing?" he cried.

"What I must do," Sigerric replied, tears streaming down his drawn face.

"Why bother?" Penda asked. "For what earthly reason should we battle now? Our Hunt is gone. Havgan is dead. Our only real course is to leave Kymru. Why fight now?"

Even as Sigerric hesitated Prince Aesc reached over and grabbed the horn. "Because we are warriors," Aesc growled. "That's why."

So Aesc sounded the horn.

And the last battle began.

Chapter Twenty-three

Gwytheryn, Kymru
Gwernan Mis, 500

Calan Llachar—midmorning

Achren fought steadily, killing Coranian after Coranian. She was not absolutely certain how long they had been fighting—she knew that in the heat of battle it was difficult to judge these things. But she had a great deal of experience, and, from the position of the now-visible sun, she guessed it had been only an hour or so since the battle was joined. Though why it had begun, when Havgan had lost the fight with Arthur, she had no idea. Prince Aesc had sounded the horn, the Coranian army had moved forward, and the battle had been joined.

Even in the confused heat of the melee, she knew exactly where the others were. Rhoram, of course, was right next to her. Her job was to protect him, and she would do it even if it killed her, which it most likely would. As with the rest of his teulu, he fought on horseback. The Coranians, as they always did, fought on foot. The advantage to the Kymri of being horsed was a small one, but they needed all the advantage they could get, she thought grimly. For they were badly outnumbered. She thought it likely that they would all be killed this day, and was merely determined to ensure she fell when Rhoram did—no sooner and no later.

Cian rode just behind Rhoram, ready to relay Arthur's telepathic orders. The once-captive Bard sat his horse calmly, as though he had been through far too much to let one battle frighten him. Achren supposed that this was true enough, for Cian had been through a great deal. He had been captured for the testing device he had carried, taken to Eiodel, and imprisoned with Anieron Master Bard. He had then been taken to Afalon and there he had endured day after day of torture. And though he had regained much of his strength his scanty hair was more gray than brown and his face was etched with lines of pain and endurance that no amount of ease could erase. But his green eyes were alert and alive.

"Arthur says we must ensure that not one single wyrce-jaga is left alive," Cian shouted to Achren.

She nodded. She saw her lieutenant, Aiden, and his new bride, Lluched, battling side by side just a few feet away. Aidan was smiling fondly at Lluched, who had just speared a Coranian through the neck. Lluched, her eyes sparkling, was momentarily vulnerable as she tugged at the spear to loosen it from the soldier's dying body. She nodded her thanks to Aidan as he deflected a blow until she could pull the spear free. Aidan snatched a kiss from her, then turned to sink his sword into another attacker.

"Aidan!" Achren called. "All wyrce-jaga must be killed. They are massed before the gates of Eiodel!"

Aidan nodded and motioned for Lluched and a group of warriors to follow him. Achren motioned a contingent of warriors behind her to fill in the line where Aidan had been.

Grimly, Achren fought on. She saw Geriant a few feet ahead of her battling like a madman. Princess Enid's token, tied to his left arm, was no more than a bloodstained rag. Geriant killed the enemy with a single-minded determination that told Achren he was not really fighting Coranians as much as he was fighting his own private battle—or, rather, Enid's battle.

Rhoram saw Geriant, too, and reined in his horse. He dropped back a little, then rode behind Achren and up to his son. He reached out and placed his hand on Geriant's arm. Geriant whipped around with his sword, almost slicing off his father's hand.

"Da!" he gasped. "Don't sneak up on me like that!"

"Sneak up on you?" Rhoram demanded. "Just how would I do that?"

"You know what I mean."

"I do. And when I tell you to ease down, you know what I mean."

Geriant opened his mouth, but thought better of it.

"Wise, my son. Very wise."

Rhoram would have lost his life at that moment if Achren hadn't been at his back. The Coranian axe swung through the air with a vicious shriek, but was stopped just inches from Rhoram's neck by Achren's blade. The weapons rang out as they connected so hard the Coranian lost his balance and fell to one knee. Achren's knife hissed through the air, burying itself in the man's neck. He went down in a welter of blood. Achren leaned down as he fell, and pulled her knife from his neck.

"Get back to work!" she shouted at Rhoram. "You, too, Geriant. This is no time for idle talk."

Before they could answer her, if they even intended to, she saw an axe fly through the air and bury itself in the chest of Cadell, Rhoram's Dewin. The Dewin fell off his horse, astonishment written on his face. He raised a hand to Rhoram as he fell. But he was dead before he hit the ground.

While above them, the Wild Hunt hovered silently in the sky.

Fear lodged in Cai's throat, filling his mouth with a heavy, coppery taste. His heart beat so fiercely he thought it might fly out of his chest. Sweat beaded his brow and threatened to cloud his vision.

But his hand did not shake as he deflected blow after blow, as he shadowed Queen Morrigan, as he ensured that he kept the glint of Susanna's red-gold hair in his sight.

He was charged with the safety of his queen and of his wife, and he would keep them alive. This time it would be different. This time those that he loved best would not be taken from him. It would not be—it could not be—as it had been in Tegeingl three years ago. It would not—it could not—happen again.

That was the fear that drove him even as he cursed himself and called himself a coward. Because though he was afraid for the lives of these two women, he was more afraid for himself. He was afraid that he would be required to bear the pain again, the kind of pain he experienced the day his first wife and his beloved son had been killed. He had seen it happen. And he had killed the Coranian soldier who had done it. But that had changed nothing. A few days later he had been forced to abandon his king, and Uthyr had died in a battle Cai had not been allowed to be in. Instead, he had still been forced to go on alone, to keep living, to fulfill his destiny as the captain of Gwynedd, to keep his promise to Uthyr.

His wife, his son, his ruler, these had been taken from him before. Had he known whom to beg, he would have begged that it not happen to him again.

For Susanna was now his wife. And her son, Gwyhar, who he had come to love, was also in this battle, fighting in the way of the Y Dawnus with Arthur. And his ruler was now Morrigan, by whose side he fought.

Oh, how easily it could all be taken away from him again.

And it likely would be, for he knew—they all knew—how badly they were outnumbered. Arthur himself had known it before this battle, but had chosen to fight anyway. If the High King had a plan to win this battle, Cai hoped he would unveil it soon. Before it was too late.

A cry of anguish and horror pierced his brain. A woman's frenzied scream pierced his heart. Frantically he looked around and found the source. He saw his nephew, Bedwyr, fall from his horse, his right hand attempting to staunch the blood spurting from the place where his left arm had once been. Bedwyr's young wife, Tangwen, vaulted off her horse, her scream still echoing across the battlefield, and caught her husband as he fell.

Morrigan and Cai, with Susanna following, flew off their horses to ring Bedwyr, protecting him as Neuad, Morrigan's Dewin, laid her hands on the socket where his arm had been, trying to staunch the bleeding. She closed her eyes and Life-Read, while the rest of them held their breath. At last she opened her eyes and spoke to Tangwen.

"I have done what I can to halt the blood loss," she said quietly. "If we can get him to the Dewin with Arthur he may live."

"Then take him," Morrigan said. "Neuad, take two warriors

and go with him. Come back as soon as you can."

Tangwen reluctantly released her hold on her husband as two warriors picked him up. She started to follow them but Morrigan put a hand on her arm and pulled her back.

"Not you," Morrigan said harshly. "We can't spare you."

Tangwen narrowed her eyes and opened her mouth to reply. But she did not. Instead, she nodded to Morrigan, then mounted her horse. Her blue eyes were cold and hard as sapphires, and murder was written on her beautiful face as she focused her gaze on the advancing Coranian warriors.

For Morrigan was right. They needed every warrior they had. And then some. For the Kymric army, valiantly as it fought, was losing. Slowly, inexorably, they were being pushed back. Soon the lines would break and be overrun. Very soon.

He only hoped he would not live long enough to see everyone else die.

While above them, the Wild Hunt hovered silently in the sky.

TRYSTAN'S SWORD HISSED through the air and buried itself in the neck of the advancing Coranian warrior. He jerked the blade out of the dying warrior's body and turned his horse swiftly to kill another advancing Coranian. There were so many to choose from—too many of them, far too many.

He was too far away from the Y Dawnus clustered behind the High King to know if they were still safe, but he thought his heart would know if Sabrina had fallen. He wished he could have fought near her, but his duty, as captain of Rheged, was clear.

He kept Owein in his sight even as the battle raged all around him. He would never allow himself to get too far from his king. Owein's golden horse gleamed under the brightened sky, and the opals on his golden helmet flashed as he lifted his spear time and again and spitted warrior after warrior. Owein's young wife, Sanon, fought tirelessly beside her husband, though her shining blond hair was muted now with beads of enemy blood.

The two of them were a formidable couple indeed, Trystan thought. And winced as he was reminded of another formidable couple he had known—King Urien and his wife, Queen Ellirri. These two had fought together in the last battle of Llwynarth, and had died beneath the axes of the Coranians. He put that thought from his mind as swiftly as he could and killed yet another warrior.

"Trystan!"

He turned his horse, for he knew that voice as he knew the beat of his own heart. Esyllt, Owein's Bard, stared up at him, her beautiful face pale with fear.

"What?" he asked impatiently, when she did not immediately speak.

"Arthur says to have the eastern flank fall back. He wants to open a gap between Owein's and Elen's forces. Then have the two armies close the gap and kill those caught inside. He says there will be wolves and wild horses to help."

Trystan nodded and motioned for his lieutenant, Teleri, and her husband, Gwarae. He directed them to carry out Arthur's orders and they spurred their horses east. Esyllt grabbed Trystan's stirrup before he could turn his horse away.

"Oh, Trystan, I'm afraid," she said.

Trystan rolled his eyes. Had he really ever thought her charming? "You can't possibly be serious."

"I—"

"Does this look like the time or place for that?" he shouted. "Does it?"

And it was in that moment that he heard the deadly whistle of an axe behind him. It was in that moment that he knew his life was over.

But the blow never came. Instead, even as he turned to face his death, he heard the clang of a sword grinding against the axe. And was astonished to see that the hand holding that sword belonged to March, Esyllt's husband.

Trystan stabbed the axe-wielder in the neck, and the man went down. Then he looked back at March. "You saved my life."

"As you once saved mine," March answered.

"I saved your life before because I had wronged you. Wronged you for years. You had no reason to save mine."

"Ah, what does that matter any more?" March asked. "Besides, today is Calan Llachar, and I am finally free. My marriage is officially dissolved today."

"So it is," Trystan brightened. "I had forgotten today was the day."

"Well," March said judiciously, "we've had a few other things on our minds."

A howl of grief from the west made Trystan and March whirl around. Trystan saw that the banner of Hetwin Silver-Brow, the Lord of Gwinionydd, had fallen. Briefly he closed his eyes in anguish. Hetwin had been a good man, and a good friend to the royal house of Rheged. It was Hetwin who had taken Owein in after the last battle of Llwynarth. Hetwin who had been one of the strongest of the Cerddorian, loyal and steadfast. Hetwin was the father of Neuad, Queen Morrigan's Dewin, and Cynedyr the Wild, one of Trystan's dearest friends.

The cry had come from Cynedyr, who had been chosen to guard the Y Dawnus from attack. Cynedyr had seen the banner fall, and he sat on his horse near High King Arthur, his arms outstretched to the place where the banner was now trampled to the ground, grief etched on his face.

Trystan and March spurred their horses to the place they saw Hetwin's banner fall. Hetwin was lying on the ground, a Coranian axe in his belly. The old warrior's dark eyes were open as he gazed up at the Hunt-filled sky. His breathing was shallow and his face lined with pain. Trystan and March flung themselves on the ground next to the dying man. Trystan took one of Hetwin's huge, battle-scarred hands in his own.

"Trystan, boyo," Hetwin gasped. "You should not be here."

"Where then?" Trystan asked steadily.

"Fighting. You waste your time here."

"My time is mine to waste."

"No. It is Arthur's." Hetwin closed his eyes briefly, then opened them again, trying to focus on Trystan.

"Cynedyr will be here in a moment, Hetwin," Trystan said.

"He had best not," Hetwin whispered, "or I will tan his hide."

"Hetwin—"

"I am done for. Cynedyr must stay with the Y Dawnus. He must. If the Coranians break through that line we are lost."

"They won't," Trystan said steadily.

But Trystan was wrong, and he knew it. It was true that Cynedyr would not abandon his post, for he was honor bound to guard the Y Dawnus. But all was indeed lost. For it was then that the Coranians broke through Cynedyr's men.

While above them, the Wild Hunt hovered silently in the sky.

Angharad battled steadily, ferociously, savoring the death of every Coranian that crossed her relentless path. With every sword-stroke, with every spear-cast, her rage grew; it did not lessen.

Emrys, she thought, would have pulled her back if he had been alive. Emrys would have recognized the battle rage and would have spoken to her, would have calmed her. For in her rage she was vulnerable to mistakes, and she knew it. Emrys would have seen it and would have done something about it.

But Emrys, her lieutenant, was dead. The Coranians had killed him the day the Kymri had retaken Dinmael. Emrys had loved her for all those years, never speaking of it, for he had known it was hopeless. Dear, faithful, patient, Emrys. Gone.

And though she had not loved him his death had shattered her. For it was almost as though Amatheon was dying again. She had loved Amatheon, Gywdion's younger brother, and if he had lived she would have been happy with him. Though it had been almost six years since Amatheon's death on Afalon, for her it was as though it had happened yesterday. She would grieve for him, she thought, forever and ever.

"Angharad!"

She whirled to face Talhearn, Queen Elen's Bard. "What?" she demanded fiercely.

"The Coranians have broken through to the Y Dawnus! Arthur says to take a contingent and move northwest. Cai will lead a contingent northeast and meet you. You must strengthen Cynedyr's line. It is falling!"

At that moment Queen Elen rode up. Her silvery helmet was streaked with Coranian blood, but she herself was unharmed. Prince Rhiwallon was at her side, his young face grim.

"Elen—" Angharad began.

"It's all right, Angharad," Elen said, her voice cool. "Go."

"But—"

"When I fall, I will not fall alone," Elen went on. "Rhiwallon is with me."

"And I," Prince Lludd said as he rode up, "am with her also. Go, Angharad. Elen will not fall alone."

There was no more to be said, and Angharad knew it. For though Elen's words were cold Angharad saw the grief in the young queen's eyes. Grief that Angharad knew could be seen in her own eyes. For it was ending. It was all ending and Kymru was lost.

But not, Angharad promised herself, without costing the Coranians dearly.

So she saluted Elen and turned to go. And that was when she saw an enemy warrior she recognized. He wore a helmet of silver, shaped like a boar's head with garnet eyes and silver tusks. She had seen him standing with Havgan before the battle. And she knew who he was by reputation. With a cry she launched herself from her horse and raced to confront him. The warrior turned to face her, his axe raised.

They should have fought, then. They should have fought to the death.

But they did not.

Instead they faced each other, unmoving. Penda's dark blond hair was soaked with sweat. His brown eyes were fierce, yet she saw something in them that stayed her hand. She wasn't certain what. Some knowledge, perhaps, written on her soul long ago, whispered to her. He could have killed her then, for she found herself unable to raise her sword.

But he did not. For he, too, seemed rooted to the spot. He looked into her green eyes and saw something there. But what it was, she did not know. She did not think he knew either. Perhaps Penda's soul whispered something to him, too.

It would be many years before she fully understood why she at last turned away. And why he did the same.

While above them, the Wild Hunt hovered silently in the sky.

GWYDION STOOD IN front of Arthur, a spear in his hands, warily watching the Coranians move closer. Rhiannon stood next to Gwydion, holding her bow, an arrow ready to fly into the Coranian army that slowly closed in on them. Between them Cabal, Arthur's hound, bristled and growled as the army moved closer.

Ygraine stood behind Gwydion, next to Arthur. The former Queen of Gwynedd held a sword in her hands, her dark eyes fierce. Gwen stood on Arthur's other side, a spear clutched in her hands. Her young face was hard and her jaw clenched. Though both women held their ground bravely, Gwydion could see the knowledge in their eyes as the enemy army began to break through the lines.

Arthur himself stood unmoving, his eyes open but not blinking. He held the hilt of Caladfwlch before him, his hands resting on the pommel, the tip of the sword resting on the breast of Kymru. The folds of his silvery cloak barely moved as he breathed, for he was in a trance, drawing on the power of the Y Dawnus: seeing the battle from hundreds of Dewin eyes; speaking to the commanders through their Bards; enabling the Druids to fling boulders and fire into the enemy ranks; persuading the wolves, the ravens, even wild horses to battle the enemy.

Cariadas stood behind Arthur, her cloak of raven feathers clinging to her like a shadow. Her eyes were closed as she desperately tried to make contact with the Wild Hunt, trying to get them to answer her, trying to understand why they did not join in the battle. Trying to determine what—or who—they were waiting for.

Rhufon and his son, Tybion, stood on either side of Cariadas, swords in their hands, calmly watching the enemy near. They would stand, Gwydion knew, until they were killed. They would never run.

None of them would run. But that would probably not matter.

He turned to Rhiannon, for he wanted to see her before the end. She turned to him at the same moment and smiled.

He smiled back, for the love in her emerald eyes, for the heart's-home he saw in them. To find love at last, after all this time, was surely the greatest gift he had ever been given. He remembered the dream—oh, so many years ago—when Cerridwen had told him that someday he would find someone to whom he could open his heart. She had told him that he would win by losing. And he had. He had lost his detachment, lost his barriers, lost his heart to her. And in so doing had won indeed.

Only to lose it all now.

Gwydion heard the snarling of wolves, the fierce screams of wild horses, and the cries of the ravens as these animals did Arthur's bidding and attacked the oncoming horde. But it was not enough. The lines were breaking.

While above them, the Wild Hunt hovered silently in the sky.

ELSTAR ARDEWIN WAS surprised to feel a burning in her side. She looked down, astonished to see a spear jutting out from her stomach. How ridiculous she thought, even as she fell, even as the blood spilled down her silver robe. She had a confused thought that she hoped her blood would not stain her swan feather cloak. The cloak would belong to Llywelyn next and she didn't want to see it damaged.

She was Dewin, and so automatically did a Life-Reading on herself. The spear had pierced her stomach, its point thrusting all the way through to her spine. It was hopeless.

She had never thought she would die now. And she couldn't. She really couldn't. For Llywelyn simply was not ready to lead the Dewin. He was far too young, only nineteen. And her youngest, Cynfar, still needed her for all that he thought he was a man at seventeen.

Her husband, now—well, she knew that he didn't really need her. All these years with Elidyr had been happy enough as long as she pretended not to know that he had been in love with Rhiannon ur Heyvedd all his life.

But she did know. She had always known. And was surprised that even now, even at the last, the knowledge still had the power to hurt her.

While far above her dying body the Wild Hunt hovered silently in the sky.

Gwen heard a hoarse cry and whirled to find the source. Elidyr Master Bard was running toward Elstar's dying body, his face stricken, his eyes full of anguish and the first, hot rush of grief.

She saw that he was aware of nothing else as he flung himself on the ground and took his dying wife in his arms. Fool, she thought to herself, even as tears gathered in her throat, he'll get himself killed. And though she had vowed to stay with Arthur, she knew that Elidyr's need was greater.

And so when the Coranian warrior broke through Cynedyr's lines and raised his axe to plunge it into Elidyr's back, Gwen was there. Using her hard-won druidic skills, she paralyzed the man's muscles just long enough to bury her dagger into the warrior's throat.

She grabbed Elidyr's arm, shaking him. "Get up!" she screamed. "Unless you want to die!"

Elidyr lifted his tear-stained face. "It was too late," he whispered. "She couldn't hear me."

"Whatever you wanted to tell her will wait, then!"

"Too late," he went on as though she had not spoken, rocking back and forth on his heels. "Too late. I wanted her to know. I wanted her to know that I truly did love her. Only I didn't know myself. Not until now."

Gwen rolled her eyes. It seemed to her that people were always doing that—not finding out things like that until too late. Fools.

And then she saw just how close the Coranians were to winning. And she saw how the Y Dawnus were starting to die. And she saw how near the enemy was to Arthur. And she realized that she, too, had found something out too late. And realized that there was something she should have said to Arthur before this battle began.

But it was too late now. They were all going to die.

And still, the Hunt did not move.

Sinend, heir to the Archdruid of Kymru, shook free of her trance to find that they were surrounded. Cynedyr's men were fighting fiercely, but they were losing this battle. She saw Angharad descend on the enemy with a contingent of Ederynions. And she saw Cai ride up with a contingent of warriors from Gwynedd. But she knew it was too late. Spears rained down upon the Y Dawnus. They were vulnerable, for they were locked in a trance as Arthur used their powers. Arthur must loosen them, or they would die without even having the chance to defend themselves. She took a few running steps toward Arthur, but stopped in her tracks as she saw an axe fly end over end through the air and bury itself in her father's chest.

Aergol sank to his knees, his dark eyes filled with pain. Sinend and her brother, Menw, caught him as he fell.

"Da," Sinend murmured. "Oh, Da."

Aergol's dark eyes glistened as he looked up at his children. "My very dears," he said, as he tried to smile. "Do not grieve for me. The goddess at last calls me home."

"Modron did not keep you the first time," Menw said hopefully. "Maybe she will send you back again."

"Not this time, my son," Aergol said.

And then his spirit fled his body. And he was gone.

As the lines broke, Talorcan, by sheer force of will, shook himself free of Arthur's mind.

For he was a warrior, first and foremost. True, he was learning the ways of the Dewin and he had come to terms with the truth of who he was. He had accepted that he would never return to Corania, never again see his mother, his father, his brother.

But he was a warrior, and those instincts did not—could not—die.

He saw the Coranian that stood before him lift the axe high. But the man hesitated for one brief moment as recognition flickered in his blue eyes. And that was all the time Talorcan needed.

He slammed into the warrior's chest and the man dropped his axe as they went down. But Talorcan, knowing that would happen, had already reached out and caught the weapon before it reached the ground. With one fluid moment he brought the axe down, burying it in the man's chest.

He rose to his feet and looked around. He saw that Aergol was down with his children around him. He saw Elidyr kneeling beside the body of his dead wife with Gwen standing over him. He saw Cai and his warriors, and Angharad and her warriors fly to the aid of Cynedyr's men. And he saw that they were surrounded.

And then he saw an axe fly through the air, end over end, aimed toward the man next to him. Quicker than thought he brought his own axe up and deflected the weapon. He reached down and picked it up, handing it to the man whose life he had saved.

"Thank you, boyo," Myrrdin said genially, taking the axe. "But I'm not sure this will do much good. I haven't had any experience with a weapon like this."

"Not to worry, Myrrdin," Talorcan said. "I have enough experience for the both of us."

"Yes, but Regan will have my hide if anything happens to you."

"And Neuad mine, if anything happens to you."

But Myrrdin's keen gaze pierced Talorcan as he went on quietly. "Can you kill them? These men?"

"I have to," Talorcan said fiercely. "I am Arthur's man now. Do you doubt it?"

"Never," Myrrdin said as Talorcan drove his axe into the chest of another advancing warrior.

While the Wild Hunt hovered in the sky.

GWYDION SHOOK ARTHUR's arm, jolting him awake even as Arthur's spirit returned to his body. "Arthur, you must release the Y Dawnus! The lines have been breached and they can't defend themselves."

"I know, uncle," Arthur said. "We are losing."

"They are too many! And the Hunt just sits there!"

"Why?" Arthur called up to them, desperation in his voice. "Why do you not aid us!"

The fierce cry of an eagle rang out. Arderydd, the high eagle, soared through the Hunt then plunged down toward earth, coming to rest on Arthur's shoulder. The eagle cried out again, and the horns of the Hunt rang out in answer.

But still they did not move.

Gwydion wanted to howl in frustration. Raising his fists to the sky he called out, "Why! High Kings of Kymru, why do you not come to our aid? Cerridwen and Cerrunnos, Protectors of Kymru, why do you not help us? Why?"

"We await our warleader," High King Idris answered at last.

"Without him we cannot fight," High King Macsen said.

"It is forbidden," High King Lleu called out, "to join battle without him."

"Who?" Arthur cried. "Who is he?"

Gwydion shook his head. "I do not know."

"Nothing from your dream?" Arthur asked.

Gwydion shook his head. "The last part of the dream I had that day ended with a black raven calling out to the Hunt. But the Hunt did not move."

"What did you say?" Cariadas demanded, her hand clutching his arm. "A black raven?"

"Yes. A black raven. Symbol for the Dreamer."

"But at the end of my dream it wasn't a black raven."

Gwydion, hope dawning in his face, clutched his daughter's shoulder. "What was it?" he asked eagerly.

"It was a raven. But a raven of gold."

"Oh, gods," Gwydion breathed. "Oh."

"Havgan should have been, would have been, the Dreamer," Rhiannon said quietly.

"The Golden Man," Cariadas whispered. "Of course."

Arthur threw his head back and called out, his voice suddenly huge and powerful, like the rushing of the wind across a storm-swept sky. "Havgan ap Brychan var Arianllyn! I bid you to return!"

In a flash of gold and red a figure materialized before Arthur. Havgan rode a golden horse. On his head he wore a helmet fashioned like that of a raven with ruby eyes. His cloak of gold rippled back from his powerful shoulders and his tunic and breeches were ruby red as he proudly faced Arthur. "You have called me, High

King, and I have come. What do you want of me?"

"For you to lead the Hunt. For you to drive the Coranians from our land, from the land that we both love."

"The Hunt," Gwydion said, "will not ride without you, cousin."

"It is part of the debt I must pay to Kymru. I harmed her and her people. Now, until I am released, I must lead the Hunt into battle. It is a debt I am proud to pay."

"Then begin, my blood brother," Gwydion said.

"But how? I brought the Coranians here. Though I am now ashamed of that, I cannot kill them. They are not here through their own fault, but through mine."

"Then drive them, Havgan of Kymru," Arthur said. "Drive them to sea. And see to it that they never return."

Havgan grinned. "I will, my King." He turned to Gwydion. "Blood brother, I am glad to see you still live."

Gwydion grinned back, though there were tears in his silvery eyes. "And you, Havgan."

"After a fashion. Take care of him, Rhiannon," Havgan went on, turning toward her. "For he is a fool."

"Sometimes," she said, holding Gwydion's hand in hers, "we all are."

"Indeed. Farewell." Havgan spurred his horse and the stead took to the sky, coming to a halt before the Hunt. Cerridwen and Cerrunnos each took their places on either side of Havgan. The three High Kings arrayed themselves behind, with the host streaming out behind them.

And then the Hunt, at last, descended.

ARTHUR NEARED THE closed gates of Eiodel. The bodies of black-robed wyrce-jaga littered the ground before the gates. Aidan and Lluched had done their work well—not one single wyrce-jaga had escaped death that day.

A man sat cross-legged before the gate. His head was bowed and he idly played the harp he held in his hands. He raised his head as Arthur neared, and his keen, green eyes brightened. Arthur reached out a hand and helped the man to his feet.

"Dudod," Arthur said.

"You know why I am here."

"Yes. And you are welcome."

The dark fortress brooded silently, making no protest when Arthur, with a gesture, Shape-Moved the gates, forcing them to open.

He entered the fortress, followed closely by Gwydion, Rhiannon, and, oddly, Tybion. He had said nothing as Arthur had left the silent battlefield to make his way to Eiodel; he had merely followed. Arthur was uncertain where Rhufon was, but he imagined the Steward would be along shortly.

The courtyard was filled with Lytir's preosts, but they stood silently, unarmed and uncertain. At their head stood Eadwig, the Arch-Preost. On either side of him stood Aelfwyn and Arianrod. Arianrod's face was stricken, and marked with tears. But Aelfwyn's face was cold and she held her head proudly.

"I beg for the safety of these women, High King of Kymru," Eadwig said.

"There is no need to beg," Arthur answered. "And that you should know."

Eadwig shrugged. "Perhaps I do. But it had to be said. You may kill me now."

"What for?" Arthur asked.

"For the part I have played in the subjugation of your people."

"I do not pretend to know you, Eadwig," Arthur said quietly. "But I do know of you. You believe in your God with what is a pure heart. That is something for which no man should be punished. Go, return to Corania. But I need your word that you will never return."

"Who would ever want to?"

Arthur turned to the sound of the voice that had asked that question. Penda and Sigerric had limped through the gates together. They were both wounded, how badly Arthur could not tell. Blood streaked their clothes and ran down their faces.

"Who would ever want to indeed, Penda of Lindisfarne," Arthur replied.

Sigerric drew in a breath as he saw Aelfwyn. He raised his sword and staggered to stand between the Princess and Arthur. "If you so much as touch her I will kill you," Sigerric hissed.

And though Sigerric's defiance in the face of such odds should have elicited laughter, it did not. For it was too bravely done for that. Keeping any hint of a smile from his face Arthur answered, "Your warning is well taken, Sigerric. Be assured I mean your lady no harm."

"She is not my lady," Sigerric muttered.

Aelfwyn reached out and took Sigerric's elbow, helping to steady him. "I wouldn't be too sure of that," she said.

Arthur, recognizing the sword in Sigerric's hands, nodded to the blade. "I will allow you to take the Bana's sword back with you to your Empire. And I will allow your preosts, as well as Eadwig and Penda, to go with you. Any warriors still left alive are being chased to the sea by our Wild Hunt, led, as I believe you saw, by Havgan himself."

"I saw," Sigerric rasped. "And he saw me. He smiled at me, and rode on."

"Sparing you the terror your fellow warriors are experiencing now in their race to the sea," Arthur said. He turned to the Princess. "You, Princess Aelfwyn, will ensure that they board the ships they brought with them and leave our land. And you will ensure that they never return."

"I will," Aelfwyn nodded. "And gladly."

"Your uncle, Prince Aesc, has been killed," Arthur went on.

Aelfwyn closed her eyes for a moment, and nodded. "I saw him fall."

"He fought bravely," Arthur said.

"And Arianrod?" Aelfwyn asked, her eyes glinting. "You did not mention her as one you will let go."

"No. I did not." Arthur turned to Arianrod. Her tawny hair was snarled and her gown was torn, marks of her grief at Havgan's fall, at the horrifying truth that he was her brother. Her amber eyes were hopeless and stunned and she stood silently, as though not even aware of her surroundings. Arthur turned to Gwydion.

"Uncle?"

Gwydion shook his head. "I do not know. I fear for the child she carries. It is a child of the mating of a brother and sister, and I do not know what that could mean."

"You made a promise, Arthur," Rhiannon suddenly said.

"I know."

"A promise to Havgan as he lay dying," Rhiannon pressed. "You said she would be free to go where she will."

"I recall that, Rhiannon," Arthur said irritably.

"Then you must keep it."

Arthur sighed. "Arianrod," he said gently.

She looked up at him, her eyes glazed and unfocused.

"Arianrod, where do you wish to go? Do you wish to go to Corania? Or to stay with us here in Kymru?"

"Corania," she said swiftly, her eyes suddenly keen. "I can't stay here. I can't."

"Then you will not. Aelfwyn, I charge you to take Arianrod with you. To care for her and for her child."

"I am not bound by any promise you made to my husband," Aelfwyn said coldly.

"I will be bound, then," Sigerric said. "For the sake of my dead friend."

"Very well. Take her, then, and see that no harm comes to her. And watch that child carefully." Arthur turned to Tybion, who had been standing silently at Arthur's elbow. "Tell Rhufon to arrange an escort for them to Ystrad Marchell."

"My father, I regret to say, is dead," Tybion said quietly. "I am the Steward of Cadair Idris now."

Arthur gripped Tybion's arm. "I am sorry."

"Thank you, High King," Tybion said with great dignity, though his eyes were sad. "Be assured that your orders will be carried out."

"I am, Tybion." He turned to Rhiannon. "Would you call for Sinend and Cariadas?" he asked. "I need them."

"It is time, Arthur," Dudod said firmly. "I will wait no longer to bring my brother's bones out of darkness."

"It is indeed time and past time for that," Arthur agreed.

"I will take you," Penda said. The yellow-clad ranks of the preosts parted silently to let them through. Arthur, Gwydion, and Dudod followed Penda down the dark, dank steps into the dungeons of Eiodel. The cells smelled of fear and old blood. The straw under their feet was musty. Torches flickered feebly against a darkness that seemed to be filled with tears and terror, with hopelessness and helplessness, with the acrid scent of death and terror.

Dudod, his face drawn, had tears in his eyes as Penda halted before Anieron's old cell. A skeleton lay there in the straw, the bones gleaming whitely through the rags that once clothed it. A harp lay next to the bones, glittering with sapphires. The carved face of a woman looked out from the wood, smiling gently as though in greeting.

Arthur took off his cloak and laid it on the straw as rats scurried away. Gently, reverently, Gwydion and Arthur picked up the skeleton and deposited it on the cloak, wrapping it securely. Dudod clutched Anieron's harp, tears streaming down his weathered face. He strummed the harp and the notes sounded out purely, joyfully, and oh, so tenderly.

"I came for you, brother," Dudod whispered. "At last."

And it seemed to them all that there was a sigh, from somewhere, the kind of sigh a man might give when he reached his home after a long journey, the kind of sigh a man might give when he felt the presence of those he loved, the kind of sigh a man might give when he was allowed to rest. And the words echoed in their minds.

At last.

SINEND AND CARIADAS, as well as Gwen, were there as they came up from the dungeon. Though Arthur had not called her, he was glad to see Rhiannon's daughter. Gladder than he wanted to admit. Her eyes challenged him to send her away, but he would not have even dreamed of it. Instead, he smiled at her in welcome. And she smiled back.

The new Archdruid of Kymru was pale but composed as she bowed. "The Druids are yours to command, High King," Sinend said formally.

"Tear it down," Arthur said firmly. "Tear Eiodel down, stone by stone. And use the stones to build a cairn for Havgan. Lay him here in the courtyard and then bring it all down. Leave no stone standing."

"It will be done, High King."

Cariadas asked, "What is your will, High King?"

"You must come with me to Cadair Idris. We release the spirit of Bloudewedd from the Doors before the sun sets on this day."

"Who will take her place?" Cariadas asked.

He glanced at Rhiannon. Her emerald eyes sparkled and she smiled to herself at the Dreamer's question.

"Oh, I have someone in mind," he said.

Chapter Twenty-four

Cadair Idris, Gwytheryn, Kymru
Draenenwen Mis, 500

Alban Haf—midmorning

The only thing that felt at all natural was the torque around his neck. Since the first moment he had donned it, almost six months ago, it had felt right. The large emerald, sapphire, opal, and pearl rested comfortably against his throat. The figure eight studded with onyx, symbol of Annwyn Lord of Chaos, felt cold, as it always did. He wondered if there would be a time when it would not. He doubted it—the Lord of Chaos was not, and never would be, a comfortable deity.

But a necessary one, he understood now. For chaos was as much a natural part of the Wheel as order was, for one could not exist without the other. He had been born, chosen, for such a time as this, to live through the chaos of war and to bring his country safely through it. He had done so, with the invaluable help of others, and he would not forget how closely they had come to total destruction. Yet, in the end, they had been victorious.

The final battle was over, done and finished almost five weeks ago. But Cadair Idris and its environs remained full to bursting. Thousands of Kymric warriors were still camped on the plains of Gwytheryn, most of them still recovering from wounds sustained in the fight. Soon they would begin their journey home.

The Dewin had worked long and hard to save as many men and women as possible. And they had done well. Yes, there had been those they could not save—Hetwin Silver-Brow; Cadell,

King Rhoram's Dewin; Elstar Ardewin; Aergol Archdruid. But many others had been saved—all of the rulers, their captains, and their lieutenants were still among the living, though all had been injured to a degree. Even Bedwyr would live, though he had no will to do so with only one arm. Still, he was alive. And so many others weren't.

"If you could lift your foot, my lord," Tybion was saying.

"I can very well put on breeches without anyone's help," Arthur said, unable to keep the testiness out of his voice.

"I am sure you could, my King," Tybion said coolly, "if only you were paying attention. I have been standing here holding these breeches for some time."

"Oh. Sorry," he muttered as he took the breeches and put them on. Normally he was more than content to dress himself, but today was a special ceremony, necessitating, if he understood correctly, a great deal of fuss and preparation.

After the ceremony in Brenin Llys, the High King's Hall, they would retire to the huge grove in Coed Llachar to celebrate Alban Haf, the summer solstice, by the light of the full moon.

It was to be the first festival in many years that the Kymri could celebrate in complete freedom and the first festival in hundreds of years that would be attended by a High King. Apparently, that meant a certain amount of opulence was necessary. He was required to wear breeches and a tunic of silver and gold, and his brow was bound with a band of twined gold and silver. The tunic was emblazoned with a golden eagle with eyes and beak of shining silver. His cloak was gold trimmed with silver bands and attached to his shoulders with brooches fashioned like eagles' heads. He sported rings of emerald, sapphire, opal, and pearl. Frankly, he felt like a fool.

How strange, Arthur thought, continuing with his interrupted musings, that it had been Havgan who had attempted to destroy them all, and yet it had been Havgan who held the key to their salvation. Havgan had led the Wild Hunt against the enemy and driven them to the sea. The Coranians had embarked on their ships without a murmur, glad to leave Kymru behind. Aelfwyn's pledge to keep the Coranians from returning would be enough. As future Empress, she would ensure that her word was kept. It was obvious to him that it would take a very brave man to disobey her.

It still made him uneasy that the Coranians had taken Arianrod and her unborn child with them. But he had promised Havgan, as Rhiannon had so insistently reminded him. And there was nothing to be done about it now.

As Tybion helped him put on his gold-lined boots, Arthur glanced around the huge room. The High King's chambers were opulent, opulent enough to make Arthur wonder if Idris, Macsen, and Lleu had ever been truly comfortable here. The bed was large, surely the largest one he had ever seen, with a gilt headboard. The coverlet and hangings glittered silver and gold in the light of the roaring fire in the huge fireplace. Hangings covered the walls. Spun by the woolworkers of Gwynedd, they depicted Cadair Idris in various seasons—surrounded by the first flowers of spring, by heavily laden fruit trees in summer, by blowing leaves of gold and red in autumn, and by bright snow in winter.

Massive wardrobes covered one entire wall, making Arthur wonder who would ever have enough possessions to fill them. He sighed, for he supposed that one day he would. And would, no doubt, have to wear them all in ceremony after endless ceremony.

Tybion glanced up at Arthur as he finished putting on the boots. "My lord?" he asked, at Arthur's sigh.

"Nothing," he muttered.

But Tybion smiled unexpectedly. "It is a bit much, isn't it?"

Arthur, startled to see sympathy in his Steward's eyes, grinned. "Frankly, I don't know if I'll ever get used to it."

"Perhaps not," Tybion conceded.

"It's just so huge. Almost half of one entire level."

"There is the round table in the center, where the rooms connect" Tybion pointed out. "It takes up a great deal of room. You could easily get all the rulers, their captains, your Great Ones, and their heirs around it at once."

"And isn't that a fun thought?" Arthur murmured.

"And then the rest of the level is made up of the High Queen's apartments."

For some reason, Arthur blushed. He didn't even want to determine why.

"Which are currently empty," Tybion pressed on, "but won't be empty forever."

Arthur did not answer, but became very busy, all of a sudden, adjusting his boots.

"We hope," Tybion said.

Arthur looked up suddenly, sure that Tybion was laughing at him. But his Steward's face was impassive. Had Arthur just imagined the momentary gleam of laughter in Tybion's blue eyes?

"All is ready for your journey tomorrow," Tybion said. The Steward's abrupt change of subject was more than welcome to Arthur.

"The last time I went to any of the colleges for a graduation ceremony I was only four years old. Gwydion, Susanna, and Cai accompanied me. It will be strange to be there again."

"Strange for many," Tybion said solemnly, "for it has been three years since there were any ceremonies."

"My Great Ones have done well to be ready for them in such a short time," Arthur said proudly.

"Indeed they have."

Caer Duir, though not occupied by the Coranians, was in another way the most challenging of the colleges to restore. Cathbad had corrupted the Druids, and Sinend was finishing the task of rooting out enemies within her own ranks. Her father, Aergol, had begun this assignment, for he had had intimate knowledge of the Druids truly allied to Cathbad's cause. Armed with the knowledge Aergol had left behind, Sinend had recalled all Druids to Caer Duir. Those who had not come were declared outlaw and hunted down. Those that did come were examined, and many lost their posts. Sinend refused to collar any Druids, but there were other ways to ensure that they behaved, and Arthur left that to Sinend's able leadership. For now she was assisted by her brother, Menw, but he would be leaving soon to go to Ederynion, for Queen Elen needed a Druid.

As for Neuadd Gorsedd and Y Ty Dewin, the common folk

of Rheged had proudly assisted in putting these colleges to rights. For as soon as the Coranians were routed the people began to come to the two colleges, bringing with them books and other treasures that had been saved during the death march of the Y Dawnus across Rheged. A little over a year ago, the Coranians had, by treachery, found and invaded the caves of Allt Llwyd and hundreds of Y Dawnus had been captured. Many Bards and Dewin had carried precious books and instruments for as long as they could until they had fallen, dying from exhaustion and want. But after the army had moved on, the people of Rheged had come out to claim the bodies and had saved their belongings. Now that Kymru was free again, they had triumphantly returned the belongings to their rightful colleges.

Neuadd Gorsedd, the college of the Bards, had been occupied by the wyrce-jaga, and they had done much damage. Cynfar, with the able assistance of his great-uncle Dudod, had made a great deal of progress. Cynfar's father, Elidyr, had been less helpful, for the man seemed to still be dazed by his wife's death. Without a murmur he had given up his post as Master Bard to his son. But Cynfar, though he was young, was proving to be more than able. Many said he was like Anieron Master Bard all over again. There could be no higher praise.

Y Ty Dewin, which had been occupied by the Preosts of Lytir, had been in better shape, but the gardens had suffered and there was still much that needed to be put to rights. In this Llywelyn was ably assisted by Myrrdin.

And thinking of Myrrdin had Arthur grinning.

"My lord?" Tybion asked, curious.

"I was thinking of my great-uncle Myrrdin."

At this Tybion grinned himself. Myrrdin had arrived at Cadair Idris late last night and had thus far managed to avoid the inevitable. But he couldn't avoid it forever.

"I'd bet on Neuad any day," Tybion said.

"So would I, Tybion. So would I."

Myrrdin donned his robe and settled its silvery folds. He

glanced in the large mirror in his chamber. Not bad for an old man, he thought as his reflection gazed back. His white beard, newly washed, was cut short and his dark eyes glittered in the light of the flames dancing on the small hearth.

His smile faded as he again contemplated his reflection. He could see, now, the bags under his old man's eyes put there by his journey yesterday. He had arrived late last night along with Llywelyn from Y Ty Dewin, and had gotten very little sleep thinking of what he must do today.

And he must. He had been a coward up to now, avoiding the coming moment. Avoiding the truth. Avoiding the pain he knew would soon come.

But he would wait no longer. He was determined to put an end to it—not for his sake but rather for hers.

For if it had been up to him he would never even contemplate doing what he was going to do. If it had been solely up to him, he would stay with her until the day he died. Which would, he thought, not be as far from now as he wished. And that was the problem.

Enough. He was stalling. Best to get it done. Find her, tell her, leave her, and mourn her for the rest of his life.

He marched to the door, determined at last, and flung it open, only to stop dead at the sight of her standing there.

"Myrrdin!" Neuad breathed, her beautiful blue eyes soft with love, her golden hair flowing down her slender shoulders to her slim waist.

He cleared his throat. "Neuad," he said, forcing his voice to be neutral.

She smiled, paying no attention to his tone and stepped into his arms. He had not even been aware of having opened them to embrace her, but he had. She raised her flawless face to his and kissed him passionately.

At last he drew back and cleared his throat. "Neuad," he began, more hesitantly than he meant to.

"Go ahead, Myrrdin," she said, walking past him and into his room. "I am certain that this will be interesting." She sat down on the bed and patted the mattress, inviting him to sit next to her.

Knowing better, he dragged up a chair and firmly settled into it, facing her. "Neuad, you must forget me."

"Really?" she murmured, her blue eyes gazing at him in a way that made it hard for him to breathe.

"We—we have had a lovely interlude together."

"Thank you," she said softly. "I agree, it has been lovely."

"And it has meant a great deal to me."

"Myrrdin, *cariad*, do you think you could move this along a little?" she said sweetly. "We are going to be late."

"Neuad," he said desperately, "I'm too old for you."

"There now, do you feel better?" she asked. "And are you done?"

"No," he said, raising his voice a little in frustration. "I am not done! It's over between us. As I said, these past few months have been wonderful. But it's over."

"It will never be over with us, Myrrdin," she said, her tone still sweet, but her blue eyes beginning to cool.

"Neuad—"

"I will leave Queen Morrigan's court and come to stay with you at Y Ty Dewin."

"Neuad—"

"I'm pregnant."

The words dried up in his throat. Stunned, he could only stare at her.

"My body tells me it happened the night before the battle. Do you remember that night?"

"I will remember that night for the rest of my life," he breathed.

"And it will be a boy."

"I—"

"And I will name him Lailoken. We will raise him together, you and I. And you will forget this foolish notion that you are too old for me."

"I—"

"No more talk, Myrrdin," she said softly, reaching out to gently touch his face. "There is no more to say—you are my man, and you will stay that way. Like it or not."

Mesmerized by her eyes, he leaned forward and kissed her. She drew him to her on the bed and he thought no more about leaving her. Ever again.

They were going to be late for the ceremony. Very late, indeed.

GWYDION STRETCHED OUT on the bed, hands behind his head, and watched Rhiannon brush out her long, black hair. An occasional silver strand flashed beneath her comb, strands he thought just as beautiful as the shadowy ones that shimmered in the light of the fire.

For many years he had somehow always managed to watch Rhiannon. But he would never have thought there would come a time when he didn't have to hide that fact. He would never have thought he could be so content, his heart so free, his burden lifted. So much had changed these past several weeks, he almost felt like a new man again.

For one thing, the dreams had passed from him and on to his daughter. Every night he slept soundly, dreamlessly, in Rhiannon's loving arms. Every morning he woke up in a safe place, with his beloved beside him. Every day he saw Arthur shoulder his burdens, doing what he must to bring Kymru safely through the end of the storm and into safe harbor at last.

There had been many times in the past years he had despaired of ever seeing this moment today, the moment when Arthur would confirm Kymru's Rulers and his Great Ones in their positions, the moment when the Kymri would freely celebrate one of their sacred festivals. Then they would prepare to journey to the colleges for the graduation ceremonies, secure in the knowledge that Kymru again belonged to the Kymri.

Gratitude for all Rhiannon had done to help this day come about rushed over him. He opened his mouth, and said the words that had been waiting there for so long.

"Will you marry me?"

Rhiannon's comb froze in the middle of a stroke. Slowly she put it down and turned away from the mirror to face him. Her green eyes sparkled as she gazed at him.

"Yes," she said simply.

His heart leapt, but he did not let his joy show on his face. "We have to go to Caer Dathyl for a few months after the ceremonies," he said, matter-of-factly. "Cariadas needs more training before I can leave her there with confidence."

"Of course," she said, lightly.

"And then, we can go where we will."

"Indeed."

They were silent for a moment, and he saw her eyes begin to glitter dangerously. He had expected it—indeed, he had invited it—and worked hard not to smile. The silence lengthened and he schooled himself to show a look only of polite enquiry as her brows rushed together.

"Gwydion ap Awst, you asked me to marry you and I said yes. If you don't at least act happy right now I will—"

"Give me a Mind Shout? Shoot me full of arrows? Walk out that door and never come back?"

"Yes! All of those!" She rose and made as if to leave, but he was faster. He put his body between her and the door, then laughed, his silver eyes sparkling. "Oh, Rhiannon, what makes you think I would ever let you go?" He reached for her and took her in his arms, kissing her slowly and thoroughly.

At last he drew back to look at her. "Where should we live?"

The knowledge seemed to come to him at the same moment it came to her. He could tell by the look in her eyes, by the smile on her lips. He held her to his heart and thought that it was only right that they would come to live in that place where he had lost so much. Only to have the Shining Ones return the love he had lost, and more.

GERIANT LEFT HIS rooms and walked down the corridor toward the High King's hall. He knew that she would be there, and that knowledge made it hard for him to breathe.

Would she speak to him? Or would he have to content himself with looking at her from afar? And if she did speak to him, what would she say? His heart ached at the thought that she would simply pass him by. Even if she did not—could not—love him, perhaps he could at least be her friend. Surely she would grant him that much. He did not read too much into her gesture of sending him her token to wear into battle. That was an action that was easier to take from a long way away. Face to face things would be different. Very.

But of course, in that he was wrong.

"Geriant," she said softly.

He turned at the sound of her voice. Enid stood in the center of the corridor, her auburn hair twisted into a long braid wrapped loosely with a gold ribbon. A necklet of opals rested at her throat and he noticed that they trembled slightly as she took a deep breath in response to his gaze.

"Lady of Rheged," he said slowly, his hands tightening into fists in an effort to keep from reaching out to her. He bowed slightly.

"Oh, Geriant," she said, "aren't you at all glad to see me?"

His face twisted at her words. She held his world in the palms of her hands, and she thought nothing of it. "Is it not enough that you have my heart, Enid?" he rasped. "Do you want my soul, too?"

She stood frozen, listening to him, making no move.

"For years I have loved you. Did you think I had stopped? Did you think I would ever stop? Because I won't. I will never stop loving you, even if you don't care for me."

She opened her mouth to speak, but he was not done.

"I will never ask for anything from you, if that is what you are afraid of," he said evenly. "Never. I will simply love you. Forever. Make of that what you will."

He bowed again and turned to go, for he could not bear to hear what she would say next. He had told her the truth, and expected nothing from it.

"Don't you dare walk away from me!"

Startled, he turned back.

She stepped forward until she was right in front of him, barely a handsbreadth away. "What do I have to do, Geriant? Do you want me to ask the Druids to write it in fire? Do you want me to ask the Bards to shout it to everyone in Kymru? Do you want me to beg the High King to proclaim it to the world? Or maybe that's all just too complicated for you. Maybe if I use small words you will understand."

"Understand what, Enid?" he asked, confused.

"That I love you, you dolt!" she flared. "That I can't stand one more moment without you! That I am healed from the past and want to face the future with you!"

He stood there, his mouth open, unable to speak. He knew he looked like a fool, but he couldn't seem to help himself.

"Now kiss me, you idiot," she demanded.

He did what any wise man would do—he obeyed.

Bedwyr, soon to be named Captain of Gwynedd, walked purposefully to Queen Morrigan's chambers in Cadair Idris. His right arm grasped the hilt of his sword as if for comfort. Though his left arm was gone, cut from him in that last, terrible battle, he could still feel pain shoot through the limb that was no longer there. It was an odd feeling, to say the least.

Over and over and over again he had commanded his wife, Tangwen, to leave him, to find an able-bodied man and make a life with him. At first, she would speak soothingly to him, insisting that she loved him. After a while, she would scowl at him when he spoke like that. Now, she just rolled her eyes and changed the subject. Last night, she told him that he was getting to be dull, always saying the same old thing. And she would give him something better to talk about.

She had, and now, as he walked down the corridor, he almost smiled against his will, thinking of last night.

But then he schooled himself to be stern. He had a job to do and he would do it. And no distractions from Tangwen would divert him.

He knocked on Morrigan's door and opened it. Queen Morrigan was ready for the ceremony, dressed in a gown of deep blue, with sapphires in her auburn hair. Her dark eyes were flashing in irritation brought on, Bedwyr knew, by the fact she was dressed up within an inch of her life. Morrigan had never liked that.

Ygraine stood next to Morrigan, satisfaction on her face. He knew that Morrigan's mother had fought hard to get her daughter dressed and she had a right to be pleased.

"What is it, Bedwyr?" Morrigan asked irritably, putting her hand to her elaborately braided hair.

"Stop fussing with it," Ygraine hissed. "You'll just mess it up."

"All the pins are hurting my head," Morrigan insisted.

"They are not," Ygraine said coldly.

Bedwyr cleared his throat and the two women deigned to notice him again.

"What, Bedwyr?" Morrigan asked again, adjusting the folds of her gown.

"Stop that," Ygraine insisted, lightly slapping Morrigan's hands.

Morrigan made an exasperated sound in her throat. "And just what am I supposed to be able to do in this get up?" she asked. "I can't fight, I can't ride, I can't do anything."

"For this afternoon you aren't supposed to do anything," Ygraine pointed out, "except to curtsy every once in a while and nod your head."

"Stupid ceremony," Morrigan muttered.

"Pardon me," Bedwyr began.

"What?" they both asked at the same time, exasperated.

"You can't name me as your captain!" Bedwyr shouted, exasperated in his turn.

The two women stopped sniping at each other and turned to face him. Two pairs of dark eyes suddenly gone cold examined him in such a way that he had to swallow hard and remind himself he was a brave man.

"Are you insane?" Morrigan demanded.

"You will do as you are told," Ygraine said flatly.

"I can't," he insisted. "Look at me!"

They studied him in puzzled silence.

"You look fine," Morrigan said after a moment. "In fact, you look like you are a lot more comfortable than I am! Try having to wear a dress!"

"I have told you and told you that it is your obligation today," Ygraine said to Morrigan, Bedwyr once again forgotten.

"I don't have an arm!" Bedwyr shouted, again trying to get their attention. "How could I possibly protect you with one arm! How could I possibly lead your teulu with one arm! How could I be of any use to you—to anyone—with one arm!"

"You will serve my daughter and that's the end of it," Ygraine said, her tone as hard and cold and brittle as ice.

"I will not. Because I can't. I'm sorry."

He turned to go, but the whisper of a blade cutting through the air halted him. Quicker than thought, he had his blade out and whipped around, parrying the dagger Morrigan had thrown, turning it aside in midair.

Morrigan grinned. "Can't?"

Bedwyr suddenly couldn't think of anything to say.

"I told you so," Ygraine said with satisfaction. "And I am never wrong."

"Except about this dress," Morrigan muttered.

Bedwyr left as the two began to argue again. He knew enough to know when he was beaten.

ARTHUR ENTERED BRENIN Llys, his head held high, trying to tell himself he didn't look like a complete fool. He walked slowly as the crowd—kings and queens, captains and lieutenants, Y Dawnus—all parted for him.

The gold-sheathed room shimmered. The fountain in the center sparkled and laughed as he passed it by. To the right of the steps leading up to the throne the Treasures gleamed silently. The pearls of Y Llech, the Stone of Nantsovelta, gleamed. The opals of Y Honneit, the Spear of Mabon, shimmered. The emeralds of Y Pair, the Cauldron of Modron, glistened and the sapphires of Y Cleddyf, the Sword of Taran, glittered.

His mother stood to the left of the steps. Oddly enough, Gwen stood next to Ygraine. He stopped in front of them both.

"Mam," he said, not knowing what else to say.

She gave him one of her rare smiles, her dark eyes proud. "My son," she said, reaching up to him and laying her cool hand on his check.

"Live here in Cadair Idris. Please."

Her brow rose. "Morrigan must have promised you quite a bit for that offer."

He grinned. "She did."

Ygraine actually laughed. "I am sure she did."

Arthur turned to Gwen. "You are beautiful today."

"Just today?" she asked. Her golden hair cascaded down to her waist. She wore a gown of white, trimmed with gold. A golden niam-lann bound her brow and her flawless skin gleamed. Her blue eyes pierced him, challenging him, as she always had.

"No, not just today. You have always been beautiful to me."

Before she could reply, he turned and mounted the eight steps leading up to the throne. The jewels twinkled beneath his feet as he climbed—topaz and amethyst, emerald and pearl, ruby and onyx, opal and sapphire.

Gwydion and Rhiannon stood on either side of the massive, golden throne. The upswept eagle's wings that formed the backrest glimmered as though the eagle was thinking of taking flight.

"Uncle," Arthur said to Gwydion. But Gwydion would have none of Arthur's formality and pulled Arthur towards him and embraced him. Arthur, astonished, nonetheless had the presence of mind to return the embrace. He turned to Rhiannon, cocking his thumb at Gwydion.

"What's got into him?" he asked, trying to sound casual but failing completely.

"Joy," Rhiannon answered, her smile as bright and welcome as the dawn.

"Get used to it, nephew," Gwydion said with a grin.

"I'll try!"

Arthur sat on the golden throne and surveyed the throng. The Rulers of Kymru were all there, as well as their captains and lieutenants. His four Great Ones were also there, as well as many Y Dawnus come from the colleges or recently recovered from their wounds at the battle. He saw Myrrdin and Neuad hurry in, both looking somewhat disheveled and he could not hide his grin. Nor, frankly, could many others when they saw. But Arthur, taking pity on his great-uncle, did not say what he was thinking as the two of them made their way up toward the front, hand in hand.

"My friends, brave, beautiful folk of Kymru, we gather today to witness the fruits of our labors. For we have been victorious over the enemy, and Kymru belongs to us, once again!"

Their shouts almost deafened him, and he had to wait some time for the noise to die down. He saw tears of joy on many faces, and was aware that there were some on his own.

"We begin today with returning the rightful rulers to their places. First, I declare that Queen Elen of Ederynion, onetime captive of the enemy, is confirmed as Queen."

Elen stepped forward, flanked by her brother, Lludd, and by Prince Rhiwallon. Rhiwallon offered no excuse for standing with her, but the look on his face spoke volumes.

"Queen Elen, do you have something to say?"

Elen bowed to Arthur. The silver and pearl torque of Ederynion glowed around her proud neck. "High King, I declare that Angharad ur Ednyved remains the PenAethnen of Ederynion."

Angharad stepped forward proudly, her fiery red hair confined to a severe braid, her green eyes triumphant.

"High King," Angharad called, "my Lieutenant, Emrys, was killed in the battle for Dinmael."

"We are aware of your loss, Angharad, and mourn him," Arthur replied.

"I have taken counsel with Queen Elen, and we have determined a successor for his post."

"Name him."

"We name Talorcan of Dere as lieutenant of Ederynion."

Talorcan, standing to one side with Regan, paled. His mouth fell open in shock and he stood quite still, not believing what he had heard.

"But I, I'm Coranian!" Talorcan said in astonishment.

"You are one of us, Talorcan of Dere," Arthur replied. "And as such have been called to serve your queen. Will you do so?"

"Yes!" Talorcan said quickly, his eyes gleaming. He bowed low to Elen. "I will serve you, my Queen, until the day I die. My life is yours."

"But mine first," Regan said with a laugh, and the crowd laughed with her as Talorcan flushed to the roots of his hair.

Arthur, taking pity on Talorcan, moved on. "I declare that Morrigan ur Uthyr is now restored as Queen of Gwynedd."

Morrigan stepped forward. The silver and sapphire torque of Gwynedd caught the golden light and shimmered. Arthur noticed that Prince Lludd could not take his eyes off of her.

"Cai of Gwynedd, step forward," Morrigan called.

Cai came to stand next to Morrigan. "High King Arthur," Morrigan went on, "you have asked for the services of my captain, and both he and I freely give them."

"Cai ap Cynyr, I declare you captain of the High King's teulu," Arthur said. "You who so faithfully have served my family. Who helped to conceal my whereabouts when I was a child and never breathed a word of that knowledge, who fought by my father's side, who ensured the safety of my mother and sister. We are more grateful than we can say."

Cai bowed tears in his eyes. "I am grateful, High King, for your faith in me. I will not ever give you cause to feel otherwise."

"I don't doubt it, Cai," Arthur said solemnly. "Therefore, since the post of Captain of Gwynedd is not filled—"

"That's my part, Arthur," Morrigan said reprovingly. "I didn't get this dressed up for nothing."

A ripple of good-natured laughter ran through the hall and Arthur laughed. "I beg your pardon, sister," he said and gestured for her to continue.

"Since the post of PenGwernan is now vacant, I have appointed my lieutenant, Bedwyr ap Bedrawd as captain."

Under Morrigan's, Ygraine's, and Tangwen's steady gazes Bedwyr bowed and did not dispute Morrigan's statement.

"Very wise," Gwydion murmured to Arthur.

"Yes, in the end Bedwyr knew better than to take on those

three."

"Very, very wise."

Arthur nodded at Bedwyr and then turned to gaze at Owein. "It is my pleasure to confirm King Owein and Queen Sanon in their rightful places as King and Queen of Rheged."

Owein, the gold and opal torque of Rheged clasped around his strong neck led Sanon forward and the two of them bowed.

"High King," Owein said, "I wish to confirm that my captain is Trystan ap Naf, the PenDraenenwen of Rheged."

Sabrina started to move away from Trystan so that he could join Owein and Sanon, but he refused to let go of her hand and moved to stand before Arthur with her in tow.

"High King, may I present to you my new wife," Trystan said with great pride.

"Congratulations, Trystan," Arthur said, carefully not looking over at Gwen. For some reason he did not feel equal to meeting her eyes just now.

Esyllt, Trystan's longtime lover, stood rooted to the spot, her face shocked. Arthur made a mental note to have Cynfar recall her to Neuadd Gorsedd. The last thing the new couple needed was to have Esyllt hanging about. But then he saw that Cynfar did not need telling, for the new Master Bard caught Arthur's eye and nodded almost imperceptibly.

"Lastly, I declare that King Rhoram and Queen Achren are—"

"Well, we're not, actually," Rhoram said, moving forward with Achren through the crowd.

"Not?" Arthur asked, confused.

"Certainly not," Achren declared. "I'd rather die."

"Or kill me," Rhoram said.

"Whatever it takes," Achren said, baring her teeth at her husband.

"That's my girl," Rhoram said with a grin.

"Perhaps you would care to explain, Rhoram," Arthur said pointedly.

"Not that much to explain, High King. I find that I don't really want to be king anymore. And I think I deserve a rest.

And Achren—well, Achren finds that being queen doesn't appeal to her."

"And so?" Arthur asked.

"And so, I abdicate the throne of Prydyn in favor of my son, Geriant." With that Rhoram unclasped the gold and emerald torque of Prydyn from his neck and gestured for Geriant to come forward.

Geriant, his blue eyes wide with surprise, came to stand before his father. "My son," Rhoram said with a smile, "take this torque from my hands and know that you are King of Prydyn."

As if in a dream, Geriant reached out and slowly took the torque and clasped it around his neck. Then he turned to face Arthur and bowed low.

Arthur said, "Then I declare Geriant ap Rhoram to be King of Prydyn."

"Not quite," Geriant said, finding his tongue at last.

Arthur raised a brow. "And what else did the contingent from Prydyn forget to tell me?"

"I have no idea," Rhoram said, looking with interest at his son.

"Well I do!" Princess Enid called as she moved forward to stand next to Geriant. She clasped his hand and turned to Rhoram. "Father."

After a moment of silence, Rhoram whooped with glee. "Married!"

"Once she decided we couldn't wait," Geriant said proudly.

"Ellywen did it, didn't she?" Achren demanded.

"I most certainly did," Ellywen, Rhoram's Druid, said defiantly.

Achren, her hand on her dagger, came to stand before Rhoram's formerly traitorous Druid. Then she grinned. "Good for you!" Achren said.

"Then I declare that Geriant and Enid are the King and Queen of Prydyn," Arthur said proudly. "But what will you do, Rhoram?"

"Well, as you know, my brother-in-law, Erfin, recently lost his life through a most unfortunate accident."

"The way he ran into your knife, you mean?" Arthur asked pointedly.

"He was always clumsy," Achren said helpfully.

"A shame," Geriant murmured.

"And, before he planted his backside in my hall and declared himself king, he was the Lord of Ceredigion. Since I feel responsible for the fact that Ceredigion is now without a Lord, I thought I would take his place."

"As he so graciously took yours," Arthur said.

"Indeed," Rhoram grinned.

"Elegant," Arthur went on.

"And my wife is looking forward to rebuilding the teulu of that cantref. She will be very busy. And therefore, I hope, too busy to goad me too hard."

"A forlorn hope," Achren said, her eyes glinting. "I will never allow you to get lazy."

"Is that a promise or a threat?" Rhoram said, his eyes full of laughter.

"Both, my husband. Both."

Arthur grinned and then proceeded. He gestured for his Steward to come forward. "I further declare that Tybion, descendent of Iltydd, the Steward of Lleu Silver-Hand who lost his life defending his High King, is now my Steward."

Tybion, his son Lucan with him, bowed with tears in his eyes.

"And now I call my Great Ones to me."

Sinend Archdruid, Cynfar Master Bard, Llywelyn Ardewin, and Cariadas the Dreamer came to stand before him at the bottom of the steps. At that moment Gwydion and Rhiannon moved to step down.

"No," Arthur said, putting his hand out to stop them. "To you two I owe everything. Without you both none of this would ever have happened."

"We had our part in it," Gwydion said fairly. "But so did many, many others. And our time is over. My daughter stands as Dreamer. You have your other Great Ones to work with you and to guide Kymru. I am no longer needed here."

"I will always need you, Uncle. I will always need both of you."

"Well, if you truly do find that you need us, my wife and I won't be far away," Gwydion said, glancing over at Rhiannon.

The crowd gasped.

"Not again!" Arthur said with mock ferociousness. "Just how many marriages were going on here this morning?"

"Oh, we're not married yet," Rhiannon said. "Do you think that I would marry quietly? Having accomplished such a difficult task as catching Gwydion ap Awst?"

"Difficult!" Myrrdin called out. "I would have said impossible!"

"So would we all," Arthur declared.

"Such a feat should not go unrecognized," Rhiannon went on. "We are going to have a huge wedding."

Gwydion paled. "We are?"

"Oh, my, yes," Rhiannon said.

"I will perform the ceremony," Sinend said.

"And I will stand with my mother," Gwen put in.

"Of course I will stand with Gwydion," Arthur said firmly.

"Oh, the songs the Bards will sing," Dudod said enthusiastically, rubbing his hands together.

"And the stewards will ensure that the feast is more than ample," Tybion said.

"For of course you will be married here at Cadair Idris," Ygraine declared.

Gwydion raised his hands in mock surrender. "Enough!" he cried. "You can all do what you want, as long as Rhiannon's happy."

"The perfect goal," Cariadas said with a smile.

"You said you would be close by," Arthur said curiously. "In Rhiannon's cave?"

"No," Gwydion said as he took Rhiannon's hand. "We will live on Afalon."

"Afalon!" Arthur exclaimed as everyone gave a gasp. "No one lives there. No one has ever lived there."

"We know," Gwydion said quietly. "But we have reason to believe that Annwyn and Aertan will welcome us there."

"We will build a cottage, right next to the well where Amatheon lost his life," Rhiannon went on.

"It is right. We know it in our hearts," Gwydion finished.

"Then there is no more to be said," Arthur declared. "Except that your cottage is sure to be as comfortable as Kymru can make it."

"Stocked with the wines of Prydyn," Geriant said.

"With rugs from Gwynedd on the floor," Morrigan put in.

"And glassware from Ederynion," Elen called out.

"And fine honey and ale from Rheged," Owein insisted.

"We thank you all," Gwydion said, putting a halt to the generosity. "And accept the help offered by our friends." At that Gwydion and Rhiannon made their way down to the bottom of the steps, motioning for Arthur's Great Ones to ascend.

Llywelyn, Cynfar, and Sinend went up the steps. Cariadas, after a quick hug for Gwydion and Rhiannon, followed.

"There is one more service you two can do for me," Arthur said as Gwydion and Rhiannon turned to take their places with the rest of the crowd.

"Anything," Gwydion said sincerely.

"The death song of Havgan. Do you have it?"

Gwydion bowed with sudden tears in his silvery eyes. "We do," he said quietly.

"Then sing it," Arthur said simply. "Sing it for us. Sing it for him."

In a clear, rich voice, Rhiannon began,

"Havgan the night-bringer came,
Bringing sorrow,
Bringing death.
Havgan the Cruel caused
Treacheries to Kymru.
The earth quaking,
And the elements darkening,
Bringing a shadow to the world."

Then Gwydion sang his voice full of sorrow.

"The last step
Was taken by fierce Havgan.
Going in the course of things

Among the spirits of the dead
Reunited at last
With those who loved him.
I sing farewell to
Havgan ap Brychan var Arianllyn
And what he might have been."

They were silent for a moment, all of them thinking their own thoughts, all of them offering their silence to the memory of one of their own, even if he had not known it until the very end.

"He is at peace, now," Arthur said with certainty.

"At last," Gwydion said.

"Yes," Arthur agreed. "At last."

THE FULL MOON was riding high in the sky when Arthur drifted away from the celebration in Calan Llachar. He made his way through the trees easily. He would have been able to do so even if the moon had not lit his path, for this was his forest; Cadair Idris and its environs were his home. And neither the forest nor the plain, neither the trees nor the rocks, neither the bushes nor the grass would allow him to fall.

He stepped out of the forest and moved east, past the glowing, jeweled doors to the mountain. Then he turned north to Galar Carreg, the burial mound of the High Kings.

The plain stretched out before him, moonbeams creating silvery paths through the long grasses and wildflowers. A slight breeze danced before him and he heard the faint sound of hunting horns echoing across the sky. The fierce, free cry of an eagle carried to his heart, borne to him on the wings of the clean, wild wind.

He stood in front of the mound, lost in wonder. The brooding rocks stood silently, tall and dark, reaching up to the sky. There was no sadness to this place, and he had no fear of the dead. He was welcome here among those who had gone before him. And he was proud to be here, for Kymru was free, and the price was not so very high after all.

He had given up his freedom so that Kymru could be free, and he did not mind it as much as he had thought he would. It didn't matter, really, that he was bound here as High King. No, he had never wanted it. Yes, he would rather, even now, be sitting quietly by the fire in Myrrdin's hut, having watched the sheep all day and brought them safely home at night. Yes, he would rather have worn rough homespun than the golden cloak he was wearing now.

But there were rewards. Such as how he felt right now, standing before the place where Idris, Macsen, and Lleu were buried. He felt a kinship with them he had not expected to feel. If they could do it—and they had—so could he. He thought that reward would be enough and did not think he should ask for more.

Until he heard her voice. And he knew he did want more. Much, much more.

"Tired of dancing?" she asked as she came to stand beside him.

He turned to look down at her and found he could not banter with her. He found that he had to tell her the truth. And risk everything.

"I love you, Gwenhwyfar ur Rhoram var Rhiannon. I have loved you for a long, long time. Is there any hope that one day you will feel the same?"

She did not answer at first, merely studying his face in the moonlight, searching, perhaps, for the truth in his eyes. At last, having seen what she needed to see, she lifted her face for his kiss.

And that was answer enough.

Some time later they returned to the Doors of Cadair Idris, their arms around each other. They mounted the white, shining steps and the Doors slowly opened.

"Greetings, High King," the Doors said quietly as they passed through.

"Greetings, Efa," Arthur replied to the former Queen of Prydyn.

Epilogue

Celynnen Mis, 500

Sigerric stood at the prow of the ship, his thin hands firmly gripping the oak railing. The red and white striped sails filled with the freshening wind, sending the ship cutting cleanly through the waves, propelling it swiftly toward home.

Home. Oh, how desperately he longed to return there. He had been away from Corania for a long time, far, far too long. And the things that he had done in Kymru still had the power to shame him. He wondered if he would ever feel differently, but he thought not. The best he could hope for was for the memories to fade at least a little, for the shame to lessen slightly with the passage of time. Not that the shame would ever wholly go away—and not that he would want it to. He could not be the man he was and not feel those emotions. And he didn't want to be a different man from who he was. He never had. Unlike Havgan, who had been a very different man indeed.

It was strange, he supposed, not to mourn his friend any longer. After all, hadn't he been mourning Havgan for years beyond counting? But he knew that Havgan was free, at long last. He knew that his friend's long, strange exile had come to an end. And so he could not mourn that fact that Havgan had, at long last, gone home.

The battle had ended a little over three weeks ago, and he had mostly recovered from his many wounds. Not, of course, from the wounds to his soul. He did not think he would ever recover from those. It had taken ten days for the Coranians to reach the sea. In those ten days they had experienced such terror that some warriors had died from it. For they had been harried by Havgan and the Wild Hunt, driven to the sea and allowed little rest. Remembering the sight of Havgan, cloaked in red and gold, followed by a horned god and a goddess with pitiless amethyst eyes, still had the power to make him shiver.

Of course, when all the men were loaded onto the ships, when the ships had left Kymru, one by one, Sigerric's ship had been the last to go. He had turned back to the shore for one last look. As Havgan had known he would. For the Golden Man had raised his hand in farewell and had actually smiled.

Yes, they had embarked on their ships and gratefully turned them east, glad to leave the land that had stolen their blood and their courage. In three more days they would be back in the Coranian Empire. And Sigerric did not intend to leave that land ever, ever again.

"He seems to be doing well. Unfortunately."

Sigerric, having forgotten that Penda was standing next to him, was momentarily startled to hear him speak. Not that he was sorry Penda was there. Penda's company soothed him, for they had been friends a long, long time. They had endured the little soul-deaths Havgan had meted out to them over the years, endured the sojourn in Kymru, endured the last retreat together, endured Havgan's farewell.

"It is almost a shame we found that Dewin in his boat," Sigerric said. "For I don't trust him in the least."

"Well, I didn't want to keep him alive," Penda pointed out.

"Don't rub it in, Penda. You know perfectly well why I didn't want to put Bledri to death."

"Because you had enough Kymric blood on your hands?"

"Yes," he said quietly. "Even the life of such a one who betrayed his people is one more life than I wanted to take. At least for now."

"I understand. It's what Talorcan would have done, if he had been here."

"He found his true destiny," Sigerric said. "And we can't begrudge him that."

"I don't," Penda said. "I envy him."

Princess Aelfwyn chose that moment to join them. She was wrapped warmly in a white cloak with diamonds sewn at the hem and throat. Her bright, golden hair was braided and fastened tightly to her proud head with diamond pins. Her green eyes were cool and clear as she glanced at him. Penda bowed and left Sigerric alone with his true love.

Not, Sigerric thought bitterly, that she understood that. Or ever would.

They stood silently together for some time. When he could bear it no longer, he turned to look at her. He drank in the sight of her, all the while knowing that no matter how close she came to him, she would always remain a distant, cold light—one that would never warm him, but would always beckon him on with the hollow promise of love.

And he would follow. Now and forever.

"Princess," he said, gripping the railing even harder to keep from reaching out to her.

"General," she replied evenly.

"You cannot even use my name?" he asked, his heart aching.

"And you cannot even use mine?"

"I wouldn't presume."

"I think you presume a great deal," she said. And for the first time since he had met her he saw a flash of fire in her eyes.

"I don't know what you mean."

"I think you do," she said firmly.

"Truly, I—"

"You presume, General," she interrupted, "that I am unchanged. You presume that I carry nothing in my heart, now that my goal of being rid of my husband is accomplished. You presume that I have nothing left to give. To anyone."

"I presume only that you have nothing you would give to me," he said, stung. "For you know I love you. You have known for years and years, and it has meant nothing to you."

"They call me Star of Heaven," she said quietly. "And they

presume—as do you—that I am cold and bright and distant. And they are right. But they presume that I always will be. And they are wrong. As are you."

She turned to go, and he grabbed her arm and pulled her back to face him. There were tears on her white face, and an agony in her green eyes he had never thought to see.

"Aelfwyn," he whispered. "Oh, my heart's love."

But before she could answer the air was sliced with a scream of agony.

"Arianrod," Aelfwyn said bitterly. "My husband's whore. It is her time, then."

"Then you must go to help her."

Aelfwyn laughed shortly. "Help her? I will help her into the next world, if that is what you mean. And the child, too."

"You don't mean that."

But she did not answer him. She pulled away from his grasp and went swiftly below decks, to the source of the scream.

Arianrod lay still, too spent to move. The low ceiling of the cabin hovered over her. She felt smothered but was too weak to help herself. A strong hand laid a cold cloth on her forehead and she blinked sweat out of her eyes to see who it was.

Bledri looked down at her steadily, his gray eyes uncaring. Yet he had done the best he could for her. If it hadn't been for him, she probably would have died.

"Why did you keep me alive?" she whispered. "Why?"

He smiled, his face twisted. "My Dewin training, I suppose. Mostly, perhaps, because I could sense how much you wanted to die."

"And so made sure that I lived."

"Aelfwyn was very disappointed."

"Where did she take the baby?" she asked.

"I believe she said something about drowning it," he said, his gray eyes dancing with glee, his mouth twisted with a cruel smile.

She supposed Bledri thought she would react to that. That she would start screaming. That she would—at the very least—care.

But she didn't.

Once she had desperately wanted the child she had carried under her heart for so long. But that was before. Before she had learned that her brother was the father of her baby. Before her brother had died. Before her parents had returned—not to her, but to him.

They had left her, alone. Again. Living in this world which held nothing for her.

She turned her face to the wall and waited for Bledri to leave. He did at last, closing the door behind him. She lay there for a time, gathering her strength. She knew what she had to do now. And no one would stop her.

She considered taking a moment to see the child, to swear a destiny for him. But she did not think that would matter. She already knew that the child's destiny would be dark enough. For he was the fruit of the mating of a brother Dreamer and a sister Dewin, and such a thing had long ago been forbidden—and with good reason. She had known the moment the child left her body that it had taken her life with it. That boy would take whatever lives he wanted, and laugh while he did it. Her Mordred. Her son. She would leave him as a gift to Aelfwyn.

Gritting her teeth against the pain, ignoring the blood that trickled down her legs, further staining her shift, she rose from her bed, staggering to the closed door. She had been afraid it would be locked, and was surprised to find that it was not.

She opened the door softly, cautiously putting her head outside into the narrow corridor. But no one was there. As swiftly as she could, she made her way down the corridor to the stairs leading up to the deck. The ship swayed steadily, but not violently. She moved carefully, managing to stay on her feet, gritting her teeth against the pain as she climbed, not caring that she was leaving a trail of blood behind her.

For once in her life, her luck held. For as she came up on deck there was no one to notice her. They were all gathered at the prow, pointing at what looked to be a school of dolphins. Perhaps Nantsovelta herself had sent them to allow Arianrod to do what she so desperately needed to do.

And at that moment she did indeed feel that Nantsovelta,

Lady of the Waters, Queen of the Moon, was with her. She felt a comforting presence, and for once she did not feel alone. Nantsovelta, the goddess most revered by the Dewin, was standing with her, helping her to make her way to the railing, ensuring that no one raised the alarm.

She took a deep breath, filling her lungs with the tangy scent of the salty water. Droplets nestled in her tawny hair like diamonds as she grasped the nearest taut rope. Steadying herself with the rope, she pulled herself up until she was standing on the railing. She looked down into the sea, and felt no fear.

The prayer to Nantsovelta came to her lips and she whispered,

"O vessel bearing the light, O great brightness
Outshining the sun, draw me ashore, under your
Protection, from the short-lived ship of the world."

JUST BEFORE SHE jumped, she heard the sound of a hunting horn. And she saw them. They had come for her at last. She saw her brother, flashing golden in the sun. She caught a glimpse of her father's amber eyes, of her mother's tawny hair, of the welcoming smile all three had for her.

And then she jumped. And the sea welcomed her, filling her lungs, taking her in. Her body sank like a stone. But her spirit rose up and up, straining to join them.

They had waited for her. As she had always dreamed they would. She would never be alone again.

AELFWYN STARED DOWN at the child in her arms. At Arianrod's child. At Havgan's child. At the child of the two she hated more than anyone in the world. Sigerric was mad to think she would not take this chance to rid herself of this last reminder, this vestige of all she despised most.

The sound of hunting horns drifted to her ears. Then she heard a splash and the cries of the men on deck.

She smiled, for she knew what had happened. She had heard Arianrod leave her cabin and had known where the woman was going. At last, Arianrod was now dead. Soon, this child would join its mother in the depths of the sea.

She looked down into the tiny face, framed with a thatch of tawny hair. The boy's eyes opened. They were amber, amber as Havgan's had been. Amber as Arianrod's had been. She was conscious of a dim surprise, for newborn baby's eyes are always blue at first. Always.

The amber eyes glittered in the smoky light with a yellowish tinge that made her flesh crawl, at the same time engendering a fierce protectiveness. No one would harm this child. No one. Not while she had breath in her body. This boy would be hers. She would raise him to rule the Empire.

She said the child's name as she had heard Arianrod do. "Mordred."

And though she said it with reverence, with joy, the name still tasted of ashes in her mouth. Somewhere deep down inside a part of her screamed with horror, even as she held the child to her heart.

"Mordred," she said again. "My son."

Glossary

Addiendydd: sixth day of the week
aderyn: birds
aethnen: aspen tree; sacred to Ederynion
alarch: swan; the symbol of the royal house of Ederynion
alban: light; any one of the four solar festivals
Alban Awyr: festival honoring Taran; Spring Equinox
Alban Haf: festival honoring Modron; Summer Solstice
Alban Nerth: festival honoring Agrona and Camulos; Autumnal Equinox
Alban Nos: festival honoring Sirona and Grannos; the Winter Solstice
ap: son of
ar: high
Archdruid: leader of the Druids, must be a descendent of Llyr
Arderydd: high eagle; symbol of the High Kings
Ardewin: leader of the Dewin, must be a descendent of Llyr
arymes: prophecy
Awenyddion: dreamer (see Dreamer)
awyr: air
bach: boy
Bard: a telepath; they are musicians, poets, and arbiters of the law in matters of inheritance, marriage, and divorce; Bards can Far-Sense and Wind-Speak; they revere the god Taran, King of the Winds
bedwen: birch tree; sacred to the Bards
Bedwen Mis: birch month; roughly corresponds to March
blaid: wolf; the symbol of the royal house of Prydyn
bran: raven; the symbol of the Dreamers
Brenin: high or noble one; the High King; acts as an amplifier for the Y Dawnus
buarth: circle
cad: battle
cadair: chair (of state)
caer: fortress

calan: first day; any one of the four fire festivals
Calan Gaef: festival honoring Annwyn and Aertan
Calan Llachar: festival honoring Cerridwen and Cerrunnos
Calan Morynion: festival honoring Nantsovelta
Calan Olau: festival honoring Mabon
cantref: a large division of land for administrative purposes; two to three commotes make up a cantref; a cantref is ruled by a Lord or Lady
canu: song
cariad: beloved
celynnen: holly
Celynnen Mis: holly month; roughly corresponds to late May/early June
cenedl: clan
cerdinen: rowan tree; sacred to the Dreamers
Cerdinen Mis: rowan month; roughly corresponds to July
Cerdorrian: sons of Cerridwen; the hidden organization of warriors and Y Dawnus working to drive the Coranians out of Kymru
cleddyf: sword
collen: hazel tree; sacred to Prydyn
Collen Mis: hazel month; roughly corresponds to October
commote: a small division of land for administrative purposes; two or three commotes make up a cantref; a commote is ruled by a Gwarda
coed: forest, wood
cynyddu: increase; the time when the moon is waxing
da: father
dan: fire
derwen: oak tree; sacred to the Druids
Derwen Mis: oak month; roughly corresponds to December
Dewin: a clairvoyant; they are physicians; they can Life-Read and Wind-Ride; they revere the goddess Nantsovelta, Lady of the Moon
disglair: bright; the time when the moon is full
draig: dragon; the symbol of the Dewin
draenenwen: hawthorn tree; sacred to Rheged
Draenenwen Mis: hawthorn month; roughly corresponds to late

June/early July
Dreamer: a descendent of Llyr who has precognitive abilities; the Dreamer can Dream-Speak and Time-Walk; the Dreamer also has the other three gifts—telepathy, clairvoyance, and psychokinesis; there is only one Dreamer in a generation; they revere the god Mabon, King of Fire
Dream-Speaking: precognitive dreams; one of the Dreamer's gifts
Druid: a psychokinetic; they are astronomers, scientists, and lead all festivals; they can Shape-Move, Fire-Weave, and, in partnership with the High King, Storm-Bring; they revere the goddess Modron, the Great Mother of All
drwys: doors
dwfr: water
dwyvach-breichled: goddess-bracelet; bracelet made of oak used by Druids
eiddew: ivy
Eiddew Mis: ivy month; roughly corresponds to April
enaid-dal: soul-catcher; lead collars that prevent Y Dawnus from using their gifts
eos: nightingale; the symbol of the Bards
erias: fire
erydd: eagle
Far-Sensing: the telepathic ability to communicate with animals
ffynidwydden: fir tree; sacred to the High Kings
Fire-Weaving: the psychokinetic ability to light fires
gaef: winter
galanas: blood price
galor: mourning, sorrow
goddeau: trees
gorsedd: a gathering (of Bards)
greu: blood
Gwaithdydd: third day of the week
gwarchan: incantation
Gwarda: ruler of a commote
gwernan: alder tree; sacred to Gwynedd
Gwernan Mis: alder month; roughly corresponds to late April/early

May
gwinydden: vine
Gwinydden: vine month; roughly corresponds to August
Gwlad Yr Haf: the Land of Summer; the Otherworld
gwydd: knowledge
gwyn: white
gwynt: wind
Gwyntdydd: fifth day of the week
gwyr: seeker
haf: summer
hebog: hawk; the symbol of the royal house of Gwynedd
helygen: willow
Helygen Mis: willow month; roughly corresponds to January
honneit: spear
Life-Reading: the clairvoyant ability to lay hands on a patient and determine the nature of their ailment
llachar: bright
llech: stone
lleihau: to diminish; the time when the moon is waning
lleu: lion
Llundydd: second day of the week
llyfr: book
llyn: lake
llys: court
Lord/Lady: ruler of a cantref
mam: mother
march: horse; the symbol of the royal house of Rheged
Master Bard: leader of the Bards, must be a descendent of Llyr
Meirgdydd: fourth day of the week
meirig: guardian
Meriwdydd: seventh day of the week
mis: month
morynion: maiden
mwg-breudduyd: smoke-dream; a method Dreamers can use to induce dreams
mynydd: mountain

mynyddoedd: mountains
naid: leap
nemed: shrine, a sacred grove
nerth: strength
neuadd: hall
niam-lann: a jeweled metallic headpiece, worn by ladies of rank
nos: night
ogaf: cave
olau: fair
onnen: ash tree; sacred to the Dewin
Onnen Mis: ash month; roughly corresponds to February
pair: cauldron
pen: head of
Plentyn Prawf: child test; the testing of children, performed by the Bards, to determine if they are Y Dawnus
rhyfelwr: warrior
sarn: road
Shape-Moving: the psychokinetic ability to move objects
Storm-Bringing: the psychokinetic ability to control certain weather conditions; only effective in partnership with the High King
Suldydd: first day of the week
tarbell: a board game, similar to chess
tarw: bull; the symbol of the Druids
tarw-casgliad: the ceremony where Druids invite a dream from Modron
telyn: harp
teulu: warband
Time-Walking: the ability to see events in the past; one of the Dreamer's gifts
tir: earth
triskele: the crystal medallion used by Dewin
ty: house
tynge tynghed: the swearing of a destiny
Tynged Mawr: great fate; the test to determine a High King
tywyllu: dark; the time when the moon is new
ur: daughter of

var: out of
Wind-Riding: the clairvoyant ability of astral projection
Wind-Speaking: the telepathic ability to communicate with other humans
wythnos: week
yned: justice
Y Dawnus: the gifted; a Druid, Bard, Dewin, or Dreamer
ysgawen: elder
Ysgawen Mis: elder month; roughly corresponds to September
ystafell: the Ruler's chambers
ywen: yew
Ywen Mis: yew month; roughly corresponds to November

M
edallion
PRESS

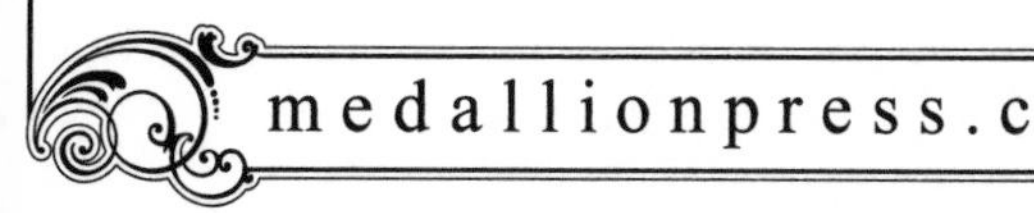

M
edallion
PRESS
®